MOMENT TO KILL

An Action Military Thriller

BARAK CHACOTY

Production by eBookPro Publishing
www.ebook-pro.com

Moment to Kill
Barak Chacoty

Copyright © 2024 Barak Chacoty

All rights reserved; no parts of this book may be reproduced or transmitted in any form or by any means, electronic or mechanical, including photocopying, recording, taping, or by any information retrieval system, without the permission, in writing, of the author.

Translation from Hebrew: Matthew Berman
Editing: Nancy Alroy

Contact: barak@chacoty.co.il

ISBN 9798304754422

Part of what is depicted in the book is based on the personal experiences of the author, who served in the Mista'arvim Duvdevan[1] unit in the early 1990s as a soldier and commander.

This book has been presented to the military censor where it was thoroughly checked for a period of six months. Part of the original manuscript has been unauthorized for publication. The remainder has undergone changes and adjustments to prevent any harm to the national security interests of Israel.

The copy in front of you has been authorized for publication by the official military censor.

---

1. Counter-terrorism unit where combat soldiers go undercover in Arab society.

CHAPTER 1
November 1993, Nablus

The red Mercedes carrying the four undercover combat soldiers slowly made its way through the southern alleys of Nablus. The local radio station was playing a song by Fairuz, the famous Lebanese singer. A *masbaha* – Muslim prayer beads – was hanging on the rearview mirror. Udi, the driver, didn't need any help navigating the city's narrow streets. Like the rest of the team, he knew the area inside out. The standard operating procedure before any operation was for the driver to receive maps and up-to-date aerial photos of the area. Arriving at the destination was the sole responsibility of the driver – any navigational error could jeopardize the entire mission. The obnoxious rain forced Udi to turn on the wipers, which squeaked horribly. Yariv, the mission commander, was sitting next to Udi. This time, Yariv was dressed up like an old Arab man: on his head he had a *keffiyeh* and *akal*,[2] with thick eyeglasses haphazardly perched on his nose, and the strands of his beard were dyed grey. He was holding today's "Al-Quds" newspaper, looking at it from time to time. A brown, worn-out, suitcase

---

2. The "keffiyeh" is the cloth headscarf worn by Muslims, and the "akal" are the bands that hold it in place on top of the head.

rested on his knees. A communications device surrounded by hard foam was hidden inside the suitcase, an additional magazine for the concealed handgun he was carrying, a pair of grenades and a small night-vision device, the latest word in the field of optics in the Israeli Defense Forces (IDF).

Yaki and Barda sat in the back seat of the Mercedes. Yaki was dressed up as a woman, as usual. To his chagrin, the blonde member of the team was usually chosen to play the role of the woman in the operations. He hated the long hours spent in front of the mirror putting on makeup, as well as the uncomfortable clothing. Truth be told, playing the woman fit Yaki like a glove: he had a thin, athletic build, blond hair and light colored eyes.

As opposed to the rest of the team, he only needed to shave every two or three days, and his blond facial hair wasn't hard to camouflage with some makeup and a bit of blush. Among the team members, Yaki, against his will, was nicknamed "Barbie." He protested, but to no avail. This time, he wore a traditional white head covering, which also served as a veil in case they got stopped at a random checkpoint by Hamas operatives.

Barda, on the other hand, was a dark-skinned country boy, short and stocky. Physically speaking, he was considered one of the strongest soldiers in the unit, and was even called "The Bull" behind his back. He held a green, plastic webbed shopping basket between his legs with a few bundles of herbs, vegetables, fruit and two loaves of bread. This was all just a cover for the basket's real purpose: a hidden pocket that was sewn into the bottom where a mini-Uzi was concealed along with a dual magazine, courtesy of the unit's weapons department. Barda was dressed up as a young man in his late twenties. The naturally-grown mustache he always sported along with a weeks' worth of dark stubble gave the young soldier a more mature look.

Neither the car nor those sitting inside stuck out in particular: anybody looking on from the side would see a family returning home from another day's work – the elderly father sitting in the front seat leafing through the paper and, next to him, his son driving the car. The rest of the family, brother and sister, sitting in the back. The rain came down harder, forcing the inhabitants of the car to close the windows entirely. Shortly after, the cold windows began to fog up, causing the soldiers to have to wipe them clear with their sleeves.

It was late afternoon on another Thursday, and the sun was about to set. Yariv, the commander, told Udi to drive faster, but it didn't matter. There was a long line of cars and trucks inching along near the Nablus market. Yariv knew that the element of time was a deciding factor during routine operations, especially that day: the force under his command, moving from the south, was supposed to connect up with the other undercover team arriving from the north, while it was still light. The other pair, Yogev and Dan, arrived two days ago and had already situated themselves in the field.

Dan and Yariv were the commanders of the two forces that were supposed to join up. The order given by Yoav, a Lieutenant Colonel and the unit's commander, to Yariv and Dan during their last briefing before heading out to the field, was clear and unambiguous: the two forces had to meet up while it was still light – it was a critical condition of the operation.

"Guys, we have been looking for Sa'id for a very long time. For anybody who has forgotten, let me remind you that we are talking about one of the most wanted, dangerous, and devious leaders of Hamas in the West Bank – as if he has nine lives. He regularly disguises himself and changes his appearance all the time. You've all received the files on him from the intelligence department, including pictures with simulations of his preferred disguises. No doubt, a very creative and brave adversary. Be certain that I want to catch him just as badly as you do," said the unit commander to his squad members. "But the safety of the soldiers comes before anything else. Keep in mind that the two undercover forces will be joining up from two different directions, north and south, which makes the chances of a friendly-fire engagement extremely high. Do you understand?" he asked, pointing to the enlarged aerial photograph of the area around Sa'id's house.

"Crystal clear," they both said. And Dan even added in a sly tone, "Yoav, maybe you forgot, but we're getting discharged pretty soon. We've already bought tickets to South America and we don't intend to let anything or anyone – certainly not Sa'id – ruin our travel plans."

Yoav, the unit commander, liked the veteran combat soldier. He remembered something he was told about Dan before his assignment: "He's as brave as he is rude. It's a package deal." Yoav knew that Dan's team, the squad of full-time soldiers, all of whom had the rank of first sergeant, would be the most suited for this operation. Even though Dan was being a smart-ass, Yoav knew that, when he was in the field, he could count on him. This time, Yoav was commanding the operation from the territorial brigade headquarters in Nablus, while Dan was one of the commanders in the field.

Dan's wisecrack broke the tension in the room a bit and put a smile on the faces of those present, including Yoav's, even though he tried to fight it. The unit commander smiled and said to him, "Dan, it may surprise you to hear this, but I'm just like you – I'm also waiting for your discharge so that I don't have to look at you anymore. I'd even be happy to get a postcard from you guys from Brazil or Peru – but, in the meantime, do me a favor? Go get Sa'id and let's finish with this already?" The soldiers nodded and left the briefing room.

The pressure level in the undercover Mercedes began to rise. "We're going to miss it because of this fucking traffic," Yariv mumbled.

* * *

Traffic was always a point of vulnerability in the undercover forces. During every training exercise, the veteran instructors repeatedly drilled into the ears of the younger combat soldiers that standing still can cause unexpected problems. Yariv even recalled when he was starting out as a soldier in the unit a few years back, he was sitting in the cabin of a commercial van that got stuck in traffic in Jenin one afternoon. There were three soldiers sitting in the cabin, and in the back – separated from the cabin – sat four more.

Two peddlers innocently crept toward the front of the vehicle and presented the passengers with whatever goods they were selling. The soldiers in the cabin graciously abstained, but just then, an unexpected event occurred: a kid, probably ten, suddenly opened the back door and asked if he could have a ride. After a split-second, when the kid saw the special equipment inside the vehicle, he immediately understood that this wasn't just some innocuous van, but a military vehicle with undercover operatives inside.

He opened his mouth to shout, but the soldier who was sitting closest to the door acted quickly, pulling the kid into the van and covering his mouth. He sat the kid down on his knees and covered his eyes with his other hand, so that he wouldn't see the rest of the specialized equipment installed in the vehicle, or be able to identify the soldiers' faces. The senior combat soldier in the vehicle, the commander of the operation, called the operation off immediately. The driver diverted the vehicle to the road's shoulder, and the team was forced to drive straight to a government military building. There, the child would remain under supervision until his parents came to pick him up. And that's how, because of traffic, that operation got cancelled – and again, one of the senior, most-wanted terrorists in Jenin slipped through the soldiers' fingers.

* * *

Udi, the car's driver, got the hint. The red Mercedes cut across the white line into the opposite lane and shot forward while ignoring the barrage of honking by the other drivers waiting in traffic, as well as those coming from the opposite direction. On Yariv's order, Udi floored it and turned left at the nearest intersection. Inside the newspaper he was holding, Yariv had a folded map of the area, laminated in plastic, and he guided Udi to their destination using a side-route.

After three minutes of fast driving, the car approached its destination. Udi slowed the Mercedes down until it came to a stop on the side of the road . The car was covered in white dust that the rain had turned to mud. Yariv, dressed as an old man, turned to the pair of soldiers in the back seat and said to Yaki, "Barbie, so, just like we agreed in the debriefing – Barda and I'll get out and walk toward Sa'id's house. I assume we will make contact with him within 30 minutes at the most, before it gets dark. In any event, I'll be in touch on the radio when I've got Sa'id. You guys are meeting us at Interchange 64, and from there, we head west out of town. Got it?"

"Okay, we'll meet there. And I'm warning you, Yariv – if you call me that one more fucking time, you can walk back from the field on your own. The vehicle simply won't be there waiting for you, so don't bother looking for us..."

Udi, the driver, tapped his fingers on the steering wheel in annoyance. "Girls," he said to Yariv and Yaki, "maybe we can have this discussion later? In case you didn't notice, it's getting dark."

"All right, Bull, let's get going," Yariv said to Barda. He pressed on the concealed communications device in the vehicle and said, "Headquarters, this is sixty. We've started walking." This was the agreed upon sign to continue on foot from the car and to join up with the other force.

Barda, dressed up like a young man, opened the back door, got out of the vehicle, and opened the front door for the "old man," Yariv. In his right hand, Barda was holding the shopping basket, and in his left, he held Yariv by the armpit, as he was pretending to have great difficulty getting out of the passenger seat. Two youths on bicycles stopped to look at them for a moment before almost immediately continuing on their way. They didn't have any reason to suspect anything: they saw a son driving his elderly, infirm father while they said their goodbyes to the rest of the family members in the car.

Yariv cleared his throat in the way that older people who are sick are accustomed to doing, and then spat behind him. The undercover Mercedes continued on its way to the meeting point. Then Yariv raised his gaze to the horizon, saw the setting sun and whispered quickly to Barda, "Let's get going, Dan and Yogev are probably there already." The two soldiers quickened their steps toward their destination.

* * *

In the proficiency course for the unit, the combat soldiers were trained in how to become familiar with large, complex areas and to navigate them within minutes. During the final exam of the navigational portion of the course, the soldiers received maps of different neighborhoods in Palestinian towns only ten minutes before they had to go navigate that same area. Yariv discovered that the time pressure caused him to concentrate better and keep his bearings, as well as helped him memorize key points in the area. The quick, unexpected change in the way in which they arrived now forced Yariv to quickly learn the new area where they just arrived. He did this all while Udi was speeding through the city's alleyways.

Out of the fog of the descending darkness, Yariv spots the house where the senior Hamas member in Nablus, Sa'id, is supposed to be hiding out. From an earlier study by the Shin-Bet[3] intelligence officer, Yariv remembered that they were talking about a driven, twenty-nine-year-old man who manages the terrorist mechanism against Israel with cruel efficiency. The information that arrived to the Shin-Bet war room two days before was priceless: their man was going to be at this house until evening prayers – and then he would change locations, as has been his way for the past two years.

Darkness was falling quickly, and their window of opportunity was closing. The operational plan was complicated, and that's why it was assigned specifically to Dan and Yariv's team, an experienced and proficient team that had already proven itself time and again: the undercover force will quietly, and unsuspectingly, surround the house and then wait in place until Sa'id leaves for evening prayers. When the senior terrorist leaves for the mosque, the two pairs of soldiers will close in on him, "pluck" him off the street quietly and leave the area in their red Mercedes. This was the only way – all previous attempts to get to this cagey terrorist using regular military tactics failed. This time, the regiment commander decided, along with the unit commander, to try something else – the undercover forces. Yariv and Barda will encircle from the south, while Dan and Yogev's force will come in from the north. When eye contact is made between the two forces, the signal to commence will be given.

The pair of soldiers got closer to the residential structure, and then they had to split up – Yariv to the right hand corner, Barda to the left. Barda waited for Yariv, the operation's commander, to give the signal. Yariv cleared his throat. Yariv waited in place just one more second to make sure that Barda's location was good, and then continued walking slowly like an old man to the right

---

3. The Shin-Bet operates similarly to the FBI in the US.

side of the yard surrounding the house. The fog and the darkness began to descend, making it harder to locate the exact location they saw earlier on the aerial photograph. The annoying drizzle got stronger. Yariv saw a low wall to his right, which didn't appear on the photograph he received prior to the operation. However, he knew that aerial photographs weren't updated daily, so as not to arouse suspicion among the residents of the area.

On the ground, Yariv identified some long and bent rebar, sacks of sand and other equipment, which testified to the fact that the area was under construction. He looked again at the wall, which suddenly looked new to him – was that added within the last few weeks? He looked around for Dan and Yogev, but didn't see them. Suddenly, he was seized with doubt, because maybe he wasn't in the right place. Could the unplanned detour that they took en-route to the destination have brought him and Barda to the wrong place?

In front of him, at a distance of a few dozen yards, was the terrorist's house. It was a long, wide two-story structure with a lot of windows. At the entrance was a broad, black iron door. In front was a welcome mat for wiping off one's shoes. To the right of the door was a large, tiled area at the end of which he could see a few fruit trees. Yariv couldn't recall if the trees appeared on the aerial photographs. The sun had almost set, and due to the pittance of light that was left outside, the lights in the house were already on.

Yariv continued past the house, stopping to try to hear what was going on inside. Sounds of a conversation could be heard, and Yariv figured that the residents were getting ready for dinner. He remembered that the idea for the operation was that both pairs – he and Barda, Dan and Yogev – would surround the house, wait for Sa'id to leave for evening prayers, and then take him quietly and meet back up at the red Mercedes where Yaki and Udi were waiting. Standard operating procedure required that once they laid eyes on the house, they were not supposed to lose eye contact until the end of the operation. Yariv was certain that he was at the corner of the correct house, but this wall that he was seeing for the first time planted a doubt in his mind. Is he really where he's supposed to be? Maybe he's at the wrong house? Suddenly he wasn't sure of himself.

Yariv was still holding on to the folded newspaper, inside of which were the hidden aerial photographs. The veteran combat soldier understood very well the significance of his next action – opening a map while camouflaged as an Arab might expose the whole force. He looked to both sides and didn't see anyone. The drops of rain got bigger and closer together. *What lunatic would go out in this rain?* he thought to himself before he decided to sneak a peek at the aerial photographs. He leaned against the fence surrounding the house, placed his tattered suitcase on the muddy ground and opened the newspaper. The map, which was folded up inside of it, slipped out and fell into a puddle and got all muddy. Yariv got down on one knee and pressed up against the fence. He opened the map and started to clean the mud off the aerial photograph with his sleeve. Wiping it off erased the tactical signs for the battle plan he had marked for himself before heading out to the operation. The raindrops, which were getting stronger, dripped onto the thick plastic that covered the photograph and made it harder to pinpoint the exact location of the terrorist's house. Every few seconds, Yariv would look up in order to maintain continuous eye contact with the house. Again and again he tried to identify the new wall that he saw in front of the house – but to no avail. Yariv knew that the aerial photograph in his hand was relatively up-to-date and photographed only a few weeks ago. If so, why doesn't this wall appear in it?

His doubts intensified, and the suspicion that he was in the wrong place grew stronger. Suddenly, he thought he heard a noise behind him. He concentrated and recognized the sound – somebody walking on gravel. Yariv peeked over the fence and saw in the light of the setting sun two figures approaching the house from the south. He looked one last time at the aerial photograph in his hands, but wasn't able to successfully conclude that he didn't make a navigational error, and that he and Barda were indeed at the right place. The uncertainty gnawed at him, but he decided that despite the fact that the photograph didn't fit the scene, he and Barda were in the right place. *I've never gotten lost before while navigating in a developed area,* Yariv thought to himself. *Why is this happening now, of all times? It seems reasonable to assume that the wall was built immediately after the photograph was taken, and that's why it doesn't appear on the aerial photograph.*

According to his calculations, Dan was supposed to be in front of him, to the north, and Barda to his left, to the west. If so, Yariv thought, the figures approaching aren't our forces. He searched again and again for Dan, but couldn't find him. His heart skipped a beat: what if Dan and Yogev got lost and are approaching the house from the wrong direction?

The two figures walking towards the house were now about two hundred yards away. *Damn.* He remembered that Barda has the Mini Uzi. He knew that, at this range, his pistol wasn't any use. He knew he had to maintain eye contact with the house, but couldn't take his eyes off the two figures that were coming closer to him. Suddenly, the two figures slowed down and split up – one continued in his direction and the other one to the left. The rain got stronger and the fog got thicker and thicker. The visibility dropped to almost zero, and Yariv lost visual contact with the approaching figure. He squinted his eyes and tried to see through the fog, but he wasn't able to see him. Time stood still and every second seemed like an eternity. He realized that he hadn't looked at the house for almost a minute, but was currently preoccupied with trying to locate the approaching figure.

Yariv decided not to take any chances: He took the gun out of his coat pocket, quietly cocked it, and even checked to make sure the bullet had indeed entered the chamber. Then, he quietly returned the hammer and released the safety. The rain continued and the drops smacked against the keffiyeh on his head. Steam fogged the inside of the thick glasses that were still perched on his nose, the water dripping slowly into his eyes. He quickly took his disguise glasses off, put them in his jacket pocket, and wiped his eyes with the back of his hand. His gun was already fitted with a silencer. The figure was getting closer, and Yariv didn't have time to open the suitcase at his feet and activate the night vision, or the communication device in it. He decided not to take a chance, and so he bent over again, pressed up against the fence, held his breath and listened closely. The sound of the intensifying rain and the rolling thunder kept him from hearing the approaching footsteps. He looked past the fence and saw that the suspicious figure had gotten close enough to be in range of his pistol. He thought about the standard operating protocol for apprehending a suspicious individual, but decided against it immediately – the sound of him shouting and a gunshot in the air would expose his whole force.

He was holding the gun's grip between his two palms. The silhouette of the figure alternated between being visible and being hidden in the heavy fog. Yariv's finger stroked the trigger. He tried to aim through the gun's metal sight, but knew that the fog would make it ineffective. Suddenly, like out of a plume of smoke, the figure burst forth from the fog: legs exposed slowly, the edge of his pants were soaked from the rain. Yariv felt the pulse in his neck explode, but decided to wait one more moment. He focused on the figure's shoes, but couldn't tell if they belonged to either Dan or Yogev.

The strong wind diverted the fog for a moment, and the experienced combat soldier's breath caught in his throat. In front of him, about twenty yards away, stood the figure. The fog was still concealing the figure's torso and head, but one thing was certain: he was holding something in his hand. The mosque wasn't that far from here – could it be some innocent bystander coming back from the mosque with a Quran in his hand? Yariv thought about whether to try and quietly apprehend the approaching figure without using his weapon. In such a case, he knew from past experience that it could quickly devolve into a noisy confrontation, right in front of a senior terrorist's house. He remembered the rule that the unit's instructors drove into the soldier's minds over and over: do everything possible to avoid having to draw your weapon – but if you've already drawn it, don't hesitate to use it. Yariv, still hidden behind the low wall, knew that he would be exposed in a few more steps. The figure came a few more steps in his direction. Yariv strained his eyes again and decided for certain: the object in the approaching figure's hand was a gun. When he identified the gun, the die was cast: he aimed his drawn pistol at the center of mass of the approaching figure and began to slowly squeeze the cold, hard trigger.

Yariv couldn't imagine that the next few moments would change his life and those of his team members forever.

CHAPTER 2
December 1993, Jerusalem

It was early in the morning, and the Jerusalem cold penetrated his bones. Gaza Street, where Yariv was walking briskly, was still devoid of people. The sidewalk was slippery because of the rain, and Yariv tried not to step in the many puddles that had formed. He was wearing jeans, a dark-blue windbreaker and sneakers. A bus sped past him, spraying him with a stream of dirty water. The cast on Yariv's right arm got all wet. Yariv hurled a juicy curse in the driver's direction and, after a moment, found what he had been looking for – building number twenty four. He stopped at the entrance to the building and shook off the drops of rain that had accumulated on him. He then saw that his sneakers and the hem of his jeans were soaked thanks to the speeding bus driver.

The stairwell was dark and cold, and Yariv felt around on the wall until he found the light switch. He pushed the red button, turning on the light in the stairwell. In the yellow light, he identified the stairs leading to the upper floors, a plastic potted plant, message board for the homeowners association, and mail slots. The building had a wide entrance, and on the other side of the entrance, he saw a red stroller for twins and mountain bikes that were chained to the peeling railing. The light went off after barely thirty seconds had passed. *Off already? What a bunch of cheapskates these wealthy folks from Rehavia are,* he thought to himself and again felt around for the light switch.

When the yellowish light went on again, he quickly scanned the mail slots: on most of the boxes there were three or four different names pasted on them, and he assumed that most of the building's residents were students who simply rented an apartment together. For a moment, he was reminded of his sister, Inbal. She was getting her masters in mathematics, and would occasionally share her stories about the weird roommates that came her way. His finger moved quickly over what was written on the mail slots until he stopped at the name he was searching for: Ravid. He felt around for the bulge of the number protruding from the mailbox beneath the sticker bearing the name and determined that it was a "6." Must be on the second floor. Yariv glanced at his watch. It was five minutes to eight in the morning. He took the steps two at a time as he hurried up to the clinic and stood in front of the door in order to catch his breath. There was a small sign on the door, and on it, written in orange, block print, was the name: "RAVID."

His fingers rolled into a fist and he extended his hand to knock on the brown door, but something stopped him. He slowly lowered his hand, and just stood in front of the closed door. He felt a familiar feeling – his racing pulse, the pounding in his temples, the dryness in his mouth. *Incredible,* he thought, *how many crazy things have I done in my life, and I'm getting all nervous about seeing a psychologist?*

The light in the stairwell went out again, and Yariv just stood there in the dark in front of the door. Like two boxers in a ring, sizing each other up before the start of the fight – that's how he felt standing there in the dark in front of the psychologist's door.

He closed his eyes, took two deep breaths, and became engrossed in the quiet of the dark stairwell.

* * *

The week before, an unusual message was waiting for him in his team's room in the combat soldier's complex: "The unit commander requests your urgent presence in his chambers." He had a bad feeling about this, but he didn't try to postpone the evil decree and immediately went to Yoav's office. He knew the office well, as well as the girls working there – he had spent many hours there being briefed and debriefed both before and after missions. Sometimes he even tried to flirt with the girls, and was even moderately successful. But this time, Yariv felt that the familiar faces weren't the same as they were before. He knocked lightly on the door and went in without waiting for an answer.

Yoav had a simple, modest office: a long, light-brown desk for meetings, and various certificates and trophies were displayed on the shelves along the walls, including one for excellence in the recent IDF championships. At the head of the table was Yoav's chair and, behind it, pictures of the unit's fallen soldiers. The bookshelf on the wall was crammed with dozens of volumes on military subjects, as well as some books Yoav received while he was visiting other units.

On the wall next to the books were many framed photos documenting VIPs who had visited the unit, among them the prime minister, minister of defense, and the chief of the general staff. Yariv remembered these visits well – in most cases, the combat soldiers were asked to prepare a demonstration in order to impress the esteemed guest. The combat soldiers actually enjoyed it – anything was better than *Krav Maga*[4] training. The team chosen

---

4. Israeli hand-to-hand combat training.

for the demonstration bought a bunch of large pretzels from one of the Arab villages in the area, wore disguises typical of what they might wear on any given mission, and turn the unit's basketball court into a model of an authentic Arab marketplace – shouts in Arabic, peddlers with carts, and fruit and vegetable stands. One team even went one step further and brought in two donkeys.

The enthusiastic visitor would be seated at the edge of the court to enjoy the demonstration and take it all in. The reactions didn't take long to arrive: even the most senior guests were like school kids, giddy with excitement. After two or three minutes, the real demonstration began: a car would come speeding into the improvised bazaar, slam on its brakes, and out would come a few combat soldiers all dressed up as Arabs, apprehend one of those present, put him in the car and quickly leave. That whole act, Yariv recalled, would only take a few seconds, and would leave the spectators shocked and enthralled. He knew that the huge impression the demonstration helped soften up whoever was in charge before asking for additional funding, special new equipment, or other advanced and innovative technological toys.

"Yariv, how's it going?" Yoav was standing there smiling a broad grin. "Come have a seat next to me."

The white cast on Yariv's right arm, a testament to what had happened in Nablus, was almost completely covered in the colorful signatures of his friends on the team.

Yoav pulled out the chair to his right and motioned for Yariv to sit. Yariv came over, shook Yoav's hand with his left hand, and they both sat down. Two other people were sitting to Yoav: the unit's doctor, Dr. Tomer, who had the rank of major on his shoulder, and next to him sat a lieutenant colonel, whom Yariv didn't recognize.

Yoav pointed to the two and said, "Okay, Yariv, Dr. Tomer needs no introduction. This is Dr. Landau, the chief psychologist of our division in the West Bank."

Yariv shook hands with both of them and said sarcastically to

Yoav, "So what's the deal, Yoav, are you opening up a field hospital here?"

Yoav's face darkened for a moment. "No, Yariv, this time it's a little bit more serious than you think." It was so quiet in the room, one could hear the wind whistling through the open window.

Dr. Landau turned to Yariv and said, "Yariv, I'm glad to meet you face to face. I'm sorry that we're forced to meet under these circumstances, but it can't wait. I've heard good things about you and your team. You guys, the combat soldiers, you don't know me personally, but I am the one responsible for the psychological and mental aspects of the professional training in the course. My team created the questionnaires that you guys filled out, and we also analyze the sociometric tests you take during the course and after. I don't need to tell you that the mental part is the one that most strongly impacts and determines your actions in the undercover operations and, in my opinion, is no less important than the physical skills you picked up during the course, such as Krav Maga, how to shoot, and operational fitness. I suppose that you aren't aware of it but, even after you finish the course, there are still evaluations regarding your mental state and your abilities to act in a combat role in the unit." He paused his flow of words for a moment, took his glasses off, and looked right at Yariv, who sat across from him and didn't flinch. "After what happened in Nablus, we received reports that you were behaving in a strange manner: you're impatient, shout a lot, have angry outbursts, joke around less and are closed off. These are classic, clear symptoms that point to a post-traumatic reaction."

"Post-trauma?!" Yariv raised his voice. "What are you talking about? So I was lightly wounded – so what? You know how many times I've been shot at or how many times I've shot at others? Doctor, with all due respect, you have no idea what you're talking about. Yoav, are you listening to this?" Yariv turned his gaze and looked right in the unit commander's direction.

Yoav signaled to him with his hand to stop speaking and then, in a quiet but declarative voice said, "Yariv, I want to ask you to listen to what we have to say until the end. No one is blaming you for what happened in Nablus. It's clear to everybody you did the best you could there. However, from the reports that I received from the squad, and also from the guys on your team, it's clear to everyone that you're going through something – and don't tell me you aren't. There's no shame and no weakness in it. We're people, not robots, and we're affected by what we go through. I think that you feel guilty or responsible for how things went and how we got to where we are. Especially in light of what happened to Dan."

When Yariv heard his best friend's name leave Yoav's mouth, he lowered his head. Yoav understood that he may have touched that very sensitive nerve too early, but he knew that he had to lay all his cards on the table.

He stopped for a moment, placed his hand on Yariv's shoulder and then continued. "Look, a few soldiers came to me and asked to talk to me in private. I'm talking about people who love you, and care about you, Yariv. These are people who grew up with you in the unit. Who fought with you in the alleyways. People who covered you with their bodies, where every one of them would take a bullet for you... these aren't strangers, or somebody from the outside. These are the people that built this unit. I have to admit, they were extremely distraught. They aren't used to seeing you like this. This isn't the Yariv that they know. Some of them expressed that you look completely different – despondent, switched off, sad. One of the soldiers even said to me that you look as if somebody emptied you out from inside and left only the husk. He even used the phrase "hollow." Listen, not one of them is a psychologist, but they sense that it's not because of the bullet you took, but because of what happened to Dan. For them also, by the way, it's not so simple: after so many successful operations where we attacked with the element of surprise and succeeded – to suddenly get hit like this. It's not simple for anybody on the team or in the unit. Until the incident in Nablus, we all felt – and I am including myself here – a type of invincibility. Lucky for us, we had a very long string of successful ops over a long time. We got used to winning every battle every time there was action. Maybe we were complacent in Nablus – we'll look into that – but that's not the issue here. The issue here is you, and how to get you to snap out of this and move on with us."

Yariv raised his downcast head. Yoav sensed that the veteran combat soldier had calmed down a bit, and continued in his quiet tone. "Yariv, allow me to let you in on a secret: when I was injured last summer during that chase after Abu-Issa in Tulkarem, I also went through a difficult period – physically, but also mentally. We all know that the situations that combat soldiers face in the field aren't easy – physically or mentally. It takes a toll, Yariv. We're aware of this and try to give you guys all the available tools to deal with these aspects of belonging to this unit. But sometimes, the experience is too much and very powerful, an injury occurs – and causes trauma. Physically or mentally. I greatly appreciate you and trust you one-hundred percent – and you know that. But, as unit commander, I have a responsibility for the lives of the other soldiers. For the moment, the physical injury you've sustained has technically sidelined you from any field activity. But at the same time, from what we understand and hear from a number of soldiers, both from the team and the platoon, it seems as if you're currently, and I emphasize currently, in a certain place mentally that makes it harder for you to operate in the field. And so, even if tomorrow your arm were to completely heal, I'm not prepared and cannot authorize your return to the field – because this is not only about you. This affects the rest of the team and could even put lives in danger. Yariv, we tend to see ourselves as machines and supermen, but I've got news for you – at the end of the day, we're flesh and blood. Unfortunately, you went through a very difficult incident two weeks ago in Nablus. Dr. Tomer, Dr. Landau and I believe that you need to undergo a period of therapy in order to get over the trauma and to make a full return to active service."

"I don't understand," insisted Yariv. "What's the difference between the other operations that we did and this one two weeks ago in Nablus? If you guys think that the consequences of these operations hurt the combat soldiers mentally, then let's close up shop and be done with it. Of course it affects us, but the soldiers, and certainly I, know how to absorb and deal with it. Excuse me, but I don't accept what you're saying," he said, raising his voice at the end.

The tension in the room increased. Dr. Tomer, the unit doctor, signaled with his eyes to Yoav that he would like to intervene in the discussion. He turned to Yariv and said quietly, "Yariv, how many years have we known each other, you and me? Almost two years since I arrived here from the reconnaissance platoon. We've spent a night or two in the field, haven't we?"

Yariv was quiet and nodded his head with a smile. All the combat soldiers in the unit liked the doctor, who always did everything he could to care for their well-being. He remembered the long nights and the ambushes when Dr. Tomer was with them in the field, just like one of the guys; he remembered him running under fire in order to treat the wounded. Dr. Tomer was the one who treated him and his team in Nablus. No doubt that this doctor deserved his trust – rightfully so. Yariv nodded in agreement, and the unit's doctor continued. "I say these things to you, first, as a friend, but also as a doctor, as a professional. You're a talented young man. You're motivation is endless, and you have abilities that not everybody has. As far as I'm concerned, Yariv, you're the Rolls Royce of the team, all right? And I say this with the utmost seriousness – I'm not kidding. But even the most sophisticated and most advanced vehicle, once in a while, needs to go to the mechanic for a tune-up, get checked out, to rest a little, and to receive supportive care. And again, I don't mean your physical injury. That isn't what worries me in the long run because, in my estimation, after you remove the cast and do some physiotherapy, you can go back to action within two or three months at the most. What worries me more are the mental consequences of the difficult incident that you experienced. Especially given what happened to Dan. It's important that you know, Yariv, that care and support are not bad words and certainly not a sign of weakness – quite the opposite. We're counting on you to continue to serve for a long time, both full service duty and reserve duty, specifically with this team – because we already know you don't want to hear about the officers' training course – and for this, we suggest that you go on a sort of vacation, whereby you will be treated by the best professionals available in the field. Think what would have happened if, God forbid, your gunshot wound was more serious – would you even be asking the question as to whether to be hospitalized and treated? Of course not. As far as I'm concerned, you were injured twice during the incident in Nablus – physically, in the arm, but in your mind as well. In your soul. Yariv, you have to get treatment and support in order to get out of this and back to yourself."

Yariv was quiet for a moment and seemed to be deep in thought. Yoav added, "Yariv, we are explaining this to you because it's important that you understand the rationale. But the bottom line, this thing, this taking a break for therapy – it's non-negotiable. I've gone over it thoroughly with the medical staff, and this is my final decision as commander of the unit, as well as theirs as professionals who are advising us. Look, I can't force you to go to psycho-therapy and talk about what happened there in Nablus but, as of now, as far as I'm concerned, you're prohibited from taking part in any operations – until you get the ok from the therapist. By the way, from my side, nobody needs to know about this. So that nobody on the team makes a big deal about it, I'm issuing a special vacation – for starters, take a month's sick leave, on the house."

Yariv raised his eyes from the table. It was beginning to dawn on him that this was a final decision, and that the matter wasn't open to negotiation. He looked at the three officers in front of him and said, "Yoav, I understand you aren't asking me, rather, you're telling me. Fine, if there's no other way, so now what?"

Dr. Landau, the division psychologist, looked at the young combat soldier and said, "We made some inquiries on your behalf, and came to the conclusion that there is one person in particular suitable to treat your case. His name is Dr. Yehonatan Ravid, and he's a very experienced clinical psychologist who has been in practice for a long time. I believe that you two will hit it off immediately. But understand – this isn't just another psycho-analyst. We're talking about a real man in the field. He was an officer in the paratroopers' brigade. During the Yom Kippur war, he enlisted as a long-serving and experienced reserve officer in the commando unit, and took part in the intense fighting in the southern front – and then was taken prisoner, and released a few months later. After he got back from captivity, he decided to study psychology and did his residency working with mental trauma in the armed forces. He did his PhD thesis on PTSD and other related symptoms. Dr. Ravid was also one of the founders of "Awake at Night," an NGO for returned POWs. I'm giving you his biographical information so you know that he's not just some clerk from the Kirya,[5] but rather someone who was a combat soldier, just like you. His background allows him to better understand what a combat soldier like you goes through during an operation because he's been there. Also, he treated and treats many of the security personnel with similar problems – special forces soldiers, Mossad and Shin-Bet operatives that have encountered emotional distress, and many other good people. You could say that he's like the "in-house psychologist" for the entire security establishment. Because of his special role,

---

5. Military compound in Tel Aviv that acts as the main military base in Israel.

he has a very high level of security clearance – you are free to tell him about everything that you've gone through and what bothers you, including anything having to do with classified matters. In the world of clinical psychology, there is no rule that says that the therapist has to have undergone an experience similar to what the patient has in order to understand him. I still think that, in a case such as yours, Dr. Ravid's military background can only help him in your therapeutic process. Yariv, go see him. Sit with him – and trust me, you'll come back to the unit and the team as good as new."

The tension in the room eased a bit. Yoav got up from his chair, placed his hand on Yariv's back and said with a smile, "You'd be surprised, but a little sick leave won't kill you. Dr. Tomer will give you as much as you need – and nobody else in the unit needs to know about this aside from the three of us. As far as their concerned, you're going on sick leave until your arm is better. We'll tell them something about rehabilitative physiotherapy that you need to do every day, and that's why you won't be here for a while."

Dr. Tomer also came over to Yariv. He gave the injured soldier a hug and said to him in a quiet voice, "Yariv, go civilian, spend time with your family and friends, get out and smell the roses. You deserve it after everything you've been through. I'll let you in on a little secret: there's life outside the unit, and outside the army, and I'm telling you that as someone who has been in the service for a while now. Get out a little, go eat a home cooked meal, go out with some girls, but most important – don't forget, there's enough bad guys for everybody."

All four in the meeting room smiled. Yoav lightly clapped Yariv on the shoulder and said, "Come on, it'll be fine, Yariv. And now, take yourself and that ugly-ass cast of yours and get out of my face already before I change my mind."

Yariv nodded, understanding, shook the hands of the two doctors with his good hand and left the unit commander's office.

* * *

The light in the stairwell suddenly turned on and Yariv heard the sounds of a baby crying. Already used to the darkness, he squinted instinctively. From the floor above, he heard the sound of a young woman trying to calm her crying baby. He looked at his watch and discovered that it was already a minute after eight o'clock. *What's happening to me?* He wondered. *I've been standing here for six minutes. What the hell am I afraid of?*

He raised his hand and knocked on the door. After a few moments, he heard the sound of approaching steps. The door opened and in front of him stood the psychologist, Dr. Yehonatan Ravid.

"Hello, Yariv. I'm glad you came. You're welcome to come in," said his host and shook Yariv's good hand.

The clinic was small and modest: light-blue curtains on the window, some pictures hanging on the walls, a small kitchenette on the right and, in the middle of the room, two armchairs. The psychologist was tall, handsome, and kept himself in decent shape for his age. Yariv assumed he was closing in on the end of his fifth decade. He had a full head of hair that had started to turn a silvery-grey and wore thin-rimmed glasses, dark-blue pants and a light-blue, checkered sweater. When he had reached out to shake hands, Yariv noticed a thin, gold wedding band.

"I see it's raining outside. Come, hang your coat over here, next to the heater. It's warm."

"Thank you, doctor."

"You can call me Yehonatan, that's fine. Did you have any trouble finding the building?"

"Not particularly. You know, I've navigated slightly more problematic areas than this…"

Dr. Ravid smiled broadly.

"I apologize for the puddles I'm leaving on your floor," Yariv said, slightly embarrassed. "A bus driver was hugging the sidewalk and arranged a second shower for me this morning." He tried pulling his cast through the jacket sleeve, but wasn't able to free it. The thick, wet cast got stuck, and Yariv had a hard time freeing himself with his good hand.

"Can I help you off with your coat?" the psychologist asked quietly, but Yariv adamantly refused. Again and again he tried by himself to get his arm with the cast out of the sleeve, and his face twisted up in pain. It was obvious that the fresh wound was indeed very painful. Dr. Ravid mulled whether to offer to help him again – but in the end he decided against it. Without knowing Yariv at all, he felt that it might be embarrassing for him and could be seen as another personal failure on his part, and an admission of his new physical limitations.

After a few additional attempts, Yariv succeeded in freeing his cast from the sleeve. He hung his coat by the heater.

"The kitchen is over there," Dr. Ravid said, pointing to the kitchen. "If you want something hot to drink – feel free."

Yariv thanked him with a nod of his head and walked slowly to the kitchen. The psychologist sat in the living room quietly when suddenly there was a loud sound of breaking glass. After a moment, Yariv appeared in the kitchen doorway, his face red with embarrassment. "I'm so sorry," he said in a quiet voice, "but the jar with the Turkish coffee slipped out of my hand and broke… understand, it's this fucking cast…" He was holding a half-full glass of steaming hot Turkish coffee in his good hand. The length of the cast was stained with coffee grounds.

Dr. Ravid smiled understandingly. "It's fine," he said. "Forget about it, Yariv. Come sit down and let's talk a bit."

Yariv placed the glass on the low table in front of him and then tried to shake the coffee grounds from his cast, but that only made it worse. He blew forcefully on the coffee grounds that remained and then sat in the armchair across from Dr. Ravid.

"So, what, doctor, where's the couch I'm supposed to lie down on and tell you about how my mother didn't breastfed me enough and it was all downhill from there, and here I am?" Yariv asked sarcastically and took a sip of his coffee.

The psychologist smiled. "You might be surprised," he answered pleasantly, "but I don't work that way. The goal of therapy is completely different. I don't investigate, I'm not a detective. I'm interested in talking with you to understand what you're experiencing. In time, I hope we can reach a point where we can also help you feel better."

"Look, doctor," Yariv said, intentionally addressing him by his title and not his first name, "the truth is that I'm here for one reason and one reason only – because they are forcing me. I don't know what they told you about me, but my unit commander dropped an ultimatum in my lap and informed me that, right now, I'm frozen out of active duty until I undergo therapy, and then everybody will see that I'm fine. That's the deal, and I really want to get back to my team and to active duty. Sorry for being direct but, in my opinion, this is all for nothing. I admit that I'm floored about what happened, but I'm not depressed, I don't have PTSD or anything else. I got shot. It's not pleasant, but it's also not the end of the world. Perhaps I'm letting you down right at the get-go, but it's important that you know my true feelings on the matter. By the way, I don't have a problem sitting here and telling you anything you want to hear, despite the fact that I think it's a waste of time. But if I have to I have to – come on, I'll tell you in ten minutes what happened during the operation in Nablus, what happened to Dan and how, and be done with it. What do you say, doctor?"

Dr. Yehonatan Ravid looked at Yariv and his body language. He was still trying to remove the last of the coffee grounds that were stuck to his cast. As if the act of removing all those coffee grounds would solve all of his problems – what happened would be erased, everything will go back to how it was, and the cast would also return to its gleaming white color. He saw that Yariv had yet to internalize his new situation. Even breaking the coffee jar – a silly mistake that could happen to anyone – was another blow to Yariv. Even though it was minor, and only symbolic, it was a blow that highlighted his bleak situation.

The experienced psychologist understood that they had a long and complicated journey ahead of them, for many reasons. Yariv reminded him of himself during the time after he was released from captivity. Even he, during those difficult times, wouldn't agree to meet with the psychologist and the rest of the professional staff, and only repeated the same mantra to everybody all the time: "Leave me alone, I'm fine." But after having persistent nightmares and genuinely understanding that something was wrong with his psyche, he began to consider the issue of therapy. Looking back, after he was exposed to the process, he discovered that he had been mistaken about how he approached the matter.

How can I successfully find the way to Yariv's heart? Dr. Ravid thought to himself. It was evident from his body language and his aggressive behavior that he was going through a difficult period. *How can I explain to him that his physical injuries are the easy part of rehabilitation, and that the mending of his mental fractures will likely take much longer to heal?*

"I understand what you're saying, Yariv," he finally said. "You went through something that isn't easy, and I believe that to completely ignore it is a mistake. I don't intend to force you to be here, that's not the point. By the way, it may surprise you and may even seem like I'm being disloyal to the system I work for but, in my opinion, "dropping an ultimatum into your lap" like you say your unit commander did, is a major, fundamental error. You can't force a person to go to therapy – and you certainly can't expect a person to willingly take an active and positive part in a touchy, sensitive process like this by using threats of one sort or another. This has to come from you, from within. You are the one who has to feel that something inside you isn't quite right, and you need to want to heal the wound that has opened in your psyche because of what you went through."

The veteran psychologist stopped talking, but watched Yariv's movements with his eyes as he sat across from him. He felt that there was somewhat of a softening of Yariv's demeanor. *This is the moment*, he thought to himself, *to push – just a little more.*

"Yariv, it's important for me to emphasize to you that the therapeutic process is not a lifelong commitment. What I mean is, the moment you feel that you want to stop – I won't stand in your way. And therefore, I suggest that we begin and see how things develop. Worst case – we stop and part as friends. What have you got to lose?"

The room was quiet. Dr. Ravid knew that he had brought the young soldier to a crossroads – and he had to let Yariv make his own choice.

"To tell you the truth, doctor," Yariv began, looking doubtful. "My limited experience with psychologists hasn't been positive, to put it mildly."

"What do you mean? Have you been in therapy before?"

"Not exactly," Yariv was quick to respond. "About a year ago, we had an incident in the unit. Some solider on my team was kicked out because he didn't try to take out an armed terrorist that was shooting at us. He preferred to hide behind a nearby brick wall. He was petrified and couldn't function. The soldier standing behind him saw what was happening, pushed him out of the way, and then he shot and killed the terrorist. That's how the incident ended."

"I understand," the psychologist responded. "And what happened afterward when you returned to the unit?"

"Of course, there was a debriefing, like after every operation.

During the debriefing, this thing came up, and the unit commander decided that, at the moment of truth, the soldier failed, and that there's no guarantee that it won't repeat itself in the future. Therefore, he kicked our soldier out of the team and transferred him to the unit's weapons department. That is – he went from being a combat soldier to being a desk jockey."

"All right, that is a rather extraordinary move, but not surprising, especially in a unit like Duvdevan. What happened after that?" asked Dr. Ravid and crossed his legs.

"What happened after that was that there was resentment among some of the soldiers – the ones who didn't agree with that decision. I won't get into the whole discussion that ensued there, but kicking him out caused discontent in the team, and the unit commander decided to take a break and send all the soldiers in that specific team for 'a week-long team development session' – that's what they called it – at the Goldmintz Institute in Netanya. It's like a vacation compound for soldiers, like the Soldier's Institute," Yariv added.

"Yeah, I know the place. I headed a few workshops for soldiers there. Okay, I suppose that at this point the army psychologist entered the picture?"

"Yes. They put a psychologist on the team, who was supposed to talk to us about our feelings and emotions about what happened. So, of course, each one of us sat down and talked about his feelings, but I felt like he didn't really believe what he was hearing."

"What made you think that? Did he say something?" the psychologist challenged him.

"Not exactly. He never said anything definitive but, from just how he said things, I got the feeling that he didn't really believe what he was hearing. Look, doctor, he had high-level clearance, so we told him about a lot of real events that we experienced in the field. But we felt that the stories we told him about what we went through and the examples we brought to make our points, in his eyes, were made up and imaginary. I'll say it again – he didn't say anything, but the feeling he projected, or at least what we picked up on from him, was that he didn't believe our stories." Yariv finished his coffee in two long gulps and placed the glass containing the coffee grounds on the table.

"And how did you feel about this?" Dr. Ravid asked.

"The truth is, I wasn't surprised. In our unit, we're used to people from the outside not believing our stories. Whenever we share what we do with outside parties, they're convinced we're putting them on. It doesn't matter if it's a journalist who came to write an article on the unit, soldiers from other units, or our civilians friends – we always get that same stare of disbelief. It's extremely frustrating. Listen, I know that some of what we do and recounting the unit's combat heritage sounds like some crazy action movie, but it's the honest truth."

"And did you bring your concerns to his attention?"

"No. No way. I just wanted that workshop to end so we could get out of there as fast as possible. Looking back, it was a mistake. I think that I should have said something to him. Maybe even started in on him a little about it," said Yariv, and made a face.

"You know, Yariv, there's an interesting phenomenon that happens to groups of people who experience something difficult and challenging together. For example, a group of people gets kidnapped, or rather – a group of survivors who all experienced a traumatic event. Within these groups, there is a solidarity the group forms as well as a "turning inward," apart from all the other members of the group and, at the same time, they tend to discount whoever isn't part of their little group. One of the consequences of this phenomenon is a feeling of 'nobody outside my group can understand me like my friends in the group, like those who were along with me and experienced the same thing.' As a professional, I must admit that it's very difficult to create an atmosphere of trust in a situation such as this, whereby the patient decides ahead of time that the therapist has no chance of possibly understanding him. Let me guess – after the psychologist gave off that vibe of 'I don't believe any bit of what you're saying,' you went back to the comfort of your team, and that just strengthened your conviction, as well as your team members' conviction, that no professional who comes from the outside could possibly understand the truth like your friends on the team." Dr. Ravid finished speaking and looked Yariv in the eye.

Yariv was quiet. It was clear that the psychologist's words made an impression on him. *He's dead on*, Yariv thought to himself. *That's exactly what I felt at that shitty-ass workshop.* The rain outside intensified and pounded on the glass window forcefully. The external metal shutters rattled loudly in the strong wind.

"Yariv," the doctor said addressing him, "have you heard of the expression 'the 81st lash?'"

Yariv was quiet for a moment, lifted his gaze to the ceiling and exhaled thoroughly. "No. That doesn't ring a bell. What is it, a book or movie?"

"No, Yariv. It's an expression from a very interesting story. Would you like to hear it?"

"Truth be told, doctor, you've aroused my curiosity. Let's have it," Yariv answered him and folded his arms across his chest.

"Okay, so the story goes like this. By the way, this story is completely authentic: during Eichmann's trial in 1961, the prosecuting attorney in the trial, Gideon Hausner, called many witnesses to the stand to testify against the Nazi criminal. The witnesses told what they saw and experienced in the death camps. Among them was a Holocaust survivor who testified that he saw one of the senior Nazi officers orchestrate a field trial held in one of the ghettos against a boy, about fifteen years old, who was accused of smuggling food into the ghetto. The boy was found guilty and whipped 80 times by a German SS officer. The witness told how, after the 80 lashes, the boy collapsed onto the floor and appeared to be dead. In addition, the witness told the prosecutor that even the German officer was sure of it, because he wiped the sweat from his brow, wound up his whip and left."

"What, is that the end of the story?" Yariv said, furrowing his brow.

"Not at all. The witness explained that, after a few minutes, the young boy lying on the floor started to move. Everybody present was surprised by what they saw. And after a few more moments, he got up and just limped away from there."

Yariv didn't say anything. From what he knew about the Nazi whippings, he was trying to wrap his head around how a fifteen-year-old boy could have taken eighty lashes and lived, but was having a hard time seeing it. He opened his mouth to say something, but Dr. Ravid continued.

"Wait, the story isn't over. After the witness finished his story, the prosecutor, Gideon Hausner as I said, turned to him and asked him, 'Sir, can you see the boy who was whipped, as per your story, in this courtroom today?' Silence filled the courtroom. The witness raised his hand and pointed to Michael Goldman, a police officer, who was the personal assistant to the prosecutor and said, 'That's him. That's the boy who took the eighty lashes.'"

"Are you serious? The investigating officer in Eichmann's trial was that boy who got whipped?"

"Indeed he was. At this point, a commotion erupted in the courtroom such that the judge had to stop the proceedings," the psychologist finished.

"Absolutely incredible. Really, fascinating, but what does that have to do with me?"

"After the gripping testimony, the press became very interested in the police investigator, Michael Goldman. He became a symbol of Jewish resistance – from a boy who was whipped and humiliated, he became the Jewish investigator who settled the score with Eichmann, the symbol of the Nazi machine of destruction. Goldman gave many interviews to the press and, in all of them, he was asked: "Why didn't you tell anyone about this incredible story?"

"Good question, what was his answer?"

"Goldman said, 'I did tell people, but nobody believed me.' He told his interviewers that when he came to Israel and told this story, he was faced with total disbelief. No reasonable person was ready to accept the story of a fifteen-year-old Jewish boy, suffering from malnutrition, cold and neglect, who withstood eighty lashes by a Nazi officer – and lived to tell about it. So he stopped telling it and kept it to himself. And here, allow me to quote Goldman: 'And this was the 81st lash.' That is, the fact that nobody in the community who heard his story believed him, for him, constituted an additional lash on top of the eighty he had already endured from the Nazi officer."

Yariv was quiet, as was the psychologist. He got the message loud and clear.

"Yariv," said the psychologist, breaking the silence. "It's clear that you're going through a rough patch. In order to help you deal with it and get you back to your regular routine, I need your full trust in me and the process. I'm here to help. It won't be a short process, and it won't be pleasant touching exposed nerves, but I feel that you're in a place where the therapeutic process is necessary for you to function. But, like I said, the ball's in your court."

Yariv remained silent. *There is something to what the psychologist sitting across from him was saying,* he thought. *Maybe, despite everything, it makes sense to give the process a chance? If it doesn't help, it certainly can't hurt. I mean, I have to be here anyway, so why not give it my best? And this doctor seems sympathetic and understanding. Like he said, what have I got to lose?*

Outside, the rain continued, and the sound of hail could even be heard smacking against the glass. "Well, if I go outside now,

I'll probably catch pneumonia. My cast will undoubtedly get wet, which they told me is strictly forbidden. Looks like I'm stuck here with you," Yariv answered with a thin smile after a few moments of silence.

The psychologist also produced a light smile. He sensed that the soldier in front of him was starting to open up, and he knew that this was the first step on the long road ahead of them. Yariv got up from his chair and stood in front of the window. Dr. Ravid looked at the young man's back. Yariv stood there a few moments, looking out at the wet street below.

Yariv's stayed silent. The psychologist was also quiet. He had spent countless hours in therapy having conversations with patients who arrived with a negative attitude about the complicated process, which requires exposing oneself, being open and being honest. Therefore, Dr. Ravid was quiet for the moment and didn't utter a word: he knew that this specific moment was critical – the moment when the patient decides to "jump into the deep end" and trust the therapist and cooperate with the demands of the therapy.

Yariv was still standing with his back to Dr. Ravid, his nose right up against the window, his good hand deep inside the pocket of his jeans, eyes watching the pounding rain outside. And then, without warning, he began spitting out a long monologue without any pauses or bothering to stop. His stream of words and breathing fogged the cold window pane with a condensation that fluctuated rhythmically with his intonations.

"Dr. Ravid, I told you that I came here because of what happened to Dan, my best friend on the team, two weeks ago in Nablus. You know when I first met Dan? It was a completely strange and odd occurrence. We were at the Adam Institute for Democracy and Peace in the Jerusalem forest toward the end of advanced training, about six months into our army service. It was a Thursday. I remember because we were in formation, heading out for a ruck march. Every Thursday we went on a ruck. This specific trek was the culmination of our advanced training – something like sixty kilometers. Not an easy march at all, carrying a lot of weight and personal equipment on our backs. The sun was about to set, which was standard, because our staff didn't want it to be too hot so that we'd have to stop the training – so they waited until sunset. We stood there in a semi-circle, stretching, and suddenly we see this guy arriving in his nice white dress uniform from the navy. He wore a tag from the base in Atlit. We didn't understand what was going on or who he was. Despite the tag from Atlit, we didn't put two and two together and make the connection that he was arriving from the naval commandos. He was carrying a large duffel bag on his back and came over to us. Next to him stood our company commander wearing his field uniform. The company commander comes over to our team commander and says to him, 'This is the guy they were talking about. His name is Dan. From now on, he's on your team. Congrats.'

"Our team commander was named Asaf. The truth is, he was a real piece of shit. Seriously, a real bastard. It was no secret that his own team couldn't stand him. They demanded that he stay away from the operational activities and so they sent him to instruct. So he was frustrated and pissy on a regular basis. It didn't matter what we did – he made our lives hell. For fun. He didn't set a personal example for shit. I swear, I don't know how they made him a commander over soldiers at all, let alone train the next generation of combat soldiers in the unit. In any event, we all were sure that at least this time he would behave humanely. We expected him to take Dan aside, say, 'Welcome, nice to meet you, go get yourself organized in the tent,' or something like that. Instead, he asked him, 'Where'd you come from?' Dan answered, 'The navy.' 'Where in the Navy?' Dan beat around the bush – you could tell that this whole thing was uncomfortable for him, but he finally answered, 'From the naval commandos.' That bastard of a team commander smiled and said, 'Ah, the naval commandos? So come show us what you're worth. You see that tent? Good, so go inside, put your vest on and come back here. You have five minutes. Move it.'

"Dan stood there, stunned. He started to say, 'But, sir, I came here because I was injured there and was on medical leave – I can't just go on a ruck right now, I'm still in my dress uniform, wearing dress shoes.' He had other logical, convincing arguments, but the team commander looked at him with hollow eyes, like only he could, and simply said to him, 'Don't bother saying anything, you've already wasted fifteen seconds of your time.'

"We were all in shock. Just in shock. Listen, that poor guy's standing there, doesn't know anybody, still in his white dress uniform with the shoes like they wear in the navy, he tells the team commander that he just arrived after being injured and that he isn't fit, and the team commander starts barking at him in front of everyone. What a disgusting welcome. Some of the guys started to say, 'But, sir, he's injured and just got here,' but our team commander, who really was a world-class asshole, said quietly, 'Shut your mouths. If he wants to stay here, that's the condition. If he doesn't, let him file a complaint and piss off. I don't need any more crybabies here. I have enough.'

"There was quiet tension. The sun was setting right over our heads. We all looked silently at Dan, like a brother in distress – despite the fact that we had only just met him. We saw in Dan's eyes that he understood only too well where he was, and who he was dealing with. He regained his composure after a moment or two, gave the team a quick once-over, and saw in our eyes that that's how it was and there wasn't anything that anybody could do about it. We saw him make a switch in his mind, and then he said, 'No problem, sir, but I need a little more time.' As if something dawned on him and he flipped the record to the other side. Just a moment ago he was a new soldier in his dress uniform, injured and on medical leave, but now he was in the game and had completely changed his attitude. The team commander smiled a big victory smile and said to him sarcastically, 'Of course, distinguished sir, you have one extra minute.' Dan pushed the button on his stop watch and said, 'Yes, sir,' and immediately ran into the nearest tent. He took one of the vests from one of the kitchen crew that wasn't going on the ruck and, indeed, after a few minutes, was standing in front of us with a vest over top of his clean, white uniform and his dress shoes, and said, 'Sir, I'm ready for the ruck, sir.'

"We looked at one another. We were in shock. It was so surreal. The commander walked around him, inspecting him. It looked like something out of an American movie. Good thing he didn't check his shave with a piece of paper or a prepaid phone card.

"The ruck began. It really was long and difficult this time. Dan had trouble walking. He didn't even have time to do a proper warm-up, because of Asaf, that useless team commander. We could all clearly see that his shoes were causing him difficulty walking on the rocky and dusty ground. He practically sprained his ankle every few minutes, and we could also see that he wasn't really in shape. The guys, who were impressed by his courage and impressive reaction to the situation he found himself in, took turns helping him out. We pushed him from behind, pulled him by his vest from the front, and made every effort that he walk next to the team commander so that gaps wouldn't open up and that he wouldn't fall too far behind.

"The ruck ended before sunrise. We were all bruised and hurting – the chafing in our groin, the blisters on our feet, the vest chafing our waists, our shoulders aching from the weight of the vest, the weapons and the stretcher that we carried at the end of the trek. Dr. Ravid, I know you were also a combat soldier – so you must know what I'm talking about. But, despite all our pain, all of us, the whole team, looked at Dan, who looked like he was going to pass out. He was completely white, pale, and barely able to stand.

Yogev and I supported him, one on either side, and held him so he wouldn't fall. Again we stood in a semi-circle, now to stretch out our muscles and summarize the trek. The team commander came over to the three of us, leaned in and whispered in Dan's ear, 'I see you're still with us. Welcome to hell.'

"The team commander went to the officers' tent and we went off to our tent. Each one sat down on his bed and started taking his boots off. Dan didn't even have a bed. His duffel bag was thrown on the ground. In this damp, green tent, in the dim light of the single lamp that still worked, I saw him sitting on the cold floor trying to get his shoes off – unsuccessfully. He couldn't even move, it was as simple as that. Could not move. All of his muscles were sore. I came over to him, picked him up off the floor and sat him on my bed, next to me. Afterward, I helped him take his shoes off – and I was horrified when I saw his feet: they were bleeding. He had two broken toes, his ankle was swollen, and even the act of taking his socks off hurt like crazy. I wanted to run to call a medic, but Dan grabbed my arm and whispered to me, 'Thanks, but no need. Don't get the medic.' 'Why not?' I asked. Dan looked into my eyes, grabbed me by my shirt collar, and whispered, 'I won't let that son-of-a-bitch commander break me. I'm here with you guys to the end. To the end. You hear me? He won't break me. Nothing will break me.' Those were his exact words, and then he said, as if reciting a mantra, 'To the end, to the end, to the end...'

"I sat on the bed in complete shock. I realized that I was sitting across from a rock, a man with a will of steel. And then I asked him, 'Tell me, how is it you didn't break? How did you not stop in the middle? Look at you, like a broken vessel, like a ragdoll. Look at your feet, Lord have mercy. How is it you didn't cry out for a break?'

"He was quiet for a moment, looked deep, deep into my eyes and then answered me. And what he said, I'll remember my whole life. He said to me, 'Yariv, I'm going to tell you something they told me in the naval commandos before one of our treks.'" Yariv stopped the flow of his speech for a moment. His nose was still right up against the frigid, cold window pane. He turned his head toward Dr. Ravid. "Do we have a few minutes or is our time over?" he asked.

The psychologist, who was riveted to his chair by the story, was surprised by the question and shaken out of the trance-like state he had fallen into while listening to Yariv. Yariv looked at him with a questioning glance. Dr. Ravid, like a child caught red-handed, answered immediately without hesitating, "Oh, yes, yes, of course. You may continue."

Yariv smiled to himself. It was clear that the story fascinated the veteran psychologist and it was more than just listening to another standard monologue from just another standard, boring patient. Yariv turned back to the window, his good hand still in his jeans' pocket. Down on the street below, he saw busses pass by, spraying rain puddles on the passersby as they sped along. He lost his train of thought. He closed his eyes, addicted to the sound of the rain smacking against the window. He took a few deep breaths and continued his story.

"So now I'm sitting across from him, across from Dan. His feet are bleeding. Various muscles are cramping up on him every few seconds, his face is twisted up in pain each time. But it doesn't look like it matters to him – he had this light in his eyes. Something that I haven't seen in anybody ever before, nor since. He had this sort of inner power, quiet, but radiating outward. Like a type of calm, an air of 'I'm here, everything's going to be fine.' Dan slowly rubbed his two bleeding feet, massaging them one at a time, and he started to tell me a story he heard from the naval commandos:

"'A number of years ago, there were two Native American tribes that claimed ownership over a wide expanse of grasslands. Each tribe claimed that the territory was theirs. All efforts to mediate between the two tribes were unsuccessful. Neither tribe was willing to discuss a compromise, and the conflict intensified.

Both sides stole cattle from the other, tools, and there were even attacks on individuals. This initiated a vicious cycle of revenge and blood feuds, and the situation rapidly deteriorated. Finally, the heads of the two tribes met, two old chiefs, and they decided to put an end to the conflict. The decided to have a very special, unique competition: both tribes would congregate in a clearing in the forest. Each chief, as per the agreement they made, would put his finger into the other chief's mouth. When the signal was given, each chief would start biting the other chief's finger. The first one to scream, loses. They brought in a chief from a third tribe to act as judge.'

"'On the night of the competition, both tribes assembled in the forest clearing. Each tribe arrived dressed in their finest attire, with tom-toms and war paint smeared on the faces of each tribe member. The judge asked both chiefs to approach him and to open their mouths. He checked to make sure that neither of them had hidden anything in their mouth to increase the suffering or pain of the other. After he gave his approval, each of the chiefs put their finger in the other's mouth. The entire crowd was silent. The tom-toms quieted down, as well as the joyful hoots and ominous shouts. A tense quiet spread over the forest clearing. In the flickering light of the bonfire, the judge began his countdown, and then he swiftly lowered his hand – the competition had begun. Both old chiefs gnashed their teeth on the other's finger. The pain was immediately evident on their faces, which were twisted up in pain and rage. Beads of sweat formed on their brows and slowly dripped off their foreheads, down their cheeks and off their chins. The bulging veins on their necks were about to explode. The crunch of breaking bones could be heard throughout the clearing and, immediately after, drops of blood started to bubble out of both chiefs' mouths. The members of both tribes stood there dumbfounded, watching the bizarre and horrifying spectacle in the orange-red light of the fire. After some time, one of the chiefs began to groan and whimper in pain. It looked as if he was about to break and start screaming at any moment. His opponent saw this and immediately increased the force of his bite. After a few seconds, a massive scream erupted throughout the forest clearing – 'Ahhhhhh!!!!!!'

"The result was clear. The weird competition had come to an end. Both of the tribes' respective healers were immediately called to the sweating chiefs, who were breathing heavily, and put wet, herbal remedies on their bleeding fingers. The next day, the winning tribe held a great celebration in the chief's honor. His finger was still bandaged in a white cloth, and it was clear that the pain had yet to subside. All members of the tribe were invited to the party and, at the height of the celebration, the head of the tribe went to bless his people. When he got up, one of the young members of the tribe raised his hand and requested permission to speak. He turned to the chief and asked, 'Chief, I'm amazed and astounded at your abilities. But I have just one question that I have to ask you: how is it that the other chief screamed and yelled – but you didn't?' The old tribal chief looked at the young man who asked him the question and gave the following incredibly wise answer. He said to him, 'My son, you're making a big mistake. I screamed and yelled and moaned and groaned – I did all of that, but I did it one second after he did...' Dan told me while sitting on my bed, his feet injured and bleeding. 'I also broke and quit. But I broke here – when I got to the tent. Not there. Not in front of him. I wasn't about to give that loser the satisfaction.' And I stood in awe before this guy, floored by his inner strength, his optimism, and his charisma, and I decided to hitch my wagon to his. I wanted to be on his team. That's the story."

Quiet again filled the room. The long monologue impressed the psychologist, who expected the process of getting Yariv to cooperate with him would take longer and be more difficult. He was surprised to find that the opposite was true. It turned out that the little push he gave Yariv resulted in the long soliloquy that he just heard. Yariv pulled his nose back from the cold window and turned toward the middle of the room, toward Dr. Ravid, who was looking at him pensively.

"Interesting story," said the psychologist, "as well as the underlying moral. Come, sit down and let's start from the beginning."

Yariv sat down in the armchair across from Dr. Ravid. "Okay, let's go back to the beginning," he said, repeating psychologist's words. "So, where exactly do you want to begin? When I started breastfeeding, when I stopped using diapers, or shall we just get right to the incident in Nablus that happened two weeks ago?" he added with a sarcastic grin.

"Yariv, there's no need to exaggerate. You don't need to start telling me about kindergarten or first grade. This isn't like that TV show 'This Is Your Life,'" Dr. Ravid responded with a thin smile. "It's important for me to hear about your team, your close friends, about the training course and what you went through together during operations. You've already mentioned your best friend, Dan. I understand that he's a significant person in your life. I'd be happy to hear about him as well. Tell me whatever you want, and whatever you think makes sense to convey. I know that you've received authorization from the field security division to talk to me about anything, so feel free to talk about anything. Professionally speaking, I would prefer to hear everything from the beginning, so things will be more organized and clear. You decide what's important and what isn't but, in order to create a logical timeline, I suggest we talk about the course and the training you underwent, about the other people on the team, and about your shared experiences in the field – physically and mentally. Later on we'll get to what happened in Nablus and what happened there to you and Dan. Okay?"

"Doctor, how much time do we have? I need like, two or three years for this," said Yariv, smiling.

"As far as I'm concerned, it doesn't matter. You aren't on a time limit – I'm listening," the psychologist answered.

"All right, if that's how it is – here you go," Yariv said, and then leaned back and started telling his story, and the stories of the members of his team, from the very beginning.

CHAPTER 3
November 1990, Unit Base Somewhere in the center of Israel

In the unit, they were known as "The Three Musketeers," but this didn't bother Dan, Yariv, or Yogev at all. From the moment they met in the training course, they never separated. It is well known that every combat unit becomes a kind of melting pot for its soldiers, but even so, the case of this trio was exceptional: the bond they had was unique, almost mystical, and it brought out the best in each member of the triangle. Initially, their commanders were opposed to the close relationship they had formed, and even tried to separate them, but they quickly realized that it would only harm their motivation and even the operational capability of each of the three.

The training course they went through together was long and grueling: in the first stage, the young soldiers went through basic training and were certified as infantry soldiers in every respect – shooting, fieldcraft, navigation and familiarity with the weapons systems in the IDF. As the level of difficulty began to get tougher, more and more of the physically and mentally weaker soldiers began to fall by the wayside.

After the initial screening process, the special training series began. The operational need to perfectly blend into the environment required every combat soldier to know the local language and be completely fluent in it. In the first phase, the team members embarked on an intensive study course to learn all aspects of Arabic – reading, writing, speaking, and memorizing various dialects, each characteristic of different geographical areas in the West Bank.

The Arabic language courses initially took place at the Shin-Bet facilities in central Israel, and later at a small language studio that was built at the unit itself, where the lessons started early in the morning and ended late at night. Each day of study began with a comprehensive quiz on the material learned the previous day, in addition to weekly summary exams. A passing grade was defined as 80 and above. Those who failed had to retake the course. In order to create an immersive experience for the soldiers, they were prohibited from speaking Hebrew on studio premises. Every word out of their mouth had to be in Arabic. Whether it was a study-related question, a request for new sheets, or seconds at lunch – all conversations were conducted solely in Arabic.

Every morning, the trainees were given a limited amount of time, about half an hour, to read various newspapers from the West Bank. Afterwards, they had a discussion in Arabic in the form of questions and answers about the material they had read. They also listened to Arabic radio broadcasts and discussed them in the studios at the Shin-Bet. They studied the Quran thoroughly and memorized famous verses and well-known sayings. The instructors familiarized them with the local culture – acceptable greetings, proverbs, different customs, and traditions unique to each area in the West Bank. Many of the soldiers were surprised to discover that an Arab from Hebron and an Arab from Jenin were completely different from each other – in their dialects, various customs, life perspectives, and religious devotion.

The next step in the studio, after learning to write Arabic in block print, was to learn to read Arabic handwriting: in many operations, hand-written intelligence materials are taken. The Shin-Bet intelligence officer is not always with the operations team, and there isn't always time to transfer it to the decryption experts in the Shin-Bet who are sitting at their desks at the various Shin-Bet facilities. The trainees had to learn to read different types of handwriting, and to glean whatever relevant information was needed for the continued operations in the field. The intensive studying paid off: at the end of the three-month course, the trainees could hold conversations among themselves in fluent Arabic, while adjusting their dialects to whatever region they would have to operate in while disguised as locals.

In the next part of the training course, the young soldiers were exposed to classified, special weapons used by the unit during undercover operations. The technical mastery of these weapons had to be perfect and exact, since the fate of the whole operation depended on it. It was explained to the young soldiers that, except for operations where terrorists were "plucked off the street" or there was an attempt to hit them physically, the unit also specialized in using innovated methods to gather intelligence. Since whole swaths of the West Bank were off-limits to the IDF, the only chance they had to penetrate these areas was in disguise. When the undercover soldiers were assimilated into the field, they had to conduct various types of intelligence gathering operations that required special means not available to the regular army units.

After that, was the hardest part, both physically and mentally: the counter-terrorism course. The purpose of the course was to turn them into combat soldiers unafraid of physical confrontation with the enemy. The nature of the Duvdevan unit's undercover operations required the soldiers to initiate contact and physically subdue many terrorists – often without using weapons. During the course, the soldiers learned many Krav Maga techniques, as well as the location of weak points in the human body. Skilled instructors showed them, for example, that a well-aimed punch to the diaphragm would cause an adversary to experience what amounted to choking for several seconds, allowing him to be neutralized. The soldiers practiced defensive techniques in combat against an opponent armed with a knife or firearm, and were even trained in how to overcome two or more attackers simultaneously.

The counter-terrorism course also included "absorption training" – a long series of exercises where the trainees learned how to absorb various blows and, more importantly, how to strike the opponent efficiently and quickly. The goal was to neutralize the opponent within a few seconds and not be drawn into a prolonged fight, which could arouse the suspicion of the locals. To practice and refine the techniques they had learned, they had to arrange real hand-to-hand combat between the soldiers: at the end of each training day, the duty trainee would announce the exact time when the trainees had to arrive at the basketball court. With the announcement, the line to the restroom began – some of the trainees couldn't handle the mental pressure and either threw up or had diarrhea. Needless to say, there wasn't a particularly strong demand for dinner on these occasions. At the appointed time, the trainees arrived at the hall. The door was locked, and the air conditioners were turned on full blast. In the corner of the hall was a pile of head guards, shin guards and, of course, groin protectors. At the instructor's command, the soldiers quickly equipped themselves. Speed was critical – there simply weren't enough guards for everyone.

Thin mats were arranged in a square on the floor in the center of the court. The instructor blew his whistle shortly and sharply, and the young fighters stood around the mats, where the instructor paired them up, one on one – and the fighting began.

Each fight lasted a few minutes, which seemed like an eternity and, except for blows to the head and groin, everything was allowed. The motto was: "There are no friends on the mat," and the soldiers attacked each other mercilessly. This was the ultimate practice for the Krav Maga techniques that they had acquired during the course. To ensure that the soldiers gave it their all in the fight, the punishment for the loser was a simple deterrent: another fight until he won. Despite the safety instructions and the protective guards, many soldiers still came away with physical injuries, mainly fractures and bruises in various parts of the body. Even in this field, Krav Maga and sheer aggression, the soldiers were required to achieve a certain grade, and those who failed had to retake the course.

At the end of this part of the grueling course, the dropout rate stood at about half of those who started it. The commanders were not pleased to see the dropout rates this high, but they couldn't afford to compromise – they knew that any concession today would mean a risk to human lives in the future.

The next phase in the course involved specialized training: every operation required a combination of different specializations, including driving the unit's special vehicles, planting explosives, and sniping from a distance in stationary and mobile positions. For several weeks, the group of young combat soldiers were split into small groups and then sent to acquire these skills in different locations, mainly at the bases of the special units division of the police force and the Shin-Bet.

The next series focused on surveillance: for the next few weeks, the soldiers were exposed to surveillance techniques that the Shin-Bet commonly used, both on foot and by car. They learned how to get rid of a tail and learned ways of following an object for days, while changing the person tailing them every few hours. The final exercise was held in the heart of the stock exchange in Ramat Gan: the force was split into two, those following and those escaping and, for a full day, an external team made up of Shin-Bet personnel evaluated their ability to surveil and slip a tail.

Afterward, some of the soldiers on the team were sent to thoroughly study break-ins: they learned various ways of breaking in to places, some using "hot" techniques (explosives) and some using "cold" techniques (like picking locks or various hydraulic or other mechanical means). At the end of the three-week training period, the trainees were able to break into any door within seconds – whether it had a standard cylinder lock or magnetic one.

The second part of the break-in series dealt with devices for eavesdropping and miniature cameras: some of the unit's activities included obtaining sensitive intelligence information by installing various advanced devices in the vicinity of whichever wanted individual in the West Bank. And so, they emphasized practicing planting concealed listening devices inside furniture, cars, houses, offices, etc. In the first part of this training series, the trainees learned they could plant an eavesdropping and tracking device on another person – what was known as "transmitting" them in professional jargon – without their knowledge by dropping a tiny device into the object's belongings or attaching it to their clothes. Here too, the final test was no simple challenge: they had to transmit police officers. The trainees approached police vehicles in central Tel Aviv and practiced attaching magnetic transmitters to the outside of the vehicle, dropping transmitters into the police cars, and even attaching transmitters to the officers' clothing.

The second part of the series, which was taught by a special expert from the technical department in the intelligence division, dealt with the special miniature cameras of the IDF. The soldiers discovered that they could install a tiny camera inside virtually any useful item: a button on a piece of clothing, cigarette lighter, backpack or watch. They learned how to activate the miniature cameras such that the picture taken would be effective, but the process of taking the photograph wouldn't arouse the suspicion of the object being photographed. In order to evaluate the young soldiers' abilities to take pictures, they were sent to the Mahane Yehuda market in Jerusalem and secretly photographed various figures from up close, whom their commanders told them about in advance.

During the training, every few months, the commanders would organize an anonymous questionnaire for the soldiers. The questionnaire was called "the sociometric test," and its purpose was to give those in command a true picture of the inter-personal relationships within the team. The results often surprised the commanders: sometimes they found that the quiet, shy soldier was highly valued by his peers, while the colorful, loud team member received very low scores. Even soldiers who had received high scores on the technical tests (for example, shooting or combat conditioning) were removed from the course if their team members indicated that they didn't feel they could trust them with their lives at the moment of truth.

In the next phase of the course, the soldiers learned the secrets of disguises and makeup. Here, they learned that using makeup correctly is a significant element in the art of undercover work, especially for more challenging characters – older people, disabled individuals, and women. After a few days, every soldier in the team knew how to use eyeliner, mascara, lipstick, and other types of makeup.

Then it was time for drama and acting training: in the end, an undercover soldier is an actor. He plays a character, whether an old man with a limp, a pregnant woman, a young student, a driver, or any other person in public. The young soldiers had in-depth conversations with Mossad agents who operated in enemy countries under a false identity, who taught them that they couldn't simply put a keffiyeh on their head in order to look like a local. The soldiers needed to be intimately familiar with the area and local customs and fully embody the character they were assuming.

To experience up close the characters they were going to portray in the field, the soldiers were sent to put on disguises and practice these roles – while still in Israel: one soldier played a beggar in the Bedouin market in Be'er Sheva, another posed as a drug addict in the Lod marketplace, two others were sent to beg in Tel Aviv, and one even disguised himself as a woman and tried to hit on passersby at the Clock Tower Square in Jaffa. From the reactions of those around them, the soldiers learned whether or not their disguises were convincing and what needed to be improved to add credibility to their new character.

At the end of the all of these other series, it was time for the centerpiece of the training – the undercover series. Initially, accompanied by a mentor – a soldier with experience – the soldiers were sent for simple missions, such as buying falafel in an Arab village or purchasing an umbrella in a shop in Ramallah. As they gained self-confidence in their undercover abilities, the demands on the soldiers increased. They went into the field in pairs, without a mentor, and carried out intelligence-gathering operations.

After each such operation, a comprehensive debriefing was conducted, lessons were learned, and the young soldiers were graded. Even at this stage, quite a few people were let go. After about two long, arduous years, fourteen new soldiers proudly stood on the unit's formation field. The guests of honor were the general of the central command and the chief of the general staff. They were also the ones who pinned the unit's wings onto the young soldiers' uniforms. In the front row stood the three musketeers: Dan, Yariv, and Yogev. No one on the team was surprised when the unit commander announced that the three had received the honor of "outstanding trainees" of the course. All three were assigned to the operational team, considered the most elite of the unit, and codenamed "Team 10."

The nickname that stuck with them, "The Three Musketeers," became their second name and was commonly used in the unit. This nickname didn't change even after the disaster that occurred in Nablus.

CHAPTER 4
February 1992, Hebron

The terror attack in the middle of Jerusalem was one of the worst the capitol had ever experienced. The suicide bomber took advantage of the bitter cold in the capitol, wrapping himself in a long, thick raincoat. He didn't arouse any suspicion among the other passengers on the bus. The cost in blood was twenty-two dead and nineteen injured.

The forensic teams of the police and the Shin-Bet collected the evidence that was left at the scene of the attack and determined unequivocally that the suicide bomber was a Hamas operative from Hebron who had recently been released after serving several years in prison for belonging to a terrorist organization. The minister of defense instructed the leaders of the Shin-Bet to locate and capture whoever planned the attack as soon as possible. After about three weeks, the long-awaited intelligence breakthrough arrived: an urgent message from the Shin-Bet headquarters to the unit's intelligence department showed that Mahmoud Kawasme, the commander of Hamas' military wing in Hebron, was supposed to make a brief visit to the tent where the suicide bomber's family was sitting in mourning.

A quick analysis of the area revealed that the suicide-bomber's home was located in one of the crowded neighborhoods in western Hebron. The unit's teams knew the place well but, this time, infiltrating there in disguise was out of the question: the senior Hamas officials had several rings of protection around them – the first consisted of lookouts and informers. Their role was to surround the area where the senior official would be, both on foot and in vehicles. Any suspicious movement in the area was immediately reported to the second, inside circle. This circle consisted of the senior official's personal bodyguards, typically two to three armed with automatic rifles and pistols. Although the unit's fighters had carried out undercover operations in this area before, there was now a real concern about exposing the force due to the extra sensitivity and the multitude of lookouts and informers.

After long discussions at the unit's headquarters with representatives from the Shin-Bet, it was agreed that, in this case, the only way to capture the senior terrorist, Mahmoud Kawasme, would be while he was traveling to or from the mourning tent. Team 10 received notice to prepare immediately for action.

* * *

The platoon commander gave the responsibility for planning the details of the operation to The Three Musketeers, and determined that they would also be the ones to manage the operation in the field. It was also decided that once they finished planning the operation, they would present it to the platoon commander and the unit commander for approval; in addition, during the execution phase, a limited number of additional soldiers from the team would join the three of them. The main goal was to bring as few fighters as possible into this specific area to avoid the chances of being "burned" – the locals knew every vehicle and every person living in the area.

The intelligence pointed to the arrival of a senior Hamas official to the area, but it did not provide solid information regarding the exact day and time. According to local custom, the mourning tent is set up by the family members, and acquaintances of the deceased visit to pay their respects and honor the memory of the deceased and their family. The intelligence information reached the Shin-Bet right after the day the perpetrator was taken down, meaning that the expected timeframe for the mentioned visit was within the coming days. In such cases, where the intelligence is received in real-time, the soldiers get into disguise and go on high alert for immediate mobilization. In IDF code, these situations are referred to as "a moment's notice." The team members prepared the undercover vehicles for the operation and waited for the call. From the moment they were ready to move out, none of them left the isolated, fenced in compound on the outskirts of the brigade's building in Hebron.

Upon their arrival at the compound, they were met by the regional Shin-Bet intelligence officer. Each Shin-Bet agent had a nickname to prevent their real names from being revealed. This particular officer was known as Captain George. The intelligence officer was a man in his forties, with a stocky build and graying mustache. He was known as a chain smoker, lighting one cigarette after another. Behind his back, the fighters in the unit referred to him as "The Chimney." Captain George gathered all the intelligence related to the western neighborhoods of Hebron and was familiar with the team members from previous operations. When he arrived at the compound, he asked to speak with them.

"Guys," he began, "this last attack in Jerusalem only emphasizes to all of us how fragile the current calm environment is. The man you're going after, Mahmoud Kawasme, is considered the mastermind behind this and other attacks. He possesses intelligence information that is of immense value – that's why you're here. If we wanted him dead, we would have taken him out long ago with a sniper or from the air, as we did with his associates. You are here for one reason and one reason only – we need him alive and breathing, even if he's wounded, but alive and breathing in the interrogation room. Of course, I do not expect this to come at the cost of any of you being killed or injured, heaven forbid, just so this innocent saint Kawasme can be captured alive, but you are the best option the IDF has for this mission. I reviewed your proposed plan for the operation with your commanders, and the idea seems original and unique. I believe that with the element of surprise, we can neutralize Kawasme's guards and capture him."

He paused for a moment, looking at the combat soldiers surrounding him, then continued. "And one last thing, guys: we might be in for a long wait, possibly even weeks. In my experience and yours, at first, everyone is alert and vigilant, but then slowly, fatigue eats away at the alertness, and the tension eases. This is a natural, human process. Please, give it everything you've got. Don't forget for a moment – many Israeli lives depend on this operation. Good luck to all of us." He shook the hands of the disguised fighters and left the compound.

The days passed and the lookouts at the mourning tents didn't see anything out of the ordinary. People came and went – but there was no sign of the senior Hamas figure or any of his entourage. The mourning period was supposed to end the next day, and it seemed as if the whole thing was going to be a bust. The suspicions of the Shin-Bet intelligence officer, Captain George, began to come true: the long wait played on the nerves of the soldiers' in the observation posts, who kept their eyes on the house day and night. This fatigue also affected the undercover fighters, who had not left the isolated compound for about two weeks.

But everything changed at once when the phone in Captain George's office rang. On the other end of the line was a voice whispering in Arabic. The speaker said just two words: "He's coming."

* * *

The garbage truck belonging to the Hebron municipality meandered slowly through the alleyways in the western part of the city. The driver, Hassan, was an older, heavyset man of about sixty, just about to retire. He had been driving the city's garbage truck for close to thirty years. Next to him sat his son, Daoud. Hassan succeeded in getting him that job through his connections in City Hall. The job allowed him to take care of his family with honor, and the hours were very convenient, despite being monotonous and boring: every few hundred yards, Hassan would stop on the side of the road next to a group of garbage bins, get out of the driver's seat, and help his son lift up the next garbage bin in line and into the truck. Hassan knew that he was lucky that he had steady work during these difficult times, where finding steady work in Hebron was little short of a miracle. It was cold, and all the residents of the city were tucked away in their homes. The streets were deserted. Hassan and Daoud couldn't have imagined in their wildest dreams what they were about to experience in the next few moments.

The garbage truck continued to move slowly through the streets of Hebron, when Daoud suddenly shouted to his father, "Watch out, Dad, there's a car that got stuck!"

In the middle of the alley, right in front of the truck, was a white Peugeot. Its hood was open, and thick, white smoke was billowing out of it. Near the car stood a woman holding a baby. Another woman was seated in the back seat, and an elderly man sat in the front seat, wiping beads of sweat from his forehead with a yellow handkerchief. The woman waved toward the truck with her free hand and shouted, "Stop, stop, I need help!"

Hassan, the truck driver, brought the vehicle to a screeching halt and pulled on the handbrake. "It looks like her car broke down," he said to his son sitting next to him. "Let's get out and help her." Daoud nodded in agreement, and both of them got out of the truck and walked quickly toward the woman and her baby. The father and son walked quickly toward the disabled car. The woman stood there, rocking the baby in her arms, stroking its head. At that very moment, an elderly man that must have been her father got out of the driver's seat and came around to the front of the engine, and Hassan and Daoud met him there, but couldn't see anything through the thick smoke. At that moment, something happened that stunned the two Arabs: the woman threw the baby on the ground and lunged at Daoud. At the same time, the old man suddenly jumped in his father's direction. Within seconds, Hassan and Daoud were on the ground, their hands bound with zip-ties, and black, cloth sacks were placed over their heads so that they couldn't see. Hassan was certain that these were Hamas men who suspected him of collaboration. The punishment for such was known to everybody – an agonizing death.

He began screaming, "I'm not a collaborator, I swear!"

His son, Daoud, also began to shout, but suddenly they both heard somebody whisper in their ears: "Quiet! We aren't Hamas, we're special forces."

The two undercover operatives, dressed as a woman and an old man, quickly put Hassan and Daoud into the empty trunk of the white Peugeot. The woman looked to both sides, but didn't see anybody in the alley. The old man went to the front of the car and picked up the white smoke grenade that had been placed there in the engine. He closed the safety mechanism on the grenade, and the smoke stopped. The old man closed the hood of the car and knocked on it twice, forcefully. The other soldier, dressed as the other woman sitting in back, was already behind the wheel. He quickly put the car into first gear and drove in the direction of the civil administration building, where the two would be detained for several hours under whatever pretext until they were done using their vehicle. The woman and the old man – Yogev and Dan – quickly got into the cabin of the garbage truck and began driving to their new destination.

* * *

The Ford Escort carrying Kawasme and his armed guards slowly traversed Hebron, traveling from east to west. In front sat the driver and next to him a guard, who was armed with a Beretta. In back, on the right side, sat Mahmoud Kawasme, senior Hamas official, and on his left was another guard holding an AK-47. The car's rear windows were tinted to prevent anybody from identifying the individuals in the car.

It was late afternoon, and the sun was just starting to set. It was very cold, and with the car windows open just a crack, the wind whistled inside. Kawasme was anxious and tense: for many months, he had tried not to take main roads during the day, for fear of being captured, but today he didn't have a choice – the mourning period was going to end in a few hours. As the one responsible for recruiting the suicide bombers, he had to come make an appearance at the mourning tent of the "martyr." There was always the popular complaint that senior Hamas officials send the youth to their death, while they themselves, the leaders and recruiters, never put themselves in harm's way. Kawasme wanted to show everybody that this was not the case. He tried looking out the dark window, but the fog on the inside part of the window, along with the drizzle from outside, made it difficult.

The guard in the front seat and the driver were the young suicide bomber's neighbors. They knew every car in the neighborhood and looked suspiciously at any car or person that they didn't recognize. When they saw somebody they didn't know, they came to a screeching halt, got out with their weapons drawn, and interrogated them about what they were doing there.

The drive wore on. Kawasme leaned over to the guard sitting in front of him. "What's going on?" he asked, angrily. "Why is he driving so slowly?"

The guard turned his head toward the senior Hamas figure. "Mahmoud," he answered, "we got stuck behind Hassan and Daoud's garbage truck. The alley is narrow and we can't go around him. In a minute we'll get to the intersection and get past them."

Kawasme leaned back and, out of the front window, saw the familiar garbage truck. Suddenly the brake lights of the truck went on and it came to a stop. The Kawasme's driver barely hit the brakes in time, and the car came to a screeching halt, practically ramming the truck. The truck didn't move. Behind Kawasme's car, the white Peugeot started honking frantically. The driver of the white Peugeot put his hand out the window and starting waving it around in annoyance. Kawasme's driver, still trying to catch his breath from almost crashing into the truck, also started honking, but the garbage truck didn't move. The honking from behind grew louder. Kawasme's driver also leaned on his horn, again and again – but to no avail.

"Go out there and see what the holdup is," Kawasme instructed his guards. "I don't have time for Hassan and Daoud's horse shit right now."

The guards got out of the car, leaving just Kawasme and the driver. The guard in front began walking to the right, in the direction of Daoud's door. The rear guard went left and quickly walked to Hassan's door. In a second, as soon as Kawasme's two guards exited the vehicle, the rear hatch of the garbage truck where the garbage was dumped started to open. Kawasme watched as the compactor began rising slowly upwards, and he couldn't believe his eyes.

Out of the garbage compactor jumped six soldiers in uniform, ski masks on their faces, and bullet-proof vests on their torsos. They had helmets with small, powerful lasers on their heads. The thin, concentrated light beams flickered on the car's windshield. Each one had a shortened Uzi sub-machine gun fitted with a silencer. The first two went right and stood about a yard from the guard who had been sitting next to Kawasme. The guard tried to aim the AK-47 he was holding and shoot them, but the soldiers shot him first with a few bullets to the chest at close range. He fell on the ground and stayed there, unmoving.

The second guard that was holding the Beretta tried to flee down a side alley, but one of the soldiers fired two bullets into his knee and he fell to the ground. The second pair of soldiers quickly ran after him, bound his hands and covered his eyes with a black cloth. The driver and senior terrorist now watched as an old Arab man and an Arab woman got out of the garbage truck's cabin, each with a gun in their hand.

The driver, who immediately regained his composure, began shouting, "Mahmoud, it's the army, it's the IDF!" The driver, who was unarmed, decided to flee. He put the car in reverse, but before he could push the gas, Kawasme and his driver felt something heavy hit them from behind. Kawasme looked back and saw that the white Peugeot behind them was accelerating, ramming his car and pushing it toward the garbage truck and the soldiers. The driver realized he had no way to escape with the car, and Kawasme immediately understood that the local vehicle behind him also belonged to the military forces. At that moment, the last pair of fighters emerged from the garbage truck and stood on the hood of the car. The two aimed their weapons at Kawasme and the terrified driver.

One of the soldiers kicked the front windshield several times. It finally broke, and the cold wind whistled into the car. Another soldier approached the driver's window, pointed his weapon at the driver's head, and shouted in Arabic, "Turn off the engine and put your hands up!" The driver obediently complied with the unambiguous demand. Kawasme now understood that he had no choice: although he had a pistol, he knew that in a shootout, one against six, he didn't stand a chance. So, he quickly opened the door of the Ford and tried to flee on foot toward the alley on the right.

Two soldiers immediately began running after him. One of the soldiers shouted in Arabic, "*Waqf, jish!*"[6] but Kawasme didn't stop, and instead ran faster down the narrow alley, which had become slippery from the rain. Suddenly, he heard a few shots in the air and felt the force of the bullets over his head. The senior Hamas terrorist suddenly lost his balance and fell on the slippery stones, slamming his knees into the ground. In an instant, he felt someone lying on his back, and then the cold barrel of the soldier's gun pressed against his neck. The soldier said in Arabic, "Don't move!" while yet another soldier also sat on top of him.

"Hold his arms," a voice from above commanded. Kawasme, who had spent time in Israeli prison, was fluent and literate in Hebrew. It wasn't hard for him to understand what the soldiers were saying. He felt his arms being grabbed tightly on both sides. One soldier had him by the hair, his face pressed against the ground, his nose and ear mashed against the wet stones. Despite this, Kawasme was still able to smell the stench of the garbage emanating from the soldier who was sitting on him.

"Search him," a voice said in Hebrew.

Kawasme felt a pair of hands quickly patting him down, his legs, stomach and back.

"Clean."

"Tie him up and turn him around for confirmation."

In a moment, his wrists were bound together with zip-ties

---

6. "Halt, it's the army!"

that seemed to have come from out of nowhere. The soldier rolled him onto his back. Across from Kawasme were a pair of light-colored eyes peering out from under the ski mask. He was also able to make out the big smile on the face of the soldier sitting on top of him through the black ski mask. The soldier put his mouth close to Kawasme's face and told him in perfect Arabic with a Hebron dialect, "*Ahalan w'sahalan, ya Mahmoud,* we missed you, *ya habibi.*"

CHAPTER 5
June 1992, Jenin

The briefing room in the brigade building in Jenin was cloudy with cigarette smoke. The intelligence briefing was classified as "top secret," so only a handful of senior officers were present. The tension was palpable. The information the Shin-Bet intelligence officer presented to the brigade commander and the others present was unequivocal and didn't leave any room for doubt: this was the best opportunity the IDF had ever had to capture Ahmad al-Jaafari, the leader of the "Black Panther" terrorist cells.

The Shin-Bet representative explained at length that through cross-referencing numerous intelligence sources, it looked like early next week, al-Jaafari was expected to spend one day at his dying mother's house in the Jenin *casbah*.

"Do not take this lightly, gentlemen," noted the intelligence officer. "The man has not been home or seen his family for about a year and a half. He knows we are hunting him relentlessly and has already escaped several of our attempts to capture him in recent years. If we miss him this time, it is likely he will disappear again for a long time."

"And what do you suggest we do this time that we haven't done before?" the brigade commander asked.

The Shin-Bet representative thought for a moment. "Look," he replied in his quiet voice, "we're dealing with a terrorist who's extremely alert and suspicious. Everything sets him off – and rightly so. The man has an entire army of bodyguards and lookouts surrounding and protecting him. At the moment, I have given an order to halt all aerial photography activity in the area so that he won't suspect anything. Furthermore, you must have heard that the successful assassination you carried out recently in Jenin has resulted in the entire casbah area being covered with tarps, meaning we don't really have an up-to-date picture or map of what's actually going on there anyway. We have no choice – we need to use Yoav's guys," he said, nodding towards Yoav, the Lieutenant Colonel who commanded the undercover Duvdevan unit. "I know it's problematic, given the difficulties," he said in conclusion, "but we really don't have a choice, gentlemen. In my opinion, there won't be another opportunity like this."

Quiet descended upon the briefing room, and the brigade commander looked to his left toward Yoav. "The decision is yours," he said to him. "You know the details. Can your guys pull something like this off?"

Yoav thought for a moment before answering. "Give me a few hours to check it out," he finally responded, "and we'll see what we can do."

* * *

At Yoav's request, the platoon commander gathered the soldiers from Team 10 into the unit's room in the combat soldiers' club. All the combat soldiers in the elite team were first sergeants serving on a full-time basis. They all had more than three years of complex and intensive operations under their belt and knew each other well. The soldiers didn't yet know what this was about, but they sensed that this was not just another routine briefing.

After a few minutes, Yoav arrived and sat down next to the soldiers. Yoav enjoyed these personal meetings with them. They reminded him of his younger days when he himself went through the same course. He grew up in the undercover unit. He started his career there as a combat soldier, then served as a team commander, a platoon commander, and so on, including command roles in regular army duty – until he reached the top of the pyramid.

When he was appointed unit commander, which during his tenure comprised only about a hundred soldiers, his predecessors told him about the loneliness of the commander. He knew that the responsibility would fall on his shoulders in the event of failure. Unfortunately, he was also intimately familiar with the bitter taste of bereavement. The commanders he replaced told him that the higher he climbed up the chain of command, the more he would inevitably distance himself from the field and the soldiers he commanded. But it wasn't like that – Yoav knew every combat soldier personally and loved them all, though deep down he knew that his greatest affection was for Team 10, the team of veteran soldiers.

Yoav always made a point of spending time with his soldiers as they approached their discharge from service. He enjoyed listening to their conversations about the future waiting for them as civilians and the tickets they had already purchased for the big post-army trip. He knew the stories about the girlfriends who broke up with their boyfriends during the long course – which led to the well-known saying that "no girlfriend has ever managed to finish the course at Duvdevan." He smiled at the small jabs and inside jokes between the team members and even remembered some of the dubious nicknames the soldiers gave each other.

In the corner of the room sat Yogev, known as "Yogi" on account of his full bodied figure that reminded them of the mythological animated bear. Another version was that the name stuck because of his incredible ability to hibernate. Sitting next to him was Doron, who when he was younger was the runner-up in the Israeli junior boxing championships, so it was only natural that he was nicknamed "Tyson." In front of him sat Yariv, who's moniker was "Newton" after his friends discovered by chance that he scored a 780 out of 800 on the psychometric test he took before the army, even though he denied it.

In the other corner of the room sat Dan. He was the acting team commander, even though he wasn't an officer. This practice of appointing an experienced, veteran sergeant as the acting team commander was common in the unit; the operational activity required extensive experience and thorough knowledge of the field. In many cases, soldiers who went through the officers' training course were effectively away from the field for many months, so the unit preferred to appoint an experienced soldier to the role.

In the case of Team 10, it was complicated: the original team commander was a lieutenant, an experienced, veteran combat soldier, who led a complicated operation that went awry in the heart of the Hebron casbah. To rescue his soldiers, the officer had to shoot several civilians, who were said to have been armed and a danger to the undercover force. After the rescue, under pressure from one of the families of the Arab casualties, a military, criminal investigation was opened. In the investigation, the prosecutor for the deceased claimed that one of them was not holding a weapon, but rather a carpentry tool that just looked like a gun. The regional commander ordered the officer's suspension until a full review of the incident was completed. Dan was the team sergeant at the time of the incident, so he was appointed as the temporary replacement for the team commander until the conclusion of the investigation.

However, the investigation dragged on, the officer was discharged in the meantime, and Dan remained the acting team commander. Yogev and Yariv were appointed the team sergeant and the team commander, respectively, in Dan's absence. The trio formed the spearhead of Team 10.

Dan lived in Caesarea, and his house was right by the sea. He was an avid diver, or as it's known a little more casually – "a sea junky." During his regular leaves and on many weekends, Dan hosted friends from the team and took them on guided dives in the area. Dan's deep love for the sea and diving initially led him to enlist in the naval commandos. During one of the diving exercises in the course, he had an accident that caused a microscopic tear in his eardrum. Initially, he did not report the pain in his ear to the medical team, fearing he would be kicked out but, as the pain intensified, he had to inform his commanders about the tear, which was getting steadily worse.

He was immediately referred for a comprehensive round of examinations, which ultimately revealed that his hearing was not impaired. However, to allow the tear to heal completely, the doctor in the commandos prohibited him from diving for at least six months. The specialist also added that there was no guarantee the tear would not recur during deep-water training dives or – worse yet – during an operation somewhere in enemy territory. Additionally, the intense land training that Dan underwent in the commandos training course also resulted in stress fractures in both shins and his right ankle. He did his best to overcome this injury without reporting it but, here too, his excess motivation was his downfall; the fractures got worse, resulting in him being shut down completely, albeit temporarily.

Dan was so upset, he didn't know what to do, and was having a hard time coming to terms with the evil decree, the implications of which were clear – he had to quit the naval commandos course. His commanding officers were also sorry to see a soldier like him not finish the course because of these kinds of problems. In an extraordinary step, the head of the naval commandos summoned him to a personal meeting in his chambers. The high level of achievement as a soldier in the training course created a situation where the upper echelons wanted to keep him in the naval commandos and, therefore, they offered him supporting roles in the navy – in the intelligence department, in the ground observation unit and in the department of weapons development – but Dan adamantly refused and pointed out that he enlisted in the army to be a combat soldier and not a pencil pusher. The head of the naval commandos felt for the distraught young soldier, and recommended that he transfer to the ground forces reconnaissance division. There, they assured him, he would end up with interesting opportunities that were no less important. The head of the naval commandos even told Dan about friends of his that dropped out because of various medical problems that came to light while they were in the naval commandos course, and today they are senior officers in other special forces units.

"We wanted you with us," the head of the naval commandos told him, "but it seems as if fate is stronger than us or our plans. You have my blessing, and of course I wish you all the success on the ground, too," he said, and concluded with a firm handshake.

Dan was transferred directly from the naval commandos to the reconnaissance division in the ground forces command, where he expressed his desire to join the Duvdevan unit. Due to his injury and the recovery period he needed to undergo, he had to repeat two cycles in the training process, and was eventually assigned to Yariv and Yogev's team. Initially, his team members called him "The Frog." Later, the nickname was upgraded to "Kermit," as a tribute to the legendary Muppets icon. At first, Dan fought against this nickname – he hated it and tried to change it – but to no avail. After a while, he gave in and had no other choice but to accepted it.

There were many other funny and original nicknames in the unit in general, and for Team 10 members in particular, but everybody agreed that Gidi, who was blessed with very impressive physical attributes, had the best nickname of all. Legend has it that immediately after the first group shower in basic training, Gidi unanimously earned the nickname "Hose." The rumor spread, and curious soldiers from other teams even came to have a peek.

Yoav enjoyed watching them goof around, tease each other, and get to know every detail of their team members' lives. Team 10 was known as a group of pranksters – until the moment the order to move was given. At that moment, they "switched programs" – in an instant, the lighthearted and carefree atmosphere was replaced with a serious, "all business" attitude. Yoav, the unit commander, could sit there all day, but time was short.

"Okay, everybody," he said, "let's get started." He laid out before them in detail the intelligence indicators and the window of opportunity that was closing, the holes in the intelligence and the lack of backup for the combat soldiers, namely aerial and ground observation. "I will say it again: from the moment you enter the area of the casbah that is covered with tarps, we won't be able to see you." Here he stopped for a moment, looked at the soldiers, and asked, "Anybody have any ideas? Come on, guys, now's the time."

In contrast to other units in the IDF, where plans of action were made exclusively by the senior command and the soldiers were basically "outsourced contractors," the practice in Duvdevan was to brainstorm before every activity, even among the team members. The wealth of experience that the combat soldiers accrued during many complex and complicated operations created a situation whereby many of the best and original ideas came from them. The accompanying motto became: "When everybody thinks the same way, it's a sign that nobody is actually thinking."

Yoav looked at the soldiers on his team. Each one of them was deep in thought, and Yoav could actually hear the gears turning in the soldiers' heads. For one moment, when all of them were using their imaginations, there was quiet – and then the ideas started coming.

* * *

A company of Golani[7] soldiers stood in a semi-circle in the hangar of the brigade building in Jenin. Their company commander, a captain, stood in the center. He quieted his soldiers and said loudly, "Guys, we don't have much time and I'd like to begin. Our mission in the coming days is to serve as an extraction force for a Duvdevan team that, in disguise, is going to the area of the casbah and Jenin market for an operation. What we're going to do now is have a meeting between the two forces, those who will be disguised and those who will perform the extraction. This meeting is called an 'identification parade.' We'll see them in their disguises, just as they will be during their operation in the field, to prevent a friendly fire engagement.

"Please, after all the jokes and laughter that will undoubtedly follow, try to remember what they look like. Try to remember noticeable features, like unusual clothing, scars, glasses, a bald head, a black tooth, etc. It could prevent a disaster – for us and for them. Besides, what you are about to see is classified military information. I'm asking you in earnest: first and foremost, keep this information exclusively to yourselves. Do not tell your friends, your parents, or anyone else. If these guys' operating methods get leaked and they are exposed, it could endanger their lives, and I mean that with utmost seriousness. Secondly – please, behave

---

7. Infantry brigade in the IDF.

maturely and avoid making smart-assed remarks. Understood?" A murmur of agreement rippled through the soldiers.

A minute later, a dust-covered jeep entered the hangar. It parked in the center of the semi-circle and it's engine was shut off. Two soldiers disguised as Arabs got out of the front seat. The first one approached the back and opened the door. Four more undercover soldiers emerged and stood in a line facing the surprised soldiers of the extraction force. The soldiers in the hangar stared at them wide-eyed, as if trying to guess what parts of the disguise were real and what weren't. The hesitation on their faces was clear and evident: was the deep scar on Dan's cheek real, or was it a result of the thorough makeup course he had taken? Was Yogev's wild hair authentic, or was it a wig? Were Yariv's yellow teeth due to severe and prolonged neglect, or did he simply apply some color to them? The murmurs of admiration from the Golani soldiers grew, along with finger pointing and suppressed giggles.

After a few moments, a taxi in the form of a silver Peugeot station wagon, dusty and dented and bearing a local license plate, entered the hangar. It had a brown-fur steering-wheel cover. The driver-side door had an eagle sticker with Arabic writing beneath it. Hanging from the rearview mirror were a pair of white, furry dice and a black Quran with gold lettering casually lay atop a reddish rug covering the length of the dashboard.

Udi, the driver, parked the Peugeot next to the jeep and turned off the engine. Two more soldiers got out. The first was Barda, who played the role of a limping old man carrying a black plastic bag, followed by Yaki.

As soon as Yaki emerged from the vehicle, every single soldier in the extraction force was staring at him, no exceptions. Yaki's head was wrapped in a traditional white scarf. His face was made up with extended lashes, meticulously applied lipstick, and light-blue eye shadow. The blush completely concealed his light-colored stubble. The blue dress he wore clung to his body and reached almost to the floor, as was customary for local women. Yaki approached the soldiers, but he was walking funny, like a duck. It was clear something was bothering him.

"Barbie, what's up, dude?" asked Barda, who was standing next to him.

"It's this cheap pantyhose again, damn it... they don't fit right, always crushing my balls – those cheapskates still won't invest a few extra bucks in me..."

Despite the company commander's earlier warnings, one of the Golani soldiers couldn't resist and loudly exclaimed, "Shit, I wish my girlfriend looked like that..."

Laughter erupted in the hangar, and even the tough Golani company commander had to suppress a smile. Yaki smiled awkwardly.

Dan raised his hand, indicating to those present that he wished for permission to speak for a moment. "Hello, everyone," he said loudly. "My name is Dan, and I am the commander of this operation. The purpose of this operation is to capture terrorists hiding in the casbah and market area of Jenin. I cannot go into the specific details of our plan, but it is important to remember that from the moment our force enters the area, until you receive other orders, do not open fire on locals – unless there is fire that is being directed at you. We will be in the casbah area for several days, and I'm concerned that not everyone will remember exactly what we look like – hence the purpose of this clear directive.

"Our force will enter the area today and blend in with the local population. Please note: to establish our credibility with the locals, we may need to throw stones at IDF forces in the area or join in protests against you. If one of your patrols passes through the area and one of you identifies a soldier disguised as an Arab, treat him like any other. In general – do not smile at us, do not wink at us, and do not point at us or the vehicles you see here. Remember that during the operation, we will be acting like locals in every way.

This means that if you are conducting a search and lining up all the men against the wall for inspection – don't give us any special treatment, conduct a search on us as well. Does anybody have any questions?"

He stopped speaking for a moment and looked at the soldiers around him. "I ask each and every one of you to use your judgment and be sensible regarding the issue of opening fire," he said, locking eyes with each and every soldier. "We don't want to find ourselves in a situation where we have to respond with fire – because usually, when we shoot, we hit our targets. Any questions? If not, then see you in the field, and good luck to us all." He nodded to the company commander to indicate he had finished speaking and said to his team members, "Alright, let's move. Get in the vehicles."

The disguised soldiers returned to the Peugeot taxi and the dusty jeep they arrived in and sped out of the hangar. The murmurs among the Golani soldiers grew louder, and the bursts of laughter that followed were hard to contain.

"Alright, ladies, show's over," said the company commander to his soldiers. "Get your gear on – we're leaving in an hour."

* * *

It was dusk. The heat was oppressive. Traffic in the casbah area of Jenin languished along. Cars were parked on the side of the street and on the sidewalks. In the background, the muezzin could be heard calling the faithful to the mosque for the late afternoon prayer. Its calls were mingled with the honking cars, tires rolling over the gravel in the square, and the voices of the people milling around.

Three armed men with masks on, who were serving as the bodyguards for the terrorist Ahmad al-Jaafari, moved among the cars, closely examining the passengers inside. They were wary of the presence of undercover operatives in the casbah area and did everything they could to monitor those entering the area by car and inspect them. They went car by car, scrutinizing the occupants, some of whom were pulled out for a brief interrogation and others were even asked to open their trunks and car doors for a more thorough search.

Suddenly, several explosions rocked the intersection. People started shouting and running in all directions. The explosions were caused by a few stun grenades, planted by a couple of soldiers in trash bins near the intersection and activated by remote control.

The three armed guards immediately stopped checking the vehicles and quickly ran toward the intersection. The mass of fleeing people got in their way, and there was commotion everywhere. No one noticed the dusty jeep parked by the roadside. Its back door was open, and four young men emerged from it. They carried bags and quickly disappeared into one of the casbah's alleys. The vehicle slowly drove away and disappeared from the area.

The four "Arabs" – Yogev, Dan, Yariv, and Doron – continued down the alley, making their way to the center of the casbah. The first part of the operation, getting the force into the area, had been successfully accomplished.

* * *

The four undercover soldiers continued on their way into the casbah. For the first time, they saw with their own eyes the primitive yet effective method used by the terrorists in Jenin – long strips of tarpaulin and burlap were stretched over the buildings of the casbah. To maintain a uniform height of this artificial roof, the residents had to place poles and sticks of varying heights on their rooftops to support the heavy tarps. Primitive or not, Yogev thought to himself, this method indeed completely neutralized the IDF's aerial surveillance and mapping abilities.

At this point, Yogev reached into the bag slung over his shoulder and activated the hidden camera inside. The goal was to produce a long and continuous video recording of the area that the air force had no ability to observe. When they returned from the operation, the footage would be taken to the Shin-Bet laboratories, where decryption experts would extract an up-to-date map of the casbah. Therefore, the veteran soldier tried to shift the weight of his body and bag from right to left and even transferred it to the other shoulder, to capture as many angles of the area as possible. His goal was to document recent changes in construction, new stores that had opened or others that had closed, knowing that he now served as the eyes of the unit.

Dan was the operation commander. Hidden in his bag were a Micro Uzi, two additional dual-magazines, and optical equipment. Each soldier carried a well-concealed handgun. In Yariv's bag, the third and last, were stun and fragmentation grenades, radios, and a hoard of other surprises.

From the intelligence briefing they received before entering the area, they learned that the target, Ahmad al-Jaafari, leader of the "Black Panther" terror cells, was supposed to arrive at the mosque on the outskirts of the casbah for the nighttime prayer. Dan knew that in Islam, there are five daily prayers. The nighttime prayer is the fourth one, and it's from complete darkness until the end of the first watch around midnight. Usually, this prayer is the least popular, and the mosques are relatively empty compared to the others. He really hoped that they could capture al-Jaafari tonight, under the cover of darkness, otherwise, they would have to spend the night and the following day here, in the casbah of Jenin.

Evening began to fall, and the team continued on their way toward the mosque. The lights of the minaret, the mosque's tower, were already twinkling in the distance, and the team members began to hear the voice of the muezzin calling the faithful to prayers. Yariv signaled to Dan that they should slow down so that they wouldn't be the first to arrive at the neighborhood mosque. Dan signaled with his eyes that he understood and then stopped at the entrance of a small café and sat on one of the chairs in the entry way, and the other three did the same. Doron pulled out a pack of local cigarettes from his shirt pocket and offered them to his friends. Yogev took one, placed it casually in his mouth, and pulled a lighter out of his pocket. He tried several times to light it, unsuccessfully. He tried again, this time sitting in a different position, but these attempts also failed. The reason was simple: the small lighter was not a regular lighter but a tiny camera. When he pressed the lighter, Yogev was photographing the café and its surroundings. His body movements were intended to capture images of the street leading to the café and its escape routes for future use by the unit's intelligence department. Doron, patiently waiting for the photo session to end, pulled out another lighter and held it out to light his friend's cigarette.

After a few moments, the café owner, an elderly man who was short in stature with white hair and a full build, came out to them. Around his waist he wore a brown apron and held several menus for the new customers. He placed the menus on the table and greeted his guests. The four soldiers returned his greeting in the local dialect and ordered coffee. Although they had been trained in the Shin-Bet studios to speak fluent Arabic, it was still not advisable to engage in too much conversation with the locals: the goal was to alleviate any doubts in the minds of the locals as to their identity with as short a conversation as possible, and then end it. The generous host bowed slightly, collected the menus he had placed on the table, and headed to the kitchen. After a couple minutes, a young man, the host's son, came out with four steaming cups of coffee, which he put on the table. The four soldiers slowly sipped their Turkish coffee, left payment with a tip on the table, and waved goodbye to the owners. It was evening, and in the background, the muezzin's calls could be heard, summoning the worshippers to congregate for the night prayer.

*　*　*

Built only a few years ago, the mosque in the casbah of Jenin was the newest and nicest one in the area. The prayer hall was rectangular, facing Mecca, the holy city of Islam. The four identified the mosque from a distance and walked slowly toward it. About a hundred yards before the mosque, they split into two pairs: Dan and Yogev would enter the prayer hall while Yariv and Doron would remain in the mosque courtyard, on guard duty. Dan handed his bag to Doron, grabbed Yogev's arm, and the two entered the mosque's courtyard. The intelligence they received said that the target, Ahmad al-Jaafari, always went with at least one armed guard and was expected to attend the nighttime prayers.

The first pair, Dan and Yogev, entered the mosque's courtyard, which was still undergoing renovations and expansion. The floor was covered with a layer of gravel that was waiting to be tiled over with traditional marble. The pair turned right towards the water basin and faucets. Islamic law requires worshippers to perform *wudu*, a short purification ritual before prayer. On weekdays, worshippers must perform a partial purification, washing their hands up to the elbow, their feet up to the ankles and, of course, the face. On Fridays, they are required to undergo a more comprehensive and thorough purification ritual. Dan liked Islamic customs and remembered that during the training course, the expert on Islam explained that the purification is supposed to cleanse and purify one's sins that are associated with the hands, feet, and mouth. He also remembered that if there wasn't any water, then they are able to cleanse and purify themselves with sand, what is called "*tayammum*."

* * *

The muezzin's call went out again from the mosque's minaret tower. Yogev looked up and saw that the green neon lights at the top of the spire were already lit. The two soldiers removed their shoes and approached the taps above the small water basin. They washed their feet, hands, and faces with the cool water. Out of the corner of his eye, Dan saw Doron and Yariv positioning themselves at the entrance of the mosque's courtyard. The muezzin gave its final call – a unique verse from the Quran, indicating that the prayer would begin momentarily.

As the muezzin finished its call, Yariv's eyes caught the figure they had been waiting so long to see: Ahmad al-Jaafari and his bodyguard, who was armed with a long M-16 rifle with a new telescopic site. They entered the mosque courtyard quickly, passing right by Doron and Yariv, who were guarding the entrance. In the fluorescent light illuminating the mosque's courtyard, Dan and Yogev saw the terrorist and his bodyguard quickly removing their shoes and hurrying over to the purification basin. The mosque courtyard quickly emptied, and the prayer hall began to fill up with dozens of people. Dan made eye contact with Yariv, the leader of the second pair. Years of joint operations had their effect, and Dan signaled his intentions with his eyes. Yariv blinked twice in Dan's direction, and then each pair of soldiers went about their assigned task: Dan and Yogev entered the mosque barefoot, while Yariv and Doron moved into the lit, empty courtyard with their bags.

* * *

The new mosque was stunningly beautiful: the direction of prayer, the *"qibla,"* facing the holy city of Mecca, was marked on the mosque wall with a special, traditional symbol – the *"mihrab,"* a niche in the wall indicating the direction of the *Ka'aba*, the black stone. According to Muslim tradition, the niche was called this because, in the past, each person that came to pray would place his sword in the mihrab. Since everyone's eyes were directed toward the Ka'aba during prayer, if anyone attempted to take his sword to kill somebody else, the others would immediately notice and intervene. In ancient times, this practice prevented bloodshed in the mosques.

The eyes of the two soldiers shifted to the right: on the right side of the mihrab stood the *"minbar"* – an elevated prayer pulpit elaborately designed and decorated, with several steps leading up to it. On Fridays, holidays, and various events, the imam would stand up there and deliver his sermon. The ornamentation in the mosque was based on the art of Arabic calligraphy: the walls and ceiling were adorned with geometric arabesques, in which the soldiers could identify entire verses from the Quran as well as the names of Allah and the prophet, Muhammad. In this mosque, as in other mosques they had been to before, Yogev and Dan saw that the floor was covered from wall to wall with thick, expensive carpets. These carpets served a dual purpose: first, since the mosque didn't have a heating system, the carpets warmed the cold floor during the winter months. The second reason had to do with the practice of *Sujud* – the act of touching the forehead to the ground during *Rakah*, or bowing down; worshipers, old and young, healthy and sick, touched their foreheads to the floor when they bowed down while praying. This practice, mentioned in the Quran itself, symbolizes a person's complete submission to Allah. At a certain point, this act of prostration becomes a distinguishing mark of devout believers, leaving a mark on their foreheads, indicating their piety. Dan remembered that the Quran promises punishment to the arrogant who refuse to bow down in this manner: on Judgment Day, according to the Quran, when these evil ones wish to seek forgiveness from Allah and worship him, their backs will seize up, their bodies will turn to stone, and thus their punishment will come.

The entire congregation stood on their feet in straight rows – and the prayer session began.

* * *

In the meantime, in the mosque's empty courtyard, Yariv and Doron located Ahmad Al-Jaafari's shoes and those of his bodyguard, which were next to them. It was no simple task, as there were dozens of pairs of shoes strewn across the courtyard, most of them similar in color and size. Yariv look around to make sure that nobody was around. Doron crouched down and placed his bag on the ground next to the bodyguard's shoes. His hand dove into the bag and pulled out a small black leather pouch. He then emptied the contents of the pouch into his palm and looked at it. In his hand rested a tiny, highly advanced tracking transmitter, the size of a pencil eraser. The transmitter was black, with a thick thumbtack on one side. Doron pulled a plastic gun the size of a cigarette pack from his back pocket and then placed the tiny transmitter in the barrel of the plastic gun. Doron looked up and in the silence made eye contact with Yariv. He then winked twice – the prearranged signal.

At that moment, Yariv began a loud coughing fit, while moving his right foot around in the gravel. He made a lot of noise. Right then, Doron took the bodyguard's shoe, quickly flipped it over, and shot the transmitter's pin into the raised part of the shoe's heel that bridged the heel and the front part of the sole. The tiny transmitter was almost entirely embedded in the black sole. After Doron confirmed by sight and touch that the transmitter wasn't sticking out, he turned the device's small head and looked into his bag. The transmitter's locator light blinked on the small screen, which was as big as an average-sized walkie-talkie. Doron saw that the device was receiving and identifying the signal source, so he placed the shoe back in its place next to Ahmad Al-Jaafari's shoes.

The placement of the transmitter wasn't random: Doron knew the bodyguard wouldn't feel the transmitter attached to his shoe while walking. Additionally, since in Islam pointing the sole of one's shoe at another person is seen as a blatant insult and sign of disrespect, there was a little chance that the transmitter would be discovered anytime soon. The working assumption was that the bodyguard would be less suspicious about being followed than the arch-terrorist, so it was decided to follow him and not Al-Jaafari, and he would lead them to him. The soldiers understood the importance of attaching the transmitter: the tarpaulin covering the casbah area would prevent the IDF drones from having any visual connection to the casbah's alleys, but it wouldn't prevent an electronic connection. From the moment the tracking transmitter was attached to the bodyguard's shoe, the drone could create a sort of "digital map" of the covered streets of the casbah, and also locate where Al-Jaafari has been hiding out.

After Doron finished installing the tracking device, the two returned to their previous position at the entrance of the mosque's courtyard. Their part of the mission was complete, and now all they had to do was to wait for the prayer session to end.

* * *

The heavy wooden door at the mosque's entrance creaked, swinging on its hinges as the people began to flow out. Some of them talked with each other about their days and swapped stories. For others, it was an opportunity to catch up on what was happening in the neighborhood – who recently got engaged, who opened a business, and who is moving out of town. Yariv and Doron saw Yogev and Dan slowly exiting the mosque and heading toward the location in the courtyard where they had left their shoes. Behind them, Al-Jaafari and his bodyguard came out, still barefoot. Perfectly organized, everybody quietly identified and put on their shoes. Then, everyone began to disperse in the direction of their homes. The arch-terrorist and his bodyguard also left the mosque's courtyard and started walking in the darkness.

Doron glanced again at the bag – the tracking signal was strong and clear on the small computer screen. After about a minute, Dan and Yogev joined up with them, and all four walked together toward another alley. Dan looked at his watch. It was already close to ten p.m. In the original plan, they had decided not to make contact with the terrorist immediately after prayers. The idea was to follow the signal from the transmitter to confirm the exact location of the apartment he was hiding out in. They would take the terrorist later, but uncovering the location of the hideout would also be important for gathering intelligence material from it.

After they had distanced themselves from the mosque, Dan looked back. Seeing that they were alone in the alley, he quietly said to his friends, "Who here booked a romantic night in a luxurious cabin, courtesy of the Israeli taxpayer, of course?"

Yogev smiled and said, "I did – and I even shaved for you, Kermit."

* * *

The "cabin" was just one of dozens of safe houses maintained by the Shin-Bet in the Palestinian West Bank. In many cases, like in this operation, it was necessary to blend into the area for several days and nights. Pulling the force out every night and getting them back in the next morning wasn't feasible due to the risk of being exposed. And so, the soldiers were equipped with large sums of cash and the basics, which they brought with them in one of the bags from the jeep, just in case they needed to stay in the area for several days.

The apartment belonged to a young Shin-Bet informant. His cooperation with the Shin-Bet didn't stem from a love of Israel; his elderly father was suffering from kidney failure and his situation was deteriorating. He was in dire need of dialysis treatment, otherwise, the doctors said, he might die within a few weeks. The devoted son approached the civil administration offices and requested permission for his father be allowed to enter Israel for treatment at Hadassah Ein Kerem Hospital in Jerusalem. Automatically, all such requests are sent to the Shin-Bet to look over the case and check it out.

A thorough check of the young man's file revealed that he lived in the center of Jenin's casbah and that he was single. He was summoned to a meeting at the civil administration offices in Nablus, where he met the regional Shin-Bet field intelligence officer. The deal offered to him was simple: he gives the security forces use of the house, and his father receives treatment in Israel. At first, as expected, the young man refused the Shin-Bet's offer. The Shin-Bet coordinator didn't pressure him to change his mind: one of the hospice nurses at the hospital where his father was being treated was a Shin-Bet informant. He obtained the sick father's medical file and passed it on to his operator, the intelligence coordinator. A review of the file showed that the father was dying and that the dialysis was critical to saving his life. At this stage, the question was only who would blink first. After about two weeks, the young man called the phone number given to him by the Shin-Bet officer in Jenin and informed him that he would be willing to make the deal: use of his apartment in exchange for treating his father's illness.

When the need to use the house arose, the informant would receive a signal from his Shin-Bet operator, and he would then leave the apartment. He would tell his neighbors that he had to go visit his sick father and that his friends would soon arrive to look after the house. The informant wasn't told that those who would come to stay in his house were undercover soldiers. The apartment was located in the heart of the densely populated area of Jenin, an ideal place for observing and staging ambushes, and an excellent exit point for all kinds of operations. In many cases, after abduction operations, the soldiers would stay in the apartment for a few days with the captive until the search for him ended, and only then smuggle him out of the area.

The four soldiers approached the informant's residential complex and performed their usual procedure of scanning and securing the area. The Shin-Bet always treated these informants with a "trust but verify" approach: there was always the concern that the informant would become a double agent and would try to clear his name, or at the very least, a clean slate – by harming the Shin-Bet operatives who were managing him. This had happened a few times in the past. Consequently, the Shin-Bet changed the directive and required a thorough scan of the safehouse. Therefore, the moment they entered the house, it was critical to check to make sure everything was in the clear.

The four disguised soldiers stood in front of the entrance door to the house. Yariv and Doron secured the right and left sides, then Dan took the house key from his pocket and slowly opened the door. Yariv, gun in hand, cautiously peeked inside, and the others followed in behind him. They quickly scanned the apartment and found no signs of booby traps or explosives. Yogev was the last to enter the apartment, and he locked the door behind him. It was already after eleven, and the four of them activated their night protocol – two awake and two asleep.

They pulled special night vision devices from the bags. Yariv took a coin from his pocket and said to Dan, "Kermit, heads or tails?" Dan called it – Yariv flipped the coin in the air and caught it on the back of his hand. Dan looked at the coin, smiled, and said, "Yogi, come to bed, my dear. As usual, the young ones take first watch."

"Go to hell... how does Kermit always win?" Doron complained to Yariv.

Dan and Yogev quickly lay down on the living room carpet. Yogev reached out, pulled one of the cushions off the sofa, placed it under his head and closed his eyes. Yariv and Doron pulled out the two Micro Uzis from the bag and sat on the floor next to their friends, who were lying down.

Dan whispered to his two friends who were awake, "Okay, so we agreed on shifts of two hours. Oh, and one more thing – I'm exhausted. So if Yogi starts snoring, you have my permission to shoot him. We'll just say it was an accidental discharge."

A smile spread across Yariv's face. "The clock is ticking, Kermit," he said to Dan. "You better hurry up and go to sleep."

* * *

As strange as it might sound, Yariv loved the night watches. Since he was a child, he had always been a night person. Yariv remembered that when he was in elementary school, his family flew to the United States to visit relatives for the summer. When they returned to Israel, he suffered from prolonged jet lag; as a child, he would fall asleep in the afternoon when he got home from school. Then, every night for months, Yariv would wake up in the middle of the night, turn on the light by his bed, and read whatever he could get his hands on until dawn. He learned to recognize the sounds of the night: the garbage truck, the distant calls of the muezzin, the humming of the refrigerator in the kitchen, and the thud of the morning newspaper hitting the neighbor's door. He discovered that these sounds existed during the day as well, but they disappeared in the daylight, swallowed up by its noises.

Even here, in the heart of an Arab apartment in the center of Jenin's casbah, Yariv bonded with the sounds of the night. Now, the barks of stray dogs in the alleys had been added to the nighttime soundtrack – the same dogs that the unit's snipers occasionally had to shoot from a distance to prevent their barking from exposing their forces sneaking through the alleyways of the villages and refugee camps.

A two hour watch in the middle of the night is a long time, especially when you're sitting passively and observing. Yariv enjoyed the conversations he got to have during this time with his team members. Most of the time, they were in a large group of eight or more people. In such a forum, he knew there was no chance of really having a personal conversation. But precisely in these moments of darkness and male intimacy, the floodgates opened up among the team members: some talked about family problems, others about stuff with their girlfriends, and a few even opened up about their fears. Yariv and Doron were old friends on the team, and both were happy when the decision was made to pair them up for this operation. Yariv knew that behind Doron's tough exterior and the nickname "Tyson," there was another side to him – sensitive, introverted, and sometimes even shy. Doron was three recruitment cycles younger than they were, but they adopted him as soon as he joined the elite Team 10. Doron, one of the few religious members of the unit, came to the unit from Kibbutz Sa'ad in the south and was a graduate of the religious education system. Initially, Yariv called him "Kippi" because of the knitted kippah proudly situated on his head, but Doron quickly made it clear that he didn't like the nickname, vetoed it, and finally threatened not to respond to the radio if referred to that way. Although Yariv accepted this, he continued to tease him about the kippah and the praying. Despite being one of the younger members of the elite team, he had earned the trust of the older guys – his courage, composure, and physical strength had saved them more than once from unpleasant situations.

"Dude, if you're tired, you can doze off a bit. I can keep watch alone. It's okay," Doron said to Yariv after a few minutes of silence. Yariv's eyes had already adjusted to the darkness, and he could see Doron's silhouette sitting cross-legged on the carpet, his back leaning against the sofa, and the Micro Uzi resting on his lap.

"Thanks, but this time I'm relatively alert. Too bad we didn't bring a thermos with coffee and some cookies, huh?"

"When we get back, the first thing I'll do is call HR and complain. We'll sue the IDF for unacceptable working conditions. They promised a cabin – look what we got instead." The two soldiers smiled in the darkness. Yariv moved closer and sat next to Doron.

"Say," he asked Doron quietly, "what's it like being religious in a sea of infidels?"

"I wouldn't define you guys as infidels," he replied. "Even though some people try to annoy me, and sometimes succeed, I manage overall. It's hard for me to convey to you the feeling, but it's not easy being the only religious person on the team."

"Did you know that I used to be religious?" Yariv asked.

"You? Used to be religious?" Doron's eyes widened in the darkness. "I would never have believed you came from a religious home."

"Why do you say that?"

"Why? Because of your anti-religious stance – and sorry if I'm being too blunt – I just can't see it."

"And maybe my anti-religious stance stems from the strict religious upbringing I had at home?"

"That's possible, you're right. But still, from someone who grew up in a religious home, I would have expected a bit more appreciation for tradition. Look, I don't expect you to come pray with me or put on *tefillin*,[8] but such a tough stance against religion, especially from someone who grew up religious? I have to admit, I'm very surprised by what you're telling me right now."

There was a moment of silence between them. Doron felt that perhaps he should have expressed himself a bit more carefully to Yariv. Finally, he broke the awkward silence. "When did you stop wearing a kippah? In the army?" he asked Yariv.

"I take it the guys didn't tell you," Yariv replied.

"Didn't tell me what?"

"About my brother."

"Your brother? What's the connection?"

"My older brother was killed in Lebanon, about two or three years before I enlisted. That's when it all started. Or rather – ended," Yariv said quietly.

"I'm sorry... I didn't know you came from a bereaved family. Hey man, I'm sorry if I said anything out of line."

Yariv sensed a little embarrassment in Doron's voice. *It wasn't fair to spring this on him*, he thought, *after all, I always asked the veterans in the team not to tell anyone else about it.* "It's okay. Forget about it, man, it's a long story and it doesn't have a happy ending."

"If you didn't notice, we aren't going anywhere for the next two hours. So if you feel like it, I'd like to hear what happened to him."

---

8. Traditional Jewish religious articles used daily during prayer.

"Okay, you asked for it, but just remember – you've been warned," Yariv said and moved closer to Doron. The two friends now sat shoulder to shoulder, with Dan and Yogev sleeping at their feet. Yariv reached out and pulled one of the bags towards him. He quietly and slowly unzipped it, pushed his hand inside, closed his eyes and felt around. After a few seconds, he pulled out two energy bars and handed one to Doron. Both of them quickly and quietly nibbled on the bars.

"Well, go on already, now I'm curious," Doron said with a smile.

"Alright, so it all started when I was in high school. In 11th grade. My brother, Yohanan, was an officer in the 101st Extraction and Rescue Platoon in the paratroopers. A real bad-ass. We lived in Karnei Shomron back then. Do you know where that is?"

"Yeah, I have a friend from the kibbutz who studied there in the joint religious studies-army service program. Pretty small town to live in."

"Smallest there is… by the way, after what happened, my parents couldn't live in the house anymore – everything reminded them of him. So we moved to Kfar Saba, the big city…"

"How was he killed?"

"His platoon was supposed to set up an ambush on Friday evening, near the Karkom outpost in southern Lebanon. His force was chosen to inspect the route to ensure that it was clear and that there were no surprises along the way. Later, it turned out that Hezbollah had planted explosives along the route, as they had opened that specific route a thousand times already. The idiot brigade commander approved the activity specifically on that route, and that was it. The explosives went off, and since he was at the front of the unit, he was mortally wounded. Afterward, Hezbollah, as usual, started shelling the shit out of them, and they just opened a stretcher, threw him on top of it while he was severely injured, and ran back to the outpost. An hour later, a helicopter arrived and took him to Rambam Hospital in Haifa. He died on the way. Honestly, I'm not angry at his guys – what could they have done there? Field surgery in the middle of nowhere? My mom was angry at them during the *shiva*[9] and blamed them. She claimed that if Yohanan had received treatment on the spot and wasn't thrown on the stretcher, he would still be alive."

"Is that true?"

"Nonsense. I personally spoke with the surgeon who received him in the emergency room. I said to him, 'Doctor, tell me straight up. Could he have been saved?' You know what he said to me?"

"What did he say?" Doron asked intently.

"He told me something I'll never forget for the rest of my life. He said, 'Listen, your brother was mortally wounded by the explosion. Even if he had landed on my operating table, we wouldn't have been able to save him.' That's how definitively the doctor put it."

"And does your mom know that? That it was hopeless?"

"Forget it, my mom completely lost it from this whole thing. And even more so from the way they let us know."

"How'd they tell you?" Doron's voice pierced the darkness.

"That was really a disgrace. Look, no one from the army comes with bad intentions and a desire to do harm, but unfortunately, that's what happened. We were living in Karnei Shomron. It's a religious community. So on Shabbat, the police guard post is closed. Besides that, there are a few more barriers on the road within the community itself. Now, check this out: he died on Friday just before sundown. Then being evacuated from the field on a stretcher, airlifted out, being treated at the hospital – all that took about four or five hours. Identifying him didn't take long because he remained relatively intact – he wasn't blown up or burned. He just suffered a massive blast and bled internally until his body completely gave

---

[9]. Week of mourning in Judaism.

out and he died. Anyway, it was in August. Shabbat starts relatively late then, around seven or eight in the evening. You know how it is – festive, Shabbat evening prayers at the synagogue singing 'Lecha Dodi' and all that, then people talking for at least half an hour at the end of prayers, catching up on all the gossip and what's going on with everyone, and from there home to sing 'Shalom Aleichem,' *kiddush*[10] and then dinner. By the end of the night, you're in your undershirt and go out to the balcony to read the newspaper, and eat watermelon and sunflower seeds. Everybody in the whole neighborhood is outside on their balconies. There was a heatwave. And then – we saw him."

"Saw who?" Doron asked, his eyes flashing as he looked at Yariv.

"What do you mean who? The army vehicle. Now, remember, this is Friday night, around eleven at night. There's no traffic on the street. No one. The moment the vehicle entered the settlement, everyone knew something had happened and looked out from their balconies at the street below. Now, since the settlement was still under construction, the streets didn't exactly have names, and there weren't necessarily house numbers. It looked like a half-built development. And then the vehicle stops in the middle of the street. People in uniforms get out. Now, it was clear to everyone what was about to happen. Dude, I swear to you, it got so quiet you could hear the heartbeats of people on the balconies. It's a small community, everyone knows everyone, and many people have sons in combat units. You know how I felt when I saw them?" Yariv said with a piercing tone and stopped.

"How?"

"Have you ever been to a casino? Have you ever played roulette?"

---

10. Jewish blessing made over the wine on Shabbat.

"Yeah, before the army, I was with some friends in Greece, and we went to a casino there. Why?"

"Do you know that moment when you bet on a number in roulette, and then the croupier throws the little silver ball? It starts bouncing between the different numbers – at first very fast, you can barely see it. Then it starts to slow down and finally lands on a number. That's how we felt: they got out of the car, looking completely lost. I could see by their faces that they didn't know where we lived. Shabbat had already started a long time ago, and it was impossible to call anyone. Despite the darkness, we felt their eyes scanning the other house numbers, and I could hear the sound of the roulette ball ticking in my heart. You tell yourself, 'God, make it someone else.' But, a second later, you feel like a piece of shit because you know everyone here. They all grew up with you in kindergarten, school, the scouts, high school. It's like a kibbutz. So what are you hoping for? That your neighbor's son dies instead of your brother? It was already clear that that's why they're here. They look at the buildings up and down the street, and slowly you feel them narrowing down the possibilities, and I could hear the tick-tick-tick of the silver roulette ball gradually slowing down until suddenly they spot our building. At that point, I felt my knees start to shake. Like someone was about to take me out to be executed. I was sure I was going to shit myself with terror, right there on the balcony. Deathly afraid in the fullest sense of the word. There was only one other family in our building with a soldier in the army, but he suffered from severe asthma and had a desk job in central command."

The darkness felt charged and the suspense was palpable. Yariv swallowed and continued. "They approached the building, and then my mother, even before they officially notified her, started screaming hysterically from the balcony. Her screams were something awful. I remember my father grabbed her forcefully and almost slapped her to try and calm her down. To this day, I still believe the notification team – the officer and his assistants that were stationed at the local army branch – would have wandered around our street for another hour if not for my mother's screaming. They got some sort of official confirmation that it was us, and then they just came up to our apartment on the second floor – and that was it. Honestly, they were very nice, the local officer and his guys. Funny, but all I could think about was: what a crappy job they have. The doctor that was with them gave my mom a shot to calm her down. It didn't help much; she was already hysterical." Yariv stopped talking.

"Yariv, it's completely understandable," Doron said quietly. He couldn't remember the last time someone on the team called him by his first name. He lost his train of thought for a moment.

"So where was I? Oh, the screaming. Anyway, they came up, officially informed us, and that was that. After that, the whole neighborhood came over, and from then on, the 'celebration' for my parents began."

"Celebration? What do you mean?" Doron asked in astonishment.

"Look, it's sort of incredible: my parents became VIPs. To be honest, with all the sorrow and as terrible as it sounds – sometimes I think they even enjoy it a little. Both of them are immigrants: my mom is American, and my dad is Argentinian. They were always treated like outsiders, even though they had been in the country for years. They were always looking for that stamp of approval from society around them. Unfortunately, it was Yohanan's death that got them into the club – and bigtime: now they get to light a torch at every Memorial Day and Independence Day ceremony in our settlement, they give lectures in schools and high schools about 'the heritage of a fallen son' and other nonsense. You know how it is with bereaved families, especially in the religious-nationalist community. They've been given holy status, and I'm not exaggerating. They smile at everyone on the outside, but at home, at night, they cry into their pillows. It's their routine," Yariv finished his story sadly.

"That sucks, dude."

"I know. I'm so over and done with the whole status thing. Just so you understand, before Yohanan was killed, nobody in the settlement really paid attention to them. Their weird accents and different mentality kept them apart from the community. But the moment we lost Yohanan –whew, what an honor. In small communities, especially religious ones, when you're a bereaved family in the IDF, you're, how should I put it delicately – set for life. I always tell everyone: if you're going to be bereaved, might as well make it an IDF bereavement... And if it happened in battle – then you really become a hero. Listen, I have a friend in the neighborhood whose brother-in-law was a logistics NCO. The poor guy died in a car accident. Do you think his family gets the same treatment we do? Let me tell you: they call my dad up to the Torah almost every Shabbat, the neighbors don't complain anymore about my little brother making noise with his drums all day, everyone is suddenly very considerate. Honestly, I'm sick of it – I want to be part of a normal family, not a family of tortured saints."

Doron nodded in understanding.

"And I'll tell you another thing," Yariv continued passionately. "By the end of the thirty days of mourning, it had gotten insane. Our neighbors were the Bezalel family, and one day I kicked a soccer ball and accidentally broke their window. Not just any window – it was an expensive stained glass deal with the Twelve Tribes. My parents gave me money to go pay them, so I went to Bezalel to apologize and pay for the window – but they wouldn't accept a penny! And this is the same guy who would trip the fuse on our electricity when we made too much noise. The same guy who yelled at me like a maniac when I accidentally scratched his car once. He used to bang on the ceiling with a broom when we made too much noise. And now – nothing. All nice and sweet. If that wasn't enough, I even left there with a cake for Shabbat that they gave us. I know it's all with good intentions – but it's so fake that I just wanted to leave everything behind and go somewhere where people in the neighborhood wouldn't look at me with pity."

"So you just got up and left? And took off the kippah along the way?" Doron said.

"Actually, it suited me, if you don't mind my saying," Yariv said with a cynical smile. "I never really connected to the whole religion thing anyway – being observant, praying and all that. The day after my bar mitzvah, my parents started driving me insane – 'Did you pray yet? Where are your *tzitzit*?[11] Why didn't you say 'grace' after eating?' They drove me nuts. I mean, it's not like they're bad parents – they just wouldn't stop. I felt like I was suffocating. Drowning. And it got worse after Yohanan was killed. I didn't want to be an asshole and shatter them completely, so I waited until the year of mourning finished. The next day I told them two things: that I was taking off my kippah and that I was going to join a combat unit. I felt like I was shedding all this weight, Yohanan and the religion, just like that. Like ripping off a band-aid. I don't know what shocked them more. My dad was completely stunned by the entire ordeal. My mom started crying and begged me to reconsider. Both the kippah and the combat unit. She threatened not to sign for me. I told them clear as a bell that I was taking off my kippah, and if they didn't sign for me, I'd cut off all contact with them. Period. Honestly, they had no choice – losing two children within two years would be too much."

"And how do you guys get along today?" Doron asked.

"Believe it or not, much better. Honestly, they've calmed down a bit regarding all the public stuff about Yohanan. Everything's kind of gotten back on track."

---

11. Fringed garment religious Jews wear.

"And why did you choose to serve here? You know what'll happen to them if something happens to you, too," Doron pressed.

"First of all, I can't live my life in Yohanan's shadow anyway. I had an older brother, and he was killed in the army – that's my reality. What can I do? Besides, in a few months, I'll be discharged – and then they'll also veto my trip to South America because that's also dangerous. And after that, I'll want to buy a motorcycle – and that's dangerous, too. What will I do then? It's never-ending."

"You're right, but still – a little consideration for your parents and their situation wouldn't hurt either," Doron said.

"Let me tell you something interesting: in my class, when we were studying Arabic in the studios during our training course, we had an elderly Arabic teacher. He retired right after our course, so it's hard for me to imagine that you met him. I'm talking about a man who must have been about seventy-five years old – old guy, white hair, wrinkled hands, but sharp as a razor. The legend was that for years he was a spy in Damascus, and Eli Cohen[12] came right after him and replaced him. Either way, he was a pro. His knowledge seemed endless – customs, dialects, language, sayings, you name it. He was also fluent in Farsi. One day, when we were talking about the dangers of undercover operations and being exposed, he asked, 'Who knows how to say 'soldier' in Farsi?'"

"I don't get it. What does Farsi have to do with anything now?" Doron asked.

"Patience, man. Wait a sec. You'll see in a second... So he asked, and of course, no one knew, and so he said that the word for 'soldier' in Farsi is *'sarbaz.'* He explained that it's actually made up of two words: *'sar'* and *'baz.'* 'Baz' means 'to play.' 'Sar' means 'head.' So, literally, 'sarbaz' means 'one who plays for his head,' meaning, one who gambles with his life. That's how we need to

---

12. Renowned Jewish spy active in Syria in the 1960s.

see it. That's the truth, man. We gamble with our lives 24/7," Yariv concluded.

Suddenly, one of the two soldiers sleeping at their feet stirred. A deep, sleepy voice said, "Will you guys shut up already? I can't get any sleep like this." It was Yogev.

"Hey, Yogi, you're alive? I was about to call Magen David Adom[13] to come check your pulse," Doron said to him.

"Shut up, junior. And you, Newton, after years of 'don't tell anyone about Yohanan,' suddenly you're having a 'This Is Your Life' moment... what's up with that?"

Yariv ignored the question and looked at his watch. Almost two hours had passed. "Yogi," he said, "do me a favor, come relieve us. I'm dying to sleep."

Yogev was already sitting on the carpet, rubbing his eyes. "Okay," he said without arguing, "Just give me a minute to pee and I'll be there. Meanwhile, wake Kermit up. He's sleeping like a corpse."

"Gladly," said Doron. He turned to the carpet where Dan was sleeping and woke him up.

"Good morning, sir. What would you like for breakfast?" Yariv asked Dan in a soft, mock-polite voice.

"That's it, two hours already?" Dan marveled, "I'm still exhausted."

"Congratulations, Kermit," Yariv said, handing Dan the Micro Uzi and added, "there's food in the bags, too. Enjoy."

Meanwhile, Yogev came back from the bathroom and took the other Micro Uzi from Doron. Yariv and Doron curled up on separate carpets in the spacious living room and within a few minutes, they were sound asleep.

Dan checked his watch. There were only two hours left until sunrise and the morning prayer. Two hours until the second and final part of the operation.

---

13. Israeli equivalent to the Red Cross.

* * *

The first rays of dawn broke. Beyond the curtain swaying in the breeze, Dan and Yogev saw the sky gradually change from black to blue, then to light blue. In the distance, the two soldiers heard the sound of the muezzin, calling everyone to rise for the morning prayer.

The two quickly woke up Yariv and Doron. Yogev opened the bag and looked at the small screen, where signals from the tiny transmitter installed in Al-Jaafari's bodyguard's shoe flickered. The signal indicated that the arch-terrorist and his bodyguard were still in their apartment. If they were going to the morning prayer at the mosque, it would happen in the next few moments. Suddenly, Dan turned to Yogev and said, "Yogi, listen. On second thought, I don't want to risk them recognizing us from yesterday after we were up their ass the whole evening prayer. Let's quickly change into the second set of clothes we brought."

The two soldiers quickly opened the second bag and pulled out the second set of disguises. They removed their old clothes and switched to the new disguises. Dan asked Doron to check the tracking screen, and after watching for about two minutes, Doron said, "They're on the move."

Dan took out the small radio from the bag and activated the frequency scrambler to prevent anybody from listening in or intercepting their signal. He waited a moment and then pressed the transmit button and said, "Kermit to Purple 3."

Silence descended on the room. Everyone waited tensely for a response from the command center. After about half a minute, it came, "Proceed, Kermit," answered Udi, the driver.

"Roger that. Our friend is heading toward the synagogue. Estimated arrival time is twenty minutes. Over."

"Over," Udi confirmed.

"The gang and I are heading out in his direction. Start your engine and meet us at junction seventeen as agreed," Dan instructed.

"Roger, seventeen."

"Also, take note that he's blinking. Make sure you have his signal."

Udi, Yaki, and Barda were in disguise and sitting in the command center. They looked up at the computer screen: the signal from the transmitter on the bodyguard's shoe was clear.

"Kermit, this is Purple 3, we have the signal."

"Roger. At present, there are two of them. The second has a long stick. You grab, and the gang and I will cover you. Make sure there's always a barrel on him – until the end," Dan concluded.

"Got it, I grab, you secure," Udi confirmed.

Everyone in the command center had been waiting for them to make contact: they hadn't heard anything from the four since yesterday morning. While arresting another terrorist at a different house in Nablus about a month ago, they found IDF listening devices and tape recordings of IDF forces. Most of the tapes contained non-classified materials – guards requesting earlier shifts, complaints to the brigade headquarters about the food quality and, of course, impressions of well-known and beloved comedy sketches and films. However, one tape contained material that was more sensitive. And so, fearing further eavesdropping, the general in command instructed the unit commander directly to minimize radio use to the bare necessities, despite using the new scrambler to prevent people from listening in. The tension in the command center eased slightly when they heard Dan's voice on the classified frequency.

Yoav, the unit commander, addressed Udi, Yaki, and Barda. "Alright, guys, this is the moment we've been waiting for. The three of you will go in with the taxi and wait for Al-Jaafari and his bodyguard at Junction 17, which is on the way from his house to the mosque. The other four will close in on the junction. Yaki and Barda – you two grab him. Udi – you cover them. Dan and the others will meet up with you there. If there's a problem, Udi, you contact me directly on frequency 2 and request assistance. The code word for that is 'potato.' Alright, let's go, and good luck." Yoav signed off with the trio of soldiers.

* * *

In the cabin, before heading out, Dan unbuckled his belt and let his pants drop to the floor. Then he took a roll of masking tape from the bag, switched the radio to silent mode, and taped the tiny device to the back of his right thigh.

"I hope the stories the communications officer told us about the radiation from this device aren't true," he said to his friends with a smile.

"Worst case we'll have hard-boiled eggs for breakfast, Kermit," Yogev replied with a laugh.

"Maybe we should get out of here already?" Yariv suggested, and the four headed towards the door. Yariv paused for a moment, took a look back to make sure they didn't forget anything, and then smiled at Doron and said, "Tyson, you cheapskate, did you not leave a tip for the cleaning staff again?"

* * *

Nidal, the bodyguard, quietly woke up his commander, Ahmad Al-Jaafari. "Hey, Ahmad, the muezzin has sounded already. We need to get up."

"*Shukran*, Nidal, give me a minute to wash my face," Al-Jaafari said, heading towards the bathroom.

Nidal had slept barefoot but kept his pants on. He quickly got up and put on his shirt and his shoes. In the darkness, Nidal didn't notice the tiny tracking device attached to the sole of his shoe. After a few moments, Al-Jaafari emerged from the bathroom, his hair wet. Nidal went into the bathroom after him, closed the door, and came out after two or three minutes.

The muezzin's calls grew louder. Nidal knew it was about a twenty minute walk to the mosque, so he tried to hurry his boss up. After a few minutes, the two went out into the dark street and began walking toward the mosque where they prayed the night before. The chill in the early dawn was pleasant, and the two walked quietly through the alleys of the casbah, which was covered with tarps.

"You know, Nidal," Al-Jaafari said to his bodyguard and friend, "before they covered the area with tarps, I felt like I was walking around the streets here naked."

"Naked? What do you mean, Ahmad?" asked Nidal.

"I felt like someone was always watching me from above, the Zionist enemy's planes. I felt they were always following me and photographing me. It drove me crazy," Al-Jaafari said.

"And now what? They can't see us anymore?"

"Apparently not," Al-Jaafari said to Nidal. "At least, I feel safer."

The two continued on their way to morning prayers. The muezzin continued to recite verses, urging people to get up and pray.

"Who's replacing you in the evening, Nidal?" asked Al-Jaafari.

"Probably Yusuf. He's after me on the list."

"Good guy, Yusuf. I hope his daughter gets better soon."

"*Inshallah*, Ahmad," replied the bodyguard.

The two noticed the alleys gradually changing from blue to light blue, a sign the sun was coming up. But it was still difficult to see very far this early in the morning.

From a distance, the two saw a vehicle that was facing them. It was shining its high beams at them. Al-Jaafari shielded his eyes with his hand and told his bodyguard to go see what was going on. Nidal grabbed his M-16, which was slung over his back, and held it with both hands. He cocked the weapon and shouted to the driver, "Turn off your lights!"

The driver immediately turned off the light and stepped out with his hands raised. "Don't shoot!" he shouted, "There's a woman giving birth in the taxi! Come and help me!"

After a moment, Al-Jaafari and his bodyguard Nidal's eyes readjusted to the darkness. From about fifty yards away, they saw the vehicle. It was a taxi – an old, beat-up silver Peugeot station wagon. Nidal was suspicious by nature, and never took his barrel off the driver, but couldn't make out what was happening inside the car in the dim light. When the two got about twenty yards from the taxi, they could hear wailing and crying coming from inside the vehicle.

"Put down the rifle and come help me," Al-Jaafari shouted to Nidal.

Nidal locked the safety on his weapon with his thumb, slung it behind his back, and the two approached the vehicle. An elderly man stood outside the car, holding a black sack. Next to him was a young woman leaning against the door, holding her stomach. The taxi driver, who had been standing by the driver's door the whole time, moved closer to the elderly man and the woman. The distance between the arch-terrorist and his armed bodyguard, and the elderly man and woman, shrank to about five meters. Nidal hesitated for a moment and grabbed Al-Jaafari's arm. It was his job – to protect him and keep him safe. He had a strange feeling. But the moment they stopped, the woman suddenly collapsed into the street and lay there. The elderly man started slapping himself in the head and crying. Al-Jaafari shook himself free from his bodyguard and immediately ran to help pick the woman up. When he got to her, he bent down and tried to pick her up.

Right then, he felt a sharp pain in his neck. He tried to lift his head and look behind him, but just then he felt a severe burning in his eyes. He shut his eyes tightly, the pain unbearable. Just before he closed his eyes, Al-Jaafari saw the elderly man extend a small, strange-looking canister towards his face and spray him with it. With his eyes closed, Al-Jaafari felt another kick between his legs. He collapsed to the ground, holding his balls. Barely a moment later, Al-Jaafari felt someone cover his nose with a piece of damp cloth. He had no doubt for a moment – it was ether, a liquid anesthetic. He could feel that he was losing consciousness, plunging into a black hole. At the last second before losing consciousness, he managed to shout, "Hey, Nidal," towards his armed bodyguard, but then felt a piece of cloth shoved into his mouth, and his voice went silent.

Nidal, who hadn't come over to the taxi, stood rooted in place, as if hypnotized by the events unfolding before him: the moment the woman fell to the ground and the elderly man began to smack himself in the head and wail loudly, Al-Jaafari lunged out of his bodyguard's grip and ran toward the taxi. As he bent down to assist the pregnant woman, the screaming old man suddenly struck him in the back of the neck, quickly pulled a small silver canister out of the black bag he was holding and sprayed something into his eyes. Al-Jaafari went down, covering his eyes with his hands. Right then, the pregnant woman deftly got up off the ground and delivered a precise, quick kick between his legs.

At this point, Al-Jaafari was lying on the ground but still making an effort to get up. The pregnant woman took a cloth out of her pocket and pressed it against Al-Jaafari's nose. He continued to struggle, but she held him down forcefully, and after a few seconds, Nidal saw Al-Jaafari drop to the ground unconscious against the taxi door. Nidal thought he heard his friend cry out for help, but in an instant, the elderly man took a rolled-up handkerchief out of his pocket and shoved it into Al-Jaafari's mouth. His friend was now lying motionless on the road, and the two – the old man and the woman – quickly picked him up and put him into the back seat of the taxi.

Nidal realized that Ahmad Al-Jaafari, whom he was responsible for protecting, had just been kidnapped before his very eyes. He quickly swung the weapon slung over his shoulder to the front of his body. He was now holding it with both hands. Just before his finger reached the trigger, he heard a loud voice on his right calling to him in Arabic, "*Waqf! eerfa'a eedak!*"[14]

Still in shock from what he had just witnessed, Nidal turned to his right. The taxi driver was standing in front of him holding a gun that was aimed right at him.

"Hands on your head!" the driver shouted in Arabic.

Nidal had no intention of giving up, but the taxi driver's gun was aimed right at the center of his chest, and he was only a few steps away. The bodyguard knew that from that short a distance, he wasn't going to miss.

The bodyguard didn't know what to do – he wasn't prepared for a situation like this, despite the training he underwent in Jordan. During training, the bodyguards always had the upper hand. Now, the situation was completely reversed: the person he was supposed to be protecting, his friend and spiritual leader, Ahmad Al-Jaafari, lay unconscious in the back of a dilapidated taxi and, standing in front of him was the driver pointing a gun at him. If he tried to shoot the driver, the driver would likely shoot him on the spot. Even if he managed to neutralize the driver, he would still have to deal with the other two, the woman and the old man. He realized that the driver didn't want him dead, otherwise he could have just shot him. Nidal knew that the only way to save Al-Jaafari would be to run to the mosque a few alleys away and get help. He decided to try and fool the driver.

"Okay, okay," Nidal shouted to the taxi driver standing in front

---

14. "Stop! Raise your hands!"

of him. "Don't shoot! Look, I'm putting the weapon on the ground," he said and slowly bent down to place the M-16 on the ground. As he finished placing the weapon on the street, he sprang and started running as fast as he could toward the mosque. However, after a few steps, he encountered four people who came out of the alley and stood in front of him like a wall. One of them, short and stocky, ran at him, grabbed him by the waist and brought him to the ground. Nidal tried to cry out for help, but a second of the four jumped on him and punched him in the head. Nidal felt dizzy and could already sense the metallic taste of blood in his mouth. After seeing what happened to his friend with the taxi, he realized that he was about to have a cloth shoved into his mouth, and soon after, he would pass out. So, he clenched his jaw tightly, closed his eyes, and tried to shake off his captors.

Suddenly, he heard an authoritative voice above him in Hebrew, "Yogi, cover his nose." With his eyes closed and his mouth bleeding, Nidal felt his nostrils being pinched shut by one of the four. After a few seconds, he couldn't hold out any longer and opened his mouth to breathe. Right then, he felt a rolled-up cloth being stuffed into his mouth. He was wary of opening his eyes because he didn't want to be sprayed. But that didn't happen. One of his captors placed a black bag over his head so he couldn't see. After a few seconds, Nidal felt his arms being pulled behind his back. He felt the zip-tie being tightened around his wrists.

"Newton, hold his head, and we'll get his legs," the voice said – and Nidal felt himself being lifted into the air. Through the black bag, he could hear the trunk door open.

"Careful, take a left. Don't use the radio," the authoritative voice said again. Nidal felt himself being thrown into the trunk. Shortly after, the trunk door slammed forcefully shut. Even though his head was inside a black bag, Nidal felt the darkness descend upon him.

Udi, the driver, was already sitting behind the wheel when the four of them – Dan, Yogev, Yariv, and Doron – got into the back seat of the station wagon and breathed a sigh of relief. Now, Udi had to turn the car around, back toward the road they took to the abduction point. Udi turned his head back and said to the four of them with a smile, "Guys, welcome to Schumacher's taxi. I hope you wiped your feet before you got in."

Udi served as the regular driver for the team. He was one of the more skilled drivers in the unit, and as part of his training for the role of team driver, he underwent an operational driving course, more commonly known as "the crazy driving course." During the course, he learned how to drive the different vehicles in the unit – very fast, but safely. Among other things, he learned how to make sharp, fast turns, the quickest methods to turn a vehicle in any direction, how to shake off pursuers, simulating driving in different emergency situations, and training to shoot with one hand while steering with the other. His extensive experience and motor vehicle skills earned him the honorary title "Schumacher," after the legendary race car driver.

All six soldiers currently in the vehicle – Yaki disguised as a pregnant woman and Barda disguised as an old man, who were sitting in the middle seat of the station wagon, and the other four, who were sitting in the back seat – felt relieved. Now the only thing left to do was to leave the casbah area quickly and quietly.

"Schumacher, do me a favor, no stupid or crazy shit now," Yariv said to Udi.

Udi looked in the rearview mirror and nodded in agreement. He shifted into reverse and drove slowly until he reached the intersection they had come from. There, he turned the steering wheel in the direction of the city exit, shifted into first, and gently pressed the gas pedal.

"Driver," Dan asked Udi with a smile, "Is there a discount for soldiers?"

CHAPTER 6
September 1992, Bethlehem

The offices of the brigade commander of the Bethlehem sector were situated in what used to serve as the police headquarters of the British during the Mandate. It was a large, impressive three-story structure with square windows facing all directions, with iron security bars over them. The office area was built as a system of multiple rooms and hallways that connected them. In the room where the brigade commander sat was a heavy, dark-brown wooden desk with reports meticulously laid out on it.

The three musketeers – Dan, Yariv, and Yogev – sat on one side of the table. Next to them sat Yoav, the unit commander. Opposite them sat the brigade intelligence officer, a bespectacled officer with the rank of major, who had placed several aerial photographs on the table. The five of them sat patiently while they waited for the brigade commander to arrive – he was at present engaged in a loud argument on the secure, red telephone. On the table were various refreshments, a stack of blue plastic cups, and a carafe filled with orange juice.

After a few minutes, the brigade commander entered the room, accompanied by the regional Shin-Bet intelligence officer.

He closed the door behind him and greeted those present in his rough voice, which was grainy from smoking. "Hello everyone, and sorry for the delay. The deputy brigade commander was sent away urgently to another incident in the sector and won't be able to make it. I apologize on his behalf. By the way, meet Captain Rami from the Shin-Bet, head of the Bethlehem sub-district. As far as I'm concerned, we can start." He turned to the brigade intelligence officer. "Yaniv," he asked, "is your briefing ready? Can we begin?"

The intelligence officer rose from his chair and selected one of the aerial photographs from the stack in front of him. "Yes, sir," he replied immediately. "I'm ready. Come on, guys, get closer. The scale here isn't very good."

The three soldiers and their commander stood up from their cushioned chairs and leaned in toward the map.

"Alright," the intelligence officer began, "as you all know, Ramadan starts this week, and we all understand the religious significance this holds for Muslims. Recently, Fatah in Bethlehem issued a call for all collaborators to come and 'confess their sins' during the holy month and if they do, they'll be completely forgiven. They call it the 'month of confession and forgiveness' for the collaborators. It turns out that this whole thing of erasing the collaborators' pasts, in exchange for a full confession and a future commitment to supporting the struggle against Israel, started in Hebron and is unfortunately gaining momentum. There's no need to explain that this is very dangerous for us. The collaborators are the ones who obtain information from the inside, and if they suddenly disappear on us, we'll be in a tough spot. With all due respect to the wiretapping and surveillance, I think we can all agree that it doesn't compare to the first-hand information obtained by a human source on the inside."

"Okay," Yoav said, turning his head to the brigade commander. "Where do we come in? Do you want us to stop the confessions?" he asked in bewilderment.

"Not at all, Yoav," the brigade commander replied. "Unfortunately, this seems like a lost cause, and we won't be able to prevent it. What we can do, however, is minimize the damage."

"What do you mean?" Yariv said, injecting himself into the conversation.

The brigade commander looked at the unit commander and the three veteran fighters, whom he knew from many operations their team had carried out in the sector. "Captain Rami," he said to the Shin-Bet officer, "please, the floor is yours."

The Shin-Bet officer smiled slightly before he started to explain. "Hello, gentlemen. So, the issue is like this: when this month of confession and forgiveness by Fatah began, we thought about trying to torpedo it by imposing a general curfew for an extended length of time, or by kidnapping Fatah leaders and so on. Several times, I sat with the heads of our think-tanks in the service, teams composed of experts in Islam and intelligence personnel, and we decided that we weren't going to actively intervene to prevent their initiative."

"Why?" asked Yogev.

"Three reasons. The first is that we can't just implement a long, general curfew on such a large population, especially since the sector has been fairly quiet as of late, knock wood," said Captain Rami, and knocked three times on the wooden desk. He stopped talking for a moment and then continued. "Similarly, a general curfew will look very bad in the international press, especially during Ramadan – and that's a problem. The second reason is that we have checked in with our sources in the field, and many of them aren't making a big deal about the whole thing. We recently upped their monetary compensation as well as the other benefits they receive, and that's likely to keep them on our side. In other words, if they aren't making a big deal out of it, there's no reason for us to cause a panic."

"Okay, and what's the third reason?" Yoav asked the Shin-Bet intelligence officer.

"The third reason has to do with one of our intelligence officers here in Bethlehem, who came up with an intriguing idea – he suggested we do the opposite."

"What do you mean?" asked Dan.

"I mean that this is a golden opportunity for us to find out who is a loyal source and who isn't. I want us to keep track of the various confessions given from our informants to Fatah, if there are any, and that way we can discover who the double agents are," said Captain Rami, finishing his piece.

"Based on what you're saying, I gather you have reason to suspect some of your sources," Yariv half-asked, half-stated.

The Shin-Bet officer looked at the brigade commander, who nodded, and the man from the Shin-Bet continued. "You're right. That's information not meant to be made public, of course, but recently there were two instances where we suspected that our sources were turned, that is, turned into double agents, and that they are feeding us bad information. In the first case, there was an attempt made on an intelligence officer that was coming to meet a source – luckily, his bodyguards were able to foil the attempt at the last moment. The second case is worse, and here we suspect that there is a collaborator that is turning in other collaborators. We don't know how he knows about them or why he's doing it, but the suspect is getting stronger and more powerful the longer it goes on. Therefore, your help here is critical. Similarly, who knows what else we'll find out after we hear for ourselves what is being said there in Fatah's confessionals."

The room went quiet. The three veteran soldiers – Dan, Yariv and Yogev – looked at the Shin-Bet coordinator. Yoav lightly scratched his head. "And how do you think you'll be able to track these confessions?" he asked. "I mean, they'll be done in secrecy."

At this point, the brigade intelligence officer brought the

aerial photograph over to Yoav. "We know where the confessions are going to take place," he said. "The problem is that the IDF has never been able to get in there."

"Where is this supposed to happen? Let's be more specific, please," Yoav said to the intelligence officer.

"City hall in Bethlehem, that compound," the intelligence officer replied and pointed to it on the map.

Yoav, who had been bent over the map, expelled all the air from his lungs, leaned back and crossed his hands behind his head. He looked at the brigade commander and the Shin-Bet coordinator. "Pardon me, gentlemen," he said, "but I thought that public institutions like this were outside the scope. In case you've forgotten, I'll remind you: three weeks ago, my team was in hot pursuit after an armed terrorist, who managed to escape while we were closing in on him – straight into City Hall here in Bethlehem. I got you on the radio directly, the brigade commander, and requested special authorization to go in after him. You told me absolutely not. You told me that places like this are absolutely off limits. I tried to protest and insisted, but you told me that as far as you were concerned, this was considered an international area and then gave me some other reasons that weren't very convincing. Either way, we gave up the chase, took the team out of the field, and now you're telling me we're allowed in there?"

"Yoav," said the brigade commander, leaning forward over the table and resting both palms on it, "you're right – until yesterday. Understand, I received a one-time, special authorization from the commanding general, who himself received a one-time special authorization from the chief of the general staff, who himself received a one-time special authorization from the defense minister. Think of it as a sniper with only one bullet. There is no second chance. That's also the reason why the representatives of Duvdevan's special unit are sitting here," and gestured with his head to the Three Musketeers. The brigade commander took a few quick sips of his orange juice and continued. "There's no room for error here. I need your team – Team 10 – to pull this off without their cover getting burned."

"All right. Let's assume it's even possible, this surveillance," Dan asked, "what did you have in mind?"

The Shin-Bet officer, Captain Rami, cleared his throat. "I'd like to say something," he began. "In my position as a sub-district head in the Shin-Bet, briefings and reports from other sub-districts come across my desk all the time. For a long time, I have been following the various operations of your elite team. I have to admit – and don't let it go to your head – but every single time, you guys surprise us, the people at the Shin-Bet, more than the last. You guys have devious minds and balls the size of watermelons – and we love it. In a moment, I'll present the general idea, but I'll tell you in advance in the clearest terms possible: if something this complicated and complex actually does take place, it can only be done by your team – Team 10. That's the operational condition – both according to the commanding general and the Shin-Bet, which I represent here at this meeting. I'll say it again: there are no second chances here, and if an undercover force gets exposed like this in a public institution, it will almost certainly become an international incident. That is, we're talking about the most sensitive operation there is here. And so if you, the operational team in the field, think that the mission can't be done, then under no circumstances do we go, because of the severe nature of the consequences. Is that clear enough?" he asked all three, as well as Yoav, as their commander.

"Thanks for the vote of confidence, Captain Rami. Let's go over the plan and see if we even have anything to discuss," Yoav responded.

The intelligence officer took a red marker out of his pocket and circled the compound at City Hall. "All right, so according to our sources, Fatah has decided to hold their confessions in City Hall.

The reason for this is simple: as you know, the economic situation in the West Bank isn't great – in Bethlehem in particular, but in general as well. The unemployment rate among young people in Bethlehem is extremely high. It's no secret that one of the largest employers in Bethlehem is the city itself. There are all kinds of projects up for bid that come up once every few years – guided tours for tourists that come to town for Christmas, security for events, internal police work, sanitation department, teaching, etc. When these projects open up for bidding, hundreds of young people flock to City Hall for interviews, hoping to get a job and escape unemployment. Fatah doesn't want to expose the identity of every collaborator to the public, and so they looked for a central place where there would be a lot of people. Everybody who wants an interview will have to first pass through the other room, the confessional. If he has anything to confess to the Fatah guys, he'll do it. If not, then he won't. But once everybody is forced to go through the confessional, nobody will suspect anybody who they saw go into that room."

"Let me guess," said Yariv to the intelligence officer, "our job will basically be to go into the confessional and plant a listening device. Right?"

The intelligence officer cast a sideways glance at Yoav, who merely lifted an eyebrow and smirked. "That's correct. That's the plan," answered the intelligence officer. He was prepared to say more, but didn't expect Yariv to blurt out the general idea so succinctly like that. He looked at the three soldiers in front of him.

"What do you think, Yoav?" the brigade commander said, turning to the unit commander. "Is it possible?"

"Gentlemen," the unit commander responded, "I trust my soldiers one hundred percent, especially the ones on Team 10. But nobody can guarantee success one hundred percent of the time. Shit happens – you guys have to understand that. And Captain Rami, if you describe a situation where there's the risk of a serious international diplomatic incident, then you need to take that into consideration."

"I understand what you're saying, Yoav," the Shin-Bet intelligence officer responded, "but the powers that be think that we need to do everything we can to pull it off. At the same time, like I said at the beginning, you guys have the last word. At the end of the day, you guys are operating in the field and your opinion on the matter is critical. Of course we'll follow the planning, authorize it, provide you with listening devices and anything you need for the operation. But at the moment of truth, only you guys are going to be there to judge."

The room was quiet. "Last thing, guys," the brigade commander's voice said, breaking through the silence, "the purpose of this operation, if it does in fact play out, is to plant a listening device in that room. That's it – nothing else. It doesn't matter who you run into there – you aren't shooting or kidnapping anybody in that building. And so we're clear, even if you run into our good friend the "engineer," Yahya Ayyash,[15] you don't take him out. You only shoot in the case where fire is effectively being directed against you. Except for that – nothing."

"All right, then let us check it out, and we'll let you know as soon as possible what we decide," Yoav said.

All present rose to their feet, shook hands all around, and went their separate ways. Duvdevan's commander and his soldiers went toward the exit, and then the brigade commander called over to them, "Hey, guys, one more thing: if everything goes down smoothly, I'll make sure that the whole team gets a special week's vacation. That's certain. I'll also recommend the whole team receive a citation for excellence. That's the only kind of bribe I can offer you as combat soldiers," he said, and winked with a smile.

---

15. Yahya Ayyash was the chief bombmaker for Hamas in the early 1990s and was killed in 1996.

* * *

Three days went by and the indecision had yet to be resolved. After they came back from the meeting with the division commander, the unit commander called in the company commander and the other combat soldiers from Team 10 into his chambers to present them with the dilemma. The meeting lasted several hours, and each person was given the opportunity to have his say. Like the rest of the combat soldiers, Yoav knew that the army was not a democracy: there are those who give the orders, such as the commanding officer, and those who must carry out those orders. However, in this unit – and especially on this team – he felt obligated to put the matter up for discussion in order to hear the opinions of all the veteran soldiers. The unit commander knew that the operation's success depended exclusively on the skills of the guys in the special unit, their cool, their daring, and in the originality of their thinking. In this instance, their diverse set of skills wouldn't help them – not their mastery over different kinds of weapons, Krav Maga, their ability to fight for a long time under fire, nor their impressive navigational abilities. None of this would help them here, since here the goal was completely different in its purpose: this time, the undercover operatives would have to penetrate the heart of a civilian city administration building in the middle of Bethlehem, in the middle of the day, to get into the room where Fatah's most wanted were going to be, plant the listening device, and to get out of there without anybody knowing.

Shit, Yoav thought to himself, *how the hell am I going to send my soldiers into a place crawling with armed terrorists where they will be heavily outnumbered? If they are discovered, who can guarantee that they come out alive?* Yoav was leaning toward not authorizing the mission. With all due respect to the Shin-Bet and their crazy ideas, he wasn't prepared to jeopardize his soldiers' lives to this extent. *This was crazy, the whole thing,* he thought to himself.

Even within the team itself, an argument broke out. Gidi, Udi, Barda and Yogev were against it. They said that the risk of being exposed was just too great. Dan and Yariv were for it, and Doron ultimately sided with them. The rest of the fighters were on the fence. The indecision was genuine and principled. Yoav knew that the combat soldiers standing in front of him had proven their courage and willingness to put their lives on the line time and again. And so he knew that their hesitancy about the mission didn't stem from fear or concern, rather from a real, fundamental discussion about the limits of their capabilities.

And that's exactly what Yoav was afraid of. As a soldier and commander of the unit, he remembered always wanting to push the limits of daring and deviousness of their operations. He knew that there were more than a few operations that were more dangerous than usual, some of which were on the edge of suicidal. What drove him and his friends to risk their lives more and more was the desire to overcome fear, to prove that they were immune to it, even though many of their friends had paid with their bodies and souls.

There were operations that went sideways, where Yoav and his team members found themselves disguised in the middle of a bustling, public Arab square surrounding by a rabid crowd threatening to take out their anger and frustration on them. It took a miracle to get out of situations like that unscathed. There were no tangible, physical wounds, or anything visible to the eye, but the mental abrasions didn't take long to show up: two of Yoav's friends on the operations team were diagnosed with PTSD, others developed various psychological problems. One in particular, simply became violent – they were all symptoms of PTSD. And therefore, Yoav felt that he needed to hit the brakes in this case, and not hurry or accelerate the process here.

Yogev asked for permission to speak. "Look, guys, we've done some crazy shit before, and I even helped plan many of those operations. Also, in cases where our cover was burned in the field – we drew weapons, shot our way out and won. But this is a totally different situation – do you guys comprehend what kind of a media shitstorm there will be if our forces get exposed? And what about the unit – how will the unit look then? This could be a mortal blow to our good name as professionals. With all due respect, nobody here is Superman, and shit happens. Does anybody have an insurance policy against the team getting exposed? It's too dangerous. Let's not bite off more than we can chew. Let's just keep doing what we do, we don't need to be taking any crazy risks because somebody in the Shin-Bet thinks that anything and everything is possible. We all know it doesn't work that way."

"I agree in principle with Yogi," said Dan, who was one of the chief proponents of the operation. "It's too dangerous. But let's remember why we're here – not because of the day-to-day things; for that, we have the regiments. Not for the special-ops, that's what we have the various reconnaissance platoons for. We're here specifically for unique operations like these. You guys all know me – I don't look for unnecessary action – but we can't give up without even trying. I think if we come up with a good enough plan, we can do it. We have to use our heads here. We've done things before that border on insanity – and we've always come out on top. I'm telling you, there's a chance we can make this work. I told you guys what Yariv and I thought about doing so, if nothing else, give it a chance. By the way, Yogev addressed what will happen if we fail. What about if we succeed? Obviously in terms of the intelligence, this will be an awesome achievement for the Shin-Bet and the intelligence department. And, obviously for us as soldiers, this would be the proverbial feather in the cap of our service. But are you grasping the importance of how much this would improve the Shin-Bet's ability to operate? Not to mention the status of our team and the unit!"

At this point, Yoav felt like the discussion had run its course; he ended it, but asked Dan and Yariv to stay behind. When the last of the soldiers left the room and closed the door behind him, Yoav addressed the two of them. "Your plan was extremely logical," he said. "I want to hear it again, this time slowly and thoroughly."

Dan looked over at Yariv, who was sitting next to him, smiling, and began explaining the idea in detail. When he finished presenting the plan and answered Yoav's many questions, Yoav pressed the intercom button on his desk and called to his assistant, "Aviv, please get the Bethlehem brigade commander for me. It's urgent."

* * *

Another week passed. The two combat soldiers, Dan and Yariv, were questioned again and again – first by their unit commander, Yoav, and after him, by the brigade commander in Bethlehem. Finally, they brought the two into the commanding general's chambers, and they presented him with their idea, the possible ways of going about the operation and their chances of actually pulling it off. The general requested to see, with his own eyes, a feasibility demonstration so that he could get an impression of the planned operation; to this end, the commanding general arrived accompanied by the brigade commander in Bethlehem and Captain Rami. The three of them sat quietly while Dan and Yariv gave their presentation. When they finished, the two were bombarded with questions and scenarios regarding situations and responses. The two veteran combat soldiers were prepared for every scenario, and answered every question thrown at them quickly and confidently.

After the feasibility demonstration, the senior officers met for a final discussion on the matter. The discussion took place in the chambers of the commanding general, and in the end, Yoav got the green light for the operation. Everything was ready to go. Now, all they needed was a new technological toy that Captain Rami promised to get them.

* * *

The senior Shin-Bet officer promised – and delivered. The day after the operational plan was approved, Captain Rami arrived at the unit with a device. He waited in Yoav's chambers for Dan and Yariv to arrive. One of the secretaries in the bureau called Team 10 on the internal line and requested that the two come immediately. The arrived a few moments later.

Captain Rami shook their hands and asked them to sit down. "Well, getting a little nervous?" he asked, smiling.

"Not a little, a lot," Yariv admitted, slightly embarrassed.

Captain Rami used to be a Shin-Bet interrogator before being promoted to sub-district intelligence officer. Thousands of hours in the interrogation rooms had honed his senses and taught him how to read between the lines. He sensed that the veteran combat soldier in front of him was very tense.

"Yariv," he said to him in a quiet but sure voice, while looking directly at him, "you guys are about to go on a very important, very complicated mission. I don't think we have ever done anything this daring before – nothing we've done before can even hold a candle to this operation. But despite the importance, if you feel at any point that you can't pull it off, you pull out immediately. And, of course, I mean both of you. Don't go being heroes just because Yoav and the guys on the team don't like it. Your operational record is impressive, and you don't need to prove anything to anyone. Even if you're in the middle of City Hall and decide that it's too dangerous – you just pack up and leave. I trust your judgement completely in the matter. Only you can decide if it can be done based on what you see with your own eyes. I prefer you retreat rather than burn your cover, and then it'll be a lot more difficult for all of us to get you out of there. And let's not even talk of the international incident it would cause."

He stopped talking for a moment, put his hand on Yariv's shoulder and continued. "We've gone over the plan in detail, and I think that your plan is excellent. Really. I would never have thought of anything like that. But, in the end, if you decide that it's not doable, I'll stand behind you and back you up on your decision."

"Thank you," Yariv said, stifling a breath. "That really means a lot. I admit that I'm a bit more nervous than usual, but I think it's going to be fine."

"Captain Rami," Dan said, interjecting, "where's that toy you promised us?" The Shin-Bet officer stuck his hand into his jacket pocket and took out a smooth, rectangular shaped black box. He placed it on the table in front of them and carefully opened it. Inside was a fancy, ivory pen. Inscribed on the pen in Arabic was the phrase "To my one and only true love." Captain Rami turned the pen around, and the soldiers saw that on the other side of the it was a sharp, thick thumbtack. They looked at the Shin-Bet officer and waited. He set the pen down on the wooden desk and began his explanation.

"What you see here, gentlemen, is a pen made by the luxury brand Mont Blanc. It costs a few thousand dollars; high-end stores import them from abroad and sell a handful of them every year. But, our sages taught us not to look at the jar, but rather, what's inside of it, right? So, inside this expensive pen is a recording device that is capable of storing many dozens of hours of recording time, as well as a powerful miniature transmitter. In addition, our experts have managed to plant a very thin battery inside it that will provide enough power to record everything, as well as transmit the information wherever we need it to. I can also tell you, off the record, that this model you have is used by the Mossad – if it works for them, there's no reason it shouldn't work for you," Captain Rami said proudly.

"Impressive," said Yariv, "but why does it look like this? And what's this thumbtack?"

"Look, guys, we want to be a hundred-percent certain that this operation won't be discovered. Let's assume you guys get in, successfully plant it and get out. Everything's fine, the recording device works and everybody's happy. But then the unexpected happens – somebody discovers the pen. If it was a regular recording device, it's reasonable to assume that whoever found it would run with it to their superiors in Fatah or Hamas, the device would be inspected, and the recording would be exposed – in other words, we're fucked. In this case, this pen looks harmless, expensive, and there's no reason why anybody should suspect it. The inscription increases the feeling that it's a personal gift to a man from his beloved wife, and therefore we assume that whoever finds it will understand that he found something nice and expensive, and so he'll either keep it for himself, or he'll go sell it to somebody else. But it won't be exposed as a recording device, at least not immediately," said the Shin-Bet officer.

"And how are we supposed to install it in the confessional room?" Yariv asked with a skeptical glance.

"You won't install it, rather, you'll tack it to the underside of the main table in the room. Here, look," he said and took a color photo of a big, long and impressive table out of his bag and placed it on the table.

"What's this?" asked Dan.

"This is the table in the confessional room," Captain Rami answered him with a sly grin.

"How do you know that?" Yariv asked and furrowed his brow.

"The table arrived by special order from abroad, and let's just say that the guys from the Mossad helped us out here a little…" the Shin-Bet officer said with half a grin.

"I got you," said Dan. "So let's get back to the table – how do you propose we insert the pen there?"

"Whoever you choose to be the one to plant it will hold on to the pen in his pocket. After the second person creates the distraction, the one planting the device with get close to the table and stick it into the bottom of the table. As you can see, the edge of the table is wide, and so it will hide the pen if it's right up against the bottom. It's a special tack, and after it's affixed strongly, it won't come loose from the pen, even if you dance on the table. What I'm telling you is air-tight, and it has been through plenty of technical tests in our labs," Captain Rami said.

Yariv took the pen in his hand and looked at it up close. He then gave it to Dan and said to him, "All right, go practice with it, Kermit, that's your job."

* * *

The last stop was to see the unit doctor, Dr. Tomer. Yariv opened his mouth as wide as he could. Dan stood behind him and held his friend's jaw still. Dr. Tomer finished installing the capsule on Yariv's molar, took off his latex gloves and threw them in the garbage.

"Okay, we're done here. Just remember, Yariv, don't chew the capsule beforehand. As soon as you do, you can't eat or drink anything – it will only impede the strength of the capsule. From my side, don't even touch it with your tongue. It's very strong stuff, this acid. And you, Dan," the doctor said, turning to the soldier standing next to Yariv, "remember to get back after he chews it

– it's going to spray in all directions. You've been warned," the doctor said, and slowly closed Yariv's open mouth.

"Try saying something for a moment; let's see how it sits there," Dan told Yariv.

"One, two, three – how do I sound?" Yariv asked.

"Actually, you sound fine. Just fine. Close tight for a sec – I also can't see anything sticking out. I think you can head out. Just don't French kiss anybody, okay?" the doctor said, joking.

"Don't worry, doctor," Dan said as he stood next to Yariv. "The women I saw in Bethlehem... I wouldn't touch them with a laser pointer."

The three of them smiled, but the doctor still sensed Yariv was more tense than usual. "Yariv, in any event, remember that in your jacket pocket is the antidote to the stuff in the capsule. If it accidentally breaks inside your mouth, you have about ten seconds until it reaches your stomach. In that case, you take the bottle that I gave you and drink all of it immediately. That will neutralize it. But don't forget that after you swallow the acid, you might feel a sharp pain in your stomach and even a bit dizzy. That's natural, don't worry about that. All right, guys, good luck."

Dan shook the doctor's hand and started walking towards the clinic's exit. Yariv also shook Dr. Tomer's hand and mumbled a half-hearted "thank you." Dr. Tomer shook his hand and added a big hug.

"Yariv, it'll be fine. You're just tense, and rightfully so. Remember, we're all behind you," he told him confidently.

The hug indeed helped Yariv a bit, and he winked at the doctor and followed Dan outside.

"Hey, where are you? Ramadan is almost over!" Dan called over to him. "Come on, let's get dressed and get into costume already and get out of here."

* * *

The Abu-Sneina neighborhood square in Hebron was bustling with people. It was eight in the morning, and dozens of passengers stood at the various bus stops scattered around the intersection. No one paid any particular attention to the elderly man walking with a stoop, holding a wooden cane with a golden knob. His black shoes had been shined, and his blue shirt had been ironed and starched. In his other hand, the elderly man held a yellow masbaha with a red tassel. He sat on the bench at the bus stop, his fingers fidgeting with the beads while quietly reciting the many names of Allah to himself.

Next to him walked a young man in his twenties. He was holding a reusable shopping bag with Arabic writing from the local supermarket. Inside the bag were a few books. The young man's scruffy beard indicated that he hadn't shaved in the past few days. He sat next to the elderly man, took out one of the books from the bag, and started reading. The book's cover was black with Arabic letters printed on it. The other passengers at the stop heading north waited patiently. After a few minutes, the bus to Bethlehem, line 124, approached the bus stop. Everyone stood up and began pushing to stand at the curb, where the bus would stop and open its doors.

As the young man looked up and saw bus 124 approaching, he quickly closed his book, put it in the bag, and went to help the old man. The old man gave his arm to the young man, used his cane with the other hand, and slowly got up from the bench. The bus stopped and the doors opened. The two waited with the crowd at the end of the line and got on; the bus was completely full and the two stood. The bus route was full of potholes and the bus swayed wildly as it avoided them. The old man could barely steady himself and almost fell onto the young passenger next to him. A kind young man got up from his place and with a gesture of his hand offered the older man his seat.

He didn't hesitate for a moment and sat in the empty seat. "Bless you, my son," he said to the kind passenger.

"May Allah extend your days, *ya sidi*,[16]" the passenger said to him.

The young passenger who was accompanying the older man also thanked the man who vacated his seat. "*Shukran, ya habibi,*" he said and added, "you know, Ramadan…"

The passenger nodded and smiled at both of them. The bus continued driving quickly and haphazardly. After a few minutes, the driver announced, "Dheisheh." The bus slowed down and entered the Dheisheh refugee camp between Hebron and Bethlehem.

"I'm getting off here. Have a nice Ramadan, ya sidi," the young man said to the old man. He smiled and nodded to the young man accompanying him, and began walking toward the rear door.

"Allah is generous, peace be with you," answered the old man, and the passenger nodded and got off the bus.

The driver looked in his mirror and saw that nobody else wanted to get off the bus. He pushed the button and the loud hiss of the air-brakes sounded. The doors closed and the driver merged into the northbound traffic to Bethlehem.

"Next stop, Bethlehem!" the driver shouted.

Dan looked at Yariv, who was sitting next to him. Yariv, the old man, held the masbaha as his fingers rapidly worked the prayer beads. Dan, the young man, knew his friend and could tell that he was very nervous, much more than usual. Dan smiled, placed his hand on Yariv's leg, and said in a voice that even the passenger behind him could hear: "Don't worry, Father. Everything's going to be fine."

---

16. A common way of respectfully referring to older people.

* * *

The bus arrived at the bus stop in Bethlehem and stopped. The driver looked in the rearview mirror and called out, "City Hall!" He opened both the front and back doors, and got up from his chair to stretch. A few people crowded around the exits and got off the bus while holding onto the folding doors.

"Come on, father, we're here," Dan said to Yariv. Yariv, the old man, got up slowly from his seat. The driver went to help him by holding his arms while he stood, while Dan took Yariv's walking cane in one hand and in the other, the bag with his books. The driver helped Yariv until he got down off the bus's steep steps.

"May Allah lengthen your days, my son," Yariv said to the kind driver when he was finally standing outside on the sidewalk.

The driver thanked him with a nod of his head, got back on the bus and closed the doors. After a moment, the bus left the stop and continued on its way.

Yariv looked into Dan's eyes. Both of them remembered the general's instructions during their last meeting in his office: "I'm fine with you not going in at all if you see that it's too dangerous and that you might get exposed. The final decision is entirely in your hands," he told them, with Captain Rami and the brigade commander sitting next to him. "But, once you go in – do whatever you can to reach that confession room and plant the listening device. I will personally be in the command center to provide real-time responses for whatever happens. Additionally, I have asked Yoav to have two of your teams set up undercover around the perimeter of the municipal building. If there's the slightest problem – they'll come get you. Each of you has an emergency button – don't hesitate to use it if things go south."

Dan, who was dressed as the young Arab, scratched behind his thigh, which also happened to be where the distress button was located. He knew that one short squeeze would call the extraction force to immediately descend upon the City Hall complex, just like the general said. Yariv put his hand under his jacket. Like Dan, he also felt the button, which was on the left side of his chest. These places, behind the thigh and the side of the chest, were carefully chosen: there was significant concern that whoever entered the confessional would be searched. They knew that in such cases, they would be looking in places where people usually conceal weapons – the waist, legs and pockets. Nobody suspects a weapon behind the thigh or on the side of the chest.

"Come on, my son, let's go find you a job," Yariv said to Dan. Dan smiled – he felt like Yariv was back to normal.

"You're right, Father, let's not be late," Dan said, and they started walking in the direction of the rusty iron gate of the complex.

* * *

It was one of the last days to interview for work at City Hall, and the swarm at the front gate was massive. Dan took Yariv by the arm and the two of them slowly made their way in the direction of the gate.

"Move, can't you see there's an old man here?" a loud shout sounded from the direction of the gate.

The two soldiers looked up towards the gate. At the entrance to the complex stood ushers that directed the people arriving to the various registration rooms. One of the ushers, a tall, dark-skinned young man who saw Yariv – an old man leaning on his cane – waiting, went over to him while pushing everybody else out of his way. After a few seconds, when he got to Yariv, he asked, "Where are you from, ya sidi?"

"Hebron. This is my son, Jamil," Yariv said in a Hebron accent and pointed to Dan, who was standing next to him.

"How nice, sir, come, you shouldn't have to stand in the sun, and during a fast no less..." the usher said and directed both of them to come with him. He went first, and parted the crowd left and right, creating a path through. Yariv walked slowly after him, his cane in his hand, and Dan after him. In one hand, Dan was holding the black sack, and in the other he supported Yariv's hunched back.

"*Shukran, isalamu eedek,*"[17] Yariv whispered to the usher as they arrived at the main gate. The usher opened the locked gate with a key he had and ushered the two inside the City Hall complex.

"One second, man," another usher said, turning to him. "What about checking their things? That's the order, you know."

"Are you crazy?" the other usher said. "He's my father's age, let him go."

"No, no, it's fine. I understand," Yariv said and opened his jacket for the second usher to inspect. Dan did the same, and put the bag he was holding on the other table in front of the other usher.

"Just a few books, that's all," Dan said and showed the usher the contents of the bag. The usher looked inside, primarily to absolve himself of his official duties, shook the elderly Yariv's hand and said in an apologetic tone, "Forgive me, sir, you understand, those are the new orders. I didn't mean any disrespect."

"*Allah itawell omrak,*"[18] Yariv blessed him with a common phrase and smiled to the embarrassed usher.

The inner gate opened, and Yariv and Dan saw the main structure of City Hall in front of them. The building was stunningly impressive. It was built at the end of the 19th century out of chiseled white stone and stood two stories tall and, in the middle, was a

---

17. May your hands be blessed.
18. May you live a long time.

high dome. In the middle of the dome were three long windows, a large clock above them with Roman numerals, and above that, a bronze statue. The front of the building was decorated with lush green grass, and on the sides were trees that had been trimmed into various shapes.

Dan felt goosebumps all over his body. He recognized the building from the photos that they received last week. Until today, so he had been told, no Israeli had been inside that building, and certainly no undercover soldier. While preparing for the operation, the two learned the plans to the building inside and out, memorizing the layout of its rooms and its hallways. They did so with the understanding that they would have no way to open a map or aerial photographs during the operation. Dan memorized the layout of the first floor, and Yariv the second. Each story had dozens of rooms, entryways, patios and various service areas and bathrooms. The two of them looked at the impressive structure for a few moments, and then the large clock in the middle of the dome began to chime. It was noon.

"We need to get going, Father, we'll be late," Dan said to Yariv, and the two of them continued to the entrance to the building itself.

* * *

The wooden door to the entrance of the City Hall building creaked on his hinge as it slowly opened. The usher at the front door turned to the old man and said, "Hello, sir, where to?"

Yariv cleared his throat and coughed lightly and finally said in a deep voice, "My son wants to register for one of the jobs advertised," he said, and pointed to Dan.

"Please, gentlemen, come in. Turn left at the end of the hallway. The room to sign up for interviews is the third from the right," he answered and pointed in the direction of the hallway to the left.

"Thank you, young man," Yariv said and shook his hand – and the two of them looked around as they entered the building. Dozens of young people were running around the entryway to the building. Signs directed those who wanted to register for interviews as well as those who came to bid on projects – an arrow to the right for various security jobs, left for sanitation, upstairs for teaching.

Yariv and Dan stood and looked at the flow of people, when they suddenly noticed something strange next to the stairwell leading up to the second floor of the building. When the two got closer, they saw three men standing next to the stairs, with various weapons casually slung over their shoulders. The first had an old but dependable Uzi, the second had a shortened AK-47 and the last one was holding an M-16.

These guys must be part of Fatah's shock troopers,[19] Dan thought. *We'll probably see them later in the confessional room.* Despite their natural instincts, the moment they saw armed terrorists in front of them – that is, guns drawn and ready to fire – the veteran soldiers remembered the purpose of the operation. Dan held Yariv's arm and they both made their way toward the registration room for the security jobs.

They turned left at the end of the hallway, just like the usher at the entrance explained, and counted three doors on the right. The third door had a small sign with handwriting on it – "Security and police work." They had no intention of actually going in and signing up – that would only increase their risk of exposure. The goal was to find the confessional room, which was supposed to be somewhere around here. But where? Dan and Yariv quickly read all the signs close to the third door and the ones on either side of

---

19. A unit of Fatah's special forces that weeds out collaborators.

it, but none of them gave any indication of being the confessional room. Many young people came in and out of the various rooms and walked past them.

Dan looked to his right toward the end of the hallway. There were a lot of people crowding into the entryway and hallway. Suddenly, his blood froze in his veins. He squeezed Yariv's arm quickly and whispered in Arabic one word: "Three."

Yariv, well versed in the team's code, understood immediately that somebody was coming from their three o'clock, or from their right. He turned his head slowly like an old man might and looked to his right, and then he saw him. About thirty yards away from them, the most wanted terrorist in Bethlehem was walking towards them: Hassan Abu-Honoud.

He was one of the most sophisticated, experienced and most ruthless terrorists that the IDF was looking for in the Bethlehem area. His nickname was "The Punisher," which he justifiably earned. Whenever anybody was accused of collaborating with the Shin-Bet, Hassan Abu-Honoud was summoned to interrogate them. The interrogation consisted of getting shot in the knees, being beaten, sometimes into unconsciousness, cutting off fingers, and some people even reported having salt or motor oil injected into their veins. Needless to say, the confession rate during these interrogations was very high. The IDF and Shin-Bet had been looking for Hassan Abu-Honoud for months, but unsuccessfully. He was surrounded by competent body guards, as well as a web of collaborators and informants. The unit also tried to trap him once, but failed. He was never where he was supposed to be. He was obsessively suspicious and had the sharp senses of a street cat.

Yariv looked Dan in the eye. The urge was too much, but both of them knew that if Abu-Honoud was in the area, then so was the confessional room. Dan pulled Yariv over to the wall and they both leaned against it. Yariv opened his jacket and took an inhaler out of his inside pocket. He put it in his mouth and gave it two quick sprays. At the same time the inhaler made its sound, Abu-Honoud passed right by them with his security guards. He didn't look in the direction of the sick old man, nor did he look at his son, who was helping him stand up. While Dan was helping Yariv with his staged asthma attack, he was able to take a look at Abu-Honoud's guys. He saw that the arch-terrorist had a Baretta on him, and another gun in his belt. His three bodyguards were the same three they saw earlier near the stairs.

Right after the terrorist and his three bodyguards walked past them, Dan and Yariv straightened up and followed them with their eyes. At the end of the hallway, the four of them stopped in front of the last door, knocked, and then went inside.

Dan looked at Yariv. Both of them now knew where the confessional was. Beads of sweat began forming on Yariv's forehead. Dan looked at him and said, "Are you all right, Father?" concerned.

"Yes, yes, my son. You know, age and all."

On their left and right, the hallway teemed with young men. Some were accompanying their friends, some were accompanying family. The two soldiers understood that the moment of truth was drawing nearer – at the end of the hallway, the confessional room was waiting for them, and in there at least four armed men, the leader of whom was one of the most dangerous terrorists currently being hunted by the IDF.

Dan felt behind his thigh, and felt the distress button for a moment. Yariv understood what Dan did. He smiled and then felt his side – the distress button was in place. Dan's gun was against his left thigh. Yariv's gun was taped to his chest with extremely strong double-sided tape. The soldiers generally didn't tape guns to their chests ,since ultimately they had to rip the tape off. The process usually involved a lot of screaming, swearing and other colorful, original vocalizations. In Yariv's case, it wasn't a problem: as opposed to most of his friends in the unit, Yariv didn't have much hair on his chest. This fact served him in two ways: he could usually take the double-sided tape off quickly and painlessly, and he was spared being called a bunch of names that his hairy friends couldn't escape – like "baboon" and "chimpanzee."

It was still not too late to change their mind. Yariv looked at Dan. "Come, my son," he said to him. "Let's go in."

Dan could feel his heart beat, and despite the poker face he showed, he could feel himself getting wrapped up in the excitement. He got his breathing under control immediately. "Okay, Father," he said to Yariv. "Just one second."

Dan put his hand in his back pocket. There, rolled up inside some tissue paper, was the expensive pen, and inside it the advanced recording device. He took it carefully out of his pocket and hid it in his sleeve. He then turned to Yariv and asked, "How is your tooth, Father?"

Yariv slowly and gently felt the back of his mouth with his tongue. There, on his back molar, his tongue could feel the capsule glued in place. He swallowed and said to Dan, "Come on, my son, it's time."

And then the two soldiers, who were disguised as father and son, began slowly walking toward the confession room at the end of the hallway.

* * *

They stood in front of the brown wooden door. On the door was a white, rectangular piece of paper with the words "Interview Room" written in large, curly writing. *Good thing they insisted on teaching us how to read Arabic handwriting in the training course*, Dan thought to himself. He looked at his friend, took a deep breath, and extended his hand to the door. He pushed the lever down, and the door swung wide open.

The room was dark and smaller than he was expecting. The table in the middle he knew well – it was exactly like the table in the picture that Captain Rami showed him.

"What are you doing here?" said a loud voice from the right side of the room.

The two soldiers turned to their right. The security guards they saw earlier by the stairs were sitting on some stools. Their weapons were on the floor next to them. Behind them sat Hassan Abu-Honoud. One of the guards got up and shouted, "Get out, now!"

Two of them picked up their weapons off the floor. "Do you have any water?" Dan asked one of the guards. "I know it's Ramadan, but my father has a heart condition and..."

"Are you deaf?" the guard said to him, and got out of his seat, the AK-47 in his hand. "Get out now!" he screamed at both of them again.

Yariv sensed that now was the time. He cleared his throat – the sign he and Dan agreed upon – and then bit down hard with his teeth, shattering the capsule affixed to his molar. His mouth filled up with white foam and Yariv swallowed his saliva – and the stuff inside the capsule.

Dan knew that he had about ten seconds before the chemical made its way into Yariv's stomach. "Please, have mercy, he's a sick old man..." he said to the armed guard in an attempt to buy time, but the guard had already cocked his AK-47 and was aiming it at the two disguised soldiers. Dan also saw Abu-Honoud himself rise from his chair. The tension in the room ratcheted up a notch. Dan could feel his pulse beating in his temples like a hammer. Time seemed to stand still. His hand suddenly gripped the pen in his sleeve tightly. He looked at Yariv, but nothing happened. A disturbing thought flashed through his mind: what if the stuff in the capsule didn't work?

But Dan's concerns disappeared in an instant once the acidic material reached Yariv's stomach. The young soldier dressed like an old man suddenly opened his mouth and a stream of vomit gushed out onto the floor of the room. He couldn't help it. The three security guards and Abu-Honoud himself were forced to step aside so that the spew of vomit didn't spatter on them. Everybody in the room stood and looked at the mess made by the shaking old man, who had just wretched his guts out. After he finished throwing up, Yariv was overcome with a fit of deep, forceful coughing. Everybody in the room stood there looking at him. Everybody except one.

When Dan saw that the distraction was successful, he quickly stuck his hand underneath the table. Holding the pen, he shoved the tack into the bottom of the table as hard as he could, making sure to locate it right up against the thick border. Dan felt the tack sink into the wood. He looked at everybody in the room, but nobody was paying attention to him. The old man throwing up in the middle of the room, the acidic smell of vomit permeating the room, and the strange sounds emanating from him as he coughed his lungs out had taken center stage at the moment.

He tried to move the pen slightly, but couldn't – it was stuck firmly in place underneath the big table. His heart skipped a beat with excitement. A commotion erupted in the room.

"Call an ambulance to get him out of here!" screamed the guard and waved his AK-47 at Dan.

Dan nodded and mumbled, "I'm so sorry, gentlemen, excuse me... he's sick, I'm sorry... don't you have any water here?" he asked while holding Yariv by the arm.

"Both of you get out of here. Now. Don't you understand when people speak to you?" the guard with the AK-47 shouted as he waved his weapon at the two soldiers.

"I'm so sorry... sorry... excuse me, a thousand pardons..." Dan said and the two of them walked backwards towards the door.

Yariv kept coughing and Dan knew that it wasn't an act – his friend was completely drained from the effect of the acidic stuff in the capsule in his stomach. In addition, the massive vomiting fit and coughing after made it harder for Yariv to walk. That actually worked out in their favor, Dan figured. At this point, Yariv really does look like a terminally ill patient – he's pale, exhausted, he's shaking and he stinks – and it will only strengthen the impression that he was indeed a sick, old man.

He opened the door and the two left the room and went into the hallway. In the background, they could still hear the curses and shouting from the angry occupants of the confessional room. The two continued on their way down the hall, and then stopped to sit on a bench at the other end.

"Are you all right, Father?" Dan asked Yariv, who was pale.

"Yes, yes, my son. Did you leave them the present?" Yariv asked.

"Thank God, yes," Dan said, smiling.

"I don't feel well, my son. Take me home, please," Yariv requested. Dan stood up, took his arms, and both of them started walking slowly in the direction of the main gate.

Despite a fierce stomach ache he had because of the cramps that the acid caused in his stomach, Yariv felt fairly uplifted. He couldn't believe that the operation was completed, and that all they had to do now was exit the City Hall compound and get to the bus stop. He felt a bit dizzy. He felt pressure in his chest – perhaps from the prolonged vomiting, perhaps from the coughing fits after, and perhaps from the mental stress he was under just now.

Dan also felt relieved. Everything was behind them. The only thing left was to exit the complex – and the rest was history. The path leading to the gate out of the City Hall complex was long and surrounded on both sides by colorful flowers, planted in low planters the whole way. After a few steps, Yariv stopped suddenly and his hand shot to his back.

"Shit!" he said in a loud whisper into Dan's ear.

Dan understood immediately that something was wrong,

He got closer to Yariv's face and asked in a quiet whisper, "What happened?"

"I think that the radio antenna was poking out of my jacket for a moment. It was about to fall, so I grabbed it quickly. Maybe too fast for an old guy like me. I fixed it as soon as I felt it, but maybe it's sticking out. Fuck..."

"Forget it, no big deal," Dan said. "It's a short black antenna, your jacket is also black. Nobody saw a thing. Relax. Keep walking like normal, and let's get the hell out of here."

The two soldiers continued walking slowly in the direction of the exit. After walking slowly for about two minutes, the two of them saw the exit out of the complex from a distance. In front of them were more and more people. The distance between them and the gate was only a few dozen yards. The end looked closer than ever. The tension was palpable – beginning with the battle plan and the lengthy preparations, through the dozens of models shown to the higher-ups, the bus ride from Hebron, getting into the secured compound, locating the interview room and the encounter with Abu-Honoud, and finally, the convincing act the two performed in the room with loaded weapons pointed at them – all this tension dissipated in an instant when they saw the gate from a distance.

Just one more minute of walking and it would all be behind them.

And then the first stone hit Yariv in the back.

*　*　*

The nightmare of any undercover operative is for their cover to be blown in the field. It usually starts with whistles. Sharp, loud whistles that get stronger and louder to let the residents of the area know that special forces are there. Your skin bristles, the blood in your veins runs cold, and you break out in a cold sweat. Immediately after come the shouts: *"Jish, jish!"*[20] And then the shit hits the fan, or in local terms, "the *fauda*" – stones and iron rods being thrown at the forces, and from the surrounding buildings, all kinds of heavy things being hurled down. Everything on the rooftops gets thrown at the forces – old washing machines, old, hardened sacks of concrete, rusty kitchen appliances, bottles and cinder blocks. Anything they can get their hands on.

In moments, the area turns from calm and quiet to a battle zone – literally. Usually, the next stage is armed locals come to wherever it's taking place and start shooting at the undercover forces. Therefore, the most important rule in undercover work is to allay the suspicion of the locals while it's still just a suspicion. In no circumstance can the suspicion be allowed to become certainty, because once the force's cover is blown and they've been exposed, the only way out is with bullets and casualties.

* * *

The rock that hit Yariv in the back was about the size of a tennis ball. He felt something hard hit him in his hunched back. Dan, who was holding his arm, quickly looked behind him. A group of boys stood there and in their hands were more rocks. Dan turned back to face forward toward the gate to exit the municipal complex. He was right there, not more than fifty yards away. And then the whistles and shouts came: "Jish, jish!"

Shit, Dan thought to himself, *right when we're so close to the exit gate*. He looked at Yariv, who got hit with the rock and kept standing hunched over like an old man with a cane. Yariv signaled to Dan with his eyes that he was fine, but they both knew that

---

20. "Army, army!"

right now, if indeed they'd been exposed, they wouldn't be able to get out of the compound without the use of force and weapons.

The problem they had right now was two-fold: first of all, the City Hall compound was closed and protected by a high wall. That is, if somebody were to close the gate in front of them, they would be trapped inside the municipal complex. Even if they were to press their distress buttons, it's reasonable to assume the extraction force would still need a few minutes to find their positions and reach them in this area. Moreover, the moment those calls reach those armed guards in the confession room, the problems would get worse. It would be very difficult to win a gun battle against multiple assault rifles. The second problem was much more significant – if they pull their guns right now or use any force to get themselves out of the compound, the operation will be exposed and planting the device will have been for nothing. So what to do?

Yariv looked at Dan. He saw that his friend was out of ideas. Time was running out. Suddenly they heard a whistle. A rock, larger than the previous one, flew by the heads of the two undercover soldiers. *It's getting serious*, Yariv thought. He looked at Dan again, who felt behind his thigh. Yariv understood immediately what his friend was trying to do – that's where his distress button is. Yariv knew that as soon as Dan pressed that button and called in the extraction team, there would be no going back. *Right now*, he thought to himself, *they only suspect us. But they aren't completely sure.* He put his hand out to stop Dan's hand from reaching behind his thigh. "No, my son, not yet," Yariv said to Dan and looked him in the eye. Dan look back at him with a questioning glance.

Yariv stopped and slowly turned around. On a low hill, about a hundred yards from them, stood a few kids. They were holding iron clubs that they found on the ground and various large rocks. Yariv sensed his mouth getting dry. *We can't get burned here*, he thought to himself, *we need to do whatever we can to plant doubt in their minds that they're wrong, and that we're Arabs.*

Time was growing short, and the jeers from the hilltop were getting louder. And then Yariv saw what he was afraid of: all the armed guards from the confession room, led by Abu-Honoud, heard the shouting and commotion outside and came running into the center expanse. Dan looked back as well, and his eyes darkened. The four of them aimed their weapons at him and Yariv.

* * *

Many people came in and out of the gate in front of them. Suddenly, Yariv identified a young man holding the hand of a small boy around five years old. He rested his other hand on Dan's hand, the one holding him by the arm, and squeezed. Dan, who got the hint, raised his hand toward the young man and his son and waved "hello" to them. The surprised fellow looked at the old man and the younger man and waved to them, but didn't recognize them. He pulled his son's hand and came over to the two of them. After a few seconds he was standing right in front of them. He didn't recognize them at all. But that fact didn't bother Yariv in the slightest.

In Eastern cultures in general, and particularly in Arab culture, there is a certain respect for the elderly. They are the ones who orchestrate the religious ceremonies, they are the judges and mediators in various disagreements, and their advanced age is given an almost magical status. And so it's normal in the Muslim world to see a blessing from an old man as being a particularly important blessing, and people consider it a big deal and a sign of fortune. Yariv remembered all that from the course they took during the training, but that's also what his experience in the field taught him. And so he didn't wait more than a moment once the Arab man and his son were standing in front of him. He put his hands out, closed his eyes, and placed his hands on the boy's head. The father, still surprised by the strange gesture, didn't object, and even pushed the boy a bit closer, so it wouldn't be difficult for the old man to give the little boy his blessing.

The undercover soldier turned to the young father. "How old is the boy, my friend?" he asked in a deep, coarse voice.

"Five, *ya sidi*," the father replied and he placed his hand on the boy's shoulder. Yariv bent down slightly toward the small boy who stood there quietly, excited from the intensity of the occasion.

"What's your name, son?"

"Musa," the boy answered.

Yariv began blessing the boy with a well-known blessing: may God help you, may Allah extend your days with goodness, may the prophet send his blessing upon your head and much, much more. When he finished blessing the boy, something unexpected happened. The young father kissed Yariv's hands and placed them on his own head.

"Bless me, too, ya sidi," he requested of Yariv in a shaking voice.

Yariv stroked the man's cheek affectionately and began to bless him. Dan looked back out of the corner of his eye: he saw the group of youngsters, the ones who had begun the fauda, standing quietly watching the old man bless the child, and then his father. Dan now saw that even the armed guards lowered their weapons, which had been aimed at the two soldiers.

Dan knew that the scheme was working: he could see the doubt creep into the hearts of the kids throwing stones and whistling and shouting at them. He saw that they started whispering among themselves. Dan waving to the man and his son demonstrated a connection between the two strangers and the two locals. The father and son coming closer to the two solidified the doubt in the minds of the youth. But blessing the boy and the father right after provided the final proof that Dan and Yariv were indeed Arabs, maybe even related to or friends of the father and son.

But Yariv didn't want to take any more chances. Immediately after he blessed the father and son, the undercover soldier brought his mouth to the young father's ear, since he was still bent over from giving the blessing, and said, "Can you believe it? What a disgrace! Those kids throwing rocks at an old man like me…" and then cleared his throat and spit behind him.

The young man lifted his head and looked in the direction of the group of kids. He shook his head right and left a few times as if in disbelief. "They have no respect, those kids, ya sidi," he said. "Wait here, please."

The young man then raised his head, placed his hand on Yariv's shoulder, and yelled to the group of kids there, "Shame on you, *ya shabab*.[21] What is this? Throwing rocks at an old, distinguished man such as this? And during Ramadan! Who raised you? Allah will repay you exactly what you deserve! Go on, get out of here!"

The group of kids just stood there, ashamed and embarrassed. More people joined in shouting and waving their hands in the direction of the kids. Some of them dropped the rocks they were holding, the others the iron bars. The armed guards, who were there and saw that indeed, this was an unfortunate case of mistaken identity, left the area and disappeared back inside the building.

The young father held his son's hand and looked at Yariv with compassion and goodwill. "May Allah lengthen your days, ya sidi," he said, meaning every word. "Be well," and with that, he went toward the municipal building.

Dan took hold of Yariv's arm again. He sensed that his friend's arm was shaking. Yariv was sweating, but that only made him that much more believable as a sick, exhausted old man.

"Come, Father, let's get you home. Mother is waiting for us," Dan said to him, and the two of them continued making their way slowly but surely toward the bus stop next to the gate leading out of the municipal complex. From a distance, Yariv saw the bus

---

21. An Arabic term used to address adolescents.

approaching the stop. He raised his hand, and the bus began to slow down and veer toward the bus stop where the two of them were waiting. Dan looked at his team member and saw that he wasn't as pale as he was a few minutes earlier, and then bent over and kissed his "father's" head.

Yariv smiled broadly, hugged Dan's shoulder, and the two of them got on the bus heading toward Hebron.

CHAPTER 7
February 1994, Dr. Ravid's Clinic, Jerusalem

For the last few weeks, Dr. Ravid and Yariv were accustomed to meeting at least twice a week. The experienced psychologist felt as if the young combat soldier was slowly beginning to open up and share more and more of his personal feelings and past experiences – and he knew that this was the best expression of trust that Yariv could demonstrate towards him. The more they met, the more Yariv began to slowly peel back the layers of defense that he had wrapped himself in, which were apparent even at their first meeting. He gradually began to trust the veteran therapist, who the system had appointed to sit across from him, and to share his feelings with him.

From his side, Dr. Ravid tried to do his job as gently as possible: when he felt that there was a subject that Yariv was steering away from, or trying to get around in one way or another, he would let it go immediately and take a step back. The sharing and exposing of secrets, which Dr. Ravid knew from years of experience, would come only from the patients' willingness to share, and never from any pressure that the therapist put on them. The opposite was true, that pressure – and this he also knew from experience – would only cause Yariv to clam up and avoid revealing any of the things he kept locked up inside.

Yariv shared with him stories about the special vibe around Team 10, about the exhausting training, the endless variety of activities, his relationships with his various team members and about his feelings and emotions. Occasionally, the psychologist would interrupt him to ask questions in order to understand something, but mostly it was just Yariv talking uninterrupted in his flowing, exact, intelligent and interesting way.

Dr. Ravid listened intently to all of Yariv's stories. Some of them sounded like science fiction – but he knew they were completely real. Each time they met, the psychologist recalled their first meeting: Yariv arrived with a cast on his arm, all beat up, the signs of that night in Nablus clearly visible from afar. He remembered the difficulty that he had taking off his jacket, how Yariv broke the coffee jar and how he cleaned up after him – but also remembered how the young soldier suddenly opened up and began sharing. Like a delicate flower, whose petals open slowly as soon as the sun's rays shine upon them, so too was Yariv in his eyes, who came to his clinic from the operational reality of the draining, intensive combat, and didn't have the time or peace of mind to stop for a moment and take care of himself. To connect to who he was before the army, before he became a hardened soldier who was whisked away to put his life in danger on an almost daily basis.

It was one minute after nine o'clock in the morning when he heard a knock on the door. Dr. Ravid got up to open it. Yariv stood in the doorway, this time without the cast.

"Hi, Yariv. I'm happy to see you," Dr. Ravid said with a smile. "Come, let's sit and talk a bit. I want to hear how you're doing and what's new since we met last week," the psychologist said and motioned with his hand in the direction of the living room.

The two of them went in and sat down, each in his regular place. On the table in front of them was a pitcher of water, two glasses and a round plate with cookies. Yariv poured water into both glasses, and then took a cookie and put it in his mouth.

"It's good, thanks," Yariv said and flashed a small smile.

"Bon appetit! I'm also glad to see that you finally got your cast off," Dr. Ravid told him.

"Yeah, glad to finally get rid of it. Now I just have to do physiotherapy – and then I can get back to the unit. I mean, of course – I also need your authorization that I'm good to go, and then I can get back to the team and action..." he said with a devious smile.

Dr. Ravid had a hard time hiding his smile. Indeed, no doubt the young man was endowed with a lot of charisma and charm. "About the physical therapy for your injury – I'm glad that's getting better. About what happens here – that's a different story altogether..." he said, this time without a smile.

"I'm just glad," Yariv said, ignoring the doubt that crept into the psychologist's words, "the orthopedic surgeon taking care of me still thinks that it should heal quickly, like he originally thought. He even told me that within two or three months, I might even be able to get back to playing sports – albeit at a less intensive level, but I can already see the end of this shitty injury."

Dr. Ravid was quiet for a moment. He knew that, for Yariv, getting the cast off was the first sign of getting back to normal, to operational activities and to his life before the injury. But he also knew that the emotional scars Yariv had were far from healed.

"Yariv, getting your cast off is an important and significant step in your healing process. I'm happy for you that your physical condition is significantly improving."

Yariv thanked him with a nod of his head, and then as if for the first time, seemed to understand the psychologist's meaning. "Important step – but..." he asked in a quiet voice, "I feel like your sentence has more to it, right?"

Dr. Ravid nodded. "Correct. There is... the physical healing is very important, but remember why you came to me in the first place. You didn't come because you hurt your arm, and you aren't here for me to treat you physically. You came to me – or rather, were sent to me – because your commanders and those close to you felt that, aside from your physical ailment, you have another injury. The trauma of an emotional wound, on a psychological level. Something that doesn't just go away just because you take the cast off, and won't be erased with physical therapy, no matter how good the professionals are. For that, I'm here, Yariv."

Yariv was quiet. All at once, it hit him that the process for healing mentally would take a lot longer than what it would take to heal physically. He really hoped that getting his cast off would be a significant first step toward getting back to the unit and the team. Now, he felt like he was playing "chutes and ladders," and that he just landed on a square that caused him to slide all the way back to the bottom, where he had to start climbing up from the beginning.

The last few months were hard for him to bear – the physical discomfort was constant. His limited mobility, the exposed nerves, the daily pain – Yariv gritted his teeth through all of it, and indeed, the pain subsided with time. Only now did he understand that he was dealing with a different struggle. A struggle with and against himself, against his demons, against his fears and concerns, against the loss of his exaggerated self-confidence that had engulfed him up until that cursed night in Nablus.

Dr. Ravid sat in silence. He saw in Yariv's eyes the unfinished struggle between the need to present a strong, powerful front as if nothing phased him, and the truth. The sad, painful truth. The moments when every small noise jerks him out of his quiet, angry outbursts, short temper toward others around him, nights where he tosses and turns in his bed and can't get a moment's peace, the nightmares that he would wake up from drenched in sweat.

The veteran therapist knew what Yariv was going through. He had been there himself, after coming back from captivity. His body was completely fine, relative to the torture he had endured, but his psyche had been damaged and battered. Signs of captivity were apparent well after the last of his physical wounds had scabbed over.

"Yariv," he began softly, "we have been meeting in this clinic a few times a week for the last, what is almost two months. You have shared with me many of your experiences in the training course, and I was happy to hear the many interesting stories about your operations. I thank you for sharing them with me, because that is, in fact, a big part of the healing process. However, I'm concerned that unfortunately, you still aren't being completely open with me regarding what you're feeling and going through emotionally throughout the day. To somebody who doesn't know the truth, you look great. You go around making jokes, functioning one-hundred percent. But those who actually know you well, know the truth. Even if it seems unnecessary right now, it's important to understand and internalize what you went through, and that it could get worse over time if it isn't treated properly, as long as the experience is still relatively fresh. True, it's not an easy process, and not a short one – but it's necessary for your mental health and for your continued functioning," the psychologist said, and kept his gaze fixed on the young soldier.

"As far as I'm concerned, repression is the solution to the problem." Yariv answered with a smile.

"No it isn't," the psychologist said. "Unfortunately, that's a common misconception. Look, repression is a way for the psyche to protect itself from overload. That is, let's say that I experienced a certain amount of trauma, and I don't have the tools to deal with it right now – and I repeat, right now – so in order to protect myself from having a total meltdown, my psyche represses whatever happened. But it's important that you understand: repression is not erasure. Repression is a process that takes energy on a regular basis. What you repress today, may come out in the future, also without our awareness, for example, in dreams or how you treat others around you. But it's not a magic bullet, because you might lash out at others around you, even at your parents or your future wife and kids at some point. It of course depends on the power of the trauma and intensity of what happened, but it's still a type of ticking time bomb that has the potential to do a lot of damage in the future. Would you want to take that chance?" Dr. Ravid posed to him.

Now it was Yariv's turn to be silent.

He understood that the physical recovery process wasn't likely the same process, just for the mental aspect of things, and he began to internalize that it would take a lot longer than he initially thought it would. Deep down, and despite his attempts to project differently, Yariv knew that the psychologist was right – he indeed wasn't the same as before, and things were far from how they were before the incident in Nablus.

Dr. Ravid also sat there quietly. He knew that he had presented Yariv with the naked truth about his situation, and now he had to make a decision about whether to continue cooperating with the therapeutic process or not.

The ball was in Yariv's court.

The quiet in the room grew louder.

In the end, Yariv raised his head up and looked at Dr. Ravid. "I understand what you're telling me," he said quietly, "and even though it isn't easy for me to admit it, you're right. I'm not in a good way. I haven't come back to who I was. It's been almost two months and I'm still not a hundred percent..."

Dr. Ravid looked at Yariv and nodded his head in appreciation. Once he let Dr. Ravid in on his inner truth, Yariv felt an immediate sense of relief. He felt like he'd had an abscess drained – even though it's scary and painful, it brings immediate pain relief.

Dr. Ravid got up and came over to Yariv, and then put his hand on the troubled soldier's shoulder. "Know that it takes a lot of guts to do what you did," he said. "Not everybody is able to do that. It's no simple thing to bare the face that's behind the mask. To share with somebody else your deepest feelings, the most intimate corners of our soul. Good for you," he said and then shook Yariv's hand warmly, placing Yariv's hand between both of his. Yariv was embarrassed. He looked down at the floor.

"It's all right, Yariv," the psychologist continued. "That's how it is in the beginning. The first time you expose something is the hardest. It's new for you, you aren't familiar with it, because you've been taught, as a combat soldier, to be a tough guy. You mustn't show emotion, it's not good to externalize one's feelings, to always have to say that everything is fine and under control. In short – to be macho. But how do you get around the fact that we all have a soul, and sometimes we need support, encouragement, a hug and even a little help?" he asked, and looked Yariv right in the eye.

Yariv was still quiet, but the veteran psychologist saw a small, rogue tear that started slowly sliding down his cheek. Yariv wiped it away quickly, like somebody caught in a lie. Dr. Ravid felt for him. He remembered himself, the young Yehonatan Ravid, post-captivity, fighting with all his strength to put out a feeling of control, of power, as if the harrowing experience he went through in captivity had no effect on his psyche at all, nor would it ever. Boy was he ever wrong…

"It's alright," he whispered to Yariv and gave his shoulder a hug. "Let it out. It won't make you any less of a man than you are, and it doesn't diminish my appreciation for you. On the contrary."

Yariv wiped his eyes, raised his head and thanked Dr. Ravid with a glance.

The psychologist poured a glass of water and handed it to Yariv. Yariv drank the water quickly, and then tried to change the subject. "So, what do you think of my stories so far?" he asked with a smile.

"Honestly, they're amazing," the psychologist answered candidly. "Sometimes they sound like a completely insane movie script, but it's important to me, professionally, to go deeper into the emotional aspects of the issue. Tell me a bit about your feelings during the time you're undercover," Dr. Ravid requested.

"Listen, it starts way before we get dressed up and head out into the field. This may sound strange to you, but sometimes the undercover aspect itself is the easiest part of the operation. The first real difficulty is planning the operation itself. So it's like this: the process begins with an intelligence briefing. We get some general information from the Shin-Bet about the object – who we're talking about, some personal details like age, married or single, hobbies, if he works and where. So we sit down and start planning what scheme we'll use this time and how we plan on getting to him. It could be shooting him in the middle of the street, a kidnapping at a certain place or while travelling somewhere, or it could be by causing an accident somewhere that will cause him to arrive at a certain place, where our forces are waiting. We always use some element of deception – and there are always a lot of possible outcomes. All the guys on the team sit around brainstorming and throw out all kinds of ideas, and slowly they start to converge towards a central idea that ends up leading the discussion and we run with it. What's nice is that all the members of the team are involved, because each one has their own crazy ideas and idiosyncrasies, and this combination only helps. When there is a plan that is more focused and formulated, we take it to senior leadership in the unit, and from there, they check to see if it's possible from an operations standpoint, or in principle," Yariv said.

"Like authorizing you to go into the municipal compound in Bethlehem, which is generally off-limits to the IDF?" Dr. Ravid asked.

"Correct. But that's just one example. There were others – like the operation in Hebron with the garbage truck. In that case, the idea to use the garbage truck was mine. When I brought up the idea to Yoav, there was a security concern that the truck's compressor might accidentally close on the soldiers hidden inside and crush them to death. So Yoav was able to get us training on this specific garbage truck model. They were also the ones to sit in the cabin and drive the truck while I commanded the five additional soldiers inside the putrid drum where the garbage was kept. You see, that was the cherry on top of the idea I came up with for using the garbage truck..." Yariv said with a broad smile.

Dr. Ravid also smiled. He was glad that the feeling in the room became lighter. The therapy would proceed more efficiently this way, he thought. "That's interesting. But why don't the officers determine the plan, and at the end have the soldiers simply carry it out, like the rest of the army?" he pressed.

"There are a few reasons for this," Yariv responded. "First of all, in many cases, the officer went through a token regular infantry course, and then an officer's course, and then all kinds of other courses, including some weird ones. Bottom line, he would learn how to command and manage on paper, but would miss months of time in the field. This creates a situation where the simple combat soldier, as you call him, has much broader operational experience than his commanding officer. Second, the uniqueness of a unit like Duvdevan is in its soldiers. They look for people who think a little less conventionally, a little crazy, and that's so they can produce all kinds of weird and unique ideas that afterwards become a working plan for the field. Understand that a lot of the crazy ideas you heard here were from these simple soldiers, your definition... and I assume you understand that in order to go undercover well enough to mix into the heart of a hostile population, you need to have a screw or two loose upstairs..."

"It is indeed original and creative thinking. I'd like to hear about how you feel when you're undercover in the field."

Yariv leaned back and stretched, folding his hands behind his head. He then exhaled out a long, slow whistle. "That's an experience that really is hard to put into words," he finally said, and then continued uninterrupted, and with a not insignificant amount of enthusiasm, given the fact that he'd been on the verge of tears a moment ago. "It's a uniquely exhilarating feeling. It starts with getting into the character itself. Each time, it's a different character, according to whatever the plan and conditions in the field call for. The variety of people on the Arab street is huge, and so everybody on the team needs to know how to play a variety of roles: you can find yourself dressed as a woman in the morning and a student in the afternoon. You can be selling giant pretzels in Dheisheh on Tuesday, and on Wednesday driving a taxi in Hebron. Sometimes you're dressed up as an old man with a cane and a hunchback, something that requires two hours in the unit's makeup department, and sometimes you just put some gel in your hair and in two minutes you can turn yourself into some common local thug. The flexibility of thinking while in an operation is endless – it's never boring. And the more you're in the field, the more ideas for characters you come back with. But it doesn't matter what character you use – your heart rate is always at two hundred, a high like you can't imagine. Peak adrenaline... suddenly you turn into somebody else completely, walking around dressed up in the middle of a hostile population, and you know that if they find out who you are, you've had it. You have to be sharp, listen and be very sensitive to everything around you. If you make the slightest mistake – it's game over. There's no second chance here. It could be your gun that sticks out for a moment by mistake, or it could be a word that you say to the salesman at the store in the wrong accent, or it could be somebody alert and suspicious suddenly starting to harass you... and it could be something technical that you didn't plan on – a flat tire that suddenly happens in the middle of a refugee camp, a car that just dies next to the central mosque, on Friday, at prayer time, and on and on," Yariv paused, with a certain amount of pride that he didn't attempt to hide.

"Getting a flat tire in the middle of an undercover operation sounds to me like a pretty serious problem," said Dr. Ravid.

"Indeed, and it happened to me once: there were three of us in the car – Barbie, The Bull, and me. This time I was dressed up like an old man and I was driving. Barbie, who was dressed as my wife, and The Bull as our daughter, who was in the late stages of pregnancy, were in back. We were on an intelligence gathering mission, relatively easy – go to one of the refugee camps in Jenin and photograph some buildings there to plan a future operation. It was a simple task, not more than an hour, and we weren't even supposed to get out of the car. It was winter, not great weather, raining a bit outside. Everything was going smoothly, but toward the end of the mission, I felt the car roll over something. I continued a few more yards and felt the steering wheel was harder to turn than usual. I stopped for a moment and got out of the car to take a look, and I saw that I must have driven over something sharp because the front tire was flat. Now, the problem was that it made no sense for an old man and two women, one in the advanced stages of pregnancy, to change a tire in the middle of the rain, right? The exit from the refugee camp was too far to drive all the way with a flat, so we weren't sure what to do."

"Well, what finally happened?"

"Simple, I got out of the car, waved at a few cars, and immediately a few young men stopped, I told them what happened, and they immediately rolled up their sleeves and helped us change the tire. The truth is, they were great, because one of the nuts was on really tight and they tried a bunch of things until they were finally able to get it loose. In the meantime, then got dirty in the mud... and not only that, a couple of them offered to drive us in their car, practically begging us so that we wouldn't have to stand in the rain, but come in and have some hot tea."

"Interesting. One minute they and their houses are being used as an object of surveillance, and the next they're changing your flat tire while inviting you into their home... odd situation," said Dr. Ravid.

"You're right. But there are many odd situations, some even scary. For instance, when I was a young soldier, we had to get to some mosque in Tulkarem to gather intelligence on somebody who prayed there. What we didn't know from the aerial photographs was that, just a few days before the operation, the city of Tulkarem decided to repave the road leading to the mosque. Just so you understand, the mosque was on top of the highest hill in the neighborhood, something that is very common in Islam, because the mosque and tower always need to be the tallest structures in the area. So we get there, and we're in a Ford Transit that the team made up so it would blend in. And then it turns out that the old asphalt has been scrubbed off the road, and the Transit can't make it all the way to the mosque. This was in the afternoon, and everybody started coming out of the mosque. When they saw us stuck in the middle of the incline, without making too big a deal about it, they just banded together and pushed us up to the top of the hill. Imagine the situation, they're making this huge effort to push us up the hill... surreal."

"Surreal indeed. But do you remember anything funny, or at least amusing from the undercover unit?" Dr. Ravid asked.

"Actually, I do. Check this out: we once had this job near Hebron. We received an order to intercept this guy and bring him to the Shin-Bet for interrogation. This was on a Thursday, which is when the markets are open, and the operation was scheduled for afternoon when the market is full of people – it's loud and there are always a bunch of people shopping. That way it's possible to intercept him quickly without anybody really noticing that somebody is being kidnapped. We spotted the guy from afar, got close to him, and then were physically right next to him. I held a jacket in my hand, which had a gun in it, and I put the jacket right up against his stomach. He turned around and looked at me, and then I whispered to him quietly in Arabic, '*Ta'al ma'i*,'[22] He couldn't believe it and, before he could even understand what was happening, Schumacher stops the car next to us, we put him inside, and started driving out of the village. After a few seconds, the initial shock wore off of him, and he came back to himself and started shouting inside the car, '*Ana moosh mita'awen, ana moosh mita'awen!*'[23] He literally started crying, and then swore to us that he was loyal to Islam, and that he wouldn't work for the *Yahud*.[24] And then my team leader, who was sitting in the front, turned to him and asked him in Arabic: 'Who do you think we are?'

"And the guy looked at him surprised and said, 'You're Hamas, you've come to interrogate me, no?'

"So my team leader says to him, 'No, we're the special forces.' Suddenly the guy looks at me – remember that I still have my gun aimed at his stomach – and he looks at me and says, 'Ah, you're the army?' And then he puts his hand on his heart and lets out this huge sigh of relief that you could hear all the way in Tel Aviv... can you believe he was more afraid of Hamas than he was of the IDF? Unbelievable..." Yariv said, smiling. That was indeed an unforgettable operation.

The psychologist smiled as well and took a sip from the glass of water in his hand. He enjoyed listening to Yariv's stories, but

---

22. "Come with me."
23. "I'm not an informant!"
24. Arab word for Jews.

also knew that the issue that brought him to his clinic had yet to be resolved. "Wow, that sounds completely insane," he finally said.

"That's just one of many stories... it's something that stays with you all the time, the duality, the double life. For example, we had this operation to gather intelligence in Kalkiliya. It started in the evening and went until late at night. The endpoint was the central commercial area next to the main square in town. When we finished, it was already dark. I got on the hidden radio with central command and they told me that there was a technical issue with the undercover car that was supposed to come get me and that I would need to spend another half hour until they arrived. Now, you have to understand – you can't just stand around for a half-an-hour in the middle of Kalkiliya and wait to get picked up. That's way too suspicious. So what most of us do is we go into some coffee shop or restaurant, and that's how we spend the time until we get picked up. The problem here is that the commercial center was mostly closed, and I didn't have anywhere to sit and drink coffee or eat a *k'nafe*,[25] and to stand around like a statue in the middle of the commercial area at night – well that wasn't going to fly."

"So what did you end up doing?" Dr. Ravid asked.

"Simple, there was a public phone booth in a relatively isolated area, so I just went over to it and called home," Yariv answered.

"You called home?! In the middle of Kalkiliya?!"

"Yep. But the best part is that I spoke to my mom... I told her that I was in the soldiers' club at the unit – and suddenly, without any prior warning, the muezzin starts the call to prayers. Turns out there was a muezzin there I didn't notice, right above the commercial center. Its speakers were really loud, and my mother was startled. So without making too big a deal, I said, 'Wait a second,' and then I pretended to be talking to my friends and said,

---

25. Popular, sweet Arab dessert.

'Guys, turn down the television, I can't hear my mother...'" Yariv said with a big smile.

The veteran psychologist also smiled at the notion of the bizarre situation.

"And there was another funny thing," Yariv continued. As soon as he remembered one, they seemed to just kept coming, one after another. "We were in an undercover car on an operation in Hebron. The plan was to grab some terrorist and bring him in for interrogation. So we are driving along the main route, and suddenly there's an IDF checkpoint. The soldier aims his weapon at us and motions for us to slow down for an inspection. We didn't worry about it, that's the way it is in general. I was dressed as an old man and sat in front. The driver, Schumacher, is slowly moving forward toward the soldier, and stops right next to him. The soldier lowers his head toward my window – and suddenly I recognize Yoel, my friend from high school! Turns out his platoon in the paratroopers was there for an operation and we just ran into each other, completely by surprise."

"Did he recognize you?" asked Dr. Ravid.

"At first, of course not. I was made up like an old man. But after a few seconds, he caught on and broke into a huge smile. I of course signaled for him to be quiet, with my finger to my lips, but he already started laughing out loud... immediately I signaled to Schumacher to get out of there. The funny part was when we came back after the operation with the guy we nabbed in the car with us. Yoel apparently let his friends in the platoon in on the cool story, and when we got to their checkpoint, all the soldiers pointed out our car and burst out laughing... fortunately for us, there weren't many cars around and our cover wasn't blown, but that could have ended very badly for us," Yariv finished.

The psychologist smiled, crossed his hands over his chest and said with a serious face, "Yariv, you have shared some very interesting stories with me, some of them even funny. Thank you for that. I'll remind you that we finished the last meeting with your story about getting into the municipal compound in Bethlehem. That's where we left off. I'd like to hear what happened after that."

Yariv was quiet. Dr. Ravid sensed that he may have touched a nerve. "It seems to me that the operational achievement of planting a listening device into Fatah's holy of holies, and afterward that stunt you pulled to evade detection on your way out of the compound – both of you deserve special recognition. Am I right?" Dr. Ravid continued in an attempt to get an answer out of Yariv.

Yariv got out of his chair, put both hands in his pants' pockets, and stood with his back against the wall. "You're right. That really was a different operation altogether. Not only the level of daring it took, but also the level of intelligence we were able to get that day. But from then on, everything started to change. Maybe that was the turning point – after that, our luck ran out and we were jinxed. Maybe we got too arrogant, maybe we tempted fate one too many times. I don't know what to tell you, really..." Yariv said, his words trailing off.

"I don't understand what you mean. You guys pulled off a huge achievement. On a personal level but also as an operational team, as well as the information you managed to get for the Shin-Bet. So why do you say that that's where it all started to change?" the psychologist wondered out loud.

"You know what? All right, I'll continue with the story about what happened after the operation in Bethlehem. You can hear it and decide for yourself," Yariv offered, and resumed recounting the travails of his team.

CHAPTER 8
September 1992, Nahal Yehudia Preservation, Golan Heights

One week after the operation in the Bethlehem municipal compound

Yogev stood standing next to the burning pyre and turned his palms toward the fire. The colorful flames flickered in front of him as he stared into the fire, as if hypnotized. He put a tape in and then pressed "play" on his Walkman, which he had hooked up to a small speaker. The crackling of the wood got stronger and the strong voice of Leonard Cohen added itself to the background with his song "Everybody Knows."

"What a voice Leonard has, and what lyrics… pure genius," said Yogev quietly, not sure if to himself or to his friends.

"Careful you nut job, you're too close to the fire," Dan yelled at him.

"Oh, man, you have no idea how much I needed this vacation,"

Yogev said and took a couple steps back. Yariv and Dan were lying on their sleeping bags that were spread out on the ground.

"Oh, we understand, just don't step on my new sleeping bag," Yariv said to him and pushed Yogev's leg aside.

The sky was cloudless. The stars were especially bright. Now it was Dan's turn to get up and come close to the bonfire. "I wouldn't have believed that Yoav was really going to give us a break. I was certain he'd cop out at the last minute with some story about another emergency in the sector, or some other excuse. But the truth is, he nailed it," he said to his two friends, while holding a long stick in his hand that he used to turn the hissing coals at the base of the bonfire.

"Kermit, do me a favor, can you take the potatoes out of the fire already instead of starting the Commander Yoav fan club? I think they're probably done," Yariv said to Dan.

Dan turned on the flashlight that was in his hand and shined it toward the bonfire. "Dude, they need a few more minutes. In the meantime, hand me a beer," he said and reached behind him.

Yogev put a cold bottle in his open hand. Dan took a few sips from the bottle and handed it back to Yogev. Afterward, he put the long stick on the ground next to him and lay back on his sleeping bag. "Believe me, you guys deserve serious props for that thing at City Hall," Yogev said and smiled over at Dan and Yariv. Behind them, smoke was still billowing up from the extinguished grill, which had plastic plates with leftover steaks and salads sitting next to it.

"Well, Yogi, now be honest: what odds did you give us this time?" Dan asked and winked at Yariv.

"Honestly, fifty-fifty. For me, I can say that I needed this vacation, so I was praying for you guys to make it. But if your cover got blown there, that would have been interesting to see how you would have gotten out of there, given the fact that you both shoot like shit," Yogev chuckled.

"Very funny, jackass. Don't forget that your ass is sitting on that sleeping bag because of us – so show a little respect, if you would," Yariv said to him.

"Guys, this is a fascinating conversation, but I have to take a piss," Dan said getting up. "Keep an eye on the potatoes."

"Yes, sir!" Yogev said and saluted him while still lying down.

The wind picked up and the tops of the trees gently swayed. A few clouds began to cover the sky. The three of them could hear the calls of the jackals in the distance.

* * *

It was already after midnight. Every so often, one of them would get up to throw another log on the fire, which started to burn almost immediately. The three looked at the colorful flames that slowly devoured the log. Suddenly, they heard a buzzing.

Dan stood up and put his right hand into his pants pocket. He pulled out his beeper and looked at the flashing signal across the small screen. "Another shooting at an IDF vehicle in Nablus. Goddammit, don't they ever get tired of it?" he said, and threw the beeper at foot of his sleeping bag.

"Kermit, do me a favor and turn that shit off. We're on vacation, aren't we?" said Yogev and yawned.

"Yeah, but Yoav asked us to be available by beeper in case anything comes up. Believe me, Yogev, I'd love to turn this thing off," Dan told him.

The sound of crackling wood got louder. The smoke rose above the fire, circling toward the stars shining above. The clouds covered and uncovered the moon. On the road, next to the overnight parking, the lights of vehicles travelling north flickered in the distance.

"You know," Yogev said turning to Dan and Yariv, "whenever

I look at the sky and see the stars, I am always reminded of that navigational series in the rain near Beit Horon. You remember? When Asaf, the team leader, insisted on pressing on despite the stormy weather forecast, and Barda and Udi ended up in the hospital with frostbite."

"How can I forget that? That guy was such a moron. We should have filed a complaint with the soldiers' representative. They would have thrown him in jail in a second," Dan said.

"Tell me, is there an open beer?" Yariv asked and fought back a yawn.

"Enough, dude, you're already drunk," Yogev said and got into his sleeping bag. "Forgive me, gentlemen, but I'm exhausted and the beer hit me a little bit. I'm going to crash for a bit. When did we set the wake up call for tomorrow?" he asked and rubbed his eyes.

"There's no wake-up call, sleeping beauty. The sun will wake you up by six, six thirty at the latest. But I'm telling you, if you start snoring here, I'm not responsible for the consequences," Dan warned him.

"All right, so good night, and do me a favor – turn the volume down," Yogev said and disappeared into his sleeping bag.

The wailing of the jackals got louder. The wind played with the bonfire's flames. The two who stayed awake, Dan and Yariv, looked at the fire in silence. After a few moments, they heard the sound of Yogev's deep breathing as he slept next to them.

"Well, did you think we would get out of that municipal compound alive? I must say, there was a time when I thought you were going to pass out on me," Dan said to Yariv.

"Just between us, we had more luck than we did brains. Even in the end, when I blessed that kid. We were very close to getting burned. And when I say 'very,' I mean it," Yariv said, and played with a toothpick. "And you know what, I'll tell you something, but this for real stays between us: I don't know about you, but I feel my luck has run out."

"What does that mean?"

"Exactly what it sounds like, dude. If, for example, we have "X" lives, or "Y" amount of luck – then I feel like that last operation used up the last of our luck. Understand that I didn't just start sweating and getting all flustered for nothing in City Hall there. I really did feel, for the first time, that I wasn't immune. That there was a chance that my luck had run out. Just like that. I don't know why, maybe we pushed just a little too far. But we have been stretching it just a little too much, pulling, and pulling – until one clear day it's just going to snap on us."

"What are you talking about? You're an awesome combat soldier, and we haven't had a single failure over the last I don't even know how many operations!"

"But that's exactly what I'm talking about: statistically speaking, at some point we're going to get slapped. Don't you agree with me?" he asked and leaned on his side. "Look, it's impossible for us to just keep succeeding and succeeding. And it doesn't matter how competent and talented we are. Statistically speaking, at some point, we have to fail. That's just the laws of nature. There's nothing we can do about it – it'll come whether we want it to or not. The only thing that's left for me to do is to pray that our discharge comes through before that failure or disaster happens. That's all," Yariv said, and lay down again on his back. His hands were crossed behind his neck and his eyes were staring up at the star-studded sky.

They were quiet. Dan was very surprised by what Yariv said. He didn't expect to hear such a surprising confession from his good friend. Even though Dan noticed Yariv being more careful and moderated during field operations recently, he chalked it up to his professionalism as a soldier, and not from concern that their luck was running out.

"I understand what you're saying. I also have times when I am scared out of my mind. What do you think? That I wasn't scared at City Hall? Of course I was scared. But I believe that if something needs to happen – it's going to happen, and it doesn't matter what you do. A specifically fatalistic attitude like this gives me peace of mind – I do what I can, and what needs to happen, will happen," Dan answered him while picking at the grass beside him.

"Understand though, dude, that I've repressed this thing about my brother's death in Lebanon for all these years. I already told you how I had that blowup with my parents before my enlistment. I always told everybody, 'It's not going to happen to me.' But now, it's all starting to float back up to the surface all over again. I feel less certain of myself, despite the fact that it's obvious that there's no good reason for it." Yariv finished speaking and sat on his sleeping bag, his hands hugging his knees.

Dan came over to him and placed his hand on his friend's shoulder. "I really do understand what you're going through. It's completely understandable. And the truth is, with your lousy hit percentage at the practice range, I'd also feel less confident..." he said with a mischievous smile.

"What an asshole you are, my God. I tell you about what I'm going through, pour my heart out, and what do I get in response? Empathy? No, God forbid. I get sarcasm. Man, it's too bad Abu-Honoud didn't spray you with a few bullets back there at the municipal compound in Bethlehem," muttered Yariv.

"All right, relax," Dan laughed, "I'm kidding. Enough already, I've already become depressed over the whole thing. What do I look like, a confessional booth? Come on, forget about it. We're on vacation, quit worrying and start enjoying yourself. Believe me, it's going to be fine. In a few months, it will all be over, and we'll be out in one piece, fly to South America, go to Carnival, find some hot dancers and get drunk until we run out of money and the foreign affairs ministry has to send in a special team to get us out. Whatever comes first."

"You're right. Never mind, let's drop all this gloomy shit. We're on vacation. Let's change the subject."

"Wait, wait," Dan said. "You just dropped some heavy shit just now, so now it's my turn, no?"

"You? Exactly what are you going to drop?" Yariv said laughing.

"Hold on tight. What I'm about to tell you I haven't told anybody. But seriously, this has to stay between us, you hear me? But I have to tell this to somebody," Dan said in what was suddenly a very serious voice.

"All right then, out with it. What gives? You won the lottery? You finally decided to come out, is that it?" Yariv said smiling.

Dan was quiet. Yariv looked at his team member's face, and saw that his countenance had become stern.

"You're making me nervous now," Yariv said when he saw the serious expression on Dan's face. "Are you about to die or something?"

"Hard negative," Dan answered. "Worse. Two weeks ago I found out my father is cheating on my mother."

Yariv was completely silent. The smile that had been on his face was gone. He was extremely surprised – not only from what he was being told, but more from Dan's sudden candor. "Are you serious? How'd you find out?" Yariv asked in a quiet, serious voice.

"You remember about a month ago, after that operation in Tulkarem when we got that early long weekend?" Dan asked him.

"You mean the operation where we nabbed the commander of the Black Eagle terror cell? The guy with the missing finger?"

"Yeah," Dan said, "that's the long weekend I'm talking about. You remember that we left the unit for the weekend during the day, for the first time ever?"

"Oh yeah, that's right, we actually did leave when it was still light... okay, so what happened?"

"So what happened was like this: I got a ride and was near my house, around seven in the evening. And so I decided that instead of going home, I would go surprise my father at his office. With my uniform on and everything. He's always going on about me and how great I am to all his friends and employees, so I figured he'd get a kick out of it."

"So what happened?"

"What happened is that by the time I got to his factory, it was already dark, and so I figured I'd go for a complete surprise, and I thought sneaking up to his window would be a great idea. Just like the busts we do in the refugee camps in the West Bank. Long story short, I sneak up to the window of his office and see a soft light coming from his desk. I was sure that he was doing paperwork or cleaning up his desk, or something like that. I got right underneath the window, and then I hear funny noises."

"What do you mean 'funny?' I don't understand," Yariv said, wrinkling his forehead.

"I see that you need an explanation, you moron. So I'll explain: I look inside and I see that my father is indeed working, even working hard – but not on the paperwork. He was working on his secretary..." Dan said, burying his face in the grass. In his right hand, he sifted a clump of cool grass he had ripped out of the ground. The night air carried the jackals' calls, mixing with the sounds of Yogev snoring.

"You think that your mom knows?" Yariv asked in a quiet voice.

"Honestly, that's not what interests me at the moment. I'm still in shock from it. Look, I'm not some naïve little kid – of course some married people cheat. That's not new. But when it happens to you, to your parents... it's not just some other tabloid headline – it's my mom and my dad. All these years, when he ran the factory and would come home late at night – now I know what he was doing all that time. And I stupidly thought that he was working long nights to take care of us. Understand, it all just hit me right in the face. My mother gave up everything for him. She never managed to work because of all his business trips out of the country, always having to be home early to take care of us, because he would come home late – and now I find out that he was having an affair behind her back! And from what I saw and heard there, that didn't seem like a one-time thing. It sounded like an actual relationship... it's killing me. Absolutely killing me. Ever since, I can't even look at him," Dan said, finishing his story, and lay down on his sleeping bag. He closed his eyes and took a deep breath.

Yariv had never seen Dan like this – hurt, vulnerable, quiet and pensive. Dan was always the driving force, the life of the party, and the social center of the team. It was clear that the weight of his intimate confession left him drained.

"I'm really sorry to hear that, man," Yariv said, breaking the silence that until then had only gotten longer. "I wish I could do something to help."

"You helped me a lot by listening. I've been walking around with this thing for a while now, and I don't have anybody to share this wonderful, happy news with," Dan said sarcastically.

"I know this won't make you feel any better," Yariv said, still not smiling, "but a good percentage of married couples have affairs. In some study I read, it said that most people would cheat, but the fear of getting caught stopped them from actually doing it."

"Wow... since when are you into studies on marriage, my single friend?"

"About a year after my brother Yohanan was killed, my parents received a vacation courtesy of some foundation for the fallen paratroopers. When they came back, I saw my mother reading some pamphlet they got there. First chance I got, I looked at it and saw a lot of interesting things there."

"Like what?"

"A lot of statistics on high divorce rates among families who had lost a son or daughter to war. In any event, the motto of the pamphlet was that it happens to the best of us – cheating, divorce, depression and just being miserable in the relationship. And even if that doesn't actually happen, a lot of people still think about it. And so they suggest that bereaved families not be afraid to go to couples therapy or see a psychologist. That's the bottom line," Yariv said, summarizing.

"And your parents, are they on good terms with one another?" Dan asked carefully.

"I guess that depends on how you define 'good terms.' It's all relative, right? At the end of the day, neither of them committed suicide after Yohanan was killed. They both function in their day-to-day. But are they happy? They aren't, but they weren't a couple of love birds before Yohanan died, either. Look, you know what's 'nice,'" Yariv made air quotes, "about the whole bereaved family business, is that now there's a good reason for everything. Relationship sucks? Well, we're just a couple of bereaved parents. Your kid failed school? Well, he's just a bereaved brother. Your marriage on the rocks? Well, what do you expect when you're a bereaved army family... so yeah, that really is something that's just hard to swallow on any scale, but suddenly every problem has an easy solution. And the best part is that nobody can argue with you about it. The only thing left is for the country to violate the sanctity of the bereaved families of the IDF. By the way, when I took my kippa off, everybody excused it as 'a deep crisis of faith that poor Yariv is going through because his brother fell in Lebanon.' And despite the fact that I told them three hundred times that it wasn't because of that, that I was going to take my kippa off anyway, it didn't matter. Everybody was sure that was the reason. Forget it, I don't have the energy anymore. I wish everybody all the best," Yariv said and started untying his shoelaces.

"That's it? We're going to sleep?"

"The alcohol's also starting to get to me. But what I wanted to say earlier is that despite the shock when you found out about your father, you have to stop looking at it from your perspective for a moment and to look at it objectively, not like a son looking at his father, but as one man looking at another. I mean, your father, like mine, is a man – long before he was your father, right? How old is he? Fifty? That's a person who worked hard his whole life, and apparently not everything is smooth between him and your mom. You'd be surprised, but what we see is different than what is really going on. And now, he had some affair. Don't misunderstand me – I'm against it. It's not okay, it's morally wrong. Period. I of course don't justify it, but I think that one can at least understand it. That's all. He's not leaving the house, you know that happens more often than it should. That is, he's aware of and recognizes the importance of the family unit he has. Bottom line, don't get into it. With all the hurt involved – that's between them, you aren't a party to it," Yariv said while finishing taking his hiking boots and socks off. He put the socks inside his boots.

"You know what, there's something to that. I must say, I feel a little better after telling somebody. By the way, if he doesn't let me drive his new Jeep on the weekends – I'll threaten to tell my mother..." Dan said with a smile.

"That's how I like to see you, Kermit," Yariv said and got into his sleeping bag.

"Wait, before you pass out – what are we doing tomorrow? Are we heading north or south?"

"I think we should hit the pool in the morning, and then see about what to do after. In any event, we'll get up and go with it. Worst case we'll head to the Kinneret," said Yariv and yawned widely.

Dan nodded his head and unzipped his sleeping bag. He got in and curled up in it without zipping it back up.

"Good night, Kermit," Yariv said with a smile.

Dan meant to answer him, but at that moment the familiar buzz sounded again. He put his hand into his pocket and pulled out the beeper that was still vibrating in his hand.

"Oh, now what?" Yariv asked him in a sleepy voice. "A shooting? Explosives on some road? Aren't you sick of them already?"

Dan looked again and again at the small screen. After a few seconds of silence, he threw the beeper to Yariv. "Mother fucker," he said. "Take it, honey, enjoy."

Yariv caught the beeper and looked at the lit screen. He read the message out loud: "Tomorrow at exactly noon, the three of you have to meet me at the gas station at the Glilot junction just north of Tel Aviv. Come in civilian clothing. Please don't tell the rest of the team. Yoav."

CHAPTER 9
The next day, Glilot junction

The Jeep carrying the Three Musketeers entered the gas station at Glilot junction. It was eleven fifty five. The three of them got out of the Jeep and stretched after the long drive from the Golan Heights. Yogev looked out at the cloudless blue sky. "Newton," said Yariv, "why can't we have a normal vacation in this unit without getting called back in the middle of it, huh?"

After a few minutes, a white Subaru with civilian plates entered the covered area of the gas station and parked next to the Jeep. The three of them looked in the car – Yoav, the unit commander, who was dressed in jeans and a white t-shirt, got out of the car. The three of them were leaning against the Jeep as he came over.

"What's up, guys?" Yoav asked, shaking hands all around.

"Actually, it was great until you brought us back here," Yogev answered, smiling.

"I don't remember the last time I saw you dressed as a civilian, Yoav. That just proves we all work too hard," Yariv added.

"We thought you'd take pity on us this time and that we'd be able to have at least one vacation without any interruptions," Dan said.

"Guys, listen. I know that you were up north and I want to thank you for the effort it took to get here. So that you'll be at ease, I personally promise to make it up to you next time. Don't worry – it's on me. But in the meantime, I have to talk to you about something very important that came up recently."

"You're making me nervous, Yoav. And why isn't the rest of the team here?" Yogev asked.

"Look, the whole team got a break after the last operation in Bethlehem, and for sure they deserve it. Everybody worked hard on the mission to bring it home. But aside from the bonus of having the leave after a very successful operation, I had another reason: I wanted to talk to the three of you – without the rest of the team. So the only way to do that was to give the rest of them leave, and then pull just the three of you back. That way we can sit privately without the risk of anybody else hearing or seeing or knowing this meeting is even taking place."

"Why the secrecy? What are we talking about?" Yariv asked with a surprised look on his face.

"This isn't the place to have this discussion. Get in your vehicle and follow me," Yoav directed.

"Where are we going, Yoav?" Dan asked. A trace of worry was evident in his voice.

"In the general direction of Herzliya. Follow me," Yoav answered and got into the white Subaru.

After driving for a few minutes, the Subaru slowed down. Dan, who was driving the Jeep behind Yoav, slowed down as well. On the right side of the road, the three of them saw a large, grey, five-story building. On the roof the soldiers saw some tall antennas and some big satellite dishes in various colors. Security cameras were installed on the second and third floors, and they were aimed at the sidewalks that surrounded the building. The building's windows were extraordinarily shiny in the sunlight, a sign that they were one-directional. On the edge of the sidewalk, there was a low iron barrier that prohibited unauthorized vehicles from getting too close to the building. Two guards in blue suits approached Yoav's Subaru. They were both holding M4 carbines, the shortened version of the M-16, and were wearing ear pieces. One of the guards signaled with his hand for Yoav to open the window.

"Yeah, who do you need?"

"Jerry. Please tell him that Yoav and his friends are here, thanks," Yoav said and pointed to the Jeep behind him.

"Wait one sec, I'll check," the guard said. He went into his guard post at the entrance to the parking lot and, after a few moments, came back out. "All right," he said to Yoav. He pointed to a large, imposing iron gate up past the building. "Go on in, park over here to the right and wait for him in the lobby," he said.

The other security guard pressed a small button, the orange light above the gate began to blink, and the heavy gate slowly began to open with a loud screech. Yoav drove slowly forward toward the opening gate, the Jeep and its occupants right behind him. Yoav slowed down and spotted two vacant parking spots next to the building's wall, and parked in one of them. The Jeep swung into the space next to the Subaru and out popped Dan, Yogev and Yariv. The screeching gate clanked shut behind them and locked.

"What's going on here, Yoav? Where have you brought us?" Dan asked in a tense, quiet tone.

Yoav approached the three of them and placed his hand on Dan's shoulder. "Patience, my young friends," he said quietly. "Have you forgotten the famous Arabic saying, '*Al ajalay min a-shaytan?*'"[26]

The unit commander and the three soldiers approached the entrance to the building. In front of them was a heavy, black iron door. Yoav pressed the intercom twice and waited. After a moment,

---

26. Haste is the work of the devil.

he heard a buzz and then pushed open the heavy iron door, and they entered the building's foyer.

The entry hall was spacious and impressive in its size. The ceiling was very high, and a large circular chandelier with dozens of round bulbs hung from it. A large Israeli flag with gold embroidery along the edges stood in the corner of the entry hall. The marble floor, with its chessboard pattern, were shiny from having been recently cleaned, reflecting the lights from the chandelier.

On the other side of the entry hall was a large aquarium, with fish of various sizes in it. At the bottom of the large aquarium were two models of wrecked warships and a diver, and next to them was an oxygen tube with a stream of little bubbles floating up from it. Next to the aquarium was the information desk, and stationed there were two young women in their twenties. On the right, the four saw a sign that read "Visitors' waiting area." Underneath the sign was a long turquoise sofa. Yoav pointed toward it, and the three of them went over and sat down. Yoav went straight over to the information desk and talked with the two girls behind the counter.

"Looks like he knows this place. It doesn't look like his first time here," Yogev said to his friends in a low voice.

"This whole thing is really strange," Yariv half-whispered in response.

After a few seconds, the elevator opened and a tall man with an athletic build came out. He had light-brown hair and his yellow button-down, short-sleeved shirt exposed a pair of tanned, muscular arms. The man, who must have been in his sixties, looked well-preserved for his age, and didn't seem to have even the slightest beer gut. He stopped for a moment, scanned the broad entry hall, and then recognized Yoav. He called out to him and waved. Yoav went over to him, and the two shook hands warmly. Both had big smiles on their faces.

"Who's this model and how does he know Yoav?" Dan

whispered to his two friends, who were sitting next to him on the long sofa.

"Dude, it's the nineties – maybe that's his lover..." Yogev answered in a whisper, and the three of them laughed.

For the next few seconds, Yoav and the tall fellow stood whispering to each other, and then they turned and came toward the three soldiers, who in the meantime had gotten off the sofa and stood up.

"Guys," Yoav said to them, "Meet Jerry. He's basically the one guilty of ruining your vacation."

Yogev, Dan and Yariv each shook Jerry's hand in turn.

"It's nice to meet you," said Jerry. "I admit, I'm guilty... let's go up to my office. We can talk privately there."

Jerry waved to the two girls at the information counter, and they smiled back at him. The familiar ring of the elevator sounded, and the doors opened. The five of them – Yoav, Jerry, and the Three Musketeers – got in.

The elevator was well lit and large, about the size of a small room, and the entire back wall was a mirror. Jerry pressed the button for the fifth floor, there was a sound, and then the elevator began its ascent. After a few seconds, it reached the fifth floor and stopped.

The elevator doors opened to a lobby area covered in light-brown carpeting that stretched from one wall to the other. The five of them got out of the elevator and walked down the quiet, empty hallway with Jerry in the lead. Nobody said anything. After a short walk, they arrived at an opaque glass door. To the right of the door was a black box with a slight depression in it and next to it a keypad. Jerry placed his right thumb on the depression and, with his left finger, rapidly entered a five-digit code. He kept his thumb in the depression until they heard a short buzz. After a few seconds, a metallic, female computerized voice came from the box: "Identification complete. Entry authorized." Jerry quickly pushed on the handle of the opaque glass door but, as he pushed it forward a bit, he then stopped for a moment, turned to the three soldiers standing behind him and said in a quiet, deep voice, "Gentlemen, you are about to enter the holy of holies of the security establishment. Welcome to the Mossad headquarters."

* * *

Jerry pushed the opaque door wide open. The three soldiers stood in the doorway and stared wide-eyed at what they saw: the room was spacious and devoid of windows, but lit with strong fluorescent lighting. It was clear that it functioned as a war room for operations. Dozens of people were running around here and there, some of them holding files of paperwork, others cradling small portable computers. There was a lot of activity. Telephones ringing from every direction along with the buzz of printers and fax machines contributed to the general noise in the room. The sound of documents being shredded stood out above the din. Dozens of large, black televisions hung on the walls, and above each screen was a large sign with the name of a different region in the world, both in Hebrew and in English. Next to the region was a clock that displayed the local time in that particular location.

The first screen showed a moving picture of two commercial ships from above. The lettering above it stood out in particular: "IRAN." The second screen was especially large, and above it appeared the lettering: "SYRIA." Under each large screen were a few computer stations, a fax machine and a telephone, which were manned by a handful of people. Further on down the room were other large screens of Europe, North Africa, and South America. Dan, Yogev and Yariv stood as if rooted in place and couldn't take their eyes off of what was happening in the room.

"Come on, guys, my office is over here," said Jerry with a smile and pointed to a heavy wooden door. On the right side of the door was a blinking red light. Jerry pulled out a magnetic card with his photo on it from his shirt pocket and touched it to the light for a few seconds until there was a short, sharp beeping – and the light turned green. He pushed the door knob and opened the door. The three of them and Yoav entered the room and stood in the corner.

In the center of the rectangular room was a dark wooden table, unusually long and wide, and around it, elegant office chairs with wide arm rests and long metal legs perched on a base of four wheels. Next to each chair was a small, flexible hose-like microphone sticking out of a small hole in the table. This room didn't have any windows either. On two walls in the room were giant TV screens, which, at the moment, were turned off. On the third wall hung a world map, and each country was a different color. Next to the map hung a framed copy of the Israeli Declaration of Independence.

Against the ceiling on all four corners of the room were four state-of-the-art security cameras pointed at the table and whoever was sitting there. A few small microphones hung from the ceiling. Jerry slowly closed the heavy wooden door. With the door shut, suddenly the noise of the war room outside disappeared. Yariv, who was surprised by the sudden silence, looked at the door and noticed that it had a thick rubber seal around it, soundproofing the room.

"Welcome, my young friends. Sit wherever you want. What do you want to drink?" Jerry asked.

Yoav asked for a Turkish coffee. Yariv and Yogev asked for cold water, and Dan asked for a Coke. Jerry pushed the intercom next to the head of the table, ordered the drinks, and a few minutes later a full-bodied woman in her fifties with her hair pulled up brought them their drinks. In addition to the drinks, the woman put out a bunch of plates with various refreshments – fruit and cookies.

Yariv and Yogev sat down and took their drinks. Yoav sat down next to Jerry. Only Dan remained standing. He went to the far corner of the room. There was a cabinet with glass doors there and inside were a bunch of certificates of merit, trophies and framed pictures. Dan got closer to the glass shelves and looked closely at the different pictures. In the first one was Menachem Begin and, next to him, Jerry, when he was a few years younger with thick, black hair. At the bottom of the picture was a handwritten note: "To the people of secrecy and mystery, thanks to whom the Jewish state stands firm. Sincerely, Menachem Begin." In the second picture, Dan immediately recognized the facial features of President Yitzhak Navon. Jerry was standing next to him and on the bottom of the picture was inscribed: "The guardian of Israel neither slumbers nor sleeps. In endless appreciation of your efforts for the security of the State of Israel, Y. Navon."

Next to this picture Dan saw a picture of Yitzhak Rabin, who was shaking Jerry's hand. Here too was a handwritten dedication: "To Jerry, for again making the impossible, possible. Well done! Yitzhak Rabin."

Dan stook a few more seconds, the pictures and inscriptions from the general chiefs of staff of the IDF from past years peering at him from behind the dark glass: Rafael Eitan, Dan Shomron, Ehud Barak. Next to them, the veteran soldier identified the pictures of the last ministers of defense: Moshe Ahrens and Shimon Peres, and the photo of President Chaim Herzog. In every picture there was a personal dedication to the agents of the Mossad, and Jerry personally.

"Very impressive. Quite a piece of history you've got here," Dan said while his eyes skipped around the pictures.

"Right indeed. We worked very hard for that," Jerry answered him.

"Come on, Dan, sit down so we can start," Yoav said to Dan,

who was still standing in front of the large trophy case. Dan sat down, picked up his can of Coke and drank it all in one gulp.

"If you'd like more to drink or eat – just ask," Jerry said.

"Thanks, I'm good," Dan replied and added with a smile, "but we'll try to kill as much time as we can here, and then order lunch, on you..."

Jerry smiled. As an operations guy and former combat soldier, even he was a sucker for the youthful antics displayed by the young men that he worked with over the years. As he got older and ran up the ranks of command, he sensed that he was becoming distanced from his direct connection with the field, the soldiers, the real action. That was the price for climbing up the pyramid, he always reminded himself.

Quiet prevailed for a moment, and then Jerry began by saying, "Like I told you, my name is Jerry. You guys are currently in the main headquarters of the Mossad. Before we begin our discussion, I am required by our guidelines to tell you a few things – and only then can we continue. All right?"

The three nodded in agreement.

"What you are about to hear today in this room is classified as top secret. As you can see," he said and pointed to the cameras in the corners of the room and the microphones dangling from the ceiling, "everything in this room is being recorded twenty-four hours a day for operational purposes such as investigations and debriefings. Prime ministers, defense ministers, chiefs of the general staff, senior members of the security establishment and senior members of foreign spy organizations that we work with, as well as IDF generals have sat in the chairs you're sitting in right now. This is the room where decisions are made – if you'd like, you can call this the Mossad's 'pit.' I am obligated to tell you this before we begin our meeting for a simple reason: everything said today needs to stay in this room. It is absolutely critical that nobody but you are privy to this meeting even taking place, and under no circumstances can the information discussed make its way outside. To anybody. Not your friends in the unit or your operational team."

Yogev, Dan and Yariv looked stunned at the mention of their team members and guys in the unit, and their surprise was clearly etched upon their faces.

"I repeat and emphasize this again," Jerry continued, "so that there won't be any misunderstandings: the existence of this meeting is most top secret, and you are prohibited from speaking about it or any of the content discussed here today with any living soul, not your friends in the unit, or, specifically, your operational team members on Team 10. Any mention of or passing on of any information of any sort is considered a serious breach of national security laws and all that it implies – and we don't intend to be flexible about it. There's no need to elaborate, but we're talking about an offense that could carry with it time in prison. I'm sorry that I have to say these things to you in such an extreme way before we've even started, but it's important for me to lay these things out as clearly as possible. And so, if any of you think that this isn't you're thing, now's the time to walk out that door. Anybody here fit that description?"

"Mr. Jerry... may I call you that?" Yariv asked the man from the Mossad.

"There's no need for formality. Jerry is just fine. What's the question, Yariv?"

"Thanks. So, Jerry, I don't understand – how do you expect us to agree to keep a secret when we don't know what it's about?"

"You're right, there is a bit of a chicken-or-the-egg paradox here, but I still have to emphasize that this is protocol. What I mean is, even if after you hear everything said here and decide that the whole thing doesn't suit you, you're still bound to secrecy by the restrictions I mentioned. Is that clear?"

Yoav looked at the three soldiers who were sitting there

quietly, confused. It was clear to everybody that something big was happening, but what exactly? Each of them wondered separately.

"Jerry, may I add something?" Yoav asked.

"Sure, please."

Yoav addressed the three and said, "Look, guys, I didn't just call you out here in the middle of your vacation for nothing. I didn't ask you to come in your civilian clothes for nothing, and I didn't isolate you from the rest of the soldiers in the unit for nothing. We're talking about a very serious matter. We, Jerry and I, have been working on this for a while, and right now we're at the point where we want to put the theory into practice. I suggest that you listen to what we have to say, and then you can decide if you want in or not. That's what I think, but you're big boys and I can't and certainly don't want to impose my opinion on you. In any event, I reiterate Jerry's opening words: what is said here, whether you agree to continue the process or not, doesn't leave this room," Yoav said in a quiet, but definitive voice.

"I want to hear what the deal is. After that, I'll decide for myself what to do," Yogev said out loud and leaned back in the padded chair.

"I'm also in," said Dan after a moment of silence. "If nothing else, I'm curious."

Everybody in the room looked at Yariv. The veteran soldier lowered his head and looked at the table and not at the others present. He cracked his knuckles making loud snapping noises that resonated in the closed room.

"I'm not prepared for these two jackasses to know something I don't. I'm also in," he said when he lifted his head in Jerry's direction. "So can we finally hear what this is about?"

"Excellent," Jerry said smiling. "If that's how it is, I think it's time we put all our cards on the table"

The three sat stretched out on the armchairs. The feeling in the room was tense as the three expectantly waited for Jerry to speak.

"My job in the Mossad is head of the operations department," Jerry said.

"Isn't that the assassination wing for international hits, 'Caesaria?'" Yariv asked.

Jerry smiled at the implication. "First off," he said, "it isn't 'the assassination wing,' to quote you. I serve as head of the operations wing. Some are intelligence operations like those or others, and some are more a part of the Mossad's operations, where there are different units: surveillance, listening in and other things. And it's true that in Caesaria, there are those who are known to take out those who are looking to take us out."

"One second," Yariv said to Jerry, "head of the division is basically like a general in the IDF. Am I correct?"

"True. The division head in the Mossad is the parallel rank to a general in the IDF. The war room you saw outside is the operations war room, and from here, we basically direct all of our operations all over the world. Here, most of the decisions you have never heard of are made, and I'm hopeful that you never will hear about them."

"Okay, and how are we connected to this whole story?" Dan wondered out loud.

"Straight to the point. My kind of guy," the Mossad division head said and winked before continuing. "Have any of you heard of SHC?" he asked the three soldiers. All three shook their heads.

"I didn't think so. Very few people have heard of it. I'm talking about the Service Heads Committee. It goes like this: After the Yom Kippur War and the major upheaval that followed, the state investigation committee, the Agranat Commission, raised the serious issue of the lack of coordination and cooperation among Israel's security agencies – the IDF, Shin-Bet, the intelligence division and the Mossad. The investigative committee discovered that each security branch kept the information it had to itself, and didn't share it with the others. The most absurd aspect of the whole thing was that instead of being tightly coordinated and in close contact that would unite, enrich and upgrade the capabilities of the various intelligence and security branches of Israel, Judge Agranat found that each branch did the opposite – each branch kept the others in the dark. In effect, nobody told anybody else about any of the results of their operations, how they operate, what information they uncovered, about any advanced technological developments and operational and intelligence insights. That is, instead of cooperation, a secret competition developed among the various Israeli security branches."

"Are you serious? That sounds completely surreal," Yariv said.

"Wait, that's nothing: in the classified part of the investigative report, which was never disclosed or made public, the committee discovered that there were even instances where the same source in an enemy country was being used twice by Israel – once via the Mossad and once via the intelligence division or via the 504th Unit – at the same time! It should be obvious that such a distorted method of operating caused us to lose many sources, wasted a ton of resources, and of course led to exposures that cost many sources their lives, and us the loss of precious intelligence information. In other cases, the committee uncovered other severe breakdowns. For example, in another classified part of the report it was written that in Egyptian enemy territory, several different units were working on planting the same classified means – with no coordination among them. It created a real danger to the lives of the soldiers who were sent into enemy territory, and increased the chances of exposing what was planted there. That is, instead of sending in one unit one time for a single mission, each branch sent its own unit, to the same area, to basically plant the same thing – and all because of the rampant lack of coordination and information sharing. The people on the committee, who were astounded by what they discovered, determined that Israel's world intelligence picture was a one-thousand piece puzzle. Only by cooperating and giving each security branch access to all the pieces of the puzzle in its possession could the leaders of the country have a true, full and accurate picture of what's going on."

"What you're telling us here is incredible and troublesome," Dan said. "And what happened after the report came out?"

"The report, as I mentioned, had two parts to it – the revealed and the hidden. The revealed part had to do with things like empty emergency equipment depots, non-enlistment of reservists, preparations for emergency situations and things like that. You all heard about that type of thing I'm sure, because it would have been all over the news back then. The hidden part has to do with what I told you at many other points, and this isn't the place or time to discuss that. One of the immediate conclusions was the forming of a joint committee that would meet at a set time, and include representatives from each of the intelligence branches in Israel. The purpose of regular, fixed meetings was to create a system of actual, meaningful cooperation among all parties. For example – the idea was that the Shin-Bet would sit and talk about how they operate, and then maybe the guys from the Mossad would also learn something from that and, at the same time, the Mossad would talk about technological means they have been developing – and so too, the representatives from the intelligence division and the Shin-Bet could benefit from the same things, etc. The idea is clear – no more keeping things secret from each other and no more ego wars, rather a deep understanding that only by joining forces and minds can we serve the best interests of the people of Israel and their security."

"That's a nice idea on paper, but does this intelligence cooperation actually work, or are ego wars still being waged?" Yariv asked.

"Look, ultimately we're talking about people. And between us, just like there is covert competition between you guys and the operations unit of the Shin-Bet, same with us. But, if I'm being truthful, once all those committee meetings are recorded and transcribed, you have to be as transparent as possible, whether you want to or not."

"How often are these meetings?" Yogev asked, curious.

"About once a month. You see, I've been in the system for a number of years now, and served under many ministers of defense – starting with Shamir and ending with Moshe Arens, whom you can also see in the pictures in the cabinet there. I can tell you that the committee of foreign affairs and defense are very strict about that. And Defense Minister Rabin and current head of the Mossad, Shabtai Shavit, are especially strict about that. Neither is the type to cut corners in this regard."

"Hand on your heart, Jerry, are you telling me that you guys in the operations division of the Mossad are really learning from the other branches, the ones that are less professional?" Dan asked, and stole a glance at Yoav.

"Like a good Jew, I will answer a question with a question," Jerry responded easily. "Will you allow me to tell you a Native American legend that was told to me years ago by one of the heads of the Mossad that I worked under?"

The three of them smiled at each other and nodded in agreement.

"Excellent," Jerry said and began his story. "Once, many years ago, there was a small Native American village. One day, two brothers, ages six and ten, went out for a walk in the nearby forest to go berry picking and bring some back to the village. Suddenly, the bigger brother fell into a deep hole. The little brother – I'll remind you, he's only six – didn't know what to do. He started crying out of worry and panic. The older brother yelled up to him from the hole that he should connect a bunch of vines together and lower it down the hole. So that's what he did – the little brother started running around gathering all kinds of vines and tying them together until he was able to make an improvised rope. He lowered the rope into the hole and, after a long and prolonged struggle, managed to pull his older brother out. The sun began to set, and the two brothers hurried back to the village. Of course, they arrived many hours later than expected and the whole village was concerned about them – perhaps something had happened. When they arrived, the adults asked them why they were late. They told them everything – about falling into the hole, about the rope and about how the little brother pulled his big brother out. And the adults started laughing at them saying, 'Don't be ridiculous, how can a six-year-old pull a ten-year-old out of a hole like that by himself?!'"

Jerry paused his story a looked at each of the three soldiers. They looked fascinated, as did Yoav. He continued with a satisfied look on his face. "Suddenly, the old chief of the tribe walked by. He saw the kids were sad and that the adults were making fun of them, he raised his hand – and everybody went silent immediately. Then the chief looked at the small hands of the younger brother, which had cuts on them, and he saw the grooves that the improvised rope wore into his hands, the sweat still apparent on his forehead, the boy's dirty clothes and the truth shining in his eyes. And then the chief turned to the adults and said, 'I'm an old man, long have been my days, and one of the skills I picked up over the years is the ability to discern the truth, even when it's difficult and seems illogical. I believe this little boy. He indeed succeeded to pull his older brother out by himself. And you know why he succeeded? He succeeded because of one small but important reason. He succeeded to do the unbelievable by virtue of the fact that you, the adults of little faith, weren't with him when he did it. Had you been there, you would have certainly made fun of him and said, 'Oh, sweetie, don't bother, you have no chance! There's no way a child of six can lift a ten-year-old boy from a deep hole.' But he was lucky that you weren't there to destroy his belief in himself, his initiative, and in his strength and ability to adapt, that you didn't belittle him – and only because of this was he able to do the unbelievable.' And, with that, the chief finished speaking, kissed the little boy on the forehead, and went back to his tent," Jerry said, finishing the story.

He looked at the three soldiers and said, "Guys, I've been in special-ops for over thirty-five years. I'll let you in on a secret: the higher you go up the chain of command and the older you get, unfortunately, we lose our creativity, and sometimes also the guts that borders on insanity to do the unimaginable. So you may be surprised, Dan, but the answer to your last question of can we, the Mossad, the ones who can do anything on the outside, learn anything from others? – is affirmative. King David wrote in the Book of Psalms almost 3,000 years ago: 'From all my teachers, I learned something.' I found that sometimes we, the folks in the Mossad, are sure that we know best, and that we know better than anybody else what to do, and suddenly – surprise! And to our topic at hand, in the last year, the representatives of the Shin-Bet and IDF have told us during these service heads committee meetings about a team of first sergeants in Duvdevan who are miracle workers. Especially, so say the representatives of the IDF and Shin-Bet, the core and brains behind the team – three veteran soldiers who are very experienced, with incredible imaginations, balls of steel, and a lot of gumption. What particularly amazed me as a veteran operations man was hearing that despite not having access to the technology or the budget the Mossad has, these veteran soldiers have succeeded in reinventing the wheel each time to get the job done. That's what surprised us, and so we asked to meet you. And now it's time to let the cat out of the bag: after all that we've heard about you, we came to the conclusion that the Mossad would be happy if you and your abilities would help us out."

Yoav, the unit commander, who had been sitting quietly next to Jerry until now, suddenly smiled a broad smile. Dan, Yariv and Yogev sat stunned in their seats, exchanging confused glances among themselves. The shock and surprise that gripped the three combat soldiers was apparent. They sat in total silence and didn't utter a sound. Every so often, they would look at Yoav, still sitting with his arms crossed, still beaming proudly.

"I must tell you that this is the first time in my life that I have seen you three like this – speechless," Yoav joked. "It's a refreshing change. You guys always have some smart comment or some sarcastic jab, and finally somebody managed to shock you into silence. What's the matter, cat got your tongue?"

"Yoav, I'm in shock. I have to admit that I didn't think this was the direction Jerry's talk was heading," Dan said in response.

"Guys, it's obvious to me you weren't expecting this. It's natural and even warranted to be a little taken aback. You guys want to take a small break for a breather?" Jerry asked the three of them.

"No, that's all right. That was quite the surprise. Didn't see that one coming. Well played," said Yogev who stood up to stretch his legs a bit after sitting for so long.

"I second Yoav's sentiment. Well done on ambushing us like that," Yariv said with a thin smile.

"So, shall we continue?" Jerry asked. "I'll remind you that, at any stage, you can opt out of the game if you aren't interested."

"Leave now? After what we just heard? You crazy?" Yogev asked with a wink. "I'm for continuing." The other two soldiers nodded in agreement.

The man from the Mossad looked at them and continued talking. "All right, so if that's how it is, we'll continue, and I remind you that the information remains strictly in this room. Where were we? Ah, I told you about the service heads committee and their conclusions. In any event, the process of operational and intelligence cooperation became stronger among the different branches of the security establishment, and it developed into a way to share ideas and operational methods among the various members of the security sectors," Jerry explained.

"I don't understand," Dan asked in amazement. "You want to recruit us to the Mossad?"

"No, not at all," Jerry said and laughed. "The truth is, I'd be happy if you worked with us. You look like good guys, and from what I've read and heard about you, not bad soldiers either," Jerry added with a wink. "But you guys are the property of the IDF, and that's where you'll stay."

"Okay, so what do you need from us? You want us to develop a new combat doctrine for you?" Yogev asked and then sat back down in his chair.

"Not exactly. What we at the Mossad need from you is help testing new weapons we've developed. That is, you'll be a sort of laboratory and will try out all kinds of new toys that we developed – before we use them abroad."

"One second," Yariv interrupted, "You guys already have an operations unit – why do you need us specifically? And apart from that – it's no secret that you're already working closely with the general staff special forces, Shaldag[27] and the naval commandos. So if you have them, why do you need us?"

"I'll explain. You see, the scope of your operations is the largest in the IDF. I mean in terms of small operations – two to four soldiers per operation – and also the quick turnaround: in the elite units you mentioned, there are battle procedures that extend for months or even years. With you guys, it's on demand. Always. That's how you guys roll in Duvdevan. Nobody else does what you guys do, and certainly not with the intensity you bring. With all due respect to the other elite units – you can't compare what you guys do to what anybody else does. Take the naval commandos or Shaldag, for example, where many soldiers are active in each operation," Jerry explained.

---

27. A special forces unit in the IDF.

"Why not? What are they less good at?" Yogev asked unbridled pride, that almost made his question rhetorical.

"I'm not saying they're less good, God forbid," Jerry replied seriously, "but I'm looking for a unit that will be as similar as possible to what my guys and I are doing abroad. Let's go back for a moment to the example of the naval commandos or Shaldag. When they go out and do an operation in enemy territory, they take with them a relatively large fighting force, and of course a lot of heavy equipment: optical gear, sniper rifles, machine guns, grenades, and even RPGs, food and water for a few days, the entire air force is at their service to help and extract, and on and on. As you know, the guys in the naval commandos also don't go into operations with just a handful of guys, but rather with a full barrage of soldiers, drones, snipers, advanced weaponry, etc. What they do is very important, but it's not what I'm looking for and it's not what I need. I need a different model of operation, and a different model of soldiers and methods."

Yogev looked up at the ceiling, pondering what Jerry was saying. After a moment, he nodded to himself and said to Jerry, "Go on," with a smile. He was obviously pleased with what he was being told.

"Our methods in the Mossad are very similar to what you do here in the West Bank: when my guys operate abroad – say, intercepting somebody, planting listening devices, or putting surveillance on somebody – we're always talking about lone agents. We never put a bunch of agents into the same area because the chances of blowing their cover is too high. When they go into an operation, it is very similar to the unique way in which you guys work: always going in disguise or under a different identity. That's also how it is abroad – our guys go into the field, do what they need to do, and get out. That is, after the operation, nobody knows who was responsible for it. And there's another similarity: both you guys and my guys go in with handguns, concealed, and relatively small. Like, you guys won't go undercover with a grenade launcher, just like you won't see a Mossad agent head out with a machine gun, for instance," Jerry said.

"Okay, I got you," Dan said. "What else?"

"I'll give you another example," Jerry said. "Take for example your operation with the garbage truck in Hebron. The operation with Kawasme, remember?"

"Come on, are you really asking if I remember it?" Yariv laughed. "Trust me, Jerry, it took me two weeks to get the smell of garbage off me. Look at the world we live in: these two princesses, Kermit and Yogi, are sitting in the cabin like royalty while your devoted servant was stuck like a dog in the back of the nasty garbage truck for a few hours, until they finally located Kawasme's car and took him down. The worst part was that the whole idea to use the garbage truck was mine. So instead of rewarding me by letting me ride in the cabin, as the mastermind behind the operation, Yoav decides that I need to command the five other fighters that are also in the back of the mobile garbage dump. It smelled so bad in there, you have no idea. We almost puked our guts out in there."

"What are you crying about, Newton?" Yogev said with a smile. "Be thankful that we didn't turn the compactor on. We'd have turned you into juice back there…"

Jerry smiled but immediately returned to his train of thought. "In any case, let's go back to the garbage truck. I'm certain that by the time one of the locals figured out what happened there, where Kawasme disappeared to and what happened to him and his security guards, you guys were already back at the base smoking a cigarette and drinking a cup of coffee. That's the idea with us as well – hit them and immediately disappear. Without a trace."

"Okay," said Yogev. "I get the comparison and general idea."

"By the way, I have to ask you something I've been curious about," said Jerry to the three of them. "How did you manage not to throw up in there? When I read the report on your operation, I was reminded of an operation I led a few years ago in some other country. There was a Syrian intelligence agent that we needed to grab for interrogation. The idea was to get close to his house by walking through the sewer system that passed right underneath it. In any event, the operation was a total disaster, because all three of us who went into the sewer simply puked our guts out and weren't able to carry out the operation. That was something we didn't foresee when brainstorming possible 'scenarios and reactions.' So tell me: how did the six of you guys not puke your guts out?"

"It's simple, Jerry," Yariv answered. "In high school, I worked in kibbutz Ramat HaKovesh for a veterinarian who needed help. He would autopsy all the carcasses for research and disease discovery. Believe me, Jerry, a cow's carcass or a donkey after two days stinks like you can't even imagine. In high school, I was studying biology, so one time he invited me to watch him dissect a carcass in order to rule out a disease that might be spreading in our region. He put eye guards on, like somebody remodeling a house, and put a nylon robe on over his white one. I asked him what that was for, and he pulled out an electric saw and started cutting into the foul-smelling corpse. Blood sprayed all over him – absolutely disgusting. Trust me, I almost became a vegetarian right then and there. Anyway, the guts of the carcass were already full of maggots and stunk in general. I almost threw up, and then he opened a side drawer and took out a tube of something that looked like toothpaste. He squeezed, about a centimeter-long blob came out of the tube and he smeared it just under his nose and mine, like a mustache. It took me a second or two to understand what he was doing, but in a moment I got it: I couldn't smell a thing. Turns out that the cream has a very strong ingredient in it that nullifies the acrid stench. So before the operation with the garbage truck, I got some of that cream, smeared a bit on each of our upper lips, and that solved most of the problem with the stench."

"Nice," Jerry said to him and then turned to Dan and Yogev. "You understand? That's exactly what I meant – that's a simple yet good example that proves that no single branch has a monopoly on intelligence. It's possible and necessary to learn from other professionals. There's no shame in that – on the contrary."

* * *

The conversation went on and on, and Jerry got everybody more to drink and some light snacks. The tension that was in the room dissipated a bit, and everybody enjoyed the refreshments.

"Say, Jerry," Yogev asked, "is this the first time that you're integrating soldiers into your ancillary operations? We're the strike force in this case?"

"Not at all. Let's differentiate between the ancillary operations, as you called them, and our primary operational activities," Jerry replied.

"Okay, you've succeeded in confusing me," Dan said with a smile. "What exactly do you mean by that?"

"All right, let's start from the beginning, shall we?" Jerry said to the three of them. They nodded their heads in response.

"Yoav," Jerry turned to the unit commander and asked, "how much time do we have?"

"As much as we need, my friend – it's already coming out of their vacation time…" Yoav answered with a wink.

"Excellent. If that's the case, then we aren't pressed for time. Allow me a moment to go back to where I left off – cooperation between the IDF and the Mossad. This cooperation with the IDF isn't new, but rather an important integration that has resulted in a lot of successful operations in the past."

"What exactly do you mean?" Yariv asked.

"It's like this: the Mossad has a few agents that carry out our special operations. I'm talking about a few dozen individuals, and the entire burden of operations falls on them. Of course they are backed up by technical squads, and various professionals in other areas, but at the end of the day, we only have a relatively small number of people. They are the best of the best, but despite their experience and time they've been here, we still have some things that require soldiers or officers. I'll give you an example: you were pretty young then, but you've no doubt heard of an operation called 'Springtime of Youth,'" Jerry said to the three soldiers.

"Yeah, I've heard of that. Ehud Barak dressed up like a blonde woman, right?" Dan asked.

"That's right. He and Amiram Levin[28] dressed up as women for this operation. This was in 1973. In this case, the goal was to attack specific Fatah and other Palestinian terrorist targets in the Beirut and Sidon regions. The IDF integrated special forces that participated in the incursion – naval commandos and paratroopers. Everybody came by sea, and our agents were waiting for them with local vehicles on the beach; they were the ones who drove the forces through the alleyways and backroads to their destinations. Without the IDF, we wouldn't have been able to conduct our operation. We planned everything and were responsible for gathering intelligence before the operation, but in the end, we relied on the IDF to help us conduct the operation. And I'll give you another example: you remember when we eliminated Abu Jihad, right?"

"That was in Tunis, a few years ago, right?" Yogev asked.

"Very good. April 1988. By the way, Israel never officially authorized any involvement in the matter – and that's also our official stance now and into the future. However, since we're having an open discussion, I can tell you that all the intelligence for the operation was provided by our guys, but the operation

---

28. Former IDF general who served in one of the most elite special-ops units.

itself was carried out by IDF special forces. In order to pull off such a challenging endeavor, we had to sail a very large force from Israel to Tunis, and afterward, we needed to land that force on the beach, secure the area while closing off travel arteries all around, and then go in and take out Abu Jihad. As you can see, we needed a massive amount of people with different capabilities – and here as well, we got help from the IDF," Jerry finished, and poured himself some water from the glass pitcher on the table.

"Okay," Dan said, taking over after a moment of silence, "it's clear that in many instances, the Mossad brings the information and the IDF acts on it. That's no secret – for example, the attack on the nuclear reactor in Iraq or the Entebbe operation. So, can I take a stab and say that you're interested in doing some sort of operation together?"

"Right you are," Jerry responded and addressed the other two soldiers. "Look, here's the point: there's a division within the Mossad's technical department that makes all kinds of gadgets and special devices for us, in order to put them to use in sensitive areas outside the country. In the past, there were some screwups during the technical part of these operations in the field. Some were published in the press, but most never come to light, for obvious reasons. Because of this, the prime minister and minister of defense decided to establish a special cooperative committee that would be in charge of creating rules for introducing new devices for use in the field. The directives that the prime minister's office and the defense ministry's special committee came up with was that before any of these devices are used, they need to be field-tested to prove viability – that is, a wet run. The goal was clear: we have to see it work. Now, here at headquarters we've discussed the matter extensively and two critical questions came up. First, where can we test these technologies that we have developed in real time, and the second is, assuming we find the time and place, who's going to do it? I mean, it's not feasible to pull our agents, who are up to their ears in complicated operations in other countries, out of there just to come back to Israel and do a few experiments for us. Every time we pull them out and put them back into the field adds to the risk of exposing them, which would derail whatever operation they're taking care of at present. In other words," Jerry said while looking sternly at each soldier individually, "you guys are going to get your hands on a few things developed by the Mossad, try them out on the terrorists you go after in the West Bank, and let us know what you think and if it's ready for field use or not."

"And that's why we're here. We're going to be your field testers," Yogev said.

"Correct. That's the idea. That's why you're here. We'd be glad if you'd agree, and would understand if you opt out – the decision is yours. That's the whole of it," Jerry said and again looked at the three soldiers.

"Excuse me for a moment, Jerry, but I have to add a few things," Yoav said and addressed the soldiers. "Look, this is a highly classified matter. As Jerry mentioned at the beginning, just talking about this could damage the country's national security. Whether or not you agree, nobody else in the unit can know about this, not even the rest of the team, not any of the company commanding officers, nor the soldiers – nobody. Only you three have been brought into the discussion, and secretly at that. Only the four of us in the unit know about this. If you agree, you'll have to sign nondisclosure agreements and undergo a higher level security clearance check than what you've already passed. You'll undergo comprehensive and unique training on special operations – here, in the Mossad's technical lab. Not in the unit. It's highly likely that we will have to extend your service by a few extra months. I'm telling you that up front. It will depend on your level of operational preparedness after the study program, working in the lab and going through the Mossad's field training. In other words, you need to perform a very specific number of trials, and only then will you be discharged," Yoav explained.

"Wait, I don't understand," Yariv said, his eyes open in astonishment. "You mean to say that, from the moment we start this process, we'll be taken out of the unit and be under the command of the Mossad?"

"No, not at all. The opposite, actually. The unit and the team will become our acting testing lab and your cover story. You will stay in Duvdevan as combat soldiers in every way, including the undercover operations you perform all the time. I'm just telling you that we don't want to expose more soldiers to the classified aspect of things. Jerry and the development team in the lab will decide on a specific number of devices for you to test out, and only then will you start the training program under the direction of the Mossad, execute their trials successfully, show everybody that they work as intended – and get discharged."

"How much more time will our service be extended, do you think?" Dan asked Yoav.

"Dan, I don't have an answer for you right now, because it depends on a lot of factors, some of which are completely unknown to us right now. For instance, will the devices be ready for the field? Assuming they will be, will the trial in the field work the first time you test them? If not, will they ask us to do another trial to improve the results of the first? And what will be the situation in the West Bank irrespective of our trials?" Yoav responded.

Jerry added, "It really depends on our development team here at the Mossad. They are developing new toys all the time. We, too, have our own internal process of checks we run before we put anything out for field testing. Some of our gadgets don't meet the minimal demands of our lab tests, and so we shelve them or improve them. Right now we have two or three projects that we'd really like to test out. That is, two or three that have been put through laboratory testing and are ready for feasibility testing in the field. I'd like to use your professional experience and expertise, but I understand that I can't expect you to extend your service forever. At present, I'm in agreement with Yoav – take into account that you might indeed have to extend the length of your service by a few months in order to complete the task we came here to discuss. I know that this is a lot of time to ask for, but it really is important for the country's security."

"A few more months? Are you serious? That's so long..." Dan said.

"I know, and I completely understand the dilemma – but that's the situation. Understand, the extra training, the whole point of which is to familiarize you with the new equipment, takes time. That will be the first step. The second step, after you are proficient with the gear under laboratory conditions, you'll have to come up with a plan to use them in the field. The plan must be approved by Yoav, and after that, by me and a few more people in the system. The operational plan must be perfect, without any weaknesses. The reason should be obvious – if here in the West Bank it won't work like it's supposed to, then we're in trouble. At this point, after the plan is authorized, Yoav and you will get the green light from me. We will cover this operation by running it during one of your regular operations, but only the three of you will really know the actual goal of the operation. When I told you that getting familiar with the equipment and running an initial pilot operation in the field would take a few months, it wasn't a random guess. I'm telling you that because I know. I can tell you that, for our agents in the field, that was the average amount of time that it took them to become familiar with the equipment, to plan an operation and then to carry it out. You also need to be prepared for the possibility that the initial trial might fail, and that there will be a second, which takes more time. That also happens sometimes..." Jerry said.

"So what do you say, gentlemen?" Yoav asked the three, who were looking at him. "Are we doing this?"

Yariv looked at Yogev, who was looking at Dan. There was a tense silence in the room. Jerry knew that this was the critical moment – if the three of them refused, he would have to think of who else could run their trials. He felt that the issue of extending the length of their service was the main problem, but he couldn't get around it. Jerry hoped to God that these Three Musketeers would agree to take the project on. He looked up at Yoav, the unit commander. Jerry also saw in Yoav's eyes that same sinking suspicion that the three of them wouldn't agree to their request and would refuse to take part in the complicated process required of them. From the long conversations Jerry and Yoav had before the meeting with the three soldiers, there was a certain understanding that they might come up empty.

The quiet lingered. For Jerry and Yoav, it was not a good sign. Jerry was about to open his mouth to say something encouraging, but Yoav saw that and indicated with his eyes to wait a moment. The three continued looking at each other. The strong, deep bond among them didn't need words. Each side of the triangle knew every twitch, every movement of every other side. Yoav and Jerry thought that the three were having a conversation among themselves, but without uttering a single word or sound. Only then did the two of them understand how deeply connected the three combat soldiers were. Another moment passed and then –

"I'm in," Yogev said definitively.

"Me too," Yariv added.

"We're in," Dan said for all three, "but if we don't get overtime for this, I'm going straight to HR..."

CHAPTER 10
November 1992, Hebrew University Campus, Givat Ram, Jerusalem

The silver van slowed to a halt in front of the electric barrier. The vehicle glistened in the light of the sun. Its rear windows were tinted and there were no markers on the vehicle bearing any indication of its purpose whatsoever. The sleepy guard came out of his guard station and approached the driver's window. Jerry, the driver, pressed the button and the electric window made its way slowly down until it finally stopped. The guard looked inside the vehicle. Next to Jerry was Yoav. In the seats behind them sat Dan, Yogev and Yariv. Everybody was in civilian garb. Jerry handed the guard some certificates and paperwork. The guard took the papers, went back to his station, and picked up the phone that was hanging on the wall and started dialing. After a few moments, the guard came back to the van and handed Jerry back the certificates and paperwork. "It's fine," he said, "you guys can come on in. At the entrance, turn right and drive straight until you get to the red sign and park there. Dr. Yakobovitch's lab is the first building to the left of the parking lot."

Jerry thanked him with a nod of his head, the gate slowly opened, and he began driving into the campus according to the directions given to him by the guard. "Guys," Jerry said to the three soldiers who were sitting behind him while looking at them in the rearview mirror, "what you are about to see here is considered top secret. I remind you of your obligation to the secrecy of this project, including when it comes to other soldiers in the unit. We are about to meet a very special person. Dr. Yakobovitch is one of the leading senior researchers in the world in the field of toxicology, which is the use of toxins. He worked in our offices for many years, but a few years ago decided to return to academia to continue doing research in his profession. As a renowned researcher in his field, we, of course, kept in touch and he helps us out from time to time. His lab is one of the best in the field. Since you guys are going to deploy his materials in the field, it's important to me that everything be completely clear and understood – so feel free to ask him anything you want. This isn't the time to be shy," he said with a wide smile.

The three nodded and continued looking out the one-directional windows. The grounds outside the lab looked nice and well-maintained. The trees were meticulously pruned, the grass was clean and evenly mowed. After a few moments, the silver van parked in front of a sign that read "Toxicological Laboratory." The five of them got out of the vehicle and went inside the building.

* * *

Jerry led them down a long, well-lit hallway that had a few security cameras along its length and width. At the end of the hallway was a large red sign on the wall: "Toxicological Laboratory – Authorized Entry Only." Jerry stood in front of the door and knocked a few times. After a few seconds, the sound of a key turning could be heard, and then the door opened and out popped a head with a mop of grey hair. Dr. Yakobovitch's thin glasses were perched on the very end of his nose.

"Oh, hello there, Jerry, my friend. Hello to you, too. Come, come in and let's talk inside," said Dr. Yakobovitch and shook hands all around.

Everybody came into the lab and gathered around the entryway. They looked around: the lab was outfitted with a bunch of computers and multiple blinking display screens with various control lights and five long, narrow work tables. In the corner of the lab was a communications niche – a few telephones, fax machines and two other black communication devices. Dan looked up at the ceiling – there were some cameras up there as well documenting what went on in the lab.

"Hello everybody and welcome to our little slice of heaven," Dr. Yakobovitch said to them with a smile. "Jerry told me about you and asked me to make something special for you."

Jerry patted the old researcher on the shoulder before addressing the three soldiers. "As you may have guessed," he said to them, "in many cases, we have to send somebody to the next world, but it must be done quietly. When I say 'quietly,' I mean that the object's death needs to be medically undetectable. And so using certain weapons isn't possible here, and similarly, neither is strangulation or any other violent method. This is where Dr. Yakobovitch enters the picture. He is an expert in the negative effects of chemicals on animals. And as you know, people are also considered animals..." Jerry said, and narrowed his eyes.

"So here is where you concoct the toxins you use in assassinations?" Yariv asked, curious.

"Not only here. There are, of course, other places. But the general answer to your question is yes," Jerry answered.

"Okay, and what's our role in this?" Yogev asked.

"It's very simple," Jerry replied in a quiet voice. "Dr. Yakobovitch has been working a long time developing various lethal toxins that are impossible to identify or detect. The object being taken out ingests the toxin in some form and after a certain amount of time – can be hours or days – he develops normal symptoms that result in death."

"What symptoms, for example?" Dan asked.

"Let me answer, please," Dr. Yakobovitch said to Jerry before continuing. "Look, fellows, when a person dies, the death report has to include one important piece of data – the cause of death. The death can be from a number of factors: drowning, smoke inhalation, car accident, some disease, homicide or suicide, and on and on. According to every set of medical laws in the world, there's no such thing as releasing a body for burial without filling out a report on the cause of death. When our guys want to take somebody out abroad, they need to take into account that the body will undergo a third-party general examination, or even worse – an autopsy. During a pathological autopsy, they will look for traces of toxins, poison, alcohol, drugs, medicines and other things that may have caused the person's death. In order to get around this, we have developed various kinds of toxins that cause people to die of common, natural causes: heart attack, stroke, etc. The advantage of our toxins is that they are undetectable during an autopsy. Why? Because some of them dissolve in the blood without leaving a trace, while others disappear and evaporate after a few hours. We have a number of toxins in development, but we need to test them in real conditions in the field on actual, live people. Come, I want to show you something," Dr. Yakobovitch said to them. He started walking down the long hallway and Jerry, Yoav and the three soldiers followed behind.

"I feel like I'm in Q's lab from James Bond…" Yogev whispered to Dan and Yariv, and they smiled.

After a few steps, Dr. Yakobovitch opened a door with a rubber seal around it, and the others followed him into a large room filled with cages. The noise was distinct: the room was full of rabbits, mice, rats and guinea pigs.

"My friends, look around you," the senior scientist said. He raised his voice so he could be heard above the background noise. "Here is where we conduct our experiments. I know that it's not always pretty, and may seem unethical, but I have to tell you that we work under the strictest guidelines, both those of the health ministry as well as health organizations worldwide. I'm not trying to create a romantic picture here, and obviously the animals didn't come here of their own free will, but I can assure you that we do our best to ensure their comfort. Moreover, if they are given a death sentence during the trials, we have a very strict protocol, such that death will be quick and with minimal pain."

"What do you mean, doctor," Dan asked, looking at a while rabbit running around its cage.

"In order to explain myself better, I'll give you an example. Let's say that the decision has been made to try a deadly toxin on a certain animal. We determine in advance how much time we will allow the toxin to work. If we see that the animal still isn't dead after the effects of the toxin, and its suffering is being prolonged, we kill it immediately and therefore save it from further suffering. I know that doesn't sound very good, but that's how it is. That's the price we pay to develop toxins," the researcher said finishing his talk, and moved toward the exit.

Yakobovitch led his guests to the first research hall, and there everyone sat around a table. "Okay," Jerry said to the three soldiers, "so as you saw, the purpose of this lab is to develop toxins and to test them on lab animals. As you heard, these trials are also limited in all kinds of ways and regulated by various organizations. But this is just the beginning, because our goal is a bigger animal that weighs a lot more, with a different anatomical and physiological build than the lab animals on which the trials are performed. In other words, we know how the toxins work on mice that weigh a few ounces, or a ten pound rabbit, or even a seventy-five pound monkey. But we don't have any way of knowing how a toxin will work on a person that weighs two-hundred pounds or more. This is where you guys enter the picture – you are going to help us test this in the field," Jerry said.

"But how is it possible to determine the dosage, or the range of effects of the toxin? I mean, the trial here, on animals in a lab, is partial and limited. Perhaps the terrorist is on medication that partially counteracts the effects of the toxin? Maybe that medication he takes accelerates the death? How can is it even possible to calculate something like that?" Yariv asked Dr. Yakobovitch.

"You're absolutely right. That is indeed a problem. In order to mitigate this issue, we have built computerized models that take all these things into account. Generally, we haven't made too many mistakes and everything has gone smoothly," replied Dr. Yakobovitch.

"When you say, 'generally,' I take that to mean that we are not the first soldiers from the IDF to visit you here in your lab to perform real live field tests on human targets…" Dan said and looked at Jerry, who responded immediately.

"Dan, for obvious reasons, I can't get into that, but there is truth to what you're saying. You guys aren't the first. It's important to me that you know that the previous field experiments were very successful, and the models that Dr. Yakobovitch built have proven themselves. There's no reason that it won't work for you guys as well."

"Okay," Dan continued and turned to Yoav, "so where do we go from here?"

Yoav looked at the three soldiers and folded his hands over his chest. "Look," he said after a silent pause, "the purpose of our unit, at the end of the day, is to bring the bad guys to the Shin-Bet, preferably alive – and from there, they go to interrogation. But you also know that there are some bad guys that, when they meet us, it's the end for them. There are those who we know in advance are marked for death, and the operation is planned so that they don't come back alive, but rather to go hang out with seventy-two virgins in heaven. And so what happens now is that our intelligence division in the unit will locate a terrorist that, as far as we're concerned, should have been sent to the afterworld a long time ago. They'll build a comprehensive medical profile for him: height, weight, blood pressure, medications, a list of existing medical problems, perhaps even a genetic profile. We check with Jerry and Dr. Yakobovitch if the object fits the profile for the trial experiment. If not, we find somebody else that does. If he is indeed a match, Dr. Yakobovitch will prepare the correct formula: type of toxin, dosage, way to administer it, etc. You guys will meet with him, learn about the toxin in depth, understand how it works and how to bring it into contact with the object, and from there it's up to you. The three of you and I will sit down and think about how to administer the toxin to the terrorist," Yoav said.

Dr. Yakobovitch surveyed everybody in the room carefully. "It's important that you understand," he finally said, "that there are toxins that need to come into contact with the skin in order to be effective, there are those that need to be injected into the blood, and there are those that only work if ingested into the digestive system. There are many methods. I will prepare the specific material, the dosage, and the way the toxin must be administered to the object, and you will be the ones to carry it out it in the field. And that's why it's very important that you become thoroughly familiar with the materials. The smallest deviation could render it ineffective, and then all our work would be for nothing."

"Not to mention exposing our materials and methods," Jerry mentioned.

"Pardon me for asking," Yogev said, "but, if we're talking about such lethal toxins, how will the soldier – us – not be affected by them? We're supposed to be very close to the object..."

"You're a hundred percent correct," the researcher said, "there is an element of danger to the soldier – both when carrying the toxin and while administering it. Therefore, when we know who the object is and his medical status, we will all sit down together and think about the best way to administer the toxin, while keeping you guys safe. I can tell you one thing: each soldier that takes part in this kind of operation will, in advance, receive the antidote of any toxin he carries. That is, even in a case where, for example, the vessel holding the toxin breaks, and the toxin touches the soldier's skin, we have at least a few minutes until the toxin takes effect. In this time, the affected soldier can inject himself with the antidote and get out of the area immediately. But like I said, the chances of something like that happening are very slim, since I will try to minimize the amount of the lethal toxin to just the amount necessary to take out the object. In other words, I'm prepared for the effectiveness of the toxin to be lessened, but I'm not prepared for a soldier to be harmed by the toxin."

"So, in short, you guys are in good hands," Jerry said, smiling. "Thanks, doctor," he said. "We'll sit down with our list and I'll get you the physical details of the object very soon. Afterward, you can sit with our young friends here and go over the specific details. We'll be in touch," he said and got up.

Dr. Yakobovitch shook the hand of everybody warmly and escorted them to their silver van in the parking lot.

Jerry started the vehicle and began driving slowly in the area of the university campus, stopped the car and turned to the back seat. "I hope that you enjoyed your tour and meeting Dr. Yakobovitch," he said to the fighters. "You could say that the main reason Yoav put us in touch with each other was exactly this – to utilize your abilities and experience for these types of classified experiments in the field. And now, I will ask that you listen well to what is about to happen from now on: our next meeting will be in your home court. That is, at the unit. I'll also be there, of course, but with a slight change: in front of the rest of the guys on the team, Yoav will introduce me as Jerry from the Shin-Bet. Not from the Mossad. Only you guys will know the truth. The reason for this is simple. From past experience, we need a fairly good amount of manpower to carry out an operation as complicated as this. Therefore, what we'll do is this: Yoav will sit with the three of you, and together you'll plan the general guidelines for the operation. It's important for me to point out that you have to create an operational plan that will insert additional soldiers from your team into the picture. When the plan is ready, I'll arrive at your unit as a Shin-Bet field officer, and I'll meet the rest of the soldiers. You three will of course spearhead the operation, and you will also be the ones to administer the toxin that will be chosen by Dr. Yakobovitch for the mission. Yoav believes that the rest of the soldiers won't suspect anything, because in other operations you three are normally the operational force. Is the idea clear?"

"Wait, I missed something," Dan said. "If the operation is going to include other guys from the team, how do you intend keeping the toxin a secret?"

"I'll tell you the truth, I don't know yet," Jerry admitted. "You need to come up with an operational plan that allows you to administer the toxin without the rest of the guys in the team knowing anything about it. Do you think that's possible?"

Yoav smiled a big smile and answered for the three soldiers. "Jerry, my friend, we have a unique motto in our unit: do the hard things yourselves, leave the impossible to us. Give us time to look into it. I am certain we'll find a solution to that as well."

CHAPTER 11
January 1993, Unit's War Room, Somewhere in the middle of the country

It was dusk. The rays of the setting sun shone through the windows and light-colored curtains and cast shadows that danced upon the heavy wooden table. Dust particles sparkled and glowed in the sunlit space like tiny fireflies. Around the table in the operations room sat the members of Team 10. On the other side of the table sat Jerry, and next to him at the head of the table sat the unit commander, Yoav. There were light refreshments laid out in plates on the table, and in the corner of the room was a plastic cart with various cold drinks on it. Yoav scanned the eyes of the veteran soldiers: at the end of the table sat Udi – Schumacher – the team's mythological driver. Yoav knew that his mechanical abilities and control over the unit's vehicles more than once got the soldiers out of difficult situations.

Stretched out in the chair next to him was Yaki. Yoav liked the light-skinned, quiet soldier – his nickname "Barbie" stuck to him like a leech. To Yaki's left was Barda, "The Bull." Doron, the only religious soldier in the unit, sat next to Barda. His past as a youth boxing champion, his Krav Maga prowess, broad shoulders and bulging muscles clarified beyond all doubt why he was called "Tyson."

On the chair next to Doron, Yoav saw the jovial face of Gidi. Gidi was slimly built and athletic, and was one of the best liked on the team. Each time the reason why he was called "Hose" was mentioned, the unit commander was forced to stifle a smile. Yoav continued looking over every soldier's face, when he suddenly heard a knock on the door. After a few seconds, the wide door opened and the division intelligence officer walked in holding some rolled-up maps. He sat down beside Yoav, spread the maps out on the table and signaled to Yoav that he was prepared and that they could start the briefing.

All the soldiers present in the team, ten in total, moved closer to where the maps were spread out on the table, and Yoav began speaking. "Good afternoon, everybody. As Dan already told you guys a few hours ago, this meeting is especially urgent and important. We have information fresh out of the oven about our friend, Marwan Abu Qassam. For those who forgot, this saint is at the top of Fatah's pyramid of attempted terrorist attacks against soldiers and civilians. Unfortunately, he is very good at his job, and for the past two years, the Shin-Bet has been unable to get its hands on any reliable information. There were a few attempts in the past, but they didn't pan out. However, this morning, we got fresh information, and to that end, I want to introduce to you Jerry from the Shin-Bet." Yoav pointed to Jerry and signaled to him with his hand that the floor was his.

Jerry thanked him with a nod of his head and began speaking. "Thank you, Yoav. I'm happy to meet you all. I've heard from my colleagues in various districts a lot of good things about your team..."

Gidi smiled his broad smile. "Stop," he whispered to Doron, "you're embarrassing us, but go on..."

Yoav looked at Gidi and signaled to him to quit goofing around. Jerry, who also heard the sarcastic remark from Gidi smiled thinly and continued. "Okay, so we're in a good mood today, which is important, but let's focus for a moment on the mission. So like Yoav said, my name's Jerry. I'm the intelligence officer for the Ramallah area, and my personal project for the last two years has been Mr. Marwan Abu Qassam. He's in his thirties, very smart, very seasoned, and the problem with him is that he is surrounded by a very tight network of collaborators and informants. Every attempt to get near him has failed. I can tell you that the famous undercover anti-terror unit operation about a year ago was directed by us, and we all remember how that ended."

"You mean that operation with the officer who was killed and two soldiers who were severely wounded?" Udi asked from the other side of the table.

"Yeah, that's the one. Like I said, we're talking about a strong, smart guy, but I hope that with your help, we can finally get our hands on him."

Yaki raised his hand, and Jerry signaled to him to speak. "Hi, I'm Yaki. If you could please, what is this urgent new information that you've obtained?"

"What came in just this morning is what we call in our professional jargon 'the golden tip.' What happens is like this: we know that each terror organization needs money to function. A lot of money. The money is used to buy weapons on the black market, support the families of people who have been killed as martyrs or those who are in prison, payments to various collaborators, fuel, food, etc. In short, a complete operation. One way to dry out a terrorist organization is to cut off its financial lifeline. A few months ago, we managed to get important intelligence information about a number of bank transfers which were sent to Fatah's secret account in Ramallah. From interrogating a few terrorists we caught, it turns out that their salaries haven't been paid for months now, and that stopping those bank transfers has indeed hurt them badly. From the moment we caught on to this method of the bank transfers in conjunction with the secret account numbers, we understood that they are searching for alternative means. Their direction right now is to ditch the bank transfers and go back to the old days – that is, transferring cash. During one of the interrogations, the name of some Jordanian money courier came up, who apparently received a large sum of cash to transfer to his friends in Ramallah. Unfortunately, the information arrived too late, so his name didn't pop up on our list of people to interrogate. We failed to perform a comprehensive search for him like we should have, and this morning he entered Israel through the Allenby Bridge with the whole bundle of cash that he hid away in his suitcase."

Doron scratched his cheek. "One sec, Jerry," he said. "I don't get what the problem is. If he's already in Israel, and if you know who you're talking about, what's the problem with grabbing him now and interrogating him?" The rest of the soldiers nodded in agreement.

Jerry took a sip of the water in front of him before responding. "Look, you ask a good question. The answer is complicated for two reasons: first, from what we know, the courier has already gone to the Bank of Palestine branch in Ramallah and deposited all the cash. So to catch him now would be like locking the stables after the horses have already escaped. It might be a deterrent for the future, but not particularly effective. Second, the fact that the Jordanian entered without being checked, and even managed to deposit the money, proves to him and those who sent him that we don't know about him at all, and that he isn't even on our radar."

"Is that good or bad?" Gidi asked.

"On the one hand, it's an intelligence failure on our part, so that's not good. But on the other hand, it's fantastic!" Jerry answered. "Because now we can follow the money and that will lead us to Abu Qassam, who doesn't suspect that we've discovered the money that was sent to him. Perhaps something good will come out of this. Now we have to stop the cash from getting to Abu Qassam and his gang. He doesn't know that we know about him, and that is our advantage at the moment," he said and finished his water in one gulp.

Yoav, who had been silent until now, thanked Jerry and pointed to the maps. "Guys," he began, "the point right now is as follows: the money is in the Bank of Palestine next to Manara Square in Ramallah. All of you know the area well. You've been there for dozens of undercover operations already and, as such, we can control the square with surveillance from the nearby mountain."

"Oh, wow, that's right. We were there just two or three months ago when we grabbed Abu Qassam's driver. By the way, right in front of the bank they have the best *k'nafe* in the West Bank, Abu Hamid," Barda said, and everybody smiled. Yoav also recalled the successful operation that got them one step closer to the master murderer.

"That's right, Barda," Yoav said. "We were there not long ago, and that indeed is a big advantage, because we don't need to familiarize ourselves with a whole new area. But there is a new detail that we received from Jerry. Jerry, if you would, the stage is yours," he said and gestured with his hand in Jerry's direction.

"Indeed," Jerry continued. "There is an additional detail that I wish to expand upon for the next few minutes. Look, unsurprisingly, we discovered that the way Fatah operates in the West Bank is riddled with corruption. I mean with money that goes to the heads of the organization, sometimes even by opening bank accounts in Europe under these false names or shell companies. In light of this and in an unusual step, the Fatah commander in Jordan has decided that all cash will be deposited in Abu Qassam's name exclusively, and not like they had been doing this whole time. I can tell you that from the interrogations we have conducted on the terrorists we've taken into custody until now, Abu Qassam is very strict about this, and doesn't allow any money to leak outside. The information from this morning indicates that the money was deposited into a safe deposit box in the name of Abu Qassam – and therefore he is the only one who can physically withdraw the money from it."

"So," asked Udi, "all that's left for us to do is wait for Abu Qassam in front of the bank? That's it?"

"If only that were the situation," Jerry replied. "The concern we have is that somebody from the bank will allow somebody else to withdraw the money, and take it to the organization's headquarters in Ramallah, and we'll be screwed again. And here is the second reason that the situation works in our favor: you see, Abu Qassam and his friends don't know that we know about this deposit. And so we can perhaps follow the money until it gets to Abu Qassam himself. There's a reasonable chance that once Abu Qassam got confirmation about the large amount of cash awaiting him in the Bank of Palestine in Ramallah, he'd jump over there for a quick visit. And here is where we enter the picture – here, we need your ideas, that is, what should we do and how should we do it?"

The room went quiet. The sun was just setting and the red-orange light disappeared as if it never was. The hum of the bright fluorescent lights was monotonous. Everybody in the room looked at the aerial photographs that the intelligence officer spread out on the broad wooden table in the unit commander's chambers. Nobody spoke, and each soldier withdrew into his own thoughts.

The senior commanders, Yoav and the intelligence officer didn't disturb the silence. They knew that this was the most important part of the meeting. Yoav knew that the soldiers sitting in front of him had among them hundreds of hours of complicated operations under their belts, along with successful ideas on how to formulate an attack, and therefore they stayed quiet.

Dan, the team leader, was the first to breach the silence. "Wait, I don't understand something. If the most critical part right now is stopping the money from reaching Abu Qassam, then why don't we just walk into the bank and confiscate it?" he asked Jerry and Yoav.

Jerry volunteered an answer. "We thought about that, and unfortunately, we can't. Our legal department checked, and it turns out that for historical reasons and others, the Bank of Palestine in Ramallah is also used indirectly as an extension of the Muslim *Waqf*[29] here. In other words, according to the legal definition, the bank is like an embassy or consulate – that is, it's sovereign territory and any infringement upon it will get us in trouble internationally. Exactly like not being able to stop a convoy of diplomats and search their vehicles, despite information that they are delivering something to our enemies."

Yoav looked at Dan and added, "Dan, forget about it. We checked – it's illegal for the army to do something like this. As it is, our situation internationally is tenuous, to say the least. The idea of going in with the army and opening the safe would never pass the cabinet. And just think of how it would look in the press... IDF soldiers break into the Bank of Palestine and rob it. Forget about it."

Yaki stretched back in his chair, crossed his hands on his chest and continued. "The Arabs have a saying that I really like: if Muhammad won't come to the mountain, then the mountain must

---

29. A Waqf is an endowment specifically meant for religious purposes.

come to Muhammad. Yoav, who said that the army is going in? You hear me say the army is going in? Of course not. I'm just saying that there are bank robberies in the West Bank... it's something that happens all over the world. So why can't we go in undercover and rob the bank, including Abu Qassam's money?"

The room went silent. The idea began to percolate, and within a few seconds, everybody in the room began talking among themselves, and the noise grew louder. Gidi lightly slapped the table a few times and asked for permission to speak.

"Barbie – you're a genius, dude. I know that this sounds crazy, but think about it for a second: armed gangs in the West Bank that rob individuals, stores, and even money-changers and couriers is nothing new. What's wrong with going into the bank undercover and robbing Abu Qassam's safety deposit box? Guys, I'm completely serious. Who would think that the IDF was up to this and not some local gang?" The noise in the room renewed.

Jerry whispered something into Yoav's ear, and Yoav raised his voice over the din. "Guys, you've thrown out an original idea here, and it looks like it's worth checking out. We need to check it out legally with the relevant parties, and also operationally. Of course, there's no need to mention that what was said in this room stays in this room. Go back to your rooms in the meantime. Dan, Yogev and Yariv – stay here please for another moment with me." Yoav said to the Three Musketeers. "You're also dismissed," Yoav said to the intelligence officer, and adjourned the meeting.

The rest of the soldiers left the room and only Jerry, Yoav and the Three Musketeers remained. "Incredible team you've got," Jerry said to Dan as he closed the door behind them. "I don't think that the other soldiers suspected anything, and I didn't see that anybody suspected that we already know each other. By the way, the idea to rob the bank is excellent. I'll do what I can to get it authorized by the general and the relevant parties in the defense ministry. You three will spearhead the operation, and so we'll be able to take the money transferred to Abu Qassam and perhaps also finally get close enough to him to try the toxin that Dr. Yakobovitch developed."

"But how do you intend to integrate poisoning him with the rest of the operation? Take into account that the window of opportunity is very small this time. It may be that Abu Qassam is already on his way to the bank as we speak," Yoav said to Jerry.

Jerry got up from his chair and started pacing back and forth the length of the table. His hands were crossed over his chest and his pursed lips indicated that he was deep in thought on a quick solution to the situation.

"Listen, Yoav," he finally said, "first thing we have to do is buy time, so there won't be a situation where Abu Qassam succeeds in withdrawing that money before we rob it. I'm asking you – call the division commander and ask him to get a border police force to set up regular checkpoints in the central Ramallah area, with an emphasis on Manara Square. I assume that this won't be too rare a sight in the area, and therefore it won't raise suspicion. What it will do, is prevent Abu Qassam or his partners from getting near the bank in the immediate future. That's how we'll gain precious time – until we get our final plan together. At the same time, I'll call the toxicology lab that we took a tour of together and request that they send me the special toxin immediately, and that Dr. Yakobovitch personally give the three of you a crash course about it. About Abu Qassam and how to administer the toxin – I have an idea, but I need to check it out with our sources in the field. But the general direction of the bank robbery by an undercover force looks like it will work. Let us make a few phone calls and we'll let you know," Jerry said, and shook everybody's hand and quickly walked out of the room.

Yoav got out of his chair and patted Dan on the shoulder. "Excellent idea, guys. Seriously, well done," he said and looked at them, full of appreciation. "But we can't get complacent. The fact that you were able to get out in one piece from that business in City Hall in Bethlehem and didn't get burned is excellent, but I can't promise that the bank will be an easier target. In the meantime, head back to your rooms and prepare the guys for the operation. Organize into teams, communication equipment, divide up into pairs and everything we need to do, and start studying routes to the bank and alternative routes to get out."

The three parted ways with Yoav with a nod and quickly ran to their team members in the soldiers' living area.

CHAPTER 12
Two days later, Bank of Palestine, Manara Square, Ramallah

It was early. The sun's warm rays kissed the drops of dew on the trees and bushes, turning them to mist upon contact. A flock of black birds flew from the structure above the square, and the sound of the drivers honking announced the beginning of another work day.

Inside the bank, the clerks were getting ready for work. Some of them prepared their first coffee of the morning in the small kitchen in the back part of the bank, others were finishing up reading the headlines in the newspaper, which had been placed on their desks. The buzz of the copy machines coming to life bore witness to the fact that everything was ready for the front doors to open, and to begin receiving customers.

When it was time, the bank manager, Dr. Aziz Haidar, signaled to one of his clerks, who then quickly went to the heavy front door, turned the key in the lock, and threw it wide open. A burst of light rushed in through the streets and into the bank, which was mostly lit by a chandelier that flooded the dark marble floor with light.

Dozens of people streamed into the bank: some of them were businessmen who arrived to sign various documents, others were elderly folk who came to withdraw their social security payments, and others who came to pay bills. None of them paid any attention to the hunched old woman in the wheel chair being pushed by two young men.

The three of them stood in line and waited patiently for a teller. When their turn came, the teller signaled for them to come to a small window with bars on it. The two young men, Yogev and Dan, pushed the wheelchair, which Yariv was sitting in, up to the window.

"*Sabah al-her,*"[30] Yogev said, blessing the teller with a big smile.

"*Sabah a-nur,*"[31] the teller said in response from behind the counter. "How can I help you?"

"Our mother inherited a large amount of money recently, and we are thinking of depositing it here at your bank."

The clerk's eyes lit up. "How much are we talking about, if I may ask?" the teller asked in a low voice.

"A lot. Close to a million and a half dinars,"[32] Yogev whispered to him.

"Indeed, a sizeable sum," the teller answered him, also in a whisper. "According to our bank's directives, any amount above a half-a million dinars requires you to meet personally with the manager, Dr. Haidar, to ensure that you get the most professional, personal service the bank has to offer. One moment, I'll check if the manager is available," he said and left the counter and walked quickly to the rear area of the bank.

---

30. Good morning.
31. Traditional response to "sabah al-her" that also means "good morning."
32. Jordanian currency that is still in common use today in the West Bank.

Dan looked at Yogev and said in a quiet voice, "Yogi, I told you that the intelligence officer is the man. He knows everything about this bank."

After a brief wait, the clerk returned, straightened his tie and said with a big smile, "Dr. Haidar would be happy to see you now in his chambers. Please follow me." He pressed a button on his desk and there was a "buzz," and then the door separating the customer area from that of the employees opened. Dan and Yogev, both pushing the wheelchair, followed the clerk to the manager's office.

Right then, a young couple, who looked as if they were married, entered the bank: the girl, who stood up straight and was rather tall, wore tight black jeans, a light-blue shirt and a green head scarf. Her light eyes sparkled through the transparent veil. She held her husband's hand; he was muscular and wore a black shirt and leather jacket. The young man was carrying a bag with various pockets. The young couple didn't arouse the suspicions of the security guard at the entrance, who smiled awkwardly at the young girl's open displays of affection toward her husband. He had seen many liberal couples like this in secular, vibrant Ramallah. The couple took a number and waited for their turn. It was Yaki and Doron. The two of them situated themselves in the lobby, standing in the middle of the entryway and waited on the agreed upon signal from the other three.

* * *

Meanwhile, the bank manager emerged from his opulent chambers and approached the two young men and the old woman in the wheelchair. Dr. Haidar was an impressive man – silver hair, full-bodied, and a head taller than his clerk – and he received them gladly.

"*A-salam aleikum*, welcome!" he said, and motioned for them to enter his elegant chambers. "I understand that your mother has inherited some money," the manager said, getting right to the point. "We'd be happy if she decided to deposit it in our bank, and give us the privilege of serving you," the bank manager said in his deep voice.

Yogev first turned to Yariv, who was dressed up as the old woman in the wheelchair sitting next to him, placed his hand softly on his shoulder and asked, "Momma, what do you think? I think this will work for you."

Yariv, who was sitting on the wheelchair and wearing a traditional head covering that covered his mouth and nose, coughed lightly, as the elderly are prone to do, and asked Yogev, her "son," in a high-pitched, raspy voice, "And what if they rob the bank, son? Banks get robbed all the time... that doesn't sit well with me..." he said in a shaky, female voice.

Dan also threw some gas on the fire, saying, "Momma's right, I'm telling you, this is a bad idea. This bank is a dangerous place these days... it's better to just buy her a piece of land and be done with it."

"Gentlemen, why are you talking about a bank robbery?" the manager shouted, afraid that the opportunity for such a large deposit was slipping through his fingers. "Come, I'll show you our vault. It's got the highest level of security available in Ramallah."

"You mean that we can see the vault right now? Because we're actually in a bit of a hurry – my mother has a doctor's appointment in an hour with her cardiologist in Al-Bireh," Yogev said innocently.

"Right now, but just one moment, if you would. I have to get the security guard to come with us on any tour of the vault, as per regulations. I'll call him now," said the manager, and dialed a number from the phone on his desk. A quick ring was followed by the buzzing sound of being disconnected. The manager tried again – nothing. Dr. Haidar smiled awkwardly. "Uh, excuse me please ma'am, gentlemen, but we've been having technical issues this morning. Our phone lines are down, I've already sent somebody to check it out, but apparently they're still down…"

What the manager didn't know was that all communication lines to the building were cut off a few minutes ago by two more undercover operatives from Team 10. The purpose was, of course, to allow the team in the bank to work without any interruptions from the outside.

"Pardon me for asking," Dan said innocently, "but are there cameras set up around the vault?"

"Heaven forbid!" the manager answered. "Privacy and discretion for our clients are at the top of our priorities here at the bank. The entire bank is wired with security cameras – except for the vault." And then he turned to the old woman in the wheelchair, smiled, and said, "Ma'am, nobody will know how much money you deposit in the vault, or what's in it. Everything is completely secret and discreet."

The manager tried calling the security guard again and again, but the phone still wasn't working. The three soldiers waited patiently until Yogev signaled to Yariv with his leg.

"If now isn't a good time, we can always come back later…" the old woman said to the bank manager in a soft voice. That was the straw that broke the camel's back.

"No, no, of course not," said the manager. "Come, forget about the guard, I'll give you a tour of the vault area."

The manager, Dr. Haidar, got up and led his guests to the area where the vault was. The two walked slowly behind him while pushing the wheelchair. The vault room was in the back of the bank where it was quiet. The entrance was framed by a heavy, brown wooden door with two locks and next to it a keypad for entering the access code. The bank manager entered the code. A short buzz sounded, and then the manager took a large keyring from his pocket and opened the door, which turned slowly on its hinge with a creak, and behind it was a long, lit corridor, and inside it were hundreds of rectangular safety deposit boxes from the floor to the ceiling. The manager took a few steps into the corridor and waited for them in the center of the room.

Dan pushed Yariv in the wheelchair. After a couple seconds, Yogev also entered. As he entered the corridor, Dan slowed down in order to allow Yariv to prop the door open while Yogev, the last to enter, took a cubed chunk of clay from his pocket and quickly jammed it into the notch of the doorframe. The door slammed shut behind them, but didn't lock.

Everything was ready to go: The manager was by himself in the vault area, the door was shut but not locked, the internal and external phone lines were disconnected, and Yariv was sitting on five pounds of specialized plastic explosives that were installed under the cushion of his wheelchair – explosives that were well hidden by the pillow he was sitting on.

The bank manager, Dr. Haidar, turned to the three of them and said, "As you can see, everything is secure. We have motion detectors and intrusion sensors, smoke detectors in case of a fire, all the safe deposit boxes are protected from being broken into and, of course, our private security force conducts patrols in the bank area and are connected to the police dispatch. In case of any suspicion, even the slightest bit, we won't hesitate to involve the Ramallah police. Ma'am, your money is safe here."

The three of them looked around in all directions and saw the various sensors that the bank manager spoke of. The intelligence report that Jerry gave the soldiers indicated that Abu Qassam's safety deposit box was number 367. The three of them quickly located it – it was one of the last ones on the upper left side of the corridor. According to the intel they received from Jerry from his source at the bank, the security patrol and police would arrive between seven and ten minutes from the time any distress call went out.

The safety deposit boxes required using two keys together to open them – one held by the bank manager, the other by the client. The source provided photographs of the vault room and of the safety deposit boxes themselves. In the decryption division of the Shin-Bet, the safety deposit boxes were identified as French-made and very common in banks all over the world. They didn't have a time delay, but there was a complicated double mechanism inside, which required a great deal of force to break the cylinder. In the Shin-Bet laboratories where numerous trials to break into the boxes were conducted, they found that drilling into the front of the box and removing the door was problematic due to the relatively small dimensions of the box. Therefore, they decided to use plastic explosives.

Dan looked at his watch and sneezed. That was the sign: it's time. Yogev quickly closed the distance between him and the bank manager and delivered a powerful, accurate punch to the middle of the manager's diaphragm. A blow like that, as they were taught in the course on counter-terrorism, would knock the wind out of the victim for a few seconds. The manager indeed was surprised, fell back against the wall behind him, and collapsed onto the dark marble floor gasping for breath. Yogev didn't let up. He was on the manager immediately and put him in a choke hold for many seconds until the manager passed out and lost consciousness. Yogev knew that he had only two or three minutes before the manager woke up.

While Yogev was taking care of the manager, Yariv locked his wheelchair, stood up, grabbed the pillow he'd been sitting on, exposing the strips of plastic explosives. Dan delicately peeled the strips of explosives from underneath the chair, held them up carefully in the air, and affixed them to deposit box number 367. Then, he took the last strip from the chair, molded it into two circles about an inch wide and put them over both locks on the safety deposit box. He pressed the explosives as hard as he could into the keyholes until they were all the way in.

In complete silence, Dan signaled to Yogev to give him the detonators. Yogev put his hand into his pants' pocket, took them out and carefully handed them to Dan. Yariv looked on from the side while keeping an eye on the unconscious bank manager. Dan quickly shoved the two detonators into both sides of plastic explosives that framed the safety deposit box. Everything was ready to blow the box open, but right then the manager began to wake up. Yariv, who saw that the manager was coming to, dove into the floral handbag as part of his old lady disguise and pulled out a bottle of ether. He took a thick rag from his pocket, doused it quickly with ether, and leaned over Dr. Aziz Haidar, who was stirring. The manager partially opened his eyes, took a deep breath, and looked like he was about to scream – but Yariv was immediately on him, pushing the ether-soaked rag over his mouth and nose. The manager tried to fight off the young soldier, and even managed to scratch Yariv's arm in a few places, but in vain. Yariv didn't let up, and soon the manager was unconscious again and sank like a stone onto the cold floor.

"Let's go, Kermit, he's out. We have ten minutes at the most. Blow that thing and let's get out of here," Yariv whispered to Dan, who had just finished connecting the detonators.

He signaled to Yogev and Yariv, and the two of them quietly picked up the unconscious bank manager and moved him all the way back to the vault's closed door at the end of the corridor. Dan knew that the moment he activated the detonators, he had only a few seconds to get clear of the blast area, and also knew that the biggest problem was going to be the noise of the explosion. In the course on sabotage, the soldiers learned that the smaller the space where the explosion takes place, the louder the noise and the bigger the shockwave.

According to the bank's blueprints, which the unit's

intelligence department got with the help of Shin-Bet sources, the narrow corridor would act as a blast area for the controlled explosion. Therefore, the plan was to detonate the explosives only after the soldiers had cleared as far away as possible from Abu Qassem's safe, and it was better if they left the corridor entirely and waited outside the door.

Yogev dug around in the bag and pulled out a black plastic bottle. The bottle looked like a regular water bottle, but it contained a liquid chemical compound that immediately ignites upon exposure to fire. The bottle's covering was made of a special polymer, resistant to fire and heat of up to 400 degrees Fahrenheit. Yogev handed the bottle to Dan, who in the meantime had taken a silver Zippo lighter out of his pocket. Dan signaled to the other two to be ready, and then lit the lighter. The small flame flickered slightly, and Dan brought it up to the bottle's opening and waited. After a few seconds, the fumes from the bottle's opening ignited and a large orange flame shot out from it. Dan recoiled for a moment from the force of the flame, but immediately steadied himself and brought the flame toward the smoke alarm on the ceiling. The smoke and the flame coming out of the bottle encircled the smoke alarm, which immediately sounded an alarm that wailed throughout the entire bank, while also triggering the sprinklers that automatically began spraying water.

Multiple sprinklers burst from the ceiling in order to extinguish the fire that was detected. Yariv, who was pressed against the door, opened it just enough to get a narrow view outside into the middle of the bank. In the main area of the bank, there was big commotion – the alarms were going off loudly, the sprinkler system over there went off as well, and everybody went scrambling toward the front door, if not to escape any potential fire, at least to escape the water. The security guard was still standing at the front door trying to calm everybody down, saying "Ladies and gentlemen, please, no pushing, please exit in a calm, organized way, everything's under control," but the crowd just rushed to the exits, almost trampling him in the process.

Yariv signaled to Yogev, and they picked up the unconscious bank manager and laid him outside the vault. They stayed with him there while Dan connected the detonator to Abu Qassem's safety deposit box, carefully unrolled the detonating wire toward the door, pushed Yariv's wheelchair out of the room, and also exited the corridor. His hair and clothes were completely drenched from the sprinklers. The sound of the alarms was deafening, and the noise of people fleeing outside no less so: screaming, pushing, the sound of chairs being knocked over by people trying to get out, the sound of the sprinklers overhead – this was all supposed to create enough noise to cover up the sound of the explosion they were about to set off in the vault.

"Yogi," Dan said to Yariv, "where are Barbie and Tyson? Can you see them?"

Yogev turned to look in the direction of the main part of the bank, and suddenly saw a young couple throw a couple of shock grenades under one of the bank teller's tables. Three seconds later, two loud blasts resonated throughout the bank, startling everybody. One of the bank's windows broke, shattering into pieces with a loud noise, which only increased the hysteria among the bank's clientele, still fleeing as if their lives depended on it.

There was a logjam of people at the bank's exit, like a long bottle neck, which only added to the panic. From afar, sirens from the police and fire department could be heard. Yaki took a few smoke grenades out of his bag that were disguised as presents with red bows on the box, and set them off, throwing them in different directions. The first two he threw toward the main door of the bank, and the others he thew into the interior of the bank. The smoke quickly began billowing out of the grenade canisters, filling the bank with smoke from multiple locations – and the uproar increased. The smoke caused many of those present to cough. One man even tried shattering one of the windows by throwing a chair at it, but it was an awkward throw and the chair only cracked the window slightly before falling harmlessly to the floor. The man, apparently expecting the window to shatter dramatically, was at a momentary loss for what to do before he finally made his way to the exit like everybody else. The security guard, who felt like he was choking, left his post and darted outside.

Yaki pulled a packet of explosives from his bag. He fitted them with a few time delays and placed them under one of the desks belonging to a teller who had fled outside. He set the timer and walked away from the table. That would ensure a number of strong blasts every few seconds, which would further fuel the chaos in the bank.

Yaki and Yogev made eye contact with one another. Yogev signaled to him with his hand for them to come over to him. The two of them, Yaki and Doron, ran quickly toward the corridor of the vault.

"Barbie," Yogev said to Yaki while pointing at Dr. Haidar, who was lying at his feet, "this is the bank manager. Take him outside. He should wake up any minute now from the ether. Schumacher is waiting for you in the yellow Mercedes outside."

Doron nodded affirmatively. He and Yaki bent down and picked up the hazy Dr. Haidar, stood him up on his feet and made their way with him toward the bank's exit. The massive commotion and noise helped them get out unhindered.

* * *

The noise only got louder, and the alarms were still going off. Yariv remembered from the intelligence briefing given to them by the intelligence officer that the alarms had a time limit on them. He was worried that the time was almost up.

Yariv looked at Dan and said, "Now!"

Dan nodded, pressed the detonator connected to the plastic explosives, and the three of them pressed up against the outer wall outside the vault. The blast was powerful, with the shockwave reaching all the way to the wall that they were standing against, but it was barely audible – even overwhelmed – by the noise coming from inside the bank itself and the street. The brown, wooden door absorbed most of the recoil from blowing up the deposit box and one of its hinges was bent, making it hard to open the door.

"Newton, help me out here," Dan said to Yariv, and both of them opened the damaged door as wide as they could.

The three of them went inside and surveyed the result of their explosion: the safety deposit box had been blasted open, as well as those from several others that were adjacent to it. The air in the corridor was full of dust and there were documents and papers flying all over. There was a strong, burnt smell in the air, and darkness engulfed the room, the lights having been broken from the force of the blast.

Dan took a small but powerful flashlight out of his pocket and shined it inside Abu Qassem's safe deposit box. Inside the box they could make out many brown envelopes that were stacked one on top of the other. Some of the envelopes were thrown to the floor from the recoil of the blast, but most were still inside the safe deposit box.

Yogev reached into the deposit box, pulled out one of the envelopes and opened it. Inside were bundles of hundred dollar bills. He opened another envelope – same thing.

"Bingo!" Yogev smiled and showed the rest of the team what he'd found.

"Excellent, let's get everything loaded up and get out of here before the police arrive," Yariv said and started filling up his floral patterned bag with brown envelopes.

Yogev and Yariv quickly emptied the box of its contents while

Dan kept an eye on the crooked wooden door, making sure nobody surprised them while they were in there. After they finished emptying the box and putting it all in the flowery bag, Yariv got back in the wheelchair, placed the bag with the money in his lap, covered his face with his scarf, and waited outside the wooden door for Yogev to push him toward the exit. The deafening noise continued and people were still screaming, water was still pouring from the ceiling and the smell of the suffocating smoke had yet to subside.

"Just a second, wait a sec," Dan signaled to them.

He went back to the corridor, pulled out his small pistol that was fitted with a silencer, which was strapped to his ankle, and fired off a few rounds into other deposit boxes so that it would give the impression that other boxes were targeted also, and not just that of Abu Qassem. He scattered a bunch of documents all around, which flew all over the corridor. Dan finished and went out to Yogev and Yariv. Right then, two Ramallah police officers entered the bank, guns drawn.

"Police! Nobody move!" They shouted toward the rest of the people present, who immediately did as they were told.

Yogev stopped where he was and raised his hands in the air, but Dan kept slowly pushing the wheelchair toward the police officers, with Yariv in the wheelchair, and the bag with the money on him.

"Are you deaf? I said don't move!" the police officer yelled in their direction while aiming his gun at the two of them.

"Officer, sir, my mother is old and has lung disease, and she must get out to the fresh air immediately. If not, she'll faint," Dan answered him in the local dialect.

Yariv, the old woman, began coughing and making gurgling noises, and rolling his eyes back in his head.

The police officer frowned in anger. "We have strict orders not to let anybody out of the building without an interrogation," he said authoritatively. "Everybody stays put until the station manager and his team arrive."

Suddenly, the officer saw a puddle of urine, which began slowly forming underneath the wheelchair.

"What's going on?" The stunned officer yelled at Yariv, who was sitting in the wheelchair.

"She's unconscious and has lost control of her bodily functions. It happens to her all the time. She'll shit herself in a moment or two, now. Please, let us go!" Yogev begged the officer, his voice cracking for effect.

The officer looked around. "Fine, go, but quickly," the officer agreed, whose pity was aroused by the appearance of the sick old woman.

Yogev put his hands down slowly, "Thank you, Mr. Police Officer, sir," he said to the officer. "May Allah lengthen your days, and make them pleasant," Dan added and helped Yogev push the wheelchair toward the bank's exit.

"There you go, ma'am," the officer said, lowering his gun and stepping aside. "Be well," he said, and let the three of them pass.

The three soldiers continued on their way toward the bank's exit until they were outside. The bright sun blinded them, but they could still see the police units and firefighters arriving at the bank, closing in on it from all directions. The bag of urine, which Yariv had strapped to his inner thigh, was almost completely empty. That trick also worked.

Dan surveyed the square. Tons of people started walking toward the bank, fascinated by what was happening. People were gathering around the entryway to the bank and the crowd was large. Honking cars and people screaming and pushing congested the area. Dan signaled to Yogev and the two of them started pushing the wheelchair toward Manara Square, heading away from the bank.

From a distance, the three of them spotted Schumacher's

yellow Mercedes. This time, the car had the appearance of a local taxi. Yaki, Doron, and the bank manager, who was still unconscious, were already sitting in the car. Yogev raised his hand as if trying to hail a cab, and Udi saw him, flashed his high beams, and slowly drove toward them, stopping next to them. Its back windows were tinted. There were stickers with big eagles on the doors, on the dashboard was red carpeting with various geometric figures on it, and two turquoise-colored fuzzy dice were hanging from the rear-view mirror.

"*Ya sahbi*,[33] where do you need to go?" he asked in Arabic.

"Al-Bireh," Yogev answered loudly, in order to make sure those in the immediate vicinity heard him.

"No problem, hop in, sir," Udi said and got out in order to help Dan and Yariv put the disabled old woman into the car. Yariv held on strongly to the floral bag, and the two of them lifted him gently into the car. Udi then folded up the wheelchair and placed it in the trunk. Udi saw the unconscious bank manager in the back seat, Doron's hand on the hostages drooping head.

Udi saw that the Ramallah fire department was preparing to enter the Bank of Palestine, which still had thick smoke coming out of the exit. People were still streaming out of the building, covering their faces with articles of clothing to avoid smoke inhalation. The alarms were still going off at a deafening decibel level, but nobody seemed to notice the taxi waiting on the side of the road just three-hundred yards from the bank's entrance.

Once everybody was in the car, Udi closed all the windows that were open and locked the doors from inside. Right then, Dan pressed a button on his concealed radio and said, "Cheetah, this is Kermit. We're heading out, we've got the greenbacks."

Back at the mission control center, in an isolated room in the

---

33. My friend.

regional brigade building, Yoav broke out into a wide grin and winked at Jerry, who was standing next to him.

"Unbelievable. Those bastards did it again."

The communication device, which had been concealed on the floor of the car next to Dan's left leg, crackled for a moment, and then everybody in the car heard Yoav's voice. "Kermit, this is Cheetah. Nice job, but wait in the field, because there's a chance that the saint will arrive shortly."

The soldiers in the car were tense with anticipation. They all understood the implication: perhaps Marwan Abu Qassem, the arch terrorist, would hear about what happened at the bank as it had already been making waves on the local news in the Ramallah area, and come to make sure that his safety deposit box was intact and not damaged in the fire.

Besides the Three Musketeers, none of the other members of the team knew that Dan was carrying the special toxin that Dr. Yakobovitch had prepared. Jerry's directive was clear: the bank robbery needed to be carried out while making it appear as if there was a fire – and then to wait for Abu Qassem to catch wind of it. It seemed reasonable to assume that, in such a case, Abu Qassem would rush to the bank personally in order to see for himself that his safety deposit box was secure. Considering that he was the only one authorized to open the safety deposit box registered in his name, the senior terrorist would be forced to come to the bank personally. Therefore, Jerry planned for the three of them to take the toxin with them and if Abu Qassem indeed arrived, they would initiate contact with him and administer the toxin.

Dan didn't want to take the chance that somebody would see them administering the classified toxin. He turned to Udi and said, "Schumacher, listen to me: there are a lot of us here and we've been here too long, plus the money is in the car with us. That's not good. We have to get out of here before they get wise to what we did. So what we're going to do now is as follows: Yogev and I are getting out, and we'll stay in the field and wait for Abu Qassem. You continue on just like we planned. We'll either walk to you or take a bus. Be in radio contact with Bull and Hose and tell them to start heading in the direction of the bank. I have to have more firepower in case things go sideways. You got it?" he asked Udi.

The driver nodded affirmatively.

Then Dan turned to Yariv and said, "Newton, from now on, you're in command. Just make sure that the manager doesn't wake up by mistake and see your ugly mugs. He's supposed to get home safe and sound. *Yalla, salamat*,"[34] he said and got out of the cab.

Yogev rolled up his pant cuff and strapped his gun into his ankle holster, and then he got out and the two of them walked on the sidewalk toward the bank.

Udi then pressed a button underneath the steering wheel and said, "Hose, it's Schumacher. Head toward the party. Kermit is waiting for you there."

Gidi, the leader of the pair, heard the directive in his earpiece. He and Barda had already arrived in the field a few hours earlier. Udi drove them to the central bus station in Al-Bireh, and from there, they took another bus to Manara Square. The two soldiers hung out at a small coffee shop near the square while their friends caused the ruckus at the bank. Gidi and Barda could see the entrance to the bank from the coffee shop, and the plan was that they would join Dan and Yogev in order to help them take out Abu Qassem, as well as serve as extra firepower if things got messy. Of course, neither of them knew about the secret plan to poison him. Gidi asked for the bill, paid, thanked the waiter and then the two of them headed to the bank.

Since the coffee shop was full of people, Gidi was hesitant to answer Udi. In order to affirm that he got the message, he pressed the "transmit" button a few times. The button was hidden in his

---

34. All right, bye.

sleeve, with the communication device taped to his chest. Gidi clicked according to a predetermined code – three sets of two clicks each.

After receiving authorization from Gidi, Udi made a U-turn and headed toward the south exit of the city, in the opposite direction from all of the police units and fire trucks that were rapidly converging on Manara Square and the bank. The roads were completely empty. The taxi – and in it the bag with the money, as well as the bank manager, who was just beginning to come out of his temporary state of unconsciousness – headed quickly south. Doron, who had the bank manager slumped against him, noticed that Dr. Haidar's head was moving and said to Yariv, "Newton, he's waking up. We have to get to the pickup location now."

Yariv understood the severe implication of the ether wearing off: the unit doctor, Dr. Tomer, underscored to the soldiers that everybody reacts differently to the effects of the ether. There are those who pass out for half an hour or more, and there are others who wake up in less than fifteen minutes. The bank manager was apparently in the latter category. He explained to them that they couldn't just keep knocking him out repeatedly with ether without a doctor who is an expert in the field present. Dr. Tomer explained that additional unconsciousness requires that the patient be supplied with oxygen, and if he is repeatedly knocked out – without a medical physician monitoring the situation – the subject could suffer irreversible brain damage, and in extreme cases, even death. Therefore, the directive was clear: they were to render the bank manager unconscious just once, and after that, they had to neutralize him by some other means.

"Barbie, give me the kit," Doron said to Yaki.

Yaki fished around in the side compartment that was specially built for the car. He took out some zip ties, long flannel strips, and a black cloth sack, which he gave to Doron. Doron took the flannel strips and gagged the bank manager, who was waking up, attaching them tightly to the base of his skull. He bound Dr. Haidar's hands behind his back and then put the black sack cloth over his head. Udi continued driving quickly south.

In the meantime, the chaos only increased around the Bank of Palestine: hundreds of curious onlookers descended onto the street nearest the bank, with the fire trucks and patrol cars racing toward Manara Square. The smoke billowing from the entrance grew thicker, the noise of the screams mingled with the various alarms and sirens, and patrol officers stood with megaphones shouting instructions to the people present, as well as those still inside the bank. Many customers who heard on Radio Ramallah about the fire at the bank tried to get close to the area. The barriers put in place by the police at the entrance to the bank didn't help them maintain order. The people on the street began pushing and moving them, because the rumor on the street was that the bank's vault was damaged in the fire, including the cash and jewelry inside. The smoke and the explosions that were heard inside the bank did the trick: many people were afraid there would be looting, and so they hurried to Manara Square to make sure their money was safe. Shouting could be heard from all directions and everybody was in an uproar.

Dan and Yogev waited until the taxi left and then scanned the many coffee shops scattered around Marara Square. They were looking for the other two, Gidi and Barda. Yogev was the first to spot them walking in their direction from the east, and he signaled to Dan. Dan also got a bead on the two and made eye contact. Gidi scratched his head vigorously, signaling to Dan and Yogev that everything was fine and to continue with the operation.

* * *

During the briefing by the intelligence officer prior to the operation, it was explained to the soldiers that the Shin-Bet field agent would see to it personally that Abu Qassem knew about the bank fire. The working assumption was that Abu Qassem, the only one who knows what's in his safe deposit box, would come out of hiding and rush to the bank. When the commanding general approved the plan, there wasn't a clear indication as to which route Abu Qassem would take to the bank. It depended on a few things that the Shin-Bet had no control over. Therefore, they decided that the two pairs of soldiers would wait for Abu Qassem near the bank: one pair would cover the eastern part of the square, and the other would situate themselves to cover the western part. As unit commander, Yoav didn't want to put any more undercover operatives in the field out of fear that somebody would be discovered. After all, there would be a massive amount of local security personnel. And so they decided that only one pair would carry out the assassination, and the second pair would provide backup in case something went wrong, requiring them needing help getting out of there.

While planning Abu Qassem's assassination, the soldiers ran up against a serious problem: on the one hand, they couldn't use a sniper to shoot him from a distance because of all the civilians milling around the bank area. That meant they had to shoot him from up close. The soldiers had carried out shootings at close range in the past, but in this case, the place was crawling with police and security personnel. Getting out of a situation like that unscathed was no simple feat. So they thought about the possibility of intercepting Abu Qassem's car on the way to or from the bank, but there was a problem with this also, seeing as how they didn't know where he was hiding out – was he coming by car, or by foot?

Planting an explosive device in his car also wouldn't work, because of the possibility that he wouldn't be the only person in the car, and that there might be innocent civilians with him. Abu Qassem was known to be very careful and extremely suspicious, and he surrounded himself with assistants and security guards to protect himself. That's why a plan to kidnap him was also scrapped.

Therefore, the unit commander decided that Dan and Yogev would try to identify Abu Qassem when he got near the bank, verify from up close that it is indeed him, and then close the distance while determining whether it's possible to shoot him at close range using a silencer. If not, then they would call off the attempt, update headquarters using the radio and a predetermined code, and leave the job to the backup forces, who would try trapping him while he left the bank. This was the official summary given, so that the rest of the forces could join the briefing.

But there was also a secret arrangement that only Yoav, Jerry, and the Three Musketeers were privy to: this was a golden opportunity to take out Abu Qassem using Dr. Yakobovitch's toxin. The idea behind the operation was to bring the toxin into physical contact with Abu Qassem without him realizing anything out of the ordinary. Abu Qassem would continue on with his day, but would die from the effects of the toxin within a short period of time. The toxin would have to be administered in a way that didn't arouse the suspicions of Abu Qassem or those around him. Dr. Yakobovitch and his team in the lab put a lot of time and resources into creating this specific toxin that would be used to kill Abu Qassem, but would leave no incriminating evidence behind.

Everything was ready to go: Gidi and Barda were within a few seconds' running distance from the bank's steps, while Dan and Yogev were already in the crowd of people standing at the entrance to the bank shouting. The police were trying to push back the waves of people as the alarms and sirens wailed overhead and the series of timed blasts that Yaki arranged inside the bank were still going off, the thick smoke still funneling out the bank's windows. The local news had already arrived at the bank and was reporting on the situation while, at the same time, the fire department had organized itself at the entrance to deal with the apparent fire.

Suddenly, the sound of screeching brakes could be heard in the distance. Everybody in Manara Square turned their heads to see what that was all about. A white Peugeot was racing toward the bank when it suddenly slammed on the brakes while turning, leaving skid marks on the road. Two armed men holding AK-47s got out of the car. One of the brawny individuals opened the back door, and another man got out. The third man was tall, muscular, and wearing a tight, black polo shirt. He face was covered in stubble, and he held a gun in his right hand. Yogev recognized him immediately – it was Marwan Abu Qassem.

The three armed men headed toward the steps leading to the bank, pushing aside anybody standing in their way. One of the people they pushed aside started to say something, but Abu Qassem stuck his gun in the man's face which convinced him to keep his mouth shut and let it go.

Dan took a pair of clear plastic gloves out of his right pocket and put them on. These weren't regular gloves – they were made of thin but very strong latex. In the finger pads of the right glove were short bristles, similar to those of a toothbrush. These bristles were made of a liquid absorbing substance, which would momentarily soak up the special liquid toxin. Next, Dan pulled out of his left pocket a hard, wide test tube that resembled a round can of shoe polish. He unscrewed the top of the test tube. Inside was a viscous, clear liquid that was like Jello. Dan dipped the fingertips of his right glove into the jelly-like liquid and waited a few seconds. The little bristles swelled as they absorbed the liquid. He then carefully put the lid back on and returned it to his pocket. Abu Qassem's entourage pushed their way to the bank's entrance. The appearance of drawn weapons caused the crowd to give the three armed terrorists a wide berth and a clear path into the bank, and after a few more yards, they reached the bank's steps. There was a bottleneck of dozens of people there – some were pushing, others shouting, and others were still coughing from the thick smoke, while others were just trying to get away from the pushing and the crowd. Abu Qassem didn't wait and pressed on, pushing people out of his way while trying to get inside the bank.

This was exactly what Dan was waiting for. He began making his way into the army of people amassed at the front door to the bank, and was about two yards from Abu Qassem. People were waving their hands in the air and shouting loudly at the police and ushers. The arch-terrorist's arms were also thrown into the air, his gun still gripped in his right hand. There was a lot of commotion, with people pushing against the barricades that the police set up in front of the bank.

Dan took two more steps toward the armed terrorist. His temples pulsated, and his heart was beating so hard he thought it was going to explode out of his chest. And then, right at that moment, he took the last step, closing the remaining distance between himself and Abu Qassem, and reached out with his right hand. He grazed Abu Qassem's left arm with his gloved right hand, pressing the toxin-filled bristles into the senior terrorist. He remained in this position for another second, to make sure that the toxin indeed made contact with Abu Qassem's skin while penetrating the top layer – and immediately let go.

The agitated terrorist felt the touch, stopped pushing and shouting and looked to his left, his gun still in his right hand. He looked Dan right in the eye. The experienced soldier knew that this was the moment of truth.

Abu Qassem opened his mouth and roared, "What are you doing touching me!? You want to die today!?" and pointed his gun at Dan's chest.

"Excuse me, ya sidi... but they are pushing me! All my money is in the bank, I'm sorry. Please, excuse me..." the soldier answered him, and then cast his eyes down at the ground.

From behind, Abu Qassem's two bodyguards were getting closer. One of them spit in Dan's face, and then pushed him back with the butt of his rifle. "Get the fuck out of here, you motherfucker!" he yelled at Dan. Yogev, who was standing about a yard behind him, tensed, fearing the bodyguard would simply shoot Dan.

But right at that moment, another blast came from the bank. It was the extra detonator that Yaki placed on a timer. The thunderous blast diverted Abu Qassem and his bodyguards' attention to the bank. Dan took the opportunity to fall back. The guard spit in his direction again and then turned his attention to the bank. Yogev and Dan got out of there quickly while Dan closed his fist tightly, to make sure the deadly toxin didn't come into contact with anybody else. After they had gotten clear of the large crowd that had amassed at the bank, Dan took his gloves off and carefully folded them inward, and then returned them to the special bag he kept in his pocket – a doubly thick plastic bag to prevent the toxin from leaking out.

* * *

Gidi and Barda were witnesses to what happened in front of the bank, but from a distance. They saw Abu Qassem's guard push Dan back with the butt of his rifle, but didn't notice the gloves or the toxin. From the moment they saw Yogev and Dan leave the area of the bank, they understood that it was time for them to leave as well. Doron asked for the check, paid, and the two of them left the coffee shop. Except in an emergency, the two teams were not supposed to join forces. The reason was simple: if a pair was exposed and somebody was tailing them, any other part of the undercover team they met up with would also be burned. The forces needed to maintain visual contact, but not be physically close, such that each team could continue on with the mission, yet be able to lend a hand if necessary.

"Bull, why didn't he shoot him?" Gidi whispered in Barda's ear, after they had put a bit of distance between themselves and the coffee shop, as well as the crowd around the bank.

"I don't know. Honestly, it was very crowded there. I trust Kermit – if he didn't take the shot, I'm sure there was a good reason for it. I'm sure that during the debriefing at the unit he'll tell us what happened there with the bodyguard," Doron said quietly.

Gidi and Barda headed toward the bus station at the north end of Manara Square. Yoav, the unit commander, wanted to avoid sending in more undercover forces to the area, and so he directed them to leave the area however they saw fit. They agreed that the pickup location would be at the southern entrance to Al-Bireh. They maintained visual contact with the other two, Dan and Yogev, and saw them get on a bus to Al-Bireh. Barda raised his hand to signal to a transit van to stop. The van was a Volkswagen, and it stopped for them.

"Where to, *ya shabab*?" the driver asked Gidi and Barda with a big smile. He was a young man in his twenties, with an unkempt mustache and beard.

"We need to get to Al-Bireh," Gidi answered him, and the two of them got into the van, which started driving south.

Barda took a last look around in the direction of the bank. The firefighters had already entered the bank with their hoses. He didn't see Abu Qassem or his two bodyguards. "I hope that the interception team has more success than Kermit did..." he said quietly to Gidi, who was sitting next to him. Gidi smiled while watching the crowd, still gathered at the entrance to the bank.

"I hope so. One thing is certain – if the mountain doesn't come to Muhammad, then Muhammad must go to the mountain."

* * *

In the meantime, on the bus to Al-Bireh, Dan and Yogev sat in silence. A storm of emotion engulfed Dan: on the one hand, just a moment ago, the soldier was facing the business end of the gun of a terrorist known for his brutality. He was a hairsbreadth from taking a bullet to the head or chest. On the other hand, they achieved their goals – they robbed the safety deposit box, they had the money, and a lifeline to the terror cell had been severed due to the sophisticated heist they pulled off. In addition, despite the difficulties and the risks, the toxin came into contact with Abu Qassem's skin. Dr. Yakobovitch explained that only a few drops of the toxin he made were required to come into contact with the object's skin to cause death within hours. At this point, Abu Qassem was a dead man walking.

But the thing that caused Dan the most anguish was the knowledge that in just a few hours, when he gets back to the unit, he would have to stand in front of his teammates and lie to their faces without batting an eye. During the debriefing, he was going to have to come up with a reason as to why he didn't shoot Abu Qassem. In order to conceal the toxin, he was going to have to lie to his teammates and make up some story, something that would make sense to them and distract them from anything having to do with administering the toxin. This secret was eating him up inside. He couldn't see himself standing in front of his teammates, the only people in the world prepared to give their lives to protect him, and tell them a bald-faced lie. His heart was still pounding fiercely. He looked out the window of the bus and tried to quiet his thoughts and his conscience – but unsuccessfully. His unease dampened the success of the mission.

Yogev, who sensed his good friend's reaction, put his hand on his friend's leg and said, "Kermit, what's up?"

"I don't know, man. How am I going to lie to them in the debriefing? What will I say? I don't know if I can do that to the rest of the guys on the team. We don't have any secrets among us, and now this fucking secret is going to be on my conscience for the rest of my life..." Dan responded, dejected.

And, in truth, Yogev felt the same way. From the moment Yoav and Jerry separated them from the rest of the unit, he felt uncomfortable. Even though he well understood the importance of the goal and the massive service they were doing for the Mossad and the country, he still carried a weight around in his heart.

"Listen, I feel just like you do. I'm not comfortable with this whole thing either, but remember that we're doing this because there are things that are bigger than our team and unit. Who knows, maybe due to our experiment we can take out some arch-terrorist in Europe, or some Iranian missile specialist. Who knows..."

"Yogi, I understand perfectly well the importance of our work and this mission. Really. But I want to tell you that I'm planning on telling Yoav and Jerry that this is the last time I do something that is isolated from the rest of the team. Next time, if they want to let everybody in on it, with pleasure. Otherwise, I'm out. They can find somebody else for that. You hear me, Yogi? A few minutes ago I was face to face with the most wanted man in Ramallah. He pointed a gun at me at point blank range. I should be lying in the hospital or the morgue at this point – and what bothers me about this whole affair? That I have to lie to the guys on my team."

The bus stopped and the driver called out, "Movenpick Hotel. Next stop, Al-Bireh." Two young couples got up, thanked the driver and exited through the front door. An old woman with a basket on her head got on and sat in the back row, far from the two of them.

"What do you think?" Yogev asked Dan. "Did the toxin work? Is he really going to die from that?"

"I don't know," Dan said. "I mean, there's a good chance that he'll wind up having a heart attack when he sees that his safety deposit box is empty..."

Yogev smiled broadly. Dan's cynical humor always made him laugh. He turned his gaze outside. The bus continued driving rapidly south, and when they arrived in Al-Bireh, the two soldiers got out. Yogev got on the concealed radio with the command center, gave the code word, and received instructions on a meeting place and estimated time of arrival. The two of them entered a small coffee shop on the outskirts of town, ordered something hot to drink and some k'nafe, and waited there until they saw the undercover car that came to pick them up.

* * *

The sudden death of Abu Qassem, the mythological warrior, shocked Fatah's leadership as well as the residents of Ramallah. His picture was plastered all over people's houses, and three days of mourning were declared in the city and neighboring villages. The TV and radio stations played sad, melancholy songs and thousands of residents from all over the West Bank attended his state funeral.

The doctor, who was rushed to his secret hideout where he pronounced the sudden death, was interviewed on the news and explained that even young, healthy people can have heart attacks, and without any discernible reason or previous medical history. He surmised that the stressful lifestyle Abu Qassem lived, with the security forces constantly hounding him and the tremendous stress he must have been under, and then the whole ordeal with the bank – all that must have simply done him in. The doctor suggested performing an autopsy, but the terrorist's followers took his body from the secret location and paraded him around the entire city before his burial. The many eulogies at his funeral emphasized that Abu Qassem was so strong that only Allah was finally able to bring him down, and not the Zionist occupiers.

In a rare and unprecedented move, the Hamas leadership also published an obituary notice on the passing of Marwan Abu Qassem before his time, despite him being a member of Fatah, a rival faction. The mayor of Ramallah promised at the funeral that his widow and children would receive a generous monthly stipend, as well as have their house remodeled – all paid for by the city. In interviews, she blamed the Zionists and claimed that her husband had been poisoned. Every time any terrorist died from some medical condition, that's what people said, except this time, the widow's claim didn't garner much support, and couldn't buy her any favor with the Palestinian public: everybody knew that Marwan Abu Qassem was a master at evading the IDF and the Shin-Bet, and he hadn't been face to face with an IDF soldier for a long time. They knew that the IDF was looking for him day and night – and hadn't found him. Many simply couldn't bring themselves to believe the widow's claim, and after a few weeks, the issue of Abu Qassem's sudden death was forgotten.

Marwan Abu Qassem was buried in Ramallah in the cemetery for great Palestinian leaders and with him, the secret that led to his demise.

CHAPTER 13
April 1994, Dr. Ravid's Clinic, Jerusalem

Dr. Ravid sat there, riveted by Yariv's stories. He was so focused on the young soldier's stories that he didn't interrupt him, even to ask questions. He had the sense that Yariv was unloading a heavy weight off his shoulders. Yariv told the story with incredible precision, going into the most minute of details in an unabated, steady flow. The story bordered on the unbelievable, as if taken from a Hollywood script. But Dr. Ravid knew that the soldier was telling the truth. The way he spoke, the intense emotional investment in his story, the way he moved his hands, and his body language – all these things indicated to the experienced therapist that he was telling the truth.

As the therapy progressed, the psychologist had the feeling he was rolling a stone from the top of a volcano waiting to explode. He knew that Yariv didn't really have any other outlet to unload his sizeable emotional baggage that he carried around. On the one hand, he was proud to be the one to "crack open" the young soldier and bring him to where he was able to share with him the secrets he kept locked in his heart. But on the other hand, Dr. Ravid felt great frustration and anger at the military system that failed to provide a safe place for the combat soldier and his teammates where they could talk to somebody on a regular basis. From his long years of experience in the clinic, Dr. Ravid knew that the intense service required by the combat units, especially the elite units, leaves its mark on the soldiers. He also knew just how deep the fracture could be for even the best and most successful of the country's rising stars.

Dr. Ravid was happy that he agreed to accept Yariv as his last patient. His wife, his high school sweetheart, was diagnosed with cancer three months before he started seeing Yariv, and he was forced to notify the defense ministry that he had to close down his clinic and devote all his time to care for her. But if not for the pressure Dr. Landau, the division's doctor, was putting on him to help with this one specific case, he wouldn't have agreed to enter the picture and become Yariv's therapist. In addition to Dr. Landau's persistent pleading, Dr. Ravid also felt a sense of personal and professional duty to treat these young soldiers, upon whose shoulders the army places such a heavy responsibility, yet frequently forgets that they are young adults who are just barely over the age of twenty. He remembered the period of heavy fighting that he experienced in the southern sector during the Yom Kippur War, and how he felt in Egyptian captivity. He underwent mental and physical abuse and returned to Israel a broken vessel. After extensive therapy, the young Yehonatan Ravid was able to rehabilitate his life, and even help many returned hostages, whether by treating them in therapy or through establishing the organization "Awake at Night." When he heard Yariv's story, it took him back years, and he was more and more able to identify with Yariv's distress. But now it was time to take apart the biggest landmine that Yariv had been avoiding the whole time they had been talking – the mine where the disaster is buried.

Dr. Ravid knew that what happened in Nablus was extremely significant, but Yariv elegantly sidestepped the events that took place there and didn't get into it when Dr. Ravid tried to gently steer the discussion in that direction. Yariv talked about the training course in the unit, about the different operations, many undercover, about the innovative tactics they used to capture terrorists, about how it was being on the operations team – but he never once mentioned the wound that brought him here: what happened to Dan that rainy evening in Nablus six months ago. The psychologist understood that he didn't have any choice but to get straight to the point. He felt that it was time, and that there was an emotional intimacy between them that would allow him to broach the subject directly.

"Yariv," he began, "I have to share my thoughts with you. Is that all right?"

"Of course," Yariv answered, "and I promise not charge for it..."

The psychologist smiled lightly. *Despite everything he's been through*, he thought to himself, *he still has his sense of humor. That's very good.* "Look, Yariv, over the last few months, you've told me a lot of fascinating stories about you and your team. You shared with me your experiences, your misgivings, and your feelings. I'm glad that you've felt comfortable enough to confide in me, and I thank you for that. But, like any surgical procedure, at some point we have to get to what's actually bothering you and cut it out. I'm sorry, and this may be painful, perhaps very painful – but that's the nature of therapy. I feel as if the relationship we have developed is ready for this, and I feel that you have to keep going with the process and keep cooperating with me. Am I explaining myself well?"

Yariv let out a light sigh. "Unfortunately, I know you're right," he said while scratching his neck. "I also feel like we've talked about everything except that one important thing. I suppose you want to ask me what happened to Dan that fucking night in Nablus and why I ended up in a cast. Am I right?"

The psychologist nodded affirmatively and remained silent. He let Yariv have center stage.

"All right, here we go. You remember I told you about how I approached the courtyard wall bent over across from Sa'id's house?" Dr. Ravid nodded. "Okay, so it was raining. Correction – it was a downpour. It was very, very foggy. Like being inside a cloud. You couldn't see a thing. I saw a figure getting closer and closer to me. I couldn't say anything because I was right in front of the terrorist's house. I tried to see if I recognized the figure's shoes – and I didn't. I couldn't tell if it was Dan, or Yogev – the other two guys that we were supposed to meet up with and then close in on the house. The direction that the figure was coming from was also strange, because Dan and Yogev were supposed to be on the other side of the house. But I still had a bad feeling, that maybe one of them got turned around, or even that I was the one that got confused. I got down on my knees and pressed up against the wall – and opened the map. I saw that there were a bunch of details that didn't fit with the aerial photograph, all kinds of new walls surrounding the house and other things that weren't in the photograph. This was problematic because, on the one hand, there's somebody headed my way and closing in fast, under cover of the fog – and keep in mind that, at the same time, I'm inside Sa'id's yard, and he's who we're after. In any event, I suddenly saw that the figure was holding something in his hand, perhaps a book, perhaps a bag, maybe a gun... I wasn't sure. In the end, I decided not to take a chance – I took out my gun and cocked it quietly. I dropped the hammer back down and waited. The figure got closer. At the last second, I saw that he was holding a gun. And then I realized – I aimed at the center of mass and pulled the trigger." Yariv went silent and dropped his gaze to the floor.

"And what happened?" The psychologist asked, hanging on every word of the story.

"Nothing."

"What do you mean, 'nothing?'"

"Misfire. The bullet was a dud, I guess," Yariv said quietly. "The gun fired, but the bullet didn't discharge. Maybe the gunpowder was bad, maybe the cap was messed up. I don't know. Bottom line, the gun didn't shoot."

"Okay, what then? What about the figure that was there? Did you fire off another round?" asked Dr. Ravid.

"I didn't have time. As soon as he heard the shot – there was a sort of 'click' sound. The figure stopped for a moment, heard the noise, and immediately hit the ground, right on the other side of the wall. That is, he was six feet away from me, but on the other side of the wall. It was a crazy situation."

"I don't understand. Fixing a misfire takes a split second. You basically bang on the bottom of the magazine and re-cock the gun. I'm sure you've done that thousands of times in training. Why didn't you reload it as soon as it happened? Or did something else happen that I'm missing..." the psychologist wondered.

Yariv got up from his chair and started pacing around the room. "You know what?" he finally said, "you ask an excellent question. I also ask myself this same question all the time: what kept me from resetting the gun after the misfire? It's a relatively simply issue that only takes a few tenths of a second to fix. But I have to tell you something. When I was a kid, I loved reading about knights and the Middle Ages. I had a whole library on the subject. Me and Yochanan, my brother who was killed in Lebanon a few years before I enlisted, were crazy about stories from that period. Yochanan used to tell me all the time, 'Yariv, look at the respect enemies had for each other back then.'"

"Respect for the enemy?" Dr. Ravid asked. "What do you mean?"

"I'll give you an example," Yariv replied, and his eyes flashed for a moment. "Did you know that in ancient times, they gave a full military burial for the brave enemy soldiers? Yochanan told me once that Rommel, the senior Nazi officer, survived a daring assassination attempt where the assassin, a very brave British commando, was killed. So Rommel himself gave the order to prepare a full military funeral for his brave, would-be assassin, with an honor guard and full military etiquette. Even though the British officer came to kill Rommel, Rommel still respected him. It's sort of a code among warriors, even if they are the enemy."

"Interesting, but what does that have to do with your story?" Dr. Ravid wondered.

"So, one of the stories my brother like to tell me was about when a man was sentenced to death by hanging, like an enemy spy or something similar, they would weigh him three times before hanging him. They did that in order to determine the thickness of the rope they should use. Three times, so that they wouldn't end up in a situation where the rope breaks. But if the rope does indeed break during the hanging, the custom was to let the man go free and not to hang him again."

"Why?" The psychologist said, twisting up his face in perplexion.

"In ancient times, they believed in all kinds of symbolic things, like if the rope breaks during a hanging, that's a sign from the gods that the man is innocent, and therefore they let him go."

"So, if I follow you," Dr. Ravid said, "when you pulled the trigger and nothing happened, that's like the rope breaking, or something similar, is that it?"

"Exactly. I wasn't completely sure about taking the shot as it was. I have never taken a shot at a target that I wasn't a hundred percent sure of. So I felt like someone from above was saying to me, 'Don't shoot.'"

"Okay, so let's go back to the field in Nablus for a moment: it's pouring rain, you're pressed up against the wall, on the other side is another person, lying on the ground, and you still don't know who it is. So what happened?"

"First, I banged on the gun and re-cocked it. I reset it after the misfire. I ejected the bad cartridge from the chamber and loaded another. You can never be in a situation where you don't have a bullet in the chamber ready to go. Second, I heard his breathing, and the sound of a gun cocking on the other side. That is, both of us are lying up against the stone wall, and both of us have a bullet in the chamber. It seemed strange to me that the figure was able to get down so quickly and also to cock his gun. That isn't something that just anybody can do. I had a strong feeling that it was one of our guys. That is, I knew Barda was far from me, so it must have been either Dan or Yogev. Of course I couldn't yell, because I'm in Sa'id's backyard, so I whispered the password we agreed upon in case we met up and, after a moment, I heard from the other side of the wall the completion of the code. That is, it was one of ours."

"And then?" The suspense in the clinic was palpable.

"I got up slowly, trying to look over the wall. I whispered in Arabic, 'Who's there?' and after a second I heard, 'It's Kermit.'"

"Kermit?" Dr. Ravid asked in surprise.

"Yeah, it was Dan, in the flesh. He apparently got mixed up, the dummy, and arrived at the wrong corner of the house. That is, he arrived at my corner, not his corner."

"Unbelievable... Then what?"

"I was so happy that I forgot where I was. I got up quickly to see him, but I didn't notice that the wall was still in the process of being built. I grabbed it and leaned against it, in order to climb up to see Dan, who was still down – and that's when it happened."

"What happened?" The psychologist's voice pierced the air, as if from a distance.

"The wall was wet from the rain and I slipped. To break my fall, I held on to the upper part of the wall, but it wasn't strong enough to hold me and I fell back. There was a loud noise of rocks falling as that part of the wall collapsed because, in my colossal stupidity, I destroyed the entire upper section of the rock wall. Dan immediately understood what was happening and came to help me out. He carefully climbed over the fence, coming to clear the rocks off me before pulling me out, leaving himself completely exposed. Suddenly, the window closest to us opens, and we see somebody's head peek out at us – and immediately after, the barrel of an AK-47. The silhouette of that gun is unmistakable. Sa'id was on the second floor, I'm looking up and see that he saw us. That son of a bitch didn't think twice – he aimed his gun at us and waited a second. I looked at him and felt like I was about to pass out. I knew what was about to happen, and I wasn't wrong. Sa'id fired off two long bursts – one at me and one at Dan, who right at that moment was standing on top of the wall, fully unprotected.

"I could feel the rounds landing all around me. The rocks that had fallen on me saved me, but then I felt something hit my hand and there was electricity in my elbow. Only in hindsight did I understand that a bullet penetrated one of the rocks and blew my bone apart. But the real story was with Dan. Like I told you, he was standing on top of the wall, but with his back to Sa'id. Unlike me, who was hidden underneath the rocks, Dan's silhouette was perfectly visible against the fading rays of the setting sun behind him, perfectly tracing his form above the dark wall. Sa'id fired off the second burst at Dan. I remember everything suddenly played out like in slow motion. He looked over his shoulder in order to jump back, but he didn't make it. I remember shouting something like, 'No!' but I'm not sure. Everything happened so fast.

"When you fire off a burst, the first bullet might hit the target, but the rest of the bullets always go high. So I remember that the first bullet from the burst hit Dan in the leg, but the second one hit him in the thigh, and the third got him in the gut, with the fourth ripping through his neck. You ever see that movie 'Platoon?' The one about Vietnam? That's what Dan looked like. Just like the movie poster for Platoon. His knees buckled, his hands flew up toward heaven, and then he just fell forward, right onto me."

Dr. Ravid was quiet, as was Yariv. The silence persisted for a few moments. Tears welled in Yariv's eyes. His lips were quivering. He tried to choke off his tears, but wasn't able to. A treacherous tear rolled down his cheek. He tried to wipe it away, but another tear quickly took its place.

"I'm very sorry to hear that. Was he killed?" the psychologist asked in a very quiet voice, almost whispering.

"I wish. Worse."

"What do you mean, 'worse?' What's worse than death?"

Yariv turned toward the window. He stared hollowly at the street. He finally took a deep breath, and then continued talking. He spoke continually, barely pausing to even take a breath, as if he were trying to vomit up the tragedy from the depths of his soul.

"Dan basically ended up falling in a way that left him lying on top of me. He literally covered me like a blanket. I honestly don't know if he meant to or not, but that's what happened. And that's how he took everything that was meant for me. And the worst part is that I'm lying on my back, he's lying on top of me, and above both of us, on the second floor, that motherfucking Hamas piece of shit is just standing there shooting at us. I try to throw Dan off of me, in order to fire back at Sa'id, but I can't do it. Dan's weight, in addition to my injury... I just wasn't able to get him off me.

"The whole thing was over in a few seconds. Sa'id isn't stupid – he understood that he needed to get out of there because, if we're here, then there must be others on the way. He stopped shooting at us and then disappeared. He ran out of the building in the other direction, and there was nobody closing in from there – he just disappeared.

"I thought about going after him, but I started to feel dizzy because I'd lost so much blood, and because I didn't want to leave

Dan there. I'm no doctor but, between the two of us, he was half gone as it was. His gunshot wounds were severe, but the real problem was that he fell forward on his neck from a height of about five feet. He's lying in Hadassah Ein Kerem Hospital right now, paralyzed from the neck down," Yariv said, finishing his story by covering his face with his hands and crying softly into them.

Dr. Ravid was unable to remain professionally neutral in this situation. He got up and came over to Yariv, putting his hand on his shoulder. Yariv, surprised by the gesture, looked up into the psychologist's eyes.

"And it was all because of me, you understand?" he said in a voice that rose in pitch until it broke. "If I didn't climb like an asshole on that fucking wall, he'd be perfectly fine. If I hadn't knocked all the rocks off the wall, Sa'id wouldn't have heard a bunch of noise and come out and lit us up. Anyway, after a moment of silence, I hear Barda and Yogev meeting up with each other and shouting. Any thought of sticking to night protocol, where we're supposed to be quiet, was abandoned. I screamed at them like crazy to come over to me. I didn't care about Sa'id at that point. According to unit protocol, if there's a terrorist – especially an armed terrorist that just shot at our forces – we chase him until we confirm that he's dead. That means, basically, that I was supposed to leave everything, Dan included, and go chase after him. That's protocol. We leave the wounded and make contact, taking out the source of the threat. But, at this point, I didn't care about anything. As far as I was concerned, Sa'id could disappear – let him run – let him do whatever he wanted. I didn't care anymore. That's the truth.

"Barda got to me first, and then a moment later Yogev got there. Barda wanted to go after him, but I told him and Yogev to protect me and Dan. The locals started peeping out of their windows, and we were completely exposed at this point. We were both wounded, and I was seriously worried that somebody might come out of their house and smash a block over our heads. The rain was getting stronger and it was getting very dark. I felt like the entire world was against us. I was afraid that Sa'id would come back, perhaps with a few friends and try to finish the job. Yogev got on the radio with the unit's command center and called for immediate extraction. I remember that everything was covered in fog, and I started screaming at him in Hebrew, 'What extraction, you moron, tell them we need a chopper!' So he got back on the radio and requested a chopper.

"Dan began to convulse, but it wasn't serious. The bullet tore through the main artery in his leg, and it was spurting blood. With my last bit of strength, I tried putting a tourniquet on his leg, tying it off with my teeth because my other hand was injured and bleeding. Everything was wet from the rain and from his blood and the tourniquet kept slipping. I took a small pocketknife that I had in my pocket, and I cut his pants near his thigh and gently lifted up his leg. The entry wound was so small I could barely see it. But when I saw the exit wound, I almost blacked out. The exit wound from an AK-47 is no joke. It looked like a tiger took a bite out of his leg – the tissue was completely gone. Somehow, I managed to get my shirt off and I tied it tightly around his thigh. He started mumbling all sorts of things. I didn't understand exactly what he wanted. His gut shot is what really worried me. He started coughing up blood. I was afraid he caught a bullet to the lung and I didn't know what to do.

"People around started shouting. Somebody from the building next door threw a pan in our direction. It didn't land too far away, but seeing as how it came from one of the upper floors of the building, it could have ended badly. I was afraid that a fauda was about to start, which would end with them lynching us. We weren't mobile because it was impossible to move Dan. My elbow was killing me, but we didn't have a choice. I dragged Dan to a corner of the wall that provided some cover and continued treating his wounds as best I could. In the meantime, I saw that

Barda had taken the Mini Uzi out of the grocery basket and cocked it. Yogev also had a gun in his hand with the hammer drawn back. The shouts intensified, somebody threw a wooden drawer at us, which hit me in the foot. Barda got up, popped a couple of rounds into the window from where the drawer came and got back behind the stone wall. At this point, the whole neighborhood was at attention. The whistles began, people started throwing things, a real mess. I was busy with one thing: trying to stabilize Dan. His thigh stopped bleeding, but I noticed that he had no control over his body. When applying a tourniquet and pulling it tight, it hurts a lot. He didn't even resist, just kept convulsing. He kept whispering to me, 'I'm cold, I'm cold.' We were all cold because it was raining and we were soaking wet, so I didn't pay it any real mind. I'm not a doctor or a paramedic, but I had a feeling that something bad was happening here. Yogev got on the radio with the unit again. I could hear the stress in his voice. Suddenly I understood that all of these games were real. All this undercover stuff, as if we were supermen, invincible, that everything was going to be all right – and now, all that was over. Apparently we're not supermen, everything is very much not all right, we're stuck in the middle of some shithole in Nablus, completely exposed, with a couple pistols and a Mini Uzi. In a minute, we'll run out of ammo, and then we'll all really be fucked.

"Yogev poked his head out from behind the wall and got hit with a rock thrown from one of the houses. Luckily, it missed his eye by a few inches. Barda took out a bandage and told him to apply pressure to the wound. Actually, Barda rose to the occasion like a gladiator – he took the radio from Yogev, got back on with extraction and explained where we were while squeezing off rounds here and there at anybody who got too close. Suspicious person protocol my ass, he was shooting to kill. A shot to the center of mass. I counted at least four corpses Barda left there. But the Mini Uzi only had two dual magazines. It might sound like a lot but, in a real firefight, it's nothing. The pistols were useless at this range, especially in the dark.

"Yogev got back on the radio to extraction. Suddenly we hear brakes screeching and Udi shouting. Barda shouts back, Udi brings the Mercedes over to us. Yaki gets out of the car, still dressed like a woman. He was holding a Micro Uzi in his hand. You have no idea how happy I was to see them. Udi also pulled out his gun, cocked it quickly and started selectively, and accurately, shooting – a bullet or two in each window where he saw people. Within seconds everybody disappeared, and a sort of relative silence took over. It gave me the opportunity to try to get Dan into the Mercedes. I called to Yaki to come over to where I was. Yogev could barely see anything, because the blood from the wound in his head was bleeding into his eye.

"Barda got up and in one hand, he was holding a Mini Uzi that he was still firing off a few rounds from every so often at the houses across from us. In the other hand, he was holding our bags, because we couldn't leave anything in the field – anything. Yaki held Dan's legs, and I hugged his body from behind, and we slowly made our way to the car.

"Udi opened the back door and flattened out the seatbacks. We placed Dan in the back and he groaned loudly. It found it very strange that he didn't have any tension in his muscles, everything was relaxed, like Jello. I didn't understand why he was like that, but I assumed that perhaps it was some sort of response that the body gave in order to withstand the pain. Only looking back could I see how stupid I was – the damage to his spinal cord caused him to lose all feeling in everything from the neck down. A rock was thrown against the back windshield. Udi couldn't tell where it was thrown from. He pumped two rounds into a window that had a light on inside. There was a noise of the window exploding and then shrieks from inside the room. Apparently he hit somebody. Yoav was on the radio. Usually the girls in the war room handled communications, but Yoav apparently understood that things had gotten out of control. He said the helicopter was on its way. I told him that I wasn't waiting for a helicopter, I'd get Dan out in the Mercedes. He ordered me to wait there. He claimed that because of the gunfire, the whole area was up in arms and there was no way to drive out of there because they'd blocked all the exits. He ordered us to go into one of the nearby homes and find cover.

"I knew that he was right. Udi helped me pull Dan out. Dan was very heavy, like a bag of sand. He was on the verge of passing out. I tried talking to him all the time, just to keep him conscious, but all the blood he lost made that impossible. In the darkness, we could tell he was pale – really pale. Barda found some store next to Sa'id's house. The sign said it was a women's hair salon. Barda kicked in the iron door, but it didn't open. He pulled out his gun and put two bullets in the lock. The lock shattered, and the door opened. We went inside with Dan, and Udi parked the car at the store's entrance so we would have some sort of protection in case somebody tried shooting inside the store. Dan let out a moan. Yogev shot twice into a window with the light on and broke the window. We didn't care about anything at that point. Yoav got back on the radio. Not formal or fancy – he talked like people talk. No codes, no bullshit. He told me that the helicopter can't land near us because we're in the middle of the village, and there's no mapping of the electrical wires and the pilot can't risk landing near where we are. He asked for a detailed description of the structure we were in, and I told him to open the aerial photographs. I explained where we were.

"I lit an infrared stick-light and placed it in the doorway. After a few moments, I heard a helicopter in the air right above us. I lit another IR stick-light and waved it in an "X" pattern. Yoav told me that the pilot reported that he sees us. I heard Yoav give the order to the extraction team's commander. After a few minutes, I heard somebody knocking on the door of the salon. I looked outside –

it was Gidi. I have never been happier in my life to see somebody than I was right then. Gidi came inside, and Doron and a few other soldiers from another team in the company were behind him. They were our backup if we needed help getting out. After a few moments, we heard the sound of an engine. The extraction vehicles had arrived. We loaded everybody into the vehicles, with two soldiers joining Udi in the Mercedes, and drove out in a caravan. I held Dan's hand the whole way, until we reached the city limits. It was completely limp. His pulse was weak. Dr. Tomer was already waiting for us at the extraction point. They put Dan on a stretcher, secured him and covered him. Dr. Tomer lit the flashlight on his head and tried to get an IV into Dan's arm, but he wasn't able to. Because of how much blood he'd lost, his veins were compressed. The soldiers from special rescue unit 669 were already there with their helicopter. Their doctor cut Dan's pants off him and inserted the IV directly into the vein near his groin. Afterward, he tried asking me what happened there and when I applied the tourniquet. One of the soldiers from unit 669 put a neck brace on Dan. I remember thinking that it was funny – after all that he'd been through, now they finally put a neck brace on him.

"Anyway, they started putting Dan in the helicopter. I ran after the stretcher and told him that I wasn't leaving him. Dr. Tomer caught me and told me to leave the stretcher alone. I felt like I was in a fog. He bandaged me up and gave me a temporary splint for my elbow. Sirens and the flashing lights from the ambulances began sounding. I remember that Dr. Tomer sat me down in one of the ambulance seats and said to me, 'You did what you could, Yariv. Now let us do what needs to be done.' I listened to him. They laid me down on one of the beds and gave me something that knocked me out. Everything became foggy – the rain, the rock fence that fell apart in my hands, Dan, Sa'id, the shooting, the hair salon, the lights and the sirens, everything. I felt like I was floating. Looking back, they told me that I had also lost a lot of blood. Dr. Tomer told me afterward that I fought against the morphine shot he tried to give me, and that it took three soldiers from 669 to get me into the ambulance bed. I felt like I was going to pass out, that everything was going black around me. I stopped resisting, but I kept asking everybody 'Where's Dan? Where's Dan?' I felt like all my strength, all the adrenalin, was draining out of my body – and then I lost consciousness.

"I woke up a few hours later in a completely white room. Beams of light were coming in through the window at low angles, so I understood that it was relatively early in the morning. I looked to the sides, and then I saw my mother sitting next to me, crying. The tears were streaming from her eyes like a leaky faucet. She was completely helpless. It hurt more to see her like that than it did from my own wounds. I tried to sit up, to give her a hug, but I felt an electrical surge through my elbow. It was completely bandaged, with a cast and all kinds of crap to keep it in place. She hugged me and gave me a kiss on my cheek. I saw Yoav behind her. He had some shirt thrown on that was a few sizes too big for him, so that the people in the hospital wouldn't see that he was in costume and that they'd understand he was with us. He was a total mess. Looking back, I realized that he also made it to the field and took part in getting us out of there. He had blood stains on his pants, stubble on his cheeks but, what I remember most was his eyes – they were bloodshot. I didn't know if it was from lack of sleep or crying. It was strange seeing him like that.

"He came over to me and put his hand on my good shoulder. I asked him, 'Where am I, where's Dan, where's everybody else?' My mother gave me a hug and said, 'Yariv, you're at Hadassah hospital, everything's fine, everybody's fine.' I looked at Yoav. His eyes told a different story altogether. He diverted his gaze to the floor. I knew she was lying to me. I yelled out, 'Yoav, what's going on here? Where's Dan?' Yoav bent down and put his other hand on my chest. He looked me in the eye and said in a quiet voice, 'Yariv, you guys have had a rough night. You have to rest now. That's what's important.' I grabbed his arm with my good hand and squeezed it hard. I said to him, 'Yoav, don't talk to me like I'm six and just had my tonsils out. What is going on here, really?' Yoav looked at me and said, 'It's bad. Dan's in critical condition. He lost a lot of blood. He also has a serious spinal injury in his neck, he has shrapnel in his head and, if that's not enough, he took multiple bullets to multiple vital organs. He's in the ICU right now, in surgery, and that's all I can tell you at this point. That's the whole truth, Yariv. The doctors are fighting for his life as we speak. Aside from him, everybody else is fine. You got shot in the elbow, and it shattered the bone. You have a cast on, and they'll only be able to assess the damage to the nerves in a month. That's all. Now I am going to leave you with your mother. Your father is on the way.'

"And then Yoav left the room while my mother continued crying and kissing me, and I kept staring at the ceiling, furious with myself. After a few days of recuperation, I started going crazy. I was mad at everybody, mostly at myself. I understand that nobody knew what I was going through, so I just got up and went to the unit. I didn't want to spend my sick days in the hospital. I didn't care if my arm got better or not. I didn't care about anything. I wanted to get back to my team, my friends, the unit. We asked to visit Dan. They wouldn't let us yet. From what we heard, he was stable, but he would be a vegetable the rest of his life. It was irreversible, his condition. Dr. Tomer went to visit him. When he returned, we tried getting information out of him. He tried brushing it off, like he was going to be fine. I asked him, 'Is he basically a prisoner in his body? Without the ability to do anything? That's how he's going to live the rest of his life until he dies?' He's a good man, Dr. Tomer is, he really is a super guy, but he's a terrible liar. Just by looking at his eyes I knew that the situation was shitty and only getting worse. The damage to Dan's spine, along with the shrapnel in his head, were a death sentence for him. It was Satan's handiwork – that's how the surgeon put it.

"I started looking for medical articles about injuries like Dan's. I did a literal PhD in the field on his specific injury. I was trying to understand what he had to look forward to. I was horrified by what I found out. He wouldn't regain consciousness to full awareness like before and, even if he did – it would likely only be for very short periods of time. His ability to speak and understand were significantly debilitated. He would never be in control of his bodily functions, he would have constant bedsores, so he would need bedside care around the clock. His muscles will atrophy and disappear within six months, maximum, and he'll turn into a piece of meat. He'll have spasms, he will never raise a family, he'll never have kids… and the worst part about it is that he can live for many, many years like this. Turns out that Satan did a hell of a job – he won't die immediately, he'll just suffer.

"At the unit, I walked around like a caged tiger. I felt like everything that happened to him was because of me. That it was my fault. I wished it would have happened to me instead of him. I wished – but it happened to him. He basically took the rounds that were meant for me. He saved my life and paid with his own. The biggest joke is that, after the bank job we pulled and the toxin we got from the Mossad, we were going to tell Yoav and Jerry that no way were we continuing on with this thing and keeping everything secret from the rest of the unit. That it won't work in the long run that way. And then, without any warning, that business in Nablus comes in and everything gets fucked up anyway. And that's it, that's the situation now – I'm back at the unit in a cast, and they made me come see you. And here we are – you wanted to hear the whole story, so you got the whole story. Satisfied?"

Dr. Ravid felt as if he was sinking into his chair. It had been a long time since he had met a soldier with such fresh, deep trauma like he had sitting in front of him right now. The streaming, traumatic monologue that Yariv just delivered left him speechless. The combat soldier fired off his story at a dizzying speed, automatically, suddenly diving into intricate details without missing a beat or pausing for even a moment. He felt as if the event was still burning inside Yariv's bones, like an abscess that needed to be drained, or an extra appendage that needed to be amputated, a memory that was screaming to be taken out and disconnected from his body and mind forever.

He looked at Yariv, trying to catch his glance, but unsuccessfully. He knew that the young man had laid his heart bare on the table. The psychologist didn't expect openness like that in a session with a patient who put up such a tough demeanor, and certainly not with such a young soldier wrapped in so many layers of defensiveness. The understanding that, underneath the tough-guy exterior, Yariv was looking for a release, a refuge, a sanctuary that was willing to take him as he was, unfiltered and unmasked, like this, straight up, direct, blunt – this understanding seeped into him quickly. The combat soldier's young age stood in stark contrast to the life experience he had, the depth of his soul that he divulged during therapy and, of course, the incredible responsibility placed on his shoulders.

Yariv wept and was almost hyperventilating, and Dr. Ravid thought that he heard him mumble something. "Sorry, Yariv, I didn't hear what you said. Can you repeat that please?" he asked in a quiet tone.

Yariv raised his head and looked at the psychologist. His eyes were red and it was obvious that his sobs were caught in his throat. "I said that it's like writing on water," he replied.

"Writing on water? What do you mean? I didn't understand the comparison," the psychologist said in a quiet voice.

"Have you ever heard of Fairuz, the famous Lebanese singer?"

"I've heard the name," Dr. Ravid answered, "but I don't know any of her songs specifically. Why do you ask?"

Yariv sat and stared out the window, and was quiet for a moment before answering in a voice that sounded as if it were coming from a distance. "Fairuz is a singer that I like very much. She is the national singer of Lebanon, like their version of Shoshana Damari or Yaffa Yarkoni. She has an amazing voice, but more than that – the songs she sings are deep and powerful. They really do a number on you. She goes into the innermost feelings of the soul, and as somebody who speaks and reads Arabic, it's nice to listen to. She sings a lot about growing up in Lebanon, about Beirut, about Lebanon before the civil war... she sings a well-known song by the famous Arab writer and poet Jubran Khalil Jubran. In this song, he describes the importance of the flute in the song, and goes so far as to claim that song is the secret of the universe. This song of his became one of the greatest that Fairuz would ever sing. Long story short, at the end of the song, there's an amazing line. I'll translate it for you, even though it loses a lot of its sharpness in translation. She sings, 'People are nothing but lines written on water.'"

"An interesting and beautiful sentence, but I still don't get where you're coming from," said Dr. Ravid.

"I'll explain," Yariv said, his eyes burning. "When you put your hand into the water, like into a pool or a bucket, and move it from side to side – it's like you have an effect on the water. The water moves because you moved, and for a moment, it really looks like you can affect it. But soon enough, the water goes back to the way it was, and any effect you had was erased, gone completely. That's the idea behind Fairuz's song. The idea is that people do all kinds of things throughout their lives, and a person really thinks that their deeds will remain for a while, or even forever. But the fact is – at least, that's what the poet, who was also a philosopher says – people are just lines written on water. That is, their expectations to have a lasting impact aren't realistic, and their deeds will disappear sooner than they think, and it's a certainty that their influence will end with their death."

"Interesting point," the psychologist said, nodding his head in agreement. "But what does that line have to do with you and everything you've told me until now?"

"It has everything to do with me. In the unit, they taught us that we have a direct effect on the national security of the citizens of this country. That's true, I'm not arguing that. But we've gotten to the point where, for example, we took out the head of Hamas in Hebron – and two days later, there's a new head of Hamas. We took out the number one guy in Jenin – and two weeks later, we're called into the office of the Shin-Bet intelligence officer telling us that we need to plan another operation, another hit, this time on the person who stepped into the shoes of the guy we took out two weeks ago... it never ends. And when those close to you get hurt – that makes the frustration even greater. It's exactly like writing on water," Yariv said, and sniffed.

Dr. Ravid felt the huge, gaping hole that had opened up in the young combat soldier, and he couldn't take it anymore. At that moment, he knew that Yariv would be the last patient of his career. With no hesitation and against every professional rule or ethical standard in the world of therapy, he got out of his chair, went over to Yariv, and hugged him warmly.

CHAPTER 14
September 2006, Security Room, Israeli Embassy, Paris

Araleh, head of the Mossad's branch office in Paris, sat down at the head of the table. On his right sat Yariv, Simon and Paul, field agents from the Caesarea unit, the operations unit of the intelligence organization. For the last few years, Yariv had been serving in the Mossad's operations unit. Simon and Paul were the operational nicknames of two additional agents in the squad Yariv commanded. Both of them served as commanders in elite units, and after their discharge, they joined the Mossad's combat unit. Simon was tall, dark and thin. Paul grew up on a kibbutz in the north. He had fair hair with strong blue eyes and a fuller build than Simon.

The three of them worked flawlessly together for a few operations, and Yariv felt they were like the continuation of his days in Duvdevan. They worked again and again on the briefing for the upcoming mission, whose goal was to place a powerful explosive in the car of a senior Hezbollah operative, who was living in Marseille. The meeting took place in the "clean room," the innermost room of the embassy. The room got its name from the advanced electronic equipment installed there, which prevents anybody from listening in or recording anything that gets said there, and so it became the most secure meeting room for anything that was classified. Araleh placed a map of the region and the picture of the senior Shi'ite member on the table.

"All right, guys," he said, "meet Bilal Al-Masri, married, father of three. Despite his name, he's Lebanese. Don't let his baby face fool you – from the surveillance and what we've heard about him, it turns out that he's responsible for all of Hezbollah's activities in Europe. And when I say responsible, I mean big time. This guy has been living in Europe for a number of years now and is slowly, but thoroughly, building out the organization's infrastructure on the continent. He's not just another Arab with a scraggly beard and an AK-47 – he's the brains in Europe. Our intelligence experts claim that he is the one who has really pushed them to the next level in terms of recruiting operatives, raising money, making international contacts, and more. I can tell you that we've been on his tail for the better part of the past year. From what we've gathered on him, we can say with certainty that he was responsible for planning the two terrorist attacks in Buenos Aires in 1992. Remember those?"

"How can I forget?" Paul responded. "One on the embassy and the other in the Jewish community center building. They got us good there."

"They sure did. A real mess. Hezbollah justified it as revenge for the assassination of their Secretary-General by the Air Force in Lebanon that same year, but it doesn't change the fact that they attacked civilians – and far from the Middle East. From looking into his past, we discovered that besides his official title with Hezbollah, he also works as a freelancer and arms dealer for local crime networks. Our sources tell us that he buys all kinds of missile parts in Europe for Hezbollah, and it turns out that his organizational abilities have contributed to Hezbollah's power.

It was just a month ago that we finished fighting them on the northern border. You saw what they can do – hundreds of long range, accurate missiles, and a massive recruitment of trained fighters, unlimited resources, and on and on. A month of fighting – and they're still giving us the business. So the extensive activities of our friend, Bilal Al-Masri, has contributed to all of that."

"Jeez... recruiting volunteers, upgraded missiles, raising money – talented guy, no doubt. Why don't we just kidnap him and convert him and then hire him to work for us? A little diversity in the workforce wouldn't hurt..." Paul whispered to Simon with a smile.

"Guys, jokes and whispering afterward. Let's finish up the briefing and move on. What's different here is that he recently got into it with one of the local gangsters in the area, and that's good news for us."

"Why?" Simon wondered.

"Because it means this guy has enough enemies that, if tomorrow he ends up with a one way ticket to hell, the suspicion won't immediately fall on us. So this time, the nature of the operation is going to be to place a Semtex charge in his vicinity. We're still not sure where to get him."

"Did you say Semtex? Are you serious? Why not C4?" Yariv asked.

"Good question. You're right, it's not as good and less advanced than what we usually work with, but recently we got our hands on a small amount of Semtex, part of a larger shipment to one of the local organized crime syndicates. We'll use this material, and when the French forensics lab performs their examination, the suspicion will fall to them for the hit and away from us," Araleh replied.

"You're telling me that the small amount taken is enough to finish the job in one shot?" Simon asked incredulously.

"I was also wondering the same thing, I admit," the veteran Mossad agent said. "But when they told me that Pan-Am flight that blew up over Lockerbie in '88 only had 450 grams of Semtex, I understood that we had enough and that Mr. Al-Masri won't be able to go back to work after the blast."

"Awesome. Where are we supposed to plant the explosive?" Paul asked.

"There are a few possibilities: at home is not as good because of his wife and kids. We could do it at his office somewhere, his car, maybe with a magnet on his way to work – anything is possible. It depends on you guys," Araleh said and got out of his chair. "You guys will make a couple trips to observe him from a distance at various places he frequents and, based on that, we'll decide what to do."

"What about a mistress? Does he have anything steady? Maybe we can work that angle?" Simon offered.

"No," Araleh answered definitively. "From what we know about him, he's married with three relatively little kids. He's generally faithful to his wife, even if he does have an occasional thing here and there with confused, young French girls looking to get with some big-time revolutionary. I'll never understand those crazy girls."

"Too bad I can't find any confused French girls like that..." Yariv muttered quietly, but Simon and Paul heard him and suppressed a laugh.

"I see that the briefing has ended, and the artistic portion of the meeting has begun," Araleh said with a smile. "Come on, go already – let's get on with it."

He pressed the six-digit code on the keypad to the left of the big library, and opened the secret cupboard hidden behind the top picture. He took out three guns, two of which were FNs and the other was a CZ, and placed them on the table.

"Take whatever you're comfortable with," Araleh said to the three agents. "Knock yourselves out. These beauties arrived this morning. Fresh out of the oven."

"What do you mean they got here this morning? Santa Claus brought them?" Paul asked.

"Ask me no questions, I'll tell you no lies..." Araleh answered with a smile.

"If that's how it is, I'd rather he brought us something hot from the bakery instead of iron," Paul said, and everybody smiled.

Araleh also placed before them three state-of-the-art communications devices with transparent earpieces. "All right," he said, "there's nothing here you haven't seen before. You guys are familiar with the equipment. May I remind you that, as of now, we're strictly on a recon mission – we're not operational."

"Oh boy," Simon said, "but how will we be able to know for sure that he'll be alone when we actually go? Does he have a fixed schedule that you know of? Are there particular times of day, or days that we should do it?"

"On Sundays, he's mostly at home. Here, Sunday is their day of rest, and so he keeps a low profile from work and mostly spends time with his wife and kids, and sometimes even without a bodyguard. He feels safer at home, I suppose," Araleh said. "So Sunday is the preferred day. But let's not just blindly chance it. Just start with intelligence gathering, learn the area, where he lives, ways to approach and exit routes. Start planning the possible courses of action that you prefer, and of course various exits if we're blown and need to get out. Our regular team will continue watching the other days of the week, so we'll get an updated profile built for him."

"If the operation is going to take place in the next few days, maybe even more than a week from now, then why are we taking guns with us?" Yariv asked Araleh.

"You're no doubt familiar with the joke, 'Why does the Pope have balls?' Because it's always better to have a backup plan... seriously though, officially, the plan is to take him out with a bomb. But, if by some miracle while gathering intelligence, you have the chance to take him out – you have the green light from above to take him out that way. You understand?"

All three nodded their heads.

Araleh sat in his chair opposite Paul and continued. "Protocol dictates that we don't head out to a reconnaissance mission armed. We only take weapons when we're taking action. But there's an important update here: we have new information about our guy, and he's supposed to be leaving France within a month and relocating to Syria. We're still checking that out, but from what we know so far, it turns out that he canceled the automatic registration for his kids' school next year. Somebody planning on spending the next year in the city wouldn't do that. Maybe it's nothing, maybe it's everything. We don't know for sure yet, but we don't want to take a chance that it happens suddenly. So you guys are heading over there to carry out a background check in the field. If you guys see that the conditions to take him out are ripe, then you have the green light – take him down. If not, we wait until the set time, which is another week or two, and then we plant an explosive somewhere near him. Bottom line, the head of the Mossad authorized whatever decision you guys make in the field. Capiche?"

The three soldiers each looked Araleh in the eye. Message received.

"Yariv, you're the leader of the squad, and the commander. Your code name is as usual – Newton. Simon, you're the driver. You'll get your wheels later, somebody will be in touch about that. All right, I don't have anything more here. Exit the embassy according to protocol because there are cameras there. Questions?" Araleh raised his head and looked at the three soldiers.

Yariv put up his hand while saying, "I have a question."

"Shoot. What is it?"

"Araleh, I'm serious," Yariv began, then broke into a sarcastic smile, "what's the deal with Paul and Simon? Who in the hell is in charge of names in this organization?"

CHAPTER 15
September 2006, Second Day of Surveillance, Rural France on the outskirts of Lyon

Yariv raised his binoculars and looked from a distance at the two-story house. Bilal Al-Masri's house was surrounded by greenery in all directions. The red tiled roof sparkled in the morning autumn light and the rusted tail of the chicken on the weather vane above the petit mailbox at the front of the house swayed gently in the breeze, it's creaking audible from a distance.

The three agents – Yariv, Simon and Paul – were dressed like three technicians from one of the local cable companies: blue overalls and hats with the company's logo on them. They arrived in a commercial van that had a long ladder on its roof. There were gold stickers on the van that had the company phone number on it. At the Mossad's HQ in Paris, there was an agent whose sole job was to answer calls to this phone number so that she could give the combat team a heads up about potential problems in the area.

Yariv saw Bilal's car, a black Citroen jeep, which was idling by the front entrance to the house. Inside it, the driver was napping peacefully. The drivers, which rotated, were local Arabs known to work with Hezbollah. They saw helping the local leader strengthen their movement in Europe as their mission.

The weather was still pleasantly cool, as was usual for the beginning of the European autumn. The joyful voices of Bilal's three small children broke the pastoral silence. The three of them ran to the yard while competing among themselves as to who would reach the black car first. After arguing and pushing, they all got to the car. The driver opened the back door for them. Light Arabic music streamed out of the car. *It's been a long time since I've heard nice Arabic music like this*, Yariv thought, a thin smile spreading across his lips. The children reminded him of his little nephews at home in Israel. He always tried disconnecting the object from their personal life. It's very difficult to take somebody's life, even the most despicable murderer, when you see his wife and kids with your own two eyes. Yariv tried to get a good look at the driver's facial features and to photograph him with the camera with the telescopic lens camouflaged on the roof of the car, next to the ladder. He took a few pictures by pressing a button hidden underneath the glove box, the "click" sound registering multiple times.

"Well, did you get him?" Paul asked from the back.

"No, he keeps bending down for the kids. The sun is also against us. It's not going to work this way. He needs to come from the other side," Yariv replied.

The kids got into the car and sat in the back seat. The driver got back in his seat and closed the door.

"Come on, get out already," Paul's voice was urgent. "We can't wait here much longer."

"He's right," said Simon, who was sitting in the driver's seat. "Newton – maybe we'll get a better angle of the houses from the right. We can get another vantage point of the exit from the direction of Al-Masri's kitchen, and see the driver as well."

Yariv, who was commanding the operation, nodded affirmatively. Simon started the car and began taking them east, to the right of their target's house. It was Sunday, and it was relatively early. The soldiers knew that soon the townspeople would be heading to the local church for Sunday prayers. The plan was to observe the house, identify the preferred access point to get to Al-Masri, to identify his car and driver, and to write it all down. All this information would be put together later in a general report, in addition to whatever had been gathered on him to date.

After a few moments, the Al-Masris exited the house via the kitchen and walked to the car. His wife was wearing a long black garment, a grey hijab covering her head. Al-Masri himself was wearing sport-elegant: light-blue jeans, sport shoes and a red polo shirt. They walked over to the car, and the driver immediately got out to attend to them. This time he walked to the other side of the car to open the doors for Al-Masri and his wife. Yariv again brought the binoculars to his eyes, and this time he had a better view. He saw the facial features of his wife and took a picture. Afterward, he saw Al-Masri's face and took another picture. After they both got into the car, he angled the binoculars to get a good look at the driver's face. He had just turned around and was looking right at the commercial van where Yariv was sitting with the binoculars in his hand. Yariv felt as if his eyes were seeing the driver's eyes right up close. Yariv's breath caught in his throat for a moment, and he felt as if all of the air escaped from his lungs at once.

"Come on, take his picture already, he's leaving," Simon whispered to him.

Despite the sun and the warm air, Yariv felt a shiver throughout his whole body. A bead of cold sweat trickled down his back. He felt his hand involuntarily grip the binoculars with tremendous force.

"What's wrong? Is everything all right? Take his picture already!" Paul said, raising his voice from the back seat.

Yariv didn't respond. He sat there in his chair, petrified, looking through the binoculars as if possessed by a demon. Simon didn't wait a second longer. He took Yariv's hand off the binoculars and pressed the hidden button to take a picture multiple times. After a moment where he was looking at the van, the driver got into the car, put it into gear and drove quickly to the road. The car drove right past them and kept on going.

"Have you lost your mind? What gives?" Paul said, his face clearly showing his anger. "Why don't you say something?"

Yariv remained silent. The tremor in his hand grew stronger and his rapid heartbeat only increased. He was starting to feel slightly dizzy. He slowly put the binoculars on the floor of the van, and then stepped outside to get some air.

"What's the matter with him? He's lost it... he must have a thing for Al-Masri's wife..." said Simon with a smile.

"Not sure, it's very weird what just happened to him. I have been working with him for a while now, and I've never seen anything like that happen before. Like he saw a ghost," Paul answered in response.

Yariv stood outside the van and took deep breaths of the clean, clear air into his lungs, again and again, trying to get his rapid breathing under control. He heard the muffled sounds of his friends in the van. The sound of church bells ringing in the distance grew louder. People began coming out of their homes, dressed in their Sunday best for the festive prayers, children holding their parents' hands. A flock of birds flew overhead and Yariv heard the sound of their wings. His heartbeat was still elevated, his mouth dry, and he felt his knees lightly shaking. He felt as if the world was spinning around him, and he put his hand on the ladder on the roof of the van to steady himself.

Yariv's brain internalized what his eyes just saw through the binoculars, but his heart refused to believe it. Deep down, it set off an intense storm of emotions – fear, rage, confusion, anger. Everything burned inside him in a chaotic mixture. He wasn't able to calm down.

"Newton," Paul stuck his head out the window, "what's going on, man? Why didn't you photograph the driver? What's the deal? You're scaring me."

Yariv tried to open his mouth, but couldn't. He felt paralyzed. His emotions overwhelmed him. He tried to answer his friend, but his voice was stuck in his throat. He got into the van without saying a word and sat down heavily on the seat while rubbing the scar on his elbow. He had a distant, pensive look on his face and his eyes stared through the windshield. He looked as if he was entranced in a dream. At that moment, the confusion and surprise gripped him, and he didn't know what to tell his friends, who wanted to know what happened to him. He also didn't know what to write in the operational report summary that he would need to give to Araleh as head of the office. He hadn't even planned what excuse he was going to use as to why he froze and couldn't act at the end. All these questions and doubts were left floating in the air, like ghosts.

Yariv only knew one thing with absolute certainty: Al-Masri's driver, the man he saw that moment through the binoculars, was Sa'id.

CHAPTER 16
September 2006, Moshav Regba[35,] One week after the operation in France

Yariv parked his car at the entrance to the moshav and walked to the gate. He was on leave for the High Holidays,[36] which were evident across the meticulously kept grassy expanse where sprinklers were spraying water far and wide. There were multiple playgrounds spread out along the grounds, and kids were running barefoot from one to the next through the sprinklers, laughing and shrieking with delight. Bicycles were strewn about haphazardly. From afar, he saw an old man riding on a mobility scooter, and was momentarily reminded of his late grandfather. This time of the year, the late afternoons were the most spectacular. The sun presiding over the tops of the trees, the branches and treetops swaying as the wind gently blows, as if extinguishing summer's candle.

---

35. *Moshavs* were established as cooperative living farming arrangements. Regba is located in the north of the country, close to the Lebanese border.
36. Rosh Hashana, the Jewish new year, and Yom Kippur, the day of atonement.

Yariv turned right on the path that wound around the perimeter of the moshav and approached Yogev's house. He recognized his good friend's little twin sons, Raz and Dror. They ran toward him with outstretched arms as fast as they could, yelling at the top of their lungs, "Uncle Yariv!"

When the two little kids finally got to him, he grabbed both of them in a big hug and swung them up into the air.

"Uncle Yariv, were you on another trip? Did you bring us anything?" Raz asked, his light hair strewn about his little head, his cheeks red from the heat.

"Of course I brought you something. Here, check this out." Yariv fished around in his bag and pulled out two small action figures – one Spiderman, the other Superman. "You know who these guys are?" he asked Raz, while handing him one of the figures.

"Of course, it's Spiderman! Thanks! Dad, look what Uncle Yariv brought me!" he said and ran toward the house.

Dror, whose tiny birthmark on his chin distinguished him from his twin brother, asked, "What did you get me, Uncle Yariv?"

Yariv put his hand out and in his palm was the Superman figure. "This one's yours. Wow, look how big you've gotten, my God," Yariv said, and gave the boy a peck on his forehead. Dror thanked him by giving him a kiss on the nose, and then he too ran home to show off his new toy.

At that moment, Yogev's wife, Adi, came running out of the house. She gave Yariv a long hug and kissed him on the cheek. "Yariv, is that you? I can't believe it! We haven't seen you in ages... Yogi – come out here now, you're not going to believe who's here!" She shouted to her husband, who was just coming out of the kitchen with a red dish towel over his shoulder.

Yogev walked quickly over to his good friend and gave him a big hug. "You showed up while I'm in the middle of making schnitzel... what's up, man? Where've you been? What happened, did you forget our address? It's seriously been, like, a year since we've seen you," he said, finally disengaging from the embrace.

The twins followed right behind him playing with their new action figures that Yariv brought them, and they continued past everybody back out to the lawn.

"You're right. I had a few messes at work. I haven't been in Israel for a long time. But I'm glad to see that you're finally out of the bomb shelters..." Yariv answered.

"Yeah, it's been a rough time. They were firing missiles at us non-stop for weeks. It was especially difficult for the twins, look how much fun they're having running around on the grass!" Adi said with a big smile.

"Yeah... that sounds rough. I was abroad the whole time, working, but I kept up with events in the news and thought about you," Yariv said. His eyes smiled warmly at the couple, and only now understood how much he'd missed them.

"So, the main thing is that we're all healthy and in one piece, and back to our blessed routine. By the way, maybe be done with that already?" Adi said. "Come live her near us. Yogev is desperately looking for a partner for his architecture firm. You were pretty good in school, what do you say?" she offered while putting an arm around her husband.

"Adi, I adore you, but leave him alone already, will you? He just got here, at least give him a minute to breathe," Yogev said, winking at Yariv.

"All right, I get it, guy time. See you later. If you want something to drink, come inside. There's a bunch of good beer in the fridge. Ah, and one more thing, Yariv – I'm still waiting for an answer from you regarding Maya. She really is a catch, and somebody will grab her at some point, so you should consider it," she said, smiling, and blew him an "air kiss," before heading to the house to finish making the schnitzel.

"Wow, full on matchmaking service you've opened here for me, huh?" Yariv said and hugged his friend again.

"Exactly. Don't ever say we didn't do anything for you."

"When did I ever say anything like that?" Yariv said, giving Yogev a fake punch to the gut. "Whoa, looks like somebody's getting fat on me... I guess we didn't call you Yogi for nothing, did we?"

"Fuck off, jackass, let's see you keep in shape with twins after you twenty-four seven for a few years... God bless them, I tell you, a couple of Tasmanian devils those two. I love them to death, but in all honesty, sometimes I imagine switching places with you. Sometimes I'd like to fly around the world playing James Bond, have a girl in every port, just like you..." Yogev said, smiling.

"Yeah, just like that, a girl in every port... you think I have time for girls when I'm working? You serious? I guess you've been watching too many movies, Yogi. Besides, not everything that glitters is gold. Believe me, sometimes I get sick of all the operational stress. When I see what peace and quiet you have here on the moshav, the space, the kids running around barefoot – I swear, I just want to leave everything and come move here."

Newton," he said to Yariv, "I really am looking for a partner for the office I opened. Bro, you're perfect for it. You were always head of the class, and we did half of the work for the degree together. Maybe we could work together here? You'd make a great architect. Hear me out for a moment – forget about all the manhunts and shooting, come up north, we'll find a nice Israeli girl for you, and if you don't find a homegrown one to your liking, there are always volunteers from out of the country arriving to work here. Get married, have some kids..."

"And get fat like you?" Yariv said, teasing him.

"You motherf– why you gotta go there?" Yogev said, jumping on him and knocking him to the warm grass. The two of them wrestled around for a bit until Yariv finally was able to get Yogev, who was breathing hard from the effort, to submit.

"Okay, I get it, you're stronger. Get off me already," Yogev said, practically choking.

Yariv let Yogev out of the headlock he had him in and the two sat up on the grass, their clothes having picked up patches of mown grass.

"Man, there's nothing like the smell of fresh cut grass at Regba. The best in the world," Yariv said raising a clump of grass to his nose and inhaling deeply, closing his eyes for a moment.

The sun began dipping west and the shadows from the trees stretched out, as if sending a message of farewell.

"How about a beer? You're staying for dinner, right?"

"Sure," Yariv replied.

Yogev went inside, opened the fridge, and grabbed the first two beers he saw. He brought them back and handed one to Yariv. "Cheers," Yogev said, raising his beer.

"Cheers," Yariv said, and they clinked their beers together, each taking a sip.

"So what are you doing in Israel?" Yogev asked. "No more terrorists abroad, the Messiah came and nobody told me?"

"Mainly I came for briefings, and a bit of shooting practice that I haven't done for a very long time, and some other errands," Yariv said.

"Cool. The important thing is that you're here, even if for just a bit."

They were quiet for a moment. The two sat on the grass, sipping their beers and watching the twins run around making up villains and bad guys to subdue. Yariv didn't want to start a serious conversation only to be interrupted by the twins or Adi, so he made small talk about France and downplayed the urgency of his visit. He asked Yogev innocuous questions about life on the moshav, his career, pondering how they might work together, but mostly he was just waiting for the right moment. In the meantime, the sprinklers had stopped, and Yariv enjoyed watching his friend's twins run around on the wet grass, which was slippery. Both twins fell multiple times, with clumps of grass stuck to their wet clothes. Yariv sensed that maybe now was a good time to get the kids cleaned up to eat.

"Yogi, listen," Yariv said, finally breaking the silence. "I have to talk to you about something, but it has to stay between us. You can't tell Adi, nobody."

Yogev scooted even closer to his good friend, and his eyes didn't stray from Yariv's when he spoke. "You got it, what's the deal?"

"Let's go for a walk and talk," Yariv said, and stood up.

"Raz! Dror!" Yogev suddenly barked. The twins, who were in their own world until then, snapped to attention when their father called them and turned and looked at him, as if awaiting further instructions. "Go on inside, you need to get cleaned up for dinner. I'm going for a quick walk with Uncle Yariv, we'll be right back."

The twins ran inside as their father commanded, and the two men walked slowly toward the fence surrounding the moshav. From afar, Yariv recognized the impressive aqueduct from ancient Acre, a part of which actually passed through the moshav.

"Well, what is it? I'm curious now," Yogev said, unable to contain his budding excitement.

Yariv stopped and took a deep breath. "I found him," he said in a piercing voice.

"Who? I don't understand," Yogev whispered.

Yariv didn't answer. He just lifted his gaze to that of Yogev's. When their eyes met, they were able to continue the conversation without uttering another sound. The strong bond they had forged over years in the unit and during the dozens of clandestine, dangerous missions, strengthened with blood and sweat, had brought them to an almost telepathic state. After a brief moment,

Yariv saw Yogev's eyes light up as it dawned on him who he was talking about.

"Liar. Don't tease me," Yogev whispered.

"Swear to God, it's him. Million percent," Yariv answered quietly.

"No way. I thought that piece of shit was killed in some skirmish and finally got what was coming to him."

"That's it, he wasn't. He's alive and breathing. Yogi, I'm telling you – I saw him with my own two eyes," Yariv said, his eyes burning as he looked toward the expanse.

He looked into Yogev's eyes and then watched as the pulse in his neck became more and more elevated. He knew Yogev like the back of his hand. Yogev always had a poker face on, even during the most stressful situations. Only one thing betrayed Yogev's true feelings, and only his close friends knew how to spot it – whenever he got excited, the artery in his neck would pulsate faster, betraying what was really going on inside him.

Yogev held his head in his hands and started walking toward the fence around the moshav. He was obviously trying to digest what he'd just heard. Yariv waited a few moments and then walked after him, while keeping a safe distance. He knew Yogev well, maybe too well, and knew that right now he needed his space. Yogev paced back and forth. His head was down, his fingers interlocked across the back of his neck. He was obviously sifting through some emotions and shaken, in shock just as Yariv had been when he set eyes on Sa'id. He suddenly turned around and quickly closed the distance between him and Yariv.

Yogev demanded in a whisper, "Tell me exactly where you saw him. I don't care about classified security clearance or any other bullshit. I want to understand how it is he's alive, and where he is right now."

"I was on a job in rural France, and then..." Yariv began.

"France?!" Yogev said, raising his voice. "Did you just say

France?! Get the fuck out of here, how'd he end up in France? And how did he even get out of the country? I'm telling you, you're wrong. He's been dead a long time. I, unlike you, left that whole story behind me. That's it. Finished. What was done, was done. At Dan's funeral, we both swore to leave it behind us and get on with our lives. Remember? We swore on his grave. I always felt like you didn't really mean it, but I decided that I was finished with this whole business. Enough. You aren't the only one with scars from that shit you know. We all have scars from that night in Nablus. And I'm not talking about physical scars... but I, unlike you, understand that I don't have anything to gain by rooting around in my sorrow and misery. I went to therapy, took care of myself and my mental health, and that's it – it's behind me. I have a house, a family, I have a career. I don't know about you, man, but I don't dream at night that I'm standing in front of a terrorist, shooting him, my gun barrel bending downward like a faucet. I also don't dream that I'm shooting and the bullets are coming out in slow motion. That's it, for me, that whole thing is dead and gone. The day we buried Dan, I buried this whole thing with him. Between you and me, I know that's what he would have wanted me to do, if the situation was reversed and it was me injured or dead instead of him. Man, believe me, I've worked very hard to get to where I am and the peace of mind I have right now. I didn't just up and decide to leave the middle of the country, from the craziness of the city, and move here with Adi for nothing. She has supported me the whole way and hugged me every night when I woke up with nightmares, sweating, if I even managed to sleep. So don't come down here out of the blue opening up that old wound again. You want to keep playing cowboy until you retire? The weapons and all the action still does it for you? Is that what you need, raids in the middle of the night? Have at it, brother. But you're on your own there, because that's not me anymore," Yogev said angrily, and turned around and started walking home.

Yariv grabbed his flustered friend's arm to keep him from leaving. "Listen to me for a minute," he said in a quiet, yet forceful tone. "I'm asking you – it threw me for a loop when I saw him, even more than you. I swear, I could barely stand up. I was certain I was going to pass out. Seriously, so please, give me two minutes to explain what's going on here – and then everything will make sense."

Yogev looked around. Darkness began to descend on the moshav like a blanket, and the quiet around them intensified, except for a flock of birds flying overhead on their way back to their nests for the night. There wasn't anybody else around, and the soft light of the sun was almost gone. "Fine. So please explain to me how Mr. Sa'id got from Nablus to rural France. I'm listening," Yogev said, impatiently.

"Remember Operation Defensive Shield[37] in 2002?" Yariv asked.

"Of course I remember," Yogev answered, "but what does that have to do with France?"

"I'll explain, just listen to me and actually hear what I'm saying – drink your beer."

Yogev nodded and took a long drink from his beer.

"I'm coming to you after having done a thorough investigation and I also pulled some strings. The information you're about to hear is definitive and verified. It goes like this – a month before Defensive Shield, the twins were born, and you guys were in the neo-natal intensive care unit all the time."

"That's right, they were born a month premature, they had all kinds of problems breathing, and with their lungs because they weren't developed enough. It was an awful period. But so what?" Yogev asked, confused.

"So you weren't focused and you weren't glued to the

---

37. This was an IDF operation in the West Bank in response to the bombings during the Second Intifada.

news, and it's perfectly natural and makes sense, but one of the big stories of Defensive Shield was when a group of terrorists escaped IDF custody and holed up in the Church of the Nativity in Bethlehem. They took a few priests hostage, some nuns and perhaps two-hundred civilians that weren't affiliated with the church. The IDF, of course, didn't want to intervene, for obvious reasons. It would have been a real mess, and would have become an international incident. In the end, after a month of negotiations, an international delegation was able to reach an agreement with the terrorists – they would evacuate the holy area, some to Gaza, others to countries in Europe. It sounds crazy, but that was the solution to the crisis that they found. In any event, turns out that Sa'id was in the church and from there, he and some of his friends were flown to Europe, and today he's walking around without a care in the world in France. That's it," Yariv said, his eyes still locked on Yogev's.

Yogev stared at the ground. "Ok, so you want to tell me that, for almost a decade, the IDF and Shin-Bet were unable to locate him? Does that sound reasonable to you?" he asked without lifting his head.

"I have a few friends in military intelligence who owe me. So I checked some things out, discreetly. Turns out that the same night in Nablus, after he shot me and Dan, he fled. He understood that we were onto him, and so he dropped off the grid. I mean nothing. So the Shin-Bet wasn't able to find him during the other operations in the years that followed. Toward the end of 1999, he started getting involved with terrorism again and, unfortunately, they didn't find out in time. He joined up with other terrorists and continued hiding out for a few more years, until he joined that group at the beginning of 2001 and, in the end, found himself trapped in that church," Yariv said.

Yogev raised his gaze from the ground to the sky. The sun had set and the last rays of fire painted the sky in dark hues over the moshav. "I want to understand," Yogev said, leveling his gaze at Yariv, his eyes burning. "You saw Sa'id with your own two eyes. Our Sa'id, right? So just explain to me, please, Mr. Genius that you are, how'd you recognize him – you haven't seen him for over a decade, and the last time you met, it was at night, when Dan was lying on top of you. Explain to me, if you would, how in the hell you recognized him," Yogev demanded adamantly.

"First of all," Yariv began, "I'll never forget that face as long as I live. When somebody is standing over you with an AK-47 and shooting you and your best friend from spitting distance, that's not something you forget. But besides that, without getting into classified details, he's been photographed in an operation in France I participated in. He's the driver for a very senior figure in Hezbollah – that's the guy we're trying to get to. The pictures we have are very good, and taken in the middle of the day, so in order to verify this, I checked with the right people and cross-checked it against the Shin-Bet's database here in Israel. Our experts at the Shin-Bet verified that it's him."

"I don't understand," Yogev insisted, "how is it possible to determine something like that absolutely? It's been ten years since then. The person changes, gets older, suddenly needs glasses, maybe he's got white hair, maybe he's even gotten a little fat," Yogev said. "How can you be one hundred percent sure that it's him?"

"The ID is done using all sorts of computer programs these days. Don't ask me how they work exactly, it's not my area and so I don't really know how to answer that. Irrespective, I can't talk about it – but that's what happens. Bottom line, the identification process goes through a double verification – besides the computer, which is the most advanced there is, a team of experts verifies it," Yariv said in a decisive tone.

Yogev closed his eyes and took a deep breath. He held it for a moment before letting it out slowly. "Go to hell. Because of you, now I need a cigarette. Just when I was finally able to quit," Yogev sighed.

"You're fat *and* you smoke?" Yariv replied with a smile while taking a pack of cigarettes out of his bag, popping one out of the top and offering it to his friend.

"Oh, drop dead," Yogev said, taking it.

Yariv dug into his back pocket and produced a lighter and lit Yogev's cigarette. Yogev inhaled the smoke into his lungs, and after a moment released a pillar of smoke into the crimson sky. He offered the cigarette to Yariv. "You want it? We all die anyway. At least die happy."

"No, thanks. I knew you'd crack, so I brought the cigarettes with me," he said, laughing slightly. "And because of you, I'm the most active passive smoker in the world," Yariv added, and laughed, and finally managed to coax a small laugh out of Yogev.

Neither said anything after that, the only sound coming from the crickets, whose noise grew louder as the quiet between them lengthened. Yogev lay on his back and looked at the sky. The sun had completely set, and the darkness thickened. Yariv lay down next to him, his arms crossed behind his head.

"Look at how many stars you can see out here, man. Just for that alone it was worth leaving the city. Every night, after Chip and Dale finally go to bed, Adi and I have our own thing we do. We go out to the yard with a couple cold beers and look at the stars. It's the most beautiful and relaxing thing there is," Yogev said.

The shadows of the trees had disappeared, the darkness was almost total, and it was quiet. Above them, a street light flickered, and the buzz of the powerlines in the distance could be heard. Yariv sat up and took a folded envelope from his pocket.

"The truth is, I came to say goodbye," Yariv said and gave Yogev the envelope.

"What is it?" Yogev asked, curious.

"It's a personal letter that I'm giving you. You open it if and only if something happens to me. Everything is written inside in an organized fashion. There are clear instructions and who you'll need to contact in such a case."

"I don't understand. Why should something happen to you?"

"Because next week I'm going back to France to finish what we weren't able to in Nablus," Yariv answered in a determined, confident voice.

Yogev couldn't believe it. He grabbed Yariv by his collar forcefully, his face flushed with anger. Yariv didn't put up any resistance. After a few moments Yogev loosened his grip, looked him in the eye and finally said, "Are you out of your mind?"

"I'm completely serious," Yariv said calmly, and shook himself free of his friend's grip.

"You're crazy. I also want to finish the bastard off, but we aren't vigilantes. Certainly not the outfit you work for. They're organized, they have protocols. You know what would happen if they found out you went on a personal mission of revenge? Not to mention what would happen is something were to go wrong during your little partizan op. Who's going to help you if you get captured, or wounded, or killed, or God knows what? Dude, you've lost your mind, fucking hell. Do you understand the consequences of what you're about to do?" Yogev asked. He was angry.

"So what do you propose?" Yariv said, raising his voice over that of his friend's. "That I let that motherfucker get away again and again without paying for what he did? At first, he was able to stay off the IDF radar for a few years, and then he was able to get away from us closing in on him in Nablus, then he got a free trip to Europe, and today he's living free as a student, having fun with French girls and still plotting terror attacks against Jews, and nobody can touch him. Don't you think it's time that somebody closed his account?"

"And you, Mr. James Bond, you're going to settle the score yourself? Well what do you know, what a great idea. Does that make any sense to you? Why not let your commanding officers in on it and let them come up with a solution for you?"

"Yogi, you aren't getting it. I did some digging around and it turns out that as part of the deal they signed with the state before they were deported, they promised not to engage in terrorism, and we promised not to go after them outside the country. That's why. As far as the State of Israel is concerned, Sa'id has immunity, you understand? Immunity! After all the Jewish blood he spilled, he has a damn insurance policy sponsored by the State of Israel. So the country is officially not able to touch him. The country can sign off on a thousand pieces of paper that say that – I don't give a fuck about any agreements because I won't allow it. And may I remind you that for me, this isn't just some other target. As far as I'm concerned, he killed Dan, and that's it. That the country let it go for political reasons, fine. But as far as I'm concerned, this isn't something that can be erased, and he'll pay for it," Yariv said, determined.

"What's in the envelope?" Yogev asked suspiciously.

"Listen, man, I'm not stupid. I know that what I'm about to do goes against every possible regulation. I'm aware of the fact that the Mossad will probably throw me out on my ass, and let's not even start about what will happen if something gets fucked up abroad. That could even ignite a bunch of fires for every agent in the field, or even worse, who knows. So I put in there a sort of manifesto, whereby I explain that this was my own personal doing, and that nobody else in the Mossad or the country knows about it, and that I acted completely alone and that I take full responsibility. I also wrote that if something goes wrong and I'm captured – not to trade me for terrorists, that I release the state from any and all legal or moral responsibility regarding my future. That's all. At the end of the letter, there is a list of contacts that you should give this letter to. If they ask, tell them that I came by for a regular visit to the moshav, that you found this in one of the drawers after I left, and that you didn't know anything about it beforehand. That's all. That's why I came. If you say you aren't prepared to do that – I'll get somebody else to do this for me, but you know that you're among the very few I can count on with my eyes closed."

"Wait," Yogev said, getting up. "Before you start planning your funeral, just tell me one thing. How do you plan on taking him out? Even without being in the Mossad, it should be clear to anybody that these types of things aren't done alone. We did this dozens of times in the unit. You'll need a driver, extraction, lookouts, backup... Where are you going to get all that? What, you're going to go to your commander and say, 'Listen, I'm going to take this guy out, I have unfinished business with him, and without your authorization... just do me one favor: can I get you to sign off on a getaway driver for me?"

"I don't know. I'll figure something out, but the less you know the better. I mean, they'll question you about this visit," Yariv said, lowering his voice suddenly.

Yogev looked at his good friend. It was obvious by the look on his face that his mind had been made up, even though he was taking a drastic and dangerous step. For a moment, Yogev had a crazy notion. He looked into Yariv's eyes and whispered to him, "You know what? I'm coming with you. We'll take him out together."

Yariv grabbed Yogev forcibly, put his mouth to his ear and said, "Forget it, you fucking idiot. Period. No discussion," he said, and began walking toward Yogev's house.

Yogev ran after him, placed his hand on Yariv's shoulder and stopped him. "There's no way you're doing this alone. You know you need somebody else there. Who can you trust more than me?" he said, raising his voice.

"Tell me something, did you hit your head while we were wrestling back there? I told you, there's no way, end of discussion, and I mean it. I didn't come all the way out here to drag you into this story and make your wife a widow and your kids orphans. You're a citizen now, you're off the table as far as I'm concerned. I just came here to give you this letter in case something goes wrong. I don't need something happening to you on my conscience as well. Adi would kill me if something like that were to happen."

They continued walking and Yogev kicked a colorful ball that was lying in the grass. Then he suddenly stopped. He looked at Yariv, who kept walking a few steps more before stopping and turning around, waiting for Yogev to catch up. "Bro, I get that you're vetoing the idea. But I'm asking you to listen to me now," Yogev said, in a determined, quiet voice. "Both of us have put together operational plans in the past, and not just once or twice. It always worked perfectly. Let's put together a plan, I'll fly over and join you there for a few days, we'll finish this thing and be done with it. Nobody will know anything about it, not even Adi. If we put together a good plan, there's no reason why they should know it was us. Besides, it should be obvious to you that you need at least one other person in this thing with you. You can't do this type of thing alone. So why not me? Haven't we done a thing or two together?"

Deep down, Yariv knew his friend was right. The plan he was thinking of would require at least one other person – and he really didn't know whom to recruit to the task. He thought about going to Simon or Paul with it, but knew that they'd most likely refuse, and then he'd be in the unenviable situation of having to trust them not to rat him out. But he never once thought of Yogev as an option. First of all, he's a civilian, and as upstanding a citizen as they come – how could he drag him back into this story? And if, God forbid, something were to happen to him, how could he ever look Adi in the eye, or Raz or Dror? It sounded like absolute madness.

"I don't understand you – one minute you're yelling at me, telling me this whole thing is behind you, that you are done with it, and now you're ready to come to France with me and risk everything?" Yariv asked, perplexed.

"You're right. But that was before you told me that Sa'id was alive and within reach, and that my best friend was going after him alone. Just so we're clear, I don't intend to let you do this alone, because the chances of you getting in trouble are just too high. But if we do it together, we have a much better chance to succeed. If we're talking about a one-time operation that will take a few days and that's it, why not do it together and finish it off once and for all? If you can get me a weapon, sweet. If not, I'll be the driver or your support, and you'll have your piece from your office. In any event, that won't happen if we have to count on somebody else, we both know that. We owe it to Dan, to close his account with Sa'id," said Yogev definitively.

Yariv didn't know what to say. The emotional roller coaster was overwhelming him. He came to Regba to say goodbye to Yogev and to give him that envelope, not recruit him on a dangerous mission. But at the moment, Yogev's offer was playing in his mind like a trump card. At first, it sounded like a crazy, impossible and impulsive suggestion, but from his deep friendship with Yogev, he knew there was truth to what he was saying: he did in fact need help, because it was impossible to do it alone. Yariv knew that Yogev was an excellent fighter: imaginative, creative, brave and responsible – he was somebody that could be trusted completely. He wasn't just another mercenary, or somebody who would do him a favor by taking out Sa'id – Yogev was in for all he was worth. He couldn't ask for a better partner than Yogev on this mission.

Yogev cut into Yariv's thoughts. "How much time do we even have? How big is the window?"

"About two weeks. After that, good chance that he goes somewhere else and disappears."

"Dude," Yogev said and put his hand on his friend's arm, "this is a once in a lifetime shot. It won't come back. I don't have any intelligence on Sa'id, but I am certain that you've done all the calculations on that end. I trust you one hundred percent. We both owe Dan. If you agree – I'm in," he said, and pulled him in for a hug.

Yariv hugged him back and then whispered, "Thanks. Let me sleep on it. I want to consult with somebody else first."

CHAPTER 17
The Day After the Encounter at Moshav Regba, Beit Ha-Kerem Neighborhood, Jerusalem

The streets of the ancient Jerusalem neighborhood took on the reddish hue of the setting sun. The heavy heat that accompanied the summer slowly broke, and the air became pleasantly bearable. Yariv loved the autumn nights in Jerusalem, when the warm blanket that covers the city during the day is ripped to shreds in the evening, as the Jerusalem chill slowly returns to purify the air. Two kids on bicycles pass by him, laughing out loud together. On the other side of the street, he saw a young couple with a blue baby stroller. He kept walking the neighborhood streets until he saw the address he was looking for. He pushed the door to the building open and went inside. A white, fluorescent light flickered in the stairwell, and he was able to quickly locate the apartment number he needed. He stood in front of the door, staring at it for a while. Finally, he knocked softly. He heard the sound of steps approaching from the other side of the door and then it opened. Standing opposite him was the psychologist, Dr. Yehonatan Ravid.

He looked more bent over than Yariv remembered, his hair was now completely white and, despite the fact that the passage of time had no doubt left its imprint on him, he looked fantastic and well-cared for at his advanced age. His eyes were sharp and his gaze stopped on his guest's face, which he recognized immediately without missing a beat.

"Yariv!"

* * *

His living room was pleasantly decorated. A large brown grand piano stood to the right, and on the left was a tall bookcase that practically kissed the high ceiling. Yariv took a look around – a lot of professional literature in Hebrew and English, but also other books as well. The door leading out to the porch was slightly ajar. The wind played with the light colored curtain, blowing it gently back and forth against the wall. A heavy grandfather clock was hanging on the opposite wall, and its rhythmic sound added a dramatic aspect to the room. Oil paintings dotted the walls, but Yariv couldn't make out the name of the artist who signed them.

Two armchairs were placed side by side, the floors were clean and shiny, and the light-colored rug in the center of the room accented the legs of the glass coffee table resting on top of it. On the coffee table, Yariv saw a few pictures of the psychologist alongside an attractive woman who obviously took care of herself. They were hugging each other while being photographed at various places and landmarks around the world. He assumed she was his wife. Next to the pictures of the elderly couple, Yariv saw what must have been the Ravid children along with their children – his grandchildren.

One picture stuck out in particular. Unlike the smaller ones on the coffee table, this one was on the wall in a large black frame – a photograph of a pretty little girl with blue eyes and freckles on her nose, her light colored hair in tight pigtails. She was holding a doll, and on her head was a wreath of flowers, as if it was her birthday.

Dr Ravid was alone in the apartment. There was the soft sound of classical music coming from the kitchen. *Probably a radio station*, Yariv thought to himself. He stood awkwardly in the middle of the room, his hands shoved into his pockets.

"Come, sit down," Dr. Ravid said, "I was just making myself something to drink, what can I get you?"

"Something cold, doesn't matter what, thanks," Yariv said.

Just then, the shrieking tea kettle interrupted them, and Dr. Ravid turned and made his way to the kitchen, turned off the radio, and before long returned holding a small tray with two cups on it – one with Dr. Ravid's tea, and another with cold water for Yariv. Next to them were some decorative glass plates with an assortment of cookies on them.

Dr. Ravid motioned with his hand to a small sofa, and Yariv sat down. The unnatural, strange situation created an awkward silence.

"I must admit, I'm pleasantly surprised that you even remember me, Dr. Ravid," Yariv said.

"I'll tell you something you don't know, Yariv," the old psychologist replied as he patiently stirred sugar into his tea. Yariv waited anxiously for him to continue. "You were my last patient as chief psychologist in the security establishment and the IDF. The last. The truth is, even before you were referred to me, I had let the Ministry of Defense know that I was retiring. But then Dr. Landau, who was then the psychologist for the West Bank division, gave me a call. We did our residencies together back in the day, and we had an excellent personal and professional relationship for many years. He told me your story and, in contrast to today, the media didn't always report to the public about what goes on in the West Bank. A lot of events went unreported, for all kinds of reasons. I won't get into it now, but that's the way it was then. They called it a 'media blackout.' They didn't want people to know too much about what they were up to. It doesn't matter. The point is that as a citizen, I didn't know about your thing there in Nablus. Dr. Landau only told me a very little bit about you, and urgently asked that I treat you. Obviously I was against it, but not because of anything having to do with you, heaven forbid. Because of my family situation that I was engulfed in at the time."

"Wow, I didn't realize that. What happened, if I may ask?" Yariv inquired.

"You may, it's no secret. My wife was diagnosed with cancer at the time, and she had started radiation treatment. I needed to be with her more, and so I requested to be released from my role in the Ministry of Defense. I was one foot out the door when you arrived for our first appointment, all wet from the rain."

Yariv recalled that appointment. Everything was still raw and oozing, right after everything that happened in Nablus. *More than a decade had passed*, Yariv thought, *and that night still bleeds inside me.* Yariv looked at Dr. Ravid and took a long sip of water from his glass. "I'm sorry to hear that," he said, finally. "How is she doing?"

"To my great regret, she passed away after a year of agony. Absolute hell. We were married close to thirty years. We had a special bond. But in the end, her condition deteriorated day by day. Not that there's a 'happy ending' when somebody dies, but in her case, it was especially sad. She was a wonderful wife, a special woman and an exceptionally good mother to our children. She had a very developed artistic sense. She played piano in the philharmonic and painted the rest of the time. A delicate soul that left the world before her time."

"I'm sorry to hear that. My condolences. And to think they dumped me on you at such a time... if I would have known, I wouldn't have taken up so much of your time and energy that you dedicated to me back then," Yariv said in a quiet voice.

"It's all right. Truth is, I felt like it was the right thing to do. For sure for you, because of how broken you were when you came to me. But, believe it or not, it was also the right thing for me. The period I went through with my wife was long and unbearable. With you, I felt that I was saving a soul. It also got me out of my routine of taking care of my wife, and took me to a completely different place. Besides, maybe deep down, I was hoping that somebody or something from above would pay back my deed and save my wife. But that didn't work."

Yariv picked up a cookie and took a bite. He reveled in the taste – it had been a while since he'd tasted homemade cookies like this. Dr. Ravid noticed and pushed the plate towards Yariv, encouraging him to take another. Yariv obliged and thanked him with a nod of his head.

"But forget about me for a moment, I'm not important here. I'm just an old coot. What are you doing here? And how did you find out where I live?" asked the psychologist.

"The place I served in the army and the place I work now locate people all the time... including people who don't want to be found, even if they're out of the country, if you know what I mean," Yariv said with a mysterious grin.

"Why do I get the feeling that you're not working as a mailman for the Israel Postal Service?" Dr. Ravid asked with a thin smile. Both of them felt the tension dissipate a bit. "Now, for real, what are you doing here? If you came all this way, you obviously did some homework, and so you're certainly aware of the fact that I've been out of the system for a few years now. Even many, I'd say. Unfortunately, since I retired, I don't have the authority to officially treat anybody in the security establishment. I'll remind you, it's been more than ten years since I treated you then, after your injury. Ten years is a long time."

"It is, but you're the only one who really understands me, who was able to get me – the fact is, you managed to get me back on my feet after what happened in Nablus. I'm not sure I would have been able to make it without you. Seriously. I'm going through something at the moment, and the only person I thought of who can help me is you, doctor," Yariv said. His eyes radiated absolute honesty.

"First," the psychologist said, "thank you for the compliment. I'm happy to hear that I helped. Second, you're in my home, so don't call me 'doctor.' Call me Yehonatan, please."

"So, Dr.... uh, sorry, Yehonatan. Seriously, you did help me. I was pretty young, and to tell you the truth – pretty stupid. But you were the only one who finally was able to traverse the minefield that I surrounded myself with then, and reach me. I hope you can help me this time as well. If it doesn't sit well with you, just say so and I'll leave – I'll understand completely. Really. But it's something that is very important to me, and the only one I really trust is you. Please," Yariv said, and he looked at Dr. Ravid with a pleading gaze.

Dr. Ravid got up from his chair and stood in the corner of the room. With his arms folded across his chest, he looked at the yard before turning to Yariv. "Yariv, since you had the audacity to show up out of the blue at my home, I assume it's important enough. What are we talking about?"

Yariv also stood up. He walked over to where Dr. Ravid was standing and said, "Yehonatan, you're not going to believe this, but I found him. Sa'id. The bastard who shot me and Dan. I found him, and now I don't know what to do with myself," he said, looking away, but the old psychologist noticed his eyes welling up with tears.

He looked at the younger man standing before him. His muscular frame shook, tears streamed from his eyes and spattered on the floor. It was clear that Yariv was going through an emotionally tumultuous ordeal. Dr. Ravid didn't intervene during the first minute, but just looked on from the side and let Yariv unpack the mental distress he was carrying around. He remembered their therapy sessions and the long way they came together until Yariv was able to heal and return to the unit. He knew all too well how deeply it hurt Yariv to see Sa'id get away, not to mention the heavy price he and his friends paid, most of all Dan, for their operational failure that rainy night in Nablus.

For the duration of the therapy, over months of long meetings and deeply personal conversations, the veteran psychologist tried to get him to understand that success always comes with failures. Statistically speaking, even the best unit in the world will experience failure at some point. During the conversations, the psychologist shared personal stories with Yariv – how he was taken captive and went from a vigorous combat soldier in the paratrooper commando unit, to a broken vessel at the hands of his captors. The horrific torture, continual starvation, interrogations, breaking him down psychologically, the nightmares – all this was just Dr. Yehonatan Ravid's destiny.

He told Yariv about the hard feelings he had when he came back home, where the intelligence investigators swarmed him like flies, desperate to learn what he told them under interrogation. Though he suffered horribly to protect the state secrets that he held in his mind and in his heart, that didn't protect him from the disrespectful and even humiliating reception he received from the state investigators. He told Yariv about his difficult and even unstable emotional situation when he returned from captivity, about the nightmares and about the difficulty of telling his friends, or even his family, what he went through as a hostage. With all this going on, he ultimately decided to take matters into his own hands. He studied psychology, finished his degree with honors, and started out on his life's new mission – he recruited other rescued hostages and together they formed the organization "Awake At Night."

They embraced those who returned from being held hostage and gave them the ability to feel good, that they were wanted, that they're okay, and that they aren't disposable – that they're heroes, heroes who survived captivity and came out sane, humane, and loyal to the country and the army, despite the difficult, painful and high mental cost.

From his personal experience and that of his friends, Yehonatan Ravid knew that the healing process could take many years. He knew that it required patience, taking it one step at a time, slowly but consistently – and more than anything, something he often repeated to Yariv at the time, the need to forgive oneself, to understand that he did the best he could, and to internalize the fact that the tough result doesn't signify failure on his part, and in no way is his friend's blood on his hands. Yariv listened intently, opened up, told his story, shared, considered – but didn't internalize it.

Dr. Ravid knew that getting closure by killing Sa'id would cauterize the open wound. But he also knew that taking the law into his own hands was absolutely forbidden, certainly when done outside of Israel, and could end up disastrously for him personally, perhaps even for the country. Yariv stopped crying. He lifted his head and looked at Dr. Ravid, and in his eyes was the look of somebody who was caught doing something wrong, the tears blurring the tough façade he always wore.

Dr. Ravid looked at Yariv from a distance before approaching him. He placed a gentle hand on his shoulder, massaged it softly, and finally said in a quiet voice, "It's all right. It doesn't make you any less of a man than you were a minute ago. Think of it as a special cleansing for the soul. Your mind is working very hard, all the time. That's how it disconnects and airs itself out. It needs it sometimes. Let it, don't take that away from it."

Yariv took a tissue from the colorful box on the piano, blew his nose and mopped up the remaining tears from his eyes.

"Do you feel better now? Tell me the truth..." the psychologist said, smiling.

"I do actually. It is liberating, at least a bit," Yariv admitted and blew his nose again.

"Adopt the habit. Shed a tear once in a while, it will only help. I won't tell anybody, trust me..." said Dr. Ravid and clapped Yariv lightly on the back.

The two of them sat down opposite one another. Yariv asked for another glass of water, and Yehonatan gladly brought it to him. "Listen, Yariv," the psychologist said after a minute of silence, "I hope you realize that what's going through your head right now is confusing and frustrating. On the one hand, settling the score and getting revenge is a logical, human emotion. On the other hand, think of the potential consequences – you're a smart guy who knows that something like this could end with serious criminal charges, including a long prison sentence, let alone even worse scenarios. I understand that this is something that's burning in your bones, but I have to tell you honestly that I care more about you than getting revenge for Dan."

"Dan's not looking for revenge, he's not with us anymore. He died a few years ago," Yariv said, looking down. It was silent in the room again.

"I... I'm very sorry to hear that. I didn't know he had passed away," Yehonatan said in a whisper.

"No, it's fine, I didn't expect you to know. It wasn't in the newspapers. Turns out that even the death of a decorated combat soldier has a statute of limitations. If it doesn't happen at the time, then the write-up is tossed into the last few pages of the paper," Yariv said bitterly.

"But how did that happen?" Yehonatan asked.

"He was a vegetable for a few years, and his situation got worse and worse. It was expected. In the beginning, we visited him once a week, the whole team, to see how he was doing and to help his family. Then it became once a month, and then we all got discharged – some of us went on a year-long trip to Africa or South America, we trained all kinds of resistance movements... and then people started studying, they found work in Israel and abroad, some of the guys got married, had kids, and like the cliché says – life goes on. And this whole time, he just got worse. They took him to a full-time care facility, where the average age dropped down to eighty as soon as he arrived..."

Yariv's voice broke, and he just kept nodding his head again and again. "His body started to fall apart," he continued, his voice cracking. "We tried as hard as we could to recognize even the slightest bit of our friend that we loved, but there was nothing. It was like he'd been embalmed – that's how we felt, like he was a mummy. At first when we came to visit, we used to play songs he liked on the guitar and sing, or sing songs on Shabbat when the whole team was there, but it slowly just faded away..." Yariv said sadly.

"That's perfectly natural, and it's the way of the world. You can't hold onto something like that forever. That's the truth," Yehonatan said, trying to calm him down.

"I know in my mind that you're right, but in my heart, I can't let it go. One day we got a phone call from his mother. His system unexpectedly collapsed, and he had a heart attack. They tried reviving him there at the facility, but weren't able to. It isn't nice to say so, but it's a good thing they weren't able to. He was free from the torment and that was it," Yariv said sadly, and his eyes again welled with tears.

"That's very sad. During the war, a lot of my friends and commanding officers were killed. I know what you're going through, Yariv. Believe me, I know. I've been there," Yehonatan whispered and grasped his hand in both of his. Yariv looked at them. In his heart, Yariv was grateful for Dr. Ravid's caring and understanding toward him, both then and now. He knew without a shadow of a doubt that he had come to the right place.

"Listen, Dr. Ravid – sorry, Yehonatan. Listen, Yehonatan," said Yariv suddenly, urgently. "On second thought, I'm not sure that it is smart for me to share this story with you. If something happens and they come to you, you could get into trouble. Abetting a crime and all that crap. I prefer that you know as little as possible. But I have one request, if I may?"

"Gladly. What can I do for you?" the old psychologist said, becoming serious.

Yariv took the envelope out of his pocket containing the letter he tried to give to Yogev. With a trembling hand, he turned the white envelope over to Dr. Ravid.

"Let me guess," Yehonatan said with a bitter smile, "farewell letter?"

"Not exactly. It's sort of an insurance policy. In case something goes wrong. There is a list of contacts there that this letter is addressed to. From the head of the Mossad on down. There are phone numbers and addresses of the necessary parties. I don't want to get you into trouble – so don't mention that we met, just say that you found it in your mailbox or something like that. In any event, I wrote there that I acted alone, that the state didn't send me, and that everything that happened, transpired because of my own personal initiative and not as a representative or agent of the state, so that if something happens to me, I'm releasing the state from any responsibility for my fate..."

"Wait, stop for a moment," Yehonatan broke in. "Believe me when I tell you that I identify with what you're saying, I really do.

But I honestly don't think that you understand the full implications and possible ramifications of this course of action you're about to undertake. I'm not playing devil's advocate. Sa'id has a death sentence on him, like many other terrorists. I'm no bleeding-heart liberal, I've shot my share of terrorists, but it was always with permission and authority. This case is different. Forget about at the national level – that is, forget about any international incident this could cause. I'm talking about you now – what will happen to you if something goes wrong. You could wind up getting killed, injured, maybe captured, and in a foreign country no less... who's going to get you out of there? Who's going to back you up? Who can know how badly this thing can get screwed up, God forbid? Please, I care for you like I care for my own children – step back from this. Forget about it. It isn't worth it. I'll put it this way – what would Dan think about it? Think seriously for a minute about yourself. I didn't have the honor of knowing him, but from what you told me, he was a mature, understanding, intelligent and responsible person. Can you imagine a situation where he would expect you to sacrifice yourself and your life, your future, just to avenge his injury and ultimate death?" the psychologist said, shooting Yariv a piercing glance.

"Yehonatan, believe me, I've thought about this a lot. You know what the final straw was that convinced me to do it? I think I already told you the last time we met, but that was a while ago... you remember the song by Fairuz, the one with the line about people are nothing but lines written on water?"

"You know, I have a foggy recollection of something like that where you quoted me that line, but I don't know what you mean and how it's connected to taking out Sa'id." Yehonatan still hadn't removed his penetrating, imploring gaze from Yariv.

"Look, she claims in the song that most people are lines written on water, that most of us don't leave a mark on the world. Unfortunately, that's how I feel, that despite all the operations I was a part of, I feel that at the end of the day, I haven't left a real mark on the world. You understand? I'm just sick of writing on water. Closing the circle with Sa'id will be, at least for me, making a mark in the world. For me, but also for Dan. It could be that if he could, he would object, just like you. But I'm certain that if the situation were reversed, and I was dead, he would do it, just like I'm going to," Yariv said.

"I understand, but it still doesn't make me worry about you any less," Yehonatan said, again trying to dissuade Yariv. "If you do indeed feel dissatisfied or worthless, there are other ways to solve that – maybe it's time for you to quit this difficult and demanding line of work, perhaps you'd feel better if you were in a relationship, had kids, maybe go study... there are all kinds of things to do in order to change how a person feels, and not only by taking an extreme step like this, where who knows what the long-term consequences will be at the end of the day, both for you personally but also the country."

Yariv got up and walked to the door. "I thank you for your hospitality. And for your concern. Really. But this decision is final," he said, determined. "I only need to know that you're on board regarding the envelope. That's all. Thank you for all that you've done for me, both then and now. Really. I have to go now," he said as he stood at the doorway about to head out.

"Yariv," Yehonatan said to the younger man as he too went to the door, "wait a moment."

Yariv turned around and waited. His hand was resting on the door knob. Yehonatan got up from the sofa and went over to him and put his hand on Yariv's shoulder.

"Listen to me, Yariv. Each of us has his demons. I do too, and after I returned from captivity, I wrestled with them so as not to end up in the darkness of the past, but rather to look ahead. Not to concentrate on what was, but on what will be tomorrow. But now, you're taking your life and instead of moving forward, you're going back to the past, to what happened. Don't let what happened affect your future," said the psychologist in a quiet voice.

Yariv looked up at the ceiling.

"Look at me, dammit! I'm talking to you!" Dr. Ravid said, raising his voice, but Yariv's glance remained on some arbitrary point on the ceiling. "I'm telling you you're making a mistake. You're behaving recklessly, like a child. That's inappropriate, and even dangerous. Stop it, for the love of God!" Dr. Ravid said, now angry.

Yariv took his eyes off the ceiling and looked deep into the psychologist's eyes. "Dr. Ravid," he said coolly, "I'm going to ask you this once – trust me, okay? Please just do what I asked. That's all," he said, and opened the door.

"Don't do anything stupid!" Yehonatan practically shouted. "You could get a lot of people in trouble. By the way, what's your guarantee that I won't immediately call the appropriate authorities and tell them about this craziness that's got a hold of you? The Shin-Bet will be on you in an instant, and at the same time, they'll get a warrant barring you from leaving the country. Might be unpleasant, but at least you'll sit in jail here instead of a pit out there," he said while clutching at Yariv's jacket.

Yariv looked at Dr. Ravid. For a moment, the psychologist thought he may have gone a bit overboard with his threat, and that Yariv might harm him physically. But Yariv just stood there, and then whispered, "You wouldn't do that."

"Where is this exaggerated confidence coming from?" Yehonatan asked, surprised.

Yariv took his hand off the doorknob and walked back to the center of the living room with measured steps. He stood opposite the wall, and then raised his hand up and pointed to the picture of the pretty little girl with the freckles hanging there in the black frame. "That's Noga, right? Your granddaughter. She was murdered in the suicide bombing in Sbarro's restaurant in

Jerusalem in August 2001. She was supposed to start first grade at the end of that summer, but she was murdered there, three weeks before school started. Noga was your oldest granddaughter. Your first consolation after your wife's passing from cancer. Little Noga was there in the Sbarro's restaurant with her mother, your daughter, who was injured there and still limps and is considered legally disabled, at least partially. Maybe you don't know, I'll let you in on a little secret – Sa'id orchestrated that bombing. You're right, Dr. Ravid, I did do my homework before coming out here."

The veteran psychologist felt like his heart stopped in his chest. He wasn't expecting this at all. Noga was indeed his first granddaughter. His second great love. His connection with her was special – until she was born, he lacked the will to live in the emptiness left in the wake of his beloved wife's death. His eyes widened in astonishment. He felt his heart rate accelerate in his veins, his mouth all of sudden went dry, and he stood there in complete shock. The room began spinning around him and his legs began to shake. He held the chair next to him to keep from falling.

Yariv saw the shock gripping the old psychologist. He saw his hands shaking and legs faltering and was afraid Dr. Ravid might collapse right there and then on the floor. Yariv came over to him and suddenly the roles were reversed. The old, veteran psychologist appeared as a leaf in the wind, while Yariv, the eternal patient, became the one with the strength, the guide, the leader.

"Yehonatan," Yariv said in a quiet voice into Dr. Ravid's ear, "I'm sorry that I had to tell you that, but I had to, because now you feel just like I do. So understand, I'm doing this not just for Dan, but for her, your Noga as well."

Dr. Ravid breathed heavily. The news hit him suddenly and left him absolutely stunned. His knuckles were white from gripping the chair so that he wouldn't fall. Yariv came closer to the shaking man and gently sat him down in the chair he was holding onto.

He poured him a glass of water and placed it gently in Dr. Ravid's hand. In an instant, the veteran psychologist became a helpless old man. Yariv was moved by the old man's severe reaction. He never thought he'd see his therapist in this state.

He put his mouth close to the old psychologist's ear and then whispered to him, "You see, Yehonatan, that piece of shit continues to cause destruction and pain to so many people. Somebody has to close his account for good. For the good of everybody, and for who would be his next victims. So when I see Sa'id take his last breath with my own two eyes and pass over into the next world, I promise you that it will be for both of them. For my Dan, and your Noga. I am done writing on water." He then gently patted the old psychologist on the back and exited the apartment, leaving Dr. Ravid alone with his thoughts, still clutching the glass of water, his eyes filling with tears.

CHAPTER 18
Two Weeks after the Meeting at Dr. Ravid's House, Geneva Airport

Yogev stood in front of the carousel where dozens of suitcases of all colors and sizes revolved, waiting to be picked up. He looked to the sides – it was no longer the height of summer vacation, and the terminal had returned to its regular, sleepy state: couples that went on romantic vacations abroad just before the winter was about to break out all over Europe, ambitious travelers with massive backpacks, newly minted parents pushing baby strollers and people with suitcases hurrying to get out of the terminal and get on their way already. Every few minutes, there would be an announcement in French about something or other, and Yogev tried to figure out what they were saying, but wasn't able.

Yogev memorized the instructions that Yariv gave him, the first being to rent an out-of-the-way apartment in the pictorial French resort town of Cassis, on the Mediterranean. The town was known for its beautiful beaches and nightclubs, as well as its multitude of pubs. Yariv emphasized that nobody would suspect a single man his age who came to party for a few days in a place like this.

He spotted his suitcase and lifted it off the carousel, then made a bee-line for the Hertz counter. The gracious clerk patiently helped him fill out the details of his registration form, took a photocopy of his passport and international driver's license that he gave her, and then gave him the keys to the Peugeot that was waiting for him, and told him where to find it in the parking lot. Yogev paid cash, thanked her with a nod, and left. He found the car in the numbered spot, put his suitcase in the back, and after about five hours of driving arrived at the apartment he rented in the coastal retreat.

He unpacked his suitcase, took a shower, and napped a bit until Yariv arrived. Time dragged on and his nap turned into a deep sleep, which was cut short by a knock on the door. He woke up startled and went to the door, opening it wide.

"What's the matter with you, are you deaf? I've been out here banging on the door for an hour already!" Yariv seethed in a quiet voice as he entered the apartment.

"Oh, well, hello to you, too," Yogev said, yawning and closing the door behind Yariv.

"All right, man, go splash some water on your face and wake up. We didn't come here for a vacation," Yariv instructed, and started taking a tour around the apartment, looking out the windows to the beach below. "Jeez, Yogi, quite the place you managed to find. Maybe at the end of this thing we'll find a couple girls and bring them back to this place for a little celebration? In for a penny, in for a pound..." said Yariv, grinning.

"You're such a dumbass, I swear... the second this is over I'm out of here on the next plane. If there aren't any flights until the next morning, then I'll fucking swim," replied Yogev. He was serious, at least about leaving as soon as possible, although his mouth was full of toothpaste, which lessened the effect of his words. He spit into the sink, washed his mouth out and wiped his hands and face on a white towel that was folded neatly next to the sink.

"Ever since the wedding, you've lost your joie de vivre," Yariv said mockingly.

"That's for sure," replied Yogev.

The two of them sat down at the large table in the middle of the living room. Yariv took a map of the south of France out of his bag and spread it out on the table.

"All right, we're here. Marseille is here," he said, drawing their route with his finger. "Something like a half-hour drive. That is, we're close enough to the object but far enough from the city, in case they close it off and put up checkpoints or barriers or something. Marseille is very crowded, and there many different Muslim communities of all streams there – there are locals who were born in France, and there are many refugees from Africa and the Middle East. Some legal, like those who received refugee status, and others who are... less legal. Either way, Marseille in recent years has become very radical, so much so that the local police are afraid to go in to certain areas and enforce the law," Yariv said.

"Is that good or bad for us?" Yogev asked.

"Both. On the one hand, fewer cops is good because we can operate without any interference and get out of there without getting arrested. On the other hand, if something goes wrong, we'll be hamburger before the police finally arrive..." Yariv replied.

"Oh, well that's reassuring..." Yogev said. "Okay, so what's your plan? Where do we grab him, who does what, where do we acquire weapons?"

"So it's like this," Yariv began, "since we met on the lawn at your place, I did some checking around. Turns out that Sa'id works close with an object the Mossad is interested in. He's not only his driver, he's like a... high ranking NCO – it's through him that he connects to all kinds of other active terrorists, or the local organized crime, and whoever else... Hezbollah is investing in connections with the local crime syndicates, and the syndicates help them procure weapons. Because of the diluted police presence in Marseille, he moves freely about the city with weapons without any problems," Yariv explained.

"In other words, there's nothing new under the sun... I'd have thought that he would have learned something moving to Europe, maybe turn over a new leaf, repent for his evil ways or something... I guess I was wrong," Yogev said with a smile.

"Indeed." Yariv replied, smiling. He took another map out of his bag and placed it on top of the first one. "Look carefully here," he said to Yogev. "This is an enlarged map of the center of Marseille. You see this bay here? That's the marina. Actually, it's a nice place. I was there for a few stakeouts. Lots of tourists, lots of traffic, you can disappear into the crowd easily. Nothing we haven't done before... anyway, I pulled a few strings with one of the intelligence officers in the office, who also owes me a favor or two and, from what I found out, Sa'id has an official job – that's how he got his visa to enter France. Turns out that, officially, he's the personal driver for the CEO of the Grand Tonic Hotel, located right next to the marina in Marseille. I circled it for you here, the exact location of the hotel. As you can see, it's a relatively small hotel, only four stories, maybe thirty-forty rooms in all. The owner is some Arab tycoon who comes from a very wealthy family, and who has been linked to Hezbollah for years, and supports the organization politically and financially. The actual CEO is a French fellow, not at all related to the whole political aspect of things, but the Arab owner put Sa'id into this role, as his driver, and basically forced him upon his CEO. The hotel caters to many wealthy guests from Syria and Lebanon. So bottom line, the French CEO earns a good living from them, and basically lets Sa'id do whatever he wants."

"Nice, one hand washes the other..." Yogev remarked. "And how is this all related to the operation?"

"I think the best way for us to get to him is in the hotel," Yariv said.

"Inside a hotel full of people?! Are you crazy?!" Yogev said, jumping up.

"Wait a sec, man. Take a deep breath and hear me out. This isn't Israel. The roads out of the cities are teeming with uniformed and undercover police. There are also cameras on a certain portion of the roads. If we take him out on one of these routes around the city, that will immediately jump the authorities, because somebody will definitely report a car that is parked strangely. So that's out. We need a closed place, a place where it will take them time to figure out he's missing. In the hotel, there aren't many tourists at the moment, because the season is almost over. And so everything is much quieter than you might think, fewer eyes on us. The area here is touristy, and so everybody has it in their interest to keep things quiet, because that way everybody makes money. Apart from that, the police here in the area of the marina are mostly for the tourists – like an upgraded civilian patrol that is mostly there to prevent pickpockets and that type of thing. It's not a hard-core police department like in other major cities in France. I followed Sa'id for a bit. He has his own room at the hotel, to rest between trips with the CEO, and sometimes he even sleeps there. So bottom line is, we need to find out the room number, and go in there and finish him off. Until they realize he's missing, we'll be long gone from Marseille and as far as I'm concerned, from there you go straight to the airport and fly home," Yariv said.

"And how are we going to verify that he's in the hotel?" Yogev asked.

"I took care of that also. Turns out that if his car is parked in one of the hotel spots, more likely than not, he's there. That car is our proxy for whether the mission is a go. By the way, from the surveillance I did at the location, I discovered that the hotel has two active entrances: the first is through the lobby, which is the main entrance. The second is from minus-two, where the spa and heated pools are. There's a service entrance there, and that connects back up to the kitchen area. It's possible to exit the building from there. It's important that you remember that, come what may. Minus-two."

"Okay. Good. How do we take him out? You have a gun?" asked Yogev.

"Are you nuts? What gun? A body found shot to death at the hotel would mean an immediate investigation. That's no good for us."

"I don't understand, dude. So you want to kill him with your bare hands?" Yogev asked, astonished.

"What are you talking about, kill him with my bare hands. I'm a delicate flower…" Yariv said with a devilish grin.

"Okay, so what then, out with it already," Yogev said, his irritation showing.

Yariv took a fancy eyeglass case out of his pocket and placed it on the table in front of Yogev.

"What's this?" he asked.

"Open it up and you'll see," Yariv said calmly.

"Again with this crap… what's there to see here, it's a Ray-Ban sunglasses case. How's that going to help us kill Sa'id?" Yogev wondered, still annoyed.

Yariv placed the sunglasses to the side and took a small spray bottle with the Ray-Ban logo on it out of the case. "You see this?" he asked Yogev with a thin smile.

"Yes. Eyeglass cleaner. What's that got to do with what I asked you?"

"It's not eyeglass cleaner, dude. Remember Dr. Yakobovitch?"

"Who, the scientist from the university, the one that gave us the toxin that we used during the bank job in Ramallah?"

"Very good, I see you're awake…" Yariv said, smiling.

"Knock it off... this spray is a toxin for a hit?" asked Yogev in a quiet voice.

"Affirmative, pops..." Yariv said, nodding.

"I hope we don't have to spray it, we already saw how that worked on Khaled Mashaal..."[38] Yogev said with a smile, finally able to get a jab back at Yariv.

"I see you've brought your A-game today... the bottle is full of an especially unique toxin. It's a particularly volatile substance, so in this case, we don't spray it. What we do instead is we put it into a needle and inject it into something that will come into close contact with the object's mouth. It could be a champagne glass, a can of Coke, or even toothpaste. Within a few hours from when the toxin makes contact with the object's saliva in his mouth, he will go into anaphylactic shock, his airways will narrow, and will die suddenly without any trace that could lead back to us."

"I can't believe you're still in touch with that Yakobovitch guy. He scares the shit out of me," Yogev said with a smile.

"He deals with scary shit... anyway, the idea I came up with is, we verify that Sa'id is not in his hotel room. You stay back and secure the area from outside, I go into Sa'id's room, inject that stuff inside his toothpaste, and get out. And then both of us ride into the sunset."

"I have to ask you something, and I need you to answer honestly," Yogev said and looked Yariv in the eye.

"Of course, what is it?"

"Without getting into the operational details of your jobs with the Mossad, I assume you didn't get this toxin at the pharmacy, right? And I assume that Dr. Yakobovitch didn't give it to you like this one's on the house... so how exactly did you get it – did you steal it from your armory? What will you do if your colleagues find out about it?" Yogev wondered.

---

38. A Hamas leader the Mossad tried to assassinate in Jordan in 1996.

Yariv was quiet for a moment. It seemed to Yogev as if his questions posed no small difficulty for him. "I'll tell you the truth," he finally answered. "This whole thing is very uncomfortable for me. I have two other guys in the squad with me, great guys, and I really like them. I didn't tell them anything about this and I didn't tell them anything about our private operation. Maybe because I don't want them to get in trouble because of me if something does happen, and maybe because, deep down, I'm not one-hundred percent sure that they would be on board with this. I'm worried that one of them would rat me out, and then I'd be finished. Either way, we got equipment for a different operation. The toxin was in the operations bag, and I was able to get my hands on some. That's all. They don't know it's gone from the stash in the shared safe – but there's a chance they'll notice. Truth is, I think that one of them even suspects me a bit... but even if they find out about it, it won't matter – because we'll be carrying out our operation tomorrow morning, and I asked for the day off tomorrow. I don't think they'll connect the dots there. In any event, I left my gun there, in the safe."

"Wait a second, you don't intend to bring a weapon to this operation? You're insane, you know that?" Yogev said, dumbfounded.

"Dude, this isn't your moshav. You're in a foreign country. If you walk around without a gun, you can always make up a story or excuse. But if they catch you with a gun, you're done. And if anybody is going to have a gun, it's going to be me. But I won't carry a gun here, not even for a second. I mean, if I get caught, of course the country will get me out of here and take care of me. No chance that the country lets me sit in jail here, with everything I know about the Mossad and how they operate. If something like that were to happen, they'd make sure to extradite me immediately in a secret, back-channel deal under the radar, and without going into detail, such things have happened... I may sit in jail, but not a French one, an Israeli one. That's tolerable as far as I'm concerned.

But if you get caught here with a gun, you're done for. You're liable to end up with a life sentence in a French prison. That's no joke," Yariv answered him with a worried look.

"I don't understand, so I came here as decoration? I'm just securing the hallway to the room and that's it?" Yogev said, astonished.

"Not at all, I just planned everything already. I have some experience with that... we'll divide the operations up between us, so if and when they start looking for suspects, they won't be able to put a case file together, because any witnesses they question will describe different people. That will give us more time and cause confusion that will take them time to untangle. I go in, inject the toxin into his toothpaste, and while I'm doing that, you're securing the room from outside. The whole thing shouldn't take more than two or three minutes at the most. If everything goes well, we'll exit separately out the front door and happily ever after. But if something goes wrong, then it's me against him, physically. Either way, he isn't leaving there alive. And in that case, we'll go out through minus-two. It's quieter there. It's important that you remember that you just make sure nobody else comes close to the room, or enters Sa'id's room while I'm in there."

"All right, I trust you. If I go to jail that's fine, just imagine what my wife will do to you..." Yogev smiled and clapped his friend on the back.

"Totally... anyway, like I told you, Sa'id is the driver for an object the Mossad wants taken out. So in the meantime, don't go anywhere – I'm about to receive an indication about the object as we speak, and then I'll update you and we can go from there. I will personally verify that Sa'id's car isn't in the hotel parking lot, and that way we'll know that the room is empty and that I can enter without running into Sa'id," Yariv said confidently.

Suddenly, Yogev realized something. "Wait," he said, "something here isn't clear. Let's assume we take out Sa'id – what about the senior Hezbollah object you told me about? Won't taking out Sa'id scare him into hiding? Have you thought about that?" Yogev asked Yariv and looked at him.

Yariv got up from his chair and went to the window. The muffled sound of tourists could be heard outside. "You're right," he answered quietly. "That's presumably what will happen."

"And you don't think that catching a senior member of Hezbollah is slightly more important than taking out Sa'id? You know how much I want to settle the score with him, but fuck me, there are more important things here in the bigger picture than settling our private score with Sa'id. I want to remind you that I live in Regba. You know how many missiles fell on our heads in just two months? You understand the implications of not taking out a senior object like this?" Yogev asked and shook his head.

Yariv didn't answer him. He continued watching the golden coast, the sun that was about to set on the town's pristine shoreline. Yogev stood up and came over to where Yariv was standing. He put his hand on his friend's shoulder.

"Bro, I'm the last guy in the world that wants to see Sa'id walk away from this alive, but if you ask me who the higher priority target is, I think the answer is clear."

Yariv turned around. He looked into Yogev's eyes. "You're right. There's a good chance that our private operation here will cause the Mossad to call off their hit on the senior Hezbollah target. And it's true that more missiles will probably fall on your moshav. I'm aware of that. But on the other hand, I believe that, at the end of the day, Israel won't give up on that senior figure, and will find him one way or the other. If not today, then in the future. But Sa'id, everybody forgot about him. From the moment he left the West Bank, that was it – nobody went looking for him anymore, and what he did was erased from the history books and fell off the list of priorities of people to take care of. Just you and I remember what he did to us, and what he did to Dan. And what he did to Noga..." Yariv said in a whisper.

"Noga? Who's Noga?" Yogev asked Yariv, furrowing his brow.

"Never mind, it doesn't matter..." Yariv answered and let out the air that had been accumulating in his lungs. "Either way, this bastard must pay the price. For fuck's sake, just tell me I'm not crazy and let's finish this together," he said to Yogev.

Yogev nodded. He understood the importance of what they were about to do and the heavy price, both at the national level, but also on a personal level given the risk they were taking. He too, like Yariv, was torn over the dilemma. Despite all the years that had passed since then, he knew that, for them, the circuit was not yet complete, and that it wouldn't be as long as both of them knew Sa'id was alive.

Yariv saw the emotional struggle his friend was dealing with. It was a struggle he was intimately familiar with, for he also had been unsure for a long time. But unlike Yogev, he felt as if he had already crossed the Rubicon. He knew that Yogev needed one more little push.

"Yogi," Yariv said to him, "I want to tell you an interesting story I heard in my office from one of the veteran agents. May I?"

"Of course, shoot."

"It's like this. In Greek mythology, they say that in Sparta there were warriors that were renowned the world over for their toughness. But the true source of the warriors' power and toughness were their mothers. It's said that before going out to battle, their mothers would give their warrior sons their shields and utter only five words: 'With it or on it.' That was the farewell of the mothers to their sons going into battle."

"I don't get it," Yogev said. "What does that mean 'with it or on it?'"

"The shield used in battle was very heavy. Whoever wanted to run from the battlefield, the first thing they would do would be to throw away their shield, and then they could run fast enough to get away. But whoever would fall in battle, his brothers in arms would lay his body to rest on his shield, and that's how they would bring him back home. So what their mothers are basically telling them is this: 'My son, go to fight. Either you come back with it, that is, with it in your hand as victor, or you come back on it, that is, dead.' There is no situation where you throw away your shield, run away from the battlefield, and leave your friends to fight for you..."

The point of the story that Yariv told Yogev was razor sharp. At this moment, Yogev understood that even though what they were about to do was exceedingly problematic, in the argument between the heart and the brain, the heart won this time. At that moment, he understood that for both of them, there was no other choice.

Yogev gave his good friend a hug, wrapped his hands around his shoulders and whispered to him, "I'm with you, brother. To the end. With it or on it, with it or on it..."

CHAPTER 19
The Next Day, Downtown Marseille, Early Afternoon, The Marina

The afternoon sun was strong for autumn, and the eastern breeze created ripples on the water of the marina in the center of the city. The yachts bobbed gently with the waves that crashed against the shore, spraying white foam on the tiled sidewalks. Seagulls flew above the waves of the small bay, trying to spot a meal in the clear waters. The sky was blue and almost cloudless, and from a distance, one could hear the bellowing horns of the ships leaving port for the open sea. The few tourists that there were strolled along the promenade that encircled the marina, frequenting the coffee shops and restaurants that abutted the pier. A group of children ran next to the feeding platforms and scared off the doves that were eating there.

The lobby of the Grand Tonic Hotel was expansive, and the floor was tiled with high-quality marble. Large leather armchairs were placed the whole length of the lobby, and next to each one was a small end-table with sculpted wooden legs. In the center of the lobby hung a massive chandelier. Above the chandelier, a large ceiling fan rotated silently, creating a pleasant breeze that swirled throughout the lobby. There were a few couples sitting in the armchairs with cocktails on the low tables between them.

None of the hotel guests noticed the young man who entered the hotel carrying a luxurious box of chocolates, wrapped meticulously with a shiny red bow on it. He approached the clerk at the desk and asked, half in English, "*Si vous plait*, perhaps you can help me?"

"Of course, *monsieur*," the clerk responded.

"I have a special delivery for a person named Sa'id. He's the CEO's assistant. This is a very expensive gift, and I have to make sure that it reaches him immediately. I promised my client that I would hand-deliver it personally. Which room is he in please?"

"I'm sorry, monsieur," the desk clerk answered politely, "but we maintain the privacy of our guests and employees alike, and so I am unable to provide you with that information."

"So I'm just supposed to leave these very fine, expensive chocolates at the counter here? These are the finest chocolates available and very expensive… I'm very sorry, but I don't have authorization to leave them with you," the delivery guy said, a bit irritated.

"I understand, monsieur. Give me one moment and I will see if one of our staff is available to accommodate you," the desk clerk said, and dialed a number on his phone through the internal switchboard. After a moment during which he had a brief conversation, he addressed the delivery guy. "Monsieur, I spoke to our service department. The bellboy will arrive in a few moments.

You may leave the chocolates here. You have my personal guarantee that they will be delivered to Mr. Sa'id shortly."

"Excellent! Thank you so much, good day, *au revoir*!" the delivery guy said, and he began walking toward the exit.

Two tourists on opposite sides of the lobby watched the delivery guy as he left the hotel. They exchanged a short glance between them – part one had been accomplished successfully. Yariv was sitting on the east side of the lobby, dressed like a tourist in short, loose-fitting clothes, and was reading The New York Times. Resting at his feet was a pool bag with a green towel carelessly strewn over top of it.

Yogev was sitting on the west side of the lobby, right next to the stairwell. He was dressed as a businessman, wearing a tailored shirt and slacks. His brown shoes were brilliantly polished, and he was reading The Economist. He leafed through it attentively while slowly sipping his steaming cup of coffee.

Yariv kept his eye on the expensive delivery that was still sitting on the long reception desk. He knew that the presence of the expensive chocolates would make the concierge nervous, because this type of delivery can't just sit there, but must be delivered as soon as possible. From his corner of the lobby, Yogev was also able to sneak frequent glances at the conspicuous package. In Yogev's pants' pocket were the keys to their getaway car, which was parked in the garage on minus-two. This car – which was supposed to whisk them out of the Marseille area immediately after the operation – was the one that Yariv had rented a day earlier and paid cash for. But there was something else in Yogev's pocket – a note with the number to the Mossad's emergency dispatch in France.

***

"Listen," Yariv said to Yogev the night before, "the whole thing isn't supposed to take more than two or three minutes at the most. I go in, do the thing, go out. But as you know, there's the plan, and then there's the reality – in the real world, anything can happen. So let's get it straight between us – when I go in there, you watch the clock. If I'm not out in three minutes, it's a sign that something is wrong. Here's the number you need to call. That's our emergency office in France. Now it's very important that you listen to me: you use that only if there's no other choice. Only if shit really hits the fan. Take into account that my office is equipped to extract field agents who have gotten themselves into a bind, and usually operates efficiently and quickly. If you do call them and they arrive, take into consideration that our little partizan tryst will be exposed, and the consequences will almost certainly be a trial, and then prison for a very long time."

Yogev didn't say anything, he just nodded.

Yariv continued. "So I'm leaving this up to you, just keep that in mind. If we end up in a real bad situation and I can't function for whatever reason – call that number. Memorize it well, so that if you had to dial it blind in the middle of the night, you could. On the other end of the line, the person who will answer you is our emergency dispatch. Tell her that you want to order a personal pizza. That's the code for an agent in distress. She will ask for an exact location, and will almost certainly ask who you are. You do not, under any circumstances, identify yourself. You just say: 'I'm requesting an order for a personal pizza for Newton at the Grand Tonic Hotel in Marseille.' That's all. You say what I just said, make sure the information is received, then hang up. At that point, you've finished your job. You leave that message and get out, you understand? After you report to my office, you get into that car and drive straight to the airport. Your flight has already been booked. You don't start being a big hero, remember Lot's wife – you don't look back, you don't come to help, you just let them know and that's it. They'll already know what to do with the information. They'll find me and get me out. Or not... but the most important thing is that you get out of here before the police discover what we did and start closing everything off."

* * *

After a few moments, a tall, thin bellboy appeared in the lobby and went to the front desk. Out of the corner of his eye, Yogev saw the clerk explaining something to the bellboy. The bellboy nodded, then Yogev saw the clerk write something on a slip of paper, which he assumed was the room number, and then hand it to the bellboy. The bellboy looked at the slip of paper, put it in his pocket, and then he dutifully picked up the box of chocolates. The clerk motioned for him to wait while he picked up the phone, dialed, and waited for an answer. After a few seconds, the manager began conversing with somebody. He then put the phone back on its cradle and motioned to the bellboy that he could go on his way. The bellboy held the package carefully and went to the elevator in the lobby and pressed the button for the elevator.

Yariv, who was sitting on the other side of the lobby, also folded up the newspaper that he was reading, placed it on the wooden table in front of him, grabbed his pool bag and walked toward the elevator. After less than a minute, the elevator opened and out walked two couples, arm in arm, laughing. They nodded to the bellboy and headed toward the pool patio. The bellboy got into the elevator, and Yariv got in immediately after. The elevator went up to the fourth floor and stopped. The bellboy got out and turned right down the hallway toward Sa'id's room. Yariv got out and started walking in the other direction. He walked slowly, while stealing glances in the bellboy's direction. From the corner of his eye, he saw him knock on the large door at the end of the hallway. Bingo. That was Sa'id's room.

The bellboy knocked on the door a few times and waited. There was no answer, and the door didn't open. Yariv knew that would be the case, because Sa'id's car wasn't at the hotel. The bellboy didn't give up and knocked again on the door a few more times. He waited patiently a few more moments before turning around and heading back to the elevator, the chocolates in his hands. He pushed the button for the elevator, and within a few seconds the doors opened, swallowing him up inside and taking him back to the lobby.

Yariv placed his bag next to a random door on the other side of the hallway and searched in his pocket, as if looking for his room key. He saw the bellboy disappear into the elevator. The hallway on the fourth floor was empty. He waited a few more moments in silence, and tried to hear if there was anybody in the rooms near him. There were no sounds or voices throughout the floor. The whole area was completely silent. And then the stairwell door opened and Yogev poked his head out. He looked right and left, making sure the coast was clear. His eyes met Yariv's, who signaled that everything was clear. They both stood in the hallway against the wall.

Yariv signaled with his head in the direction of Sa'id's room. Yogev nodded. They were both completely silent, like years ago, communicating without words. Each understood exactly what the other expected and what to do next.

Yariv slowly put his hand into the bag. On the right side, underneath the towel, he felt the sunglasses case where the toxin was held. His pulse was racing. He knew that in a few moments, he would settle the score with the one who was responsible for his good friend's death, his own injuries, and the death of many others. Every muscle in his body was tense. A moment of doubt crept into his heart. He knew that what he was about to do might result in him paying a heavy price for in the future. He had one moment more to think about it, to change his mind and call it off.

But it didn't happen.

The hallway had wall-to-wall carpeting, which made it easier for him to approach the room. Yogev nodded toward Yariv, confirming that he could continue, while he stayed by the elevator and continued securing the hallway.

After a few paces, Yariv was in front of the door. He held his breath and listened. He didn't hear anything. Yariv put the sunglasses case between the towel and the bag, and took a lockpicking set from his pocket. He acted with skills acquired over many years of undercover activity, and after a few moments, he felt the lock mechanism open. He put the set back in his pocket, slowly turned the gold doorknob, and the door opened. Even though it was afternoon, the room was completely dark. The lights were off, and the curtains were closed.

He went into the room, placed the bag on the floor, hung the "Do Not Disturb" sign on the outside doorknob and closed it. After a few seconds, when his eyes adjusted to the darkness, he took the sunglasses case out of the bag and opened it. His fingers held the small bottle gingerly. He uncrewed the cap slowly and took out a syringe from the other side of the bag. He carefully pulled the toxic substance into the syringe until it was full, and then screwed the cap back on the bottle and placed it carefully back into the case.

Yariv held the syringe and went into the bathroom, which was a few yards to his left. It was only then that he noticed the beam of light peeking out from underneath the bathroom door. He continued to the doorway and then opened it slowly. The spotlight above him bathed the bathroom in a nice, soft light, and to the right, Yariv saw the bathtub, gleaming white. Yariv looked to the left side of the bathroom, and then the blood in his veins froze.

On the pristine toilet, next to the sink, sat Sa'id. In his left hand he held a gun, which was directed right at Yariv.

*　*　*

"*Eerfa'a eedak*,"[39] Sa'id commanded Yariv, while standing up.

Yariv understood that, at this point, there wasn't much to do. He didn't even try to claim that he was in the wrong room. He acceded to the order he received from Sa'id, and put his hands up.

"Turn around," Sa'id commanded. Yariv did what he was told, and turned around. The element of surprise had become Sa'id's, and Yariv was still not quite out of the initial shock from the trap that Sa'id had set for him.

This scenario, where he was in an inferior position in the bathroom with his hands raised and a loaded gun being pointed at his back, wasn't something Yariv expected. He understood that something in his original plan was flawed. His brain was working frantically, searching for a way out of the predicament he'd gotten himself into.

All at once, he was back in Nablus on that dark, rainy night.

Sa'id saw the surprise on Yariv's face. "Who are you? Who sent you? The French mafia again?!" Sa'id asked in Arabic while waving his gun at Yariv's back.

At that moment, Yariv understood that the question he just asked him was his ticket out of there.

If Sa'id had known who he really was, he would have shot him already, Yariv thought to himself. *That didn't happen, so it's obvious that Sa'id thinks I'm with the French mafia. Maybe he has some unfinished business with them, maybe a debt or something. He has no idea who I really am,* Yariv thought, *and I might be able to leverage that as a way out of this situation.*

---

39. Put your hands up.

For a moment, he thought to spin around quickly and inject the syringe into Sa'id's throat, but was afraid Sa'id might get the jump on him and shoot him first. Yariv and the rest of the field agents in his unit trained to get out of these kinds of situations, like when somebody was pointing a loaded gun at their back. There were some Krav Maga techniques where they trained how to disarm an attacker of his weapon, but that required that the attacker be within reach. Yariv needed to do something to make Sa'id come closer to him.

Sa'id continued to wave his gun around while shouting in Arabic at Yariv. "Answer me! What does the mafia want with me? I returned all their money, including the interest that Francois demanded! Tell them to leave me alone already!" Sa'id said, in a thunderous voice.

Yariv was quiet. From his preliminary stakeout of the hotel, he knew that the doors on the top floor, where the suites and business services were located, were soundproof. He knew that the more Sa'id raised his voice, the greater the chance Yogev would hear him and rush to his aid. The bathroom was large and spacious. Yariv stood on one side, Sa'id and his gun on the other, just a few yards separating them.

Sa'id was furious. He waved his gun again and again, and then came close to Yariv from behind. He pressed the barrel of the gun to Yariv's neck. "Tell me now who sent you, or I'll kill you," Sa'id whispered into his ear.

This was the moment Yariv was waiting for. He didn't waste a second to think; he just acted mechanically: quickly and with deadly accuracy, he spun to his left and struck Sa'id's hand. Sa'id lost his balance, staggering backwards, and was about to fall. Yariv took advantage of Sa'id's momentary shock and shot both his hands out over Sa'id's, which was holding the gun. Sa'id recovered and again tried to aim the cocked gun at Yariv, but it was too late.

Yariv had already grabbed Sa'id's wrist and twisted it back until he heard a "crack." His wrist snapped.

Sa'id roared in pain, dropping the gun, which fell onto the clean white floor and skid over to the corner. Yariv took the chance and sent a precise punch to Sa'id's nose, which absorbed the critical blow and splintered apart, and a stain of blood exploded onto his face. Sa'id tried to kick Yariv in the groin, but he missed, hitting Yariv in his left thigh. Yariv momentarily lost his balance, but was able to immediately regain his footing and continue pummeling Sa'id. He threw another punch, right into Sa'id's diaphragm. He struck in the exact place he intended, and Sa'id began gasping and choking for air, struggling to breathe. Yariv knew his punch landed right in Sa'id's lower diaphragm, and figured that he had a few more critical seconds before Sa'id's reflex muscles in his diaphragm unlocked and he'd be able to breathe again. He didn't wait for his enemy to recover, and shot a powerful kick into Sa'id's groin. Sa'id collapsed onto the white bathroom tile in a heap. He lay there, facing Yariv, blood pouring from his nose, breathing heavily and bent over holding his crushed testicles.

Yariv was overloaded with adrenaline. His heart rate was strong and fast, and his hand hurt surprisingly more than he would have thought from the most recent beating he administered to Sa'id. He retrieved Sa'id's gun from the corner of the room and stood over him. "Don't move!" he commanded Sa'id in Arabic.

Sa'id's eyes opened wide, and his astonishment was evident. At this point, he was certain that the man standing over him wasn't connected in any way to the French mafia. "Who are you?" Sa'id asked in a weak voice. "Who sent you?"

"*Uscoot,*"[40] Yariv commanded him. He was afraid Sa'id would shout and try to yell for help. "If you're quiet, I'll tell you everything and you'll walk out of here alive today. If you yell, you'll never see

---

40. Shut up.

the sun again," Yariv said, his hands still aiming the gun right between Sa'id's eyes.

Sa'id nodded – he got the message.

Yariv wanted to finish this as fast as possible. He didn't plan on using the gun, but now the whole point of using the toxin was irrelevant. He knew that the hotel was populated, and that anybody could have heard the sounds of their struggle and reported it to hotel management or, even worse – the police. He held Sa'id's gun in his hand and debated with himself what to do next. Now that he had been exposed to Sa'id, it was obvious he would have to kill him. But how? Taking Sa'id out of the room and killing him somewhere else was impractical.

Yariv understood that unlike the original plan, he would now have to use the gun. He knew that he couldn't shoot with this gun, that somebody would certainly hear the noise from the gunshot. He quickly scanned the bathroom. The only thing he saw that was a possibility was to grab one of the thick towels from the shelf by the bathtub, wrap it around the gun, and then shoot him. An idea popped into his head: to leave the murder weapon in his dead hand, and then it would look like suicide, at least at the critical phase when they first discovered the body.

Sa'id, who figured out pretty quickly what was going down, tried pleading for his life, but Yariv cut him off harshly by forcefully pressing the barrel of Sa'id's gun to his forehead. Sa'id exhaled deeply, practically emptying his lungs of air. He had apparently accepted his fate. Yariv looked up again to the right, toward the high shelf with the towels. The shelf was a few yards away from him. He took a step back toward the shelf and tried to reach out with his other hand to grab one of the towels.

Suddenly, without any warning, a sharp pain pierced his side near his kidney. Yariv felt a sort of electric current pass through him quickly. He looked down, and was amazed to see that Sa'id had stabbed him in the side with a small knife that resembled a dagger.

Sa'id had stabbed him frighteningly quickly and surprisingly accurately, and the knife was razor sharp. Only then did he notice the small sheath on Sa'id's ankle where the knife was hidden. The pain was immense, and his stomach had been slashed. The cut was deep and long, and Yariv quickly understood how significant it was as his shirt became blood-soaked. He felt like he was going to pass out. In a split second, Yariv made the decision to lie down on top of Sa'id, while trying with the last of his ebbing strength to smash Sa'id in the face with the butt of the gun. Sa'id grabbed Yariv's wrist, and both of them rolled around on the floor, which was now streaked with blood that was spilling out of both of them.

Yariv began to feel dizzy and no matter how hard he tried, he wasn't able to hit Sa'id in the head with the gun. Instinctively, Yariv whipped his head backward and smashed Sa'id squarely in the face with extreme force. He thought that Sa'id may have blacked out for a moment. Yariv could feel the blood slowly draining from his body. He put his hand on the wound, trying to stop the bleeding, but it was a useless endeavor. His shirt was soaked with blood, and he thought he might pass out. The room was swirling around him, and his eyes began to close. He struggled to stay awake, but his eyelids were heavy and the dizziness only got worse. Yariv felt like a kid riding on a carousel, around and around, with everything around him spinning and changing by the second. He tried keeping his eyes on Sa'id, who was lying on the floor underneath him. Sa'id uttered a slight groan and moved slightly.

Yariv started crawling toward the door. He remembered that his friend was standing at the end of the hallway, next to the elevators, securing the area for him. He reached the bathroom door where he tried to lift his hand to open the door, but right then he felt something tugging at his leg. Yariv mustered his strength and looked back, only to see Sa'id pulling at his leg. He tried to lift his other leg to kick Sa'id in the face, but his leg wouldn't heed his call. He could feel his heart rate weakening. Yariv changed direction, faced the middle of the room, and made his way towards Sa'id. He tried to raise his arm to hit Sa'id again, but he only saw black circles that got bigger and bigger. Everything was going black, and Yariv felt that he was being pulled into the void. He wasn't able to stay awake any longer – and then he passed out.

* * *

At the end of the hallway, next to the elevator, Yogev heard muffled sounds coming from inside the room. He debated with himself whether that's what he really heard, or just his imagination playing tricks on him. The noise was fairly quiet since it came from the other side of the soundproof door, but it was clear to Yogev that something wasn't right.

He didn't know what to do – should he remain where he was and continue securing the area, or should he enter the room? He looked at his watch – it had been three minutes since Yariv entered the room. This wasn't supposed to take so much time – that much Yogev knew. *Yariv has been in the room for a few minutes, and now there are strange, muffled noises coming from the room. Maybe Yariv is in some sort of trouble? Maybe we missed something in our preliminary check of Sa'id, and the room? Anything could be happening,* Yogev thought.

He wasn't armed. The only weapon they had was the syringe with the toxin, and that was with Yariv, in the room behind the closed door. Yogev was at a complete loss as to what to do. He put his hand into his pocket – and then he felt the paper. It was that small piece of paper Yariv gave him last night, with the emergency number for the Mossad.

* * *

Sa'id was also beat up and in significant pain. His broken nose throbbed, making it difficult to breath normally thanks to Yariv's incessant, precise strikes. After a few seconds, he was able to regulate his breathing. He opened his eyes and saw the ceiling of the bathroom. The bright, white light blinded him. He looked to the side where he saw Yariv, lying unconscious in a large pool of blood that was slowly expanding across the floor, which was now more bloody than not. The blows he received to his face and head hurt so badly that just moving his head amplified the pain. He heard Yariv's labored breathing and saw his chest slowly rise and fall.

Sa'id didn't know who this man who came to harm him was, but he was still breathing. Barely, but breathing. The knife wound with the small dagger proved to be deadly and efficient, but the job wasn't done yet. *I have to finish this man off*, Sa'id thought to himself.

His hands were heavy and bruised, and were shaking from the gargantuan effort it took just to get up from the cold floor. His balls still hurt a ton as well, and getting up provided a sharp reminder of that. He searched with his eyes for his gun – his gun that this stranger who spoke to him in Arabic managed to wrest from him. Sa'id saw the gun in the corner, just a few yards away. While the stranger passed out, the gun slid from his hand and came to rest in the corner between the toilet and the bathtub. Sa'id began crawling in the direction of the gun. He groaned in pain. Every movement caused him unbearable pain, but he bit his lip, mustered the last of his strength and dragged himself on across the floor.

* * *

Yogev looked at the slip of paper in his hand. He knew that if he made this phone call, he would seal Yariv's fate, and perhaps even his own. It was clear to him that, from the moment he dialed the emergency number that Yariv had given him, there was no going back.

He looked at his watch. It had been four minutes. *Something here didn't add up*, he thought to himself. His heart raced. *That's it, decide, it's time to make the call.*

Yogev took the cell phone out of his pocket, and his shaking hands made the call to the Mossad's emergency dispatch.

* * *

Sa'id continued crawling toward the gun. His body ached as he dragged himself across the blood-stained floor. He felt his shirt get wet and he smelled the metallic smell of blood, which was so familiar to him. His left hand barely responded to the commands his brain was giving to it, and he was afraid it was broken. His temples throbbed. He tried to feel his nose with his hand, and with great hesitation, he reached with his right hand to the middle of his face and was horrified when he touched his mangled nose. That only made him want to kill the formidable stranger sprawled out unconscious on the floor even more. He knew that whoever that stranger was, he was liable to wake up at any moment, and so he tried to crawl across the bloody bathroom floor as fast as he could.

Before long, he felt the butt of the gun. He was left-handed and knew he wouldn't be able to operate the gun with his damaged hand. He slowly moved the gun into his right hand and tried to sit himself up on the slippery floor near Yariv, who was still lying unconscious next to him.

* * *

Yogev finished the phone call and hung up. The pleas of the girl on the other end of the line to get Yogev to provide additional details, and that he wait with her on the line until the extraction unit arrived, fell on deaf ears. From her words, he understood that there was a pair of armed agents not far from them, and that they would be able to arrive within the hour – but he followed Yariv's instructions and hung up, then turned the phone off and put it back in his pocket.

He knew that at this point, there was no turning back – their scheme would soon be out in the open, and Yariv was going to pay a very heavy personal price. But he had no choice – he couldn't handle the current situation by himself, which was only getting worse by the moment. He also didn't understand how a Mossad extraction team was going to be able to physically get them out of the hotel, if indeed something had gone sideways in the room. Yogev clearly remembered Yariv's unambiguous instructions: report, get out, don't come in, don't play the hero. That's what he told him, in no uncertain terms. "You just report and get out, get back home to Israel."

Yogev was torn between following the clear and direct order he received, and actually carrying it out – leaving his friend in the field. He knew that if he got caught, he too could pay a heavy price. Unlike Yariv, who had an official role with the government, he was just a tourist. A tourist mixed up in criminal activity in a foreign country, with no official Israeli entity to protect him and get him out of there. However, he knew he couldn't live up to his promise. He saw no scenario in which he'd abandon Yariv in the field.

Instinctively, he understood that now, everything depended on him. Even if the team arrived within the next few minutes, which was an entirely fictional scenario, it would be too late. Yogev quickly covered the short distance to the end of the hallway and found himself standing in front of Sa'id's door. For a moment, a weird thought flashed through his head – basically, I'm the anchor in an insane relay race. A race that began a decade ago one rainy night in Nablus. A race where in the first lap, Sa'id determined Dan's unfortunate demise. The baton was then passed to Yariv, who's in trouble on the other side of that hotel room door, and who knows what his fate holds – and now it's my turn. Why are the three of us always sentenced to be shattered, again and again, each one in his own time, against this cursed rock named Sa'id?

And perhaps, Yogev thought to himself, *I have to do what Yariv said and just get out of here? Why do I have to sacrifice myself in the ancient name of revenge, which even if achieved, can never bring Dan back to life?*

His legs were shaking, his brain was telling him to get out of there, but his heart... his heart... Yogev closed his eyes for a moment, and in an instant he stopped shaking, the tension eased, his heartrate slowed. He saw Dan as if he were right in front of him, the way he remembered him – handsome, well-built, with a charming smile, as real as he had ever been. That's how he remembered his friend. Not like the broken vessel he became during the last years of his life. Through his spirit, Yogev perceived his dead friend's face, and suddenly remembered a story that Dan once told him. He couldn't even remember where they were, but it was during basic training in the unit, so many years ago.

It was the story of a Roman soldier who complained to his commander that his sword was too short, and so he wouldn't be able to defeat any enemies in battle. His commander looked at him with a smile and said, "The sword isn't too short, just take one more step forward..." That is, the victory isn't in the weapon, but in the spirit of the warrior who wields it. That's what counts, and it's the only thing that matters at the moment of truth.

With his eyes still closed, he saw a vision of his wife and the twins. For a moment, he was almost unable to comprehend how he ended up in this crazy situation: how was it that he, an upscale architect in his thirties, a family man with kids, is now standing here by himself in the middle of the hallway in a hotel in a French coastal town with his good friend who is on the other side of the door, perhaps even in a struggle with the terrorist, just to take revenge for his friend's death. In his mind's eye, he could feel the relay baton that Dan had passed to Yariv, and now, it was placed into his hand. It was as if the two of them were calling to him, whispering, "Yogev, now, it's your turn..."

He was acutely aware that, in a moment, he was about to leave behind the normalcy of the world that he had known until today, and perhaps even erase it completely. Yariv's words still echoed in his mind: "Just get out, like Lot's wife... Lot's wife..."

Yogev opened his eyes. He was still standing in front of the closed door, unarmed, and had no idea what was happening on the other side of the door, or what condition Yariv was in. He looked to both sides – the hallway had been, and still was, completely empty. He looked at his watch for the umpteenth time.

It had been five minutes.

That's it, somethings definitely wrong, he thought to himself.

Yogev opened his eyes and looked back at the round doorknob – God only knew what was waiting for him on the other side of the door. His knees started to shake again, and the shaking made its way up to his stomach and into his chest. He felt a cold sweat break out on his forehead and neck. An epic struggle broke out between what his brain was telling him and where his heart was pulling him.

He again recalled the story of the Roman soldier with the short sword and all at once sensed that this was the time to show his fighting spirit that beat deep in his heart long ago. They were three warriors, connected in heart and soul, and now Dan was gone, and

God only knows what was going on with Yariv. It was up to him to take that next step forward. Yariv's voice echoed in his mind again and again, unceasingly pounding against the walls of his head: *with it or on it, with it or on it, with it or on it...*

Yogev put his trembling hand on the doorknob. He took a deep breath, let it out slowly, and then turned the doorknob.

The door opened easily. The room was dark, the curtains were drawn, and the lights were out. From the left side of the room, Yogev could hear the muffled sounds of something being hit. The sound was coming from the direction of the bathroom, which was on the other end of the room. Yogev grabbed the decorative, metal lampshade that was sitting on the dresser next to the bed, unplugged it from the wall, and then quickly closed the gap between him and the bathroom door. Light was coming from underneath the door, but there was a shadow cast across the shining floor, indicating that something was definitely behind it.

Yogev held on to the lampshade tightly in his right hand, and then quickly opened the bathroom door. He was shocked when he saw the scene splayed out before him: what was once a white floor was now mostly smeared with blood. Two men were strewn on the floor, bleeding. He recognized Yariv immediately, lying face down on the ground, unmoving, in the middle of a large pool of blood, but it took him a moment to recognize Sa'id's bloodied and bruised face, especially since he hadn't seen him in a dozen years or so.

Sa'id, who was surprised by the stranger's sudden entrance to the room, tried to raise the gun with his shaking hand. Yogev pulled his head back at the last second before he heard the sound of a gunshot in the bathroom. The bullet sailed in Yogev's direction and lodged itself in the shining porcelain, inches above his head. The porcelain tile exploded with a loud noise, and white shards flew in all directions creating a white cloud of dust. Yogev recovered quickly, and then launched the ornament at Sa'id's head. Sa'id was knocked back from the force of the blow and the weight of the object, and the gun he had flew out of his hand and skittered on the bathroom floor. At this point, Sa'id was flat on his back and not moving, and his eyes were closed.

The bathroom was small, and the sound of the gunshot echoed again and again in Yogev's ears. He knew that, despite the insulation and soundproofing, a gunshot could still be heard throughout the floor, ultimately resulting in somebody from the hotel coming to see what the disturbance was. He instantly understood that at this moment, he needed to evacuate the room and get the injured Yariv out of there as soon as possible.

He turned Yariv over onto his back slowly. Yariv groaned in pain. He looked at his friend's stomach and shuddered. The dagger had done massive damage, his entire shirt was soaked in blood, and Yariv was very pale, a clear sign of blood loss. Yogev took one of the towels, folded it up and pressed it to Yariv's stomach.

Yariv coughed and spit out blood. Yogev knew that an injury like that required immediate medical attention at a hospital, but he didn't know what to do or how to get both of them out of there. Calling the local emergency services was not an option. Both of them would be arrested on the spot and charged with murdering Sa'id. He had to get Yariv out of there and get him to their car that was waiting for them in the parking garage underneath the building on minus-two – but how was he going to do that? Yariv looked at his friend's face, and among the winces in pain, Yogev thought he saw a look of gratitude when he was finally able to get him off the floor and standing, though with great difficulty, leaning on the porcelain wall for support.

When Yariv got into a standing position, Yogev noticed the syringe lying in the pool of blood. He took it and put it in his pocket. Yariv was breathing heavily, fighting for every breath with excruciating difficulty. *One of his lungs could be wounded*, Yogev thought. It was hard for him to tell with all the blood. Whatever it was, it was clear that he needed to see a doctor as soon as possible. But how to get him out of here like this, injured and bleeding profusely?

Yogev's brain went into overdrive, searching for a way out of this mess. Suddenly, he remembered something from what Yariv said to him yesterday, where he mentioned the alternative exit next to the spa. He had an idea: hanging on the opposite wall were two long, black spa robes embroidered with curvy, gold lettering. He took both black robes off the hangers and tried to put the first one on Yariv. Yariv groaned and squirmed. Yogev looked at his watch – almost fifteen minutes had passed since he called the emergency number. He knew that time was not on their side – a bellboy could come up at any moment, or somebody from the cleaning staff, or even a guest from the hotel, and they'd be cooked. Again and again, he tried wrapping Yariv in the robe, getting blood on himself in the process, but the pain it caused Yariv was insufferable and he failed with every attempt.

After a few more minutes, he finally succeeded. The robes were very long and covered most of the bloodied clothes, almost to the floor. Yogev tied the robe tightly around Yariv's injured body, fearing the robe might accidentally come open, revealing his bloody clothes. That act was painful for Yariv, his face twisting up in pain, but he bit his lip and suffered in silence.

"I'm sorry this hurts, but we have to get out of here," Yogev whispered into Yariv's ear. Yariv nodded weakly in understanding.

Yogev took a towel, wet it, and tried to wipe as much of the blood off of Yariv's hands as possible. Afterward, he took another towel off the shelf, wet it as well, and tried to clean the blood stains off the walls.

"What are you doing?" Yariv asked weakly.

"Cleaning up. This will make it harder in case forensics shows up. You don't want our fingerprints all over a murder scene, do you?" Yogev replied, and continued cleaning the walls and doorknobs for a few more seconds.

When he finished, he supported Yariv and they exited the bathroom. "Where is the lock-picking set?" Yogev whispered to Yariv.

Yariv pointed slowly to his back pocket. Yogev delicately reached inside the robe and fished the lock-picking set out of his back pocket. He took one of the pins and jammed it into the lock, and then broke it off inside. Yariv looked at him with a puzzled look.

"To stall whoever shows up to search the room. That way we'll buy ourselves a few extra minutes," Yogev whispered to Yariv. "Wait for me here for a moment," Yogev told his injured friend while leaning him against the wall by the door. Yogev wiped down the doorknob with the black robe, and then slowly opened the door.

The hallway was empty. Suddenly, Yogev heard the sound of the elevator arriving on their floor. He quickly, but quietly, closed the door to the room and looked through the peep hole. The hallway filled with the sound of children's voices, and they were all dressed in swimsuits with colorful floaties on their arms. They ran to one of the rooms at the other end of the hall and disappeared inside, immediately returning the quiet to the hallway.

Yogev opened the door again, slowly, and took another look outside. The hallway was empty. *Now's our chance*, he thought. He went back to the room, grabbed Yariv under his armpits and whispered to him, "Come on, we're going."

Yariv nodded weakly. His face was very pale. He was in obvious discomfort – but he didn't utter a sound, he just kept slowly walking next to Yogev toward the elevator. They walked one step at a time, heel-toe, until they reached the elevator door. Yogev pressed the button to go down, and both of them waited.

Yariv held onto Yogev's hand and every few seconds, inhaled strenuously and coughed deeply.

The elevator finally arrived, and to their great fortune it was empty. Yogev helped Yariv get into the elevator; and Yariv leaned his head toward Yogev and whispered, "Minus-two." Yogev nodded. He was encouraged that Yariv was present and conscious enough of what was going on to remind him.

Suddenly, Yariv leaned toward Yogev again and asked in a weak voice, "Did you kill him?"

"You are completely fucked! That's what you're worried about right now?" Yogev responded angrily. He then pressed the button for minus-two and didn't let go, hoping this would keep the elevator going straight down without stopping on any other floor to let anybody else on.

After a few seconds, the elevator began slowly descending with a jolt. The floor numbers were lit in red on the panel above the door, until they stopped at minus-two. After a few seconds, the doors opened, and in front of them Yogev saw a sign that read: "SPA."

To the right of the sign he saw an arrow pointing in the direction of the parking garage and the exit. He looked up to scan the area and saw that it was generally empty. He signaled to Yariv to turn to the right, and the two of them began walking slowly in the direction of their car, which was parked on the other side of the well-lit and spotless garage.

A smattering of expensive new cars sparkled in the parking spaces around them. It was obvious that the guests at the hotel were people of means. Every so often, cars would pass by, but none of them slowed down next to them. Yariv was happy to discover that they didn't arouse any suspicion.

They progressed slowly, and Yariv groaned with every step he took. It took a supreme effort on his part. His forehead was covered in small beads of sweat, partially from the lack of air in the garage, but mostly because of the shape he was in. He was very pale, and Yogev was afraid that he would pass out in his arms. Yogev held Yariv under his armpits as he limped slowly along, and they inched their way closer to the car. When they finally got there, Yogev leaned Yariv against the car, and then dug the key out of his pocket and opened the driver's side door.

Suddenly, he heard a noise behind him and turned to see two young guys appear, almost as if out of nowhere. The first was tall and thin, with a dark complexion. The second one was built thicker, and he had light hair and bright blue eyes. Yogev was surprised, because he didn't understand where these two guys came from and what they wanted.

He didn't have time to think. With the instincts he acquired over the years, Yogev threw a punch right in the middle of the light-haired fellow's face. The punch hit square on, and the mysterious fellow clutched his shattered nose and leaned against the car so that he wouldn't fall to the ground.

In the meantime, Yogev turned to his right with the goal of protecting Yariv. Yariv was standing there in shock – just walking over there was difficult, and he was breathing heavily. His vision was starting to blur, but he had a feeling he knew these guys. He picked his head up, and his eyes widened as he called out weakly, "Paul??"

Right then, the dark-skinned fellow pounced on Yogev and started choking him with an iron hand while wrestling him down to the garage floor. Yogev started choking and gasping for air. The guy applied more pressure, and Yogev felt as if he were in a vice, and couldn't free himself from his grip. He tried calling for help, but the guy clamped his mouth shut with one of his hands – the one not choking him. Yogev was unable to breathe. The garage lights slowly became blurry and began spinning. He tried to free himself again and again from the choke hold, but to no avail.

With his last bit of strength, Yogev tried to lift up his head to search for his injured friend. The effort was very difficult, because there was almost no blood flowing to his brain. Just before he lost consciousness, Yogev managed to see, through what seemed like a blurry veil, the second guy push Yariv into a commercial vehicle.

EPILOGUE
Two Weeks after the Events at the Hotel in Marseille

The floor had been cleaned until it sparkled, and the walls were painted an off-white. The chair that Yariv was sitting on was in the middle of the windowless room with its blank walls, and the dull buzz of the fluorescent lights was the only sound he heard. Yariv patted the white bandage that covered up the stitches on his right side and stomach. Despite being bandaged, it still hurt plenty. Every movement caused him to feel currents of pain in the area around the wound.

There was a metallic buzzing from the hallway, and the door opened. A man dressed in civilian garb was standing in the doorway. The man entered the room and walked over to Yariv. He took a key out of his pocket and unlocked the handcuffs around his wrists. He then motioned for him to get up, without saying a word. Yariv rubbed his wrists, sore from the handcuffs.

On the floor next to him were his crutches. Yariv leaned over to pick them up slowly, groaning from how much the stitches hurt. He picked up his crutches with his right hand, and then used them to ease himself out of the chair and into a stabilized standing position. The man signaled with his head in the direction of the door, and Yariv did as he was told. Beyond the open door, Yariv saw a long hallway, which was also windowless. Both of them started walking down the hallway.

Walking was difficult for Yariv. The stitches hurt with every step. After a few moments of walking slowly, the two of them reached a large wooden door that looked heavy. The man pressed on the black keypad to the right of the door, and another buzz sounded – the door opened with a barely audible creak.

Yariv looked inside. On a raised platform sat a stenographer, her delicate fingers already hovering over the keyboard, as if waiting patiently at attention for somebody to just say something. On the other side of the room, he saw a man standing next to a desk, and next to him were some folders and paperwork. There was a long, dark-brown wooden bench to the man's right. Nobody was sitting on the bench. The man motioned for him with his hand to come sit on the bench. Yariv walked to the bench slowly and sat down, placing his crutches next to him, and then rubbed his wrists again, which still hurt from the stiff, cold feel of iron. The man slowly closed the heavy door behind him. There was a tense silence in the room.

Yariv didn't know what the next few minutes had in store for him. He was at peace with what he had done, with the decisions he made. Despite the fact that he could feel his pulse in his temples and the cold sweat that was slowly creeping down his spine, he still breathed deeply and evenly, trying to hide, at least to everybody else, his nerves. For a few moments, the judge looked at Yariv and didn't utter a word. Yariv hoped that was, perhaps, a good sign.

But after a few more moments of tense silence, when he heard the judge announce out loud, "Case number 51178/23 – the State of Israel versus Yariv Be'eri," a tear threatened to escape from his right eye, and he held his head between his two hands as if trying to squeeze the tear back inside to stop it from rolling down his cheek.

AFTERWORD

The idea to write this book began from a collection of scrawled memories I had written to myself over the years. At first, I didn't know what I was going to do with them, if anything, but it was important for me to put into writing at least some of the unique experiences that I had during the time I served in the Duvdevan unit as a combat soldier and commander, sometime at the beginning of the '90s. The service we did, my team members and I, was packed full of extremely complex undercover operations that seemed as if they were written as crazy Hollywood scripts.

Over time, I felt that I had accumulated enough material, and so the idea to write a book began to sprout within me. I wanted to write a book that would open up a window that would allow people to take a peek inside the intense and intricate world of undercover work. A book that would describe the arduous training courses, the endless physical as well as mental preparation, the need to change ruses every time a new undercover operation was undertaken, and the use of these schemes in and of themselves, as well as the special experience and bonds formed among the soldiers on the team. However, it was also important for me to share with the reader the personal decisions the soldiers are faced with, the constant operational stress, and the complex psychological toll that the undercover work entails.

The book describes the Duvdevan unit from various angles – from the point-of-view of the combat soldiers, who are responsible for the operation in the field, but also that of the senior command, as well as the from viewpoint of the professionals in mental health care. In order to see the whole picture and broaden my understanding, I met with a wide range of people who were involved in creating the Duvdevan unit: they are high-level field commanders (who were responsible for establishing the unit, and commanding it and its soldiers on a daily basis), and professionals from various mental health fields. They actively monitored the training course for the combat soldiers in the unit over the years, and worked on building up the mental fortitude necessary to carry out the complex operations of this type, and treated those who needed therapy. Some of them are named in the next section.

I learned a lot from these meetings. I heard fascinating personal stories and was exposed to new and interesting things that I wasn't aware of back in my day. In addition, it was my privilege to have a unique experience – to see the unit I grew up in from many different perspectives. And just like the parable about the elephant and the blind men, each person I met with and each interview I conducted shined a light on a different side of the unit, from different times as well as from different perspectives. The process was extremely enriching and highly significant for me.

Writing this book was the fulfillment of a dream. It was a very long journey, arduous and complicated – but fascinating in a way like no other. The writing itself took a few years, and caused me to embark upon an exceptionally special journey, which among other things, caused me to better understand what I went through during the years of my army service.

There is no doubt that this has been the most extensive and challenging project I have ever undertaken, and the personal investment has been the greatest of my life, and I am grateful for every moment I put into it.

ACKNOWLEDGEMENTS

In writing this book, I conducted many meetings and interviews with various people in the army who were instrumental during the period in which the Duvdevan unit evolved.

It is my pleasure to personally acknowledge those among them who stand out:
- Lt. General (res.) Ehud Barak – Former Chief of the General Staff, Prime Minister, and Defense Minister
- Lt. General (res.) Shaul Mofaz – Former Chief of the General Staff and former Defense Minister
- Lt. General (res.) Moshe ("Bogi") Ya'alon – Former Chief of the General Staff and former Defense Minister

I would like to thank them for providing their unique perspectives on the process of establishing an undercover unit in the IDF, and for their operational perspective over the years in their diverse roles at the highest echelons of national security.

My beloved wife and children: You are the greatest lights in my life, and there is nothing that has brought me anywhere near the happiness you have.

A special thanks to the Creator of the World who has granted me so much good, and has allowed me to fulfill this dream.

Printed in Dunstable, United Kingdom